Voluptuous Venus

Eva Linczy

NEW ENGLISH LIBRARY
Hodder and Stoughton

Copyright © 1997 Eva Linczy

First published in Great Britain in 1997
by Hodder and Stoughton
A division of Hodder Headline PLC

A New English Library paperback

The right of Eva Linczy to be identified as the Author of
the Work has been asserted by her in accordance with the
Copyright, Designs and Patents Act 1988.

10 9 8 7 6 5 4 3 2 1

All rights reserved. No part of this publication may be
reproduced, stored in a retrieval system, or transmitted, in any
form or by any means without the prior written permission of the
publisher, nor be otherwise circulated in any form of binding or
cover other than that in which it is published and without a
similar condition being imposed on the subsequent purchaser.

All characters in this publication are fictitious
and any resemblance to real persons, living or dead,
is purely coincidental.

British Library Cataloguing in Publication Data
A CIP catalogue record for this title is available from
the British Library

ISBN 0 340 67469 5

Typeset by Avon Dataset Ltd, Bidford-on-Avon, Warks
Printed and bound in Great Britain by
Mackays of Chatham PLC, Chatham, Kent

Hodder and Stoughton
A division of Hodder Headline PLC
338 Euston Road
London NW1 3BH

Contents

CHAPTER ONE: *By Design* — 1
CHAPTER TWO: *Product Test* — 23
CHAPTER THREE: *On the Scent* — 87
CHAPTER FOUR: *Pressing Business* — 151
CHAPTER FIVE: *Home Base* — 191
CHAPTER SIX: *Shop Front* — 229
CHAPTER SEVEN: *In Camera* — 301

CHAPTER ONE

By Design

WHEN VENUS'S PARENTS HAD CHOSEN her Christian name (from the book of names that her mother had purchased during her pregnancy) in the year 2057, they had both genuinely approved of the fact that it informed them that Venus was the ancient Roman goddess of beauty and love (especially *sensual* love, it had said) corresponding to the Greek goddess Aphrodite. They were further convinced of the appropriateness of the name when they looked it up in their dictionary and read that – amongst the plethora of other meanings ascribed therein – it meant 'a beautiful or attractive woman; the desire for sexual intercourse; indulgence of sexual desire; a quality or characteristic that excites love.' It was apt, they felt, for Venus *was* the consequence of their active, vigorous and varied sexual relationship. The product, as Venus's father insisted on describing it, of their loins. A real, welcome, much-loved love child.

Twenty-three years later, in 2080, Venus had finally

decided that she both liked and approved of her Christian name, for when she revealed it to any new acquaintance it led, almost inevitably, to the discussion, first, of love and then – where appropriate – to talk of, and then perhaps indulgence in, lovemaking. Love-making was a vital and integral part of Venus's life. She spent much of her time lying on her back, with her legs apart, and she got highly paid for it.

Not – make no mistake – that Venus was a prostitute. No way. It was simply that she was the research director of a company called (again, rather appropriately) Aphrodite PLC. It was the company name that had attracted Venus to it in the first place. She had just come down from Cambridge with a first-class degree in market research, and she had been highly recommended to a headhunting concern by her tutor, Simon Menzies.

Simon had written a formal letter to the managing director of the headhunting company (who was a personal friend of his) setting out his genuinely high opinion of Venus's intellectual capabilities. But he had also telephoned his friend and told him, in confidence and at length, that Venus, if she liked a man sufficiently well, more than lived up to her rather unusual name. Not to put too fine a point on it, he said, she gave the best head of any female student who had ever granted him sexual favours. Which was a very large number. And, he added, she fucked like the proverbial stoat. He recommended that his friend give Venus an interview as quickly as possible, lest some other person should offer her the highly-paid position that her appearance and sexual abilities would

Voluptuous Venus

undoubtedly obtain for her. This the friend did immediately. Partly because he was intrigued to see this wondrous woman, but also because, if she knew her market research and was also knowledgeable sexually, she could well be the woman for whom Aphrodite PLC had been searching for some time through his agency. And, to date, without success.

To the headhunter's intense disappointment, Venus made no indication during their interview of any wish to drop her knickers for him. What she did do, however, was to talk freely, without embarrassment and with obvious expertise, about sex and her strong belief that she had both a natural penchant for the subject and a well-practised expertise in its exercise. The headhunter, with regret at his lack of opportunity to try out the lady's sexual proficiency personally but with genuine relief at having found the ideal candidate for his client's vacancy, arranged on the spot for Venus to see Aphrodite's managing director. She started work there a week later, and in six months' time she had been promoted from her original job of market research manager to research director.

Aphrodite was a result of a combination of the old so-called Space Age microchip and plastics industries to which had been added, in the early days of the third millennium, the most advanced expertise in computer software programming and in genetic engineering. Aphrodite made robots. *Sexual* robots. Male and female sex slaves. Made to measure, and programmed to order. They could and would perform any, absolutely *any*, sexual act. Expertly. Happily. Repeatedly, if you so wished. They never got headaches. They were indistinguishable from human beings. You could order a woman in any image you fancied. All you needed was money. A lot of money. In return, you would receive a robot that looked, felt, sounded, smelled and tasted like the lady (or, of course, the gentleman) of your dreams. Complete with all the appropriate orifices and appurtenances. Programmed to do whatever it was that you wanted him or her to do.

Aphrodite's electronic expertise guaranteed that your female robot would have a soft, wet tongue, to explore your mouth. Her breasts would come in whatever size or shape was your particular wish. Her nipples – ordered specifically to your desired size and shape – would harden when you sucked them or played with them. If lactating breasts were your thing, then they'd lactate. Her fingers would masturbate you, if that was what you desired. Or if you wanted to watch *her* masturbating, then her pussy would moisten and it would give off that delightful aroma of hot, wet, open cunt, tailored to your individual pleasure. You could specify vaginal depth and width, size of inner and outer labia, degree of lubrication under different circumstances and, naturally enough, length and colour of pubic hair, with choice of either straight or curly cuntal tresses. If shaved pussy was your bag, that would be available too. As to sexual acts, and sexual performance, the robots were programmable with a whole range of software. They could cater to every taste. Almost nothing was *verboten*. And they played to all your five senses.

Sight, touch, taste, hearing, smell. The men came with their penis tailored to your every wish. Circumference and

Voluptuous Venus

length were to your personal taste. Measurements could vary as much as you liked. Just insert the right microchip. You could choose either circumcised or foreskinned. Testicular details were from choice. Skin colour, naturally, was whatever turned you on. If you were a woman, your male robot would come in your mouth when you sucked him off, if that was what you liked. You could select the cubic centilitres of ejaculate. Or not. The choice was yours. He'd get an erection, fuck you, become detumescent, and then rapidly become fully erect again as you stimulated him in whatever was your favourite way. He'd fuck you non-stop for hours, without ejaculating, if that was what you wanted. All you had to do was select the right program.

Venus's job, basically, was to ensure a number of things about the Aphrodite sex robots. She was responsible to the company's board for quality control. This meant that she had to ensure that everything that the robots did was one hundred per cent realistic. She was also responsible for constant market research, designed to make certain that the sexual performance programs supplied with the robots offered anything and everything, sexually, that customers wanted. The old laws, regulations, and sexual non sequiturs had, since the development of sexual robots, long since been amended. Society – and the establishment – had decreed that it simply didn't matter what your sexual fantasies were, provided you were indulging them with a sexual robot. Paedophilia was, of course, still both completely illegal and totally taboo.

But if you wanted to buy an eighteen-year-old Aphrodite model to fuck, rape, sodomize or beat into submission before you forced her to suck your cock, then that was perfectly OK. A robot doesn't have feelings. If you wanted (and could afford to buy) a robot that was the spitting image of your mother-in-law, and you then spent happy hours fucking her anally, that was up to you. It was entirely permissible. It was a completely new way of life. Women *were* being granted divorces against their husbands on the grounds of adultery with their Aphrodite dolls, but many women – usually the older ones – were more than happy to be replaced, and thus relieved of their largely unwanted sexual duties.

But for every robot sold in the shape of someone's relative, the company sold thousands of replicas of film stars, actors and actresses, historical figures or royalty. Rita Hayworth was a favourite. Lady Di robots were so common that they were often on special offer. Marilyn Monroe, Grace Kelly and Jackie Kennedy were popular choices. And it was also Venus's responsibility to make certain that they could all be programmed to be, as her thesaurus listed it, 'arousing, beddable, come-hither, cuddly, erotic, flirtatious, inviting, kissable, naughty, provocative, provoking, sensuous, sexy, slinky, suggestive, titillating, and voluptuous!' Not to mention plain down and *dirty*. This meant that Venus spent much of her time engaged in sexual activity. She loved every minute of it and did a fantastic job for the company.

She it was who persuaded the board to increase the programming budget, in order to enable the production department to include the facility to make lactating breasts available, after she met a man who was particularly into sucking milk from women's breasts. He introduced her to his collection of magazines devoted to the subject. Venus was, initially, sceptical of the demand for such a specialized facility, but it very quickly proved to be one of Aphrodite's most popular 'specials.' Especially with customers who ordered black women with enormous tits.

She also engaged in research into the range of sexual fragrances available from the company. Venus believed that the range could be considerably extended, and had enlisted the consultancy services of one of Europe's top perfume designers.

'Look, Jacques,' she said to him, crossing her legs as she spoke. 'There is no point in trying to be polite when we're discussing this company's products. What we're talking about here is the smell of cunt. Clean cunt. Fresh cunt. Young cunt. But cunt, for all that. So let's get down to basics. You must have heard the old joke? You know the one. If little girls are made of sugar and spice and all things nice, why do they smell of kippers?'

Jacques joined in her laughter. 'My own view,' continued Venus, 'is that clean pussy *never* smells of kippers. But, first of all, *some* customers *like* pussy that smells of kippers. Dirty pussy, in other words. And dirty knickers. Hence the offers – and requests – in some of the more downmarket men's magazines for used knickers. Always "used." Never "soiled." It really turns them on. Like some men love the smell of sweaty armpits. I get requests for that, too, from time to time.'

She stopped and looked at Jacques, waiting for him to comment. He was silent for a moment. And then, 'It is none of it a problem, mademoiselle,' he told her. 'Whatever you want, I can produce for you, artificially. Smelly cunts. Smelly knickers. Smelly armpits. With variations. Also *clean* cunts. Clean knickers. A whole range. No problem. Also, if you wish it, the smell of cock, likewise in a variety of forms.'

She looked at him, and raised her eyebrows. 'Realistically?' she asked. 'Absolutely,' he replied. 'No one will know that they are not real.'

'Samples?' asked Venus. '*Certainement*,' said Jacques. 'When?' she asked. He thought for a moment. 'Three weeks,' he told her. 'Maybe sooner.'

'Terrific,' Venus said. 'We'll have a panel test. Or should that be taste? Probably both,' she decided. 'Don't forget the flavouring, will you?' She stood up, and put out her hand. 'Until the next time, m'sieu,' she said. '*Merci beaucoup.*'

Venus saw Jacques out of her office. When she sat down at her desk again, the telephone rang. 'Hey, Venus,' said the voice. 'It's Mark.' Mark was the sales director. 'Hello, Mark,' she responded. 'I think we've got a bit of a problem,' he said. 'Could you possibly spare me ten minutes? I'm in the production-line building, in Product Testing.' She looked at her watch. 'Sure, Mark,' she said. 'I'll be with you in about ten minutes.' 'Great,' he said. 'Thank you.'

She put the phone down and went on her way. When she got to Mark, he was standing by one of the testing cubicles. Each cubicle had a bed, with a mattress. On the mattress in this cubicle was a female robot. She was naked,

Voluptuous Venus

and her legs were spread. She was pretty, with nicely pointed breasts. She looked about twenty. Her chest was rising and falling rhythmically with her simulated breathing. She had blonde hair, cut short, and matching blonde pubic hair. Her genitals were moist. There was a tangle of electronic cable connecting her to a bank of testing machinery.

One of the company's male testers was standing, completely naked, beside the bed. His penis had obviously recently been erect, but it had subsided down now from full erection to what Venus was always amused to call a lazy lob.

'We've been testing out the new multiple-orgasm microchip this afternoon,' said Mark. 'Bill here doesn't think it's that good. In fact, to be honest . . .' His voice trailed away for a moment. 'You tell her, Bill,' he said. 'Tell Venus what you told me.'

Bill looked faintly embarrassed. 'Well, it's simply the fact that this version doesn't feel right,' he said. 'It's difficult to put into words. It just doesn't feel like a multiple orgasm.'

'Then what *does* it feel like?' Venus asked. Bill thought for a second or two. 'More like a double or maybe even a triple orgasm,' he said. 'But certainly not a *multiple* orgasm.'

'Could it be the chip?' Venus asked. 'Have you tried changing it?'

'Yes,' Mark answered. 'We've tried three. They're all the same, apparently. It probably *is* the chip, but if it is, it's the whole batch.'

'How many chips left untested?' asked Venus. 'Oh, I don't know exactly,' said Mark. 'Thirty, maybe. Thirty-five. Something like that.'

Venus went over to the bed and thrust her middle finger up the robot's vagina. 'She's good and wet, isn't she?' she said.

'Well, so she should be,' said Mark. 'We've had her on an electronic prosthesis penis most of the morning. She's been working overtime. Bill here didn't take over until after lunch. We thought that she might respond better to the real thing. There's obviously nothing wrong with her lubrication mode. It's simply her multiple orgasms that aren't happening properly.'

'Tell me about it,' said Venus, laughing. 'It's the story of most of us women's lives. Isolate her multiple-orgasm mode for me, and switch her on, will you please, Mark?' she asked.

Mark went over to the testing equipment, pressed a number of buttons and turned a dial or two. 'She's ready for you now,' he said, flicking a switch. The robot began to thrust her hips. Her mouth fell open, and she began to pant. 'Oh yes,' said the female robot.

'Oh, for God's sake,' said Venus. 'That's all I need. Switch her bloody voice off, will you, please, Mark?'

Mark adjusted more buttons and the robot fell silent, her hips still thrusting. Venus kept her finger inserted. Some few minutes later, it was all over.

'I see what you mean,' Venus said to Bill. 'Or rather, I feel what you mean.' She extracted her finger from the robot's vagina. 'I tell you what,' Venus said. 'I'll go back to

Voluptuous Venus

my office and get a notice e-mailed to everyone. Asking for volunteers to come and fuck their way through the rest of the batch after work this evening, and then fill in a questionnaire each. Treble time, of course. If anyone gets a proper multiple orgasm out of Annie Fanny here, let me know. If they don't, we'll have to check our entire stock of multiple-orgasm microchips. We can't afford to send out a product that can't achieve orgasm properly, now, can we?'

She grinned wryly at Mark and Bill, who grinned sheepishly back. She wondered for a moment if the sight of her with her forefinger up the lifelike robot's pulsating pussy did anything for them. She sometimes speculated as to how many of the production-line males fucked the female robots as they came off the line. And, similarly, how many of the production girls took sexual advantage of the male products they were helping to produce. Some of them, of course, were paid to do exactly that. It was called product testing, and was a vital production function. But she wasn't thinking of those.

She was thinking of the normal production staff during their lunch breaks. The night security staff. Some of her fellow executives. She knew the stories by now, of course. How the production staff, one Christmas, had got a Princess Di image robot fucked by a Boris Karloff image robot as part of the staff Christmas party unofficial cabaret. No one knew quite how, but they had managed to keep it out of the more tabloid sites on the Internet. Thank God! She laughed to herself as she made her way back to her office.

She dictated the e-mail memo to her computer and fed in the code for it to be relayed to all staff. She realized that she was more preoccupied with the upcoming media conference, scheduled for the following month, than with the current multiple-orgasm microchip problems. Let the production people work that one out. Next month, Aphrodite were introducing their newest range to the world's press. The range – in a world in which this kind of product was unbelievably competitive – was without doubt the most realistic selection of sexual robots ever marketed. The total world market was worth thousands of billions of ecus per annum. Dominated until quite recently by the Japanese, this market was now led by Aphrodite, due, in Venus's opinion – and at her behest – to their insistence upon quality in every aspect of their products.

This market had begun over a hundred years ago, way back in the early 1960s, with the German sex shops developed by Berte Uhser and first introduced to Britain by Michael ('Dandy Kim') Waterfield's protégé, Ann Summers. In those days, sex shops used to stock, among other things, horrendous plastic blow-up dolls that offered anyone deranged enough to purchase one crude mouths, even cruder vaginal and anal orifices, and – with the male dolls – vibrating penises. The gap between those and the exquisitely produced sexual robots of now was almost unimaginable. It compared with the transition from the old original wooden wind-up gramophone, of the ancient HMV advertisements and the early twentieth century, to the sophisticated, interactive, PC-run images and sounds of today.

The new Aphrodite range was unique in that, whilst the earlier models had all been programmable to specific,

Voluptuous Venus

individual tastes, that had been it. Full stop. The new range could be programmed with a whole series of individual routines, from personally designed programs to an enormous selection of standards. They also included the most sophisticated range of available extras that could be purchased anywhere in the world. The choice of robot – male or female – could come with the voice, feel, smell, touch and, naturally, the look, of anyone the customer desired.

Some months previously, Aphrodite had sent out an invitation to the world's sexual writers and interviewers to select their own particular favourite fantasy sex object, which would then be manufactured to their own, individual specification and dressed in whatever clothes were individually requested. The journalists would then be offered a weekend at some exotic location to test drive – as it were – the fantasy sexual objects of their choice.

It was an expensive operation, but the resultant publicity (assuming that the products were up to standard) would be worth millions of ecus. Venus had been particularly intrigued by the request from Australia's foremost tabloid newspaper to test drive a sexual robot with both the appearance and (at the journalist's insistence) Venus's own sexual proclivities. She had considered substituting herself, in this particular instance, for the robot. It was a great idea. But it wasn't really workable since, whilst the robots (of either sex) could indulge in *sexual* conversation, and both answer questions and say the kind of things that customers wanted their sexual robots to say, they were not able to have general conversations, on any topic.

Which meant that Venus would almost certainly have given herself away, sooner or later, if she had substituted her real self for the robot, by exceeding the robot's conversational abilities. It wasn't that the company didn't have the ability to program the robots to converse properly. It did. It was rather that such software would have tripled the already expensive cost of the models, simply to provide something that the vast majority of its customers didn't want. As well as supplying the models with individually designed sexual programs, customers could also purchase microchips to literally plug in that provided a whole range of standard sexual routines. These covered everything from sadomasochism through water sports to spanking and caning – both giving and receiving – to bondage, as well as a comprehensive range of fetishes.

The sky, sexually speaking, was the limit. The models thus became real, three-dimensional versions of the old virtual reality experience, popular back in the middle 1990s where individuals could wear a kind of electronically-controlled mask, giving the illusion of experiencing various activities including, eventually, sexual encounters. The difference between those and the new Aphrodite range was that, with the Aphrodite products, people actually *did* experience the various sexual acts, rather than simply imagining that they did. It was the vital difference between watching a video and taking part in the real action. The products were self-cleaning and completely hygienic, but needed regular servicing.

The reason for the lavish introduction of the new models to the world's media was that Aphrodite was opening up a range of company-owned and staffed outlets in major cities all over the world, offering the models on rental. The idea was that this would make them cheaply available to all. To date, their availability had been restricted to the fairly limited number of people – comparatively speaking – who could afford the high individual purchase price.

When launched, the outlets would offer a range of standard models with the full gamut of sexually programmed microchips, in return for a reasonable fee – plus a hefty deposit, taken by cash card, but held and only put through if a product was lost or damaged. Credit and residential references would be carefully checked before membership of the Aphrodite outlets – to be named 'Sexational Unlimited' – was granted. Hence everyone's worry over the production problem with the latest multiple-orgasm microchip. It could be a disaster.

Weekly rental charges from Sexational would be competitive with the cost of an evening out for two, to include a good seat at the theatre, dinner, and transport. It was easy to see why Venus privately believed that extending the company's business in this manner would eventually destroy the need not only for marriage but for genuine sexual relationships. The Aphrodite experience would be cheaper and, possibly – depending upon individual sexual tastes – more fun. Who needed repetitive sex with a real human being when he or she could, in effect, screw anyone they wanted, do whatever they wanted to those people, and change them, if they so wished, daily or weekly?

Eva Linczy

Venus had to admit to herself that she had to make an effort (which she *did* make, to be fair to her) to maintain the varied one-to-one sexual relationships that were so vital to her ability to judge the strengths and weaknesses of the microchip programs that she developed with the production people. It was so much easier to go home and switch on something that looked – but *exactly* – like her favourite movie star, with a guaranteed ten-inch erection that was six-and-a-half inches in circumference and who had been programmed to do every naughty little thing that Venus loved to have done to her. It would work her slowly and exquisitely up to a whole series of multiple orgasms, and would then go on fucking her (gently, roughly, lovingly, cruelly – whatever she felt like) for as long as she wanted. So much better than having to go through a whole evening of pandering to male pride and male ego, and probably having to suck a cock that she might well not be in the mood to suck, in exchange for a wham-bam-thank-you-ma'am two-minute mockery of a fuck. And that probably with a small prick that she could scarcely feel up inside her. *Ho hum*, she thought.

Venus wriggled her bottom on her office chair. She could feel the moisture dampening her knickers, down between her legs. *Don't be a naughty girl*, she said to herself. *It's all that thinking about ten-inch erections*. She looked up, checked that her door was closed, then slipped a hand under her skirt and on up, underneath her knicker leg. She spread her outer vaginal lips, and then slid her middle finger up inside herself. *Oooh*, she thought. *That really* is *wet*. Her finger found her clitoris.

Voluptuous Venus

To her surprise, the naughty little thing was all swollen and fully erect. She slid her finger across its bloated head. Slowly. *Ooohh. Nice.* That really felt good. She began to masturbate herself, slowly at first, and then with increasing fervour, until she felt herself coming. It was a lovely, long, intense come, and she had to bite her lip to prevent herself from shouting out. She wondered for a moment about the Australian journalist who would soon be fucking something that looked exactly like her. He'd think, reasonably enough, that he was getting her own personal sexual pleasures. But he sure as hell wasn't. She had made certain of that. She suddenly realized that she had stopped rubbing herself for a moment there, while she enjoyed the peak of her orgasm. As it slowly died away, she began to rub herself again, bringing on another, even better climax. When she had milked every last good feel out of that one, she pulled her finger out of her now even wetter pussy. She looked at her wet finger, enjoying inhaling the scent that emanated from it. The smell of hot, aroused, feminine sex. She sucked it clean, enjoying the taste of herself. *Mmmmm.* She would have to have a good fuck this evening when she got home.

She had a number of the company's products. Five or six. She forgot exactly how many. But enough to get herself fucked silly. *Maybe,* she thought, *I'll have two of them, and get fucked in two holes at the same time.* She felt her pussy twitch at the thought. She loved it up her arse. She looked around for her handbag, found it, and took from it a tissue which she then carefully bunched and thrust up inside herself. It was purely as a temporary measure, to absorb the sexual effluent that was still trickling down the inside of her thighs. She didn't want *another* wet patch staining the fabric of her expensive office chair.

To Venus's total embarrassment, the last one had attracted the office cleaning woman's attention. 'I can't think what it could be, miss,' she had said. 'You say you haven't upset tea or coffee on it. But it took me forever to get that stain off. I just don't know.'

'Go away, you silly old cow,' Venus had wanted to say. 'It's from my cunt. It comes from wanking while I'm sitting at my desk. Bugger off.' What she *had* said was, 'Don't worry about it, Mrs James. These things happen. I'm grateful for your getting it off, whatever it was.' *God forgive me*, she thought. Venus was never going to tell the Australian journalist who had ordered his Aphrodite product in her image but the busy finger-and-tongue clitoral stimulation microchip programmes now fitted to all male and female Aphrodite products were entirely based on Venus's own personal oral and digital activities. She was, privately, extremely proud of this achievement.

She was also the instigator of the fact that all Aphrodite female models built since shortly after her arrival at the company now had the built-in facility – if requested by customers – to moisten their authentically cotton-lined knicker crotches. It was one of their best-selling extras. The liquid used in this moistening process looked, tasted, and was scented exactly like Venus's own intimate sexual lubricant. Unbeknownst to Aphrodite, Venus had recently been approached by the world's largest company of retail pharmacists, who wanted her to allow them to manu-

Voluptuous Venus

facture and market the same liquid in a whole range of flavoured and scented products. These would range from sexual lubricant through male aftershave to candy, chewing gum, and cola. She remembered that there was even the suggestion, somewhere in the proposed contract document, that the company should produce and sell a range of exclusive sexy panties, aimed at male knicker-fetishists, all of which lingerie would come with its gussets pre-dampened by the solution. The suggested brand name was *Venus de Venus*. Whatever next, Venus had thought? Vaginal-fluid-scented toothpaste?

She was delaying making a decision since the project included using her real name and photograph on all the packaging. She was certainly attracted by the amount of money involved (the deal included a percentage-of-profits option). But she was uncertain of her ability to cope with the fact that, should she agree to the contract, she would almost certainly become rich but she would also forever after have to live with the fact that any man she met, anywhere, could know the taste and scent of her vaginal secretions. That would be something of a heavy load to carry.

Far from helping to calm her down, Venus's brief masturbatory session had considerably increased her randiness, to the point where she craved further sexual release. She picked up her handbag and went off to the executive female lavatory. To her relief, the six stalls were all vacant. She took the one farthest from the entrance and slid the catch inside the door. She lifted up her skirt, pulled down her knickers, and sat down on the wooden lavatory seat.

She next picked up her handbag and scrabbled around inside it until she found the small vibrator that she always carried with her to cope with emergencies just such as this. It was small enough to fit happily into even quite a little handbag, being short – about four inches long – but quite fat. Although it was fairly quiet, it still made enough noise for anyone coming into the women's lavatory to be under no illusion about what the occupant of Venus's stall was doing. So, keeping one ear cocked for the sound of anyone else entering, Venus slipped the vibrator up between her expectant, desire-swollen vaginal lips and switched it on.

She instantly felt the delightful vibrations transmitted deep into her vagina. She began to move her hips to an inner rhythm, motivated by the sensations created by the vibrator's oscillations. She shut her eyes, and gave herself up completely to what was happening to her. She imagined huge, erect phalluses, thrusting stiffly, deeply into her vagina. She opened her legs wide, offering herself completely, giving herself up to the pain and pleasure of the feelings the images brought about.

At that moment she heard the door to the women's lavatory opening. She reached down hurriedly between her legs and switched the contraption off, cursing silently under her breath. Venus grasped the end of it and began thrusting it in and out of herself, but her hurried insertions and withdrawals couldn't compare with the buzzing, humming, throbbing sensations produced by the vibrator's battery-powered motor. She cursed silently again and resigned herself to waiting out the other woman's visit.

Voluptuous Venus

She heard the opening and shutting of the cubicle's door, the metallic sliding of the latch, the rustle of clothing, and then the discreet sounds of the woman relieving herself. This was followed quickly by the sound of the woman tearing sheets off the toilet roll, the noise of the loo handle being depressed and the flush of the loo itself. Venus listened further as the woman washed and dried her hands, and then heard the sounds of her shoes on the hard tile floor. Then she was gone, the door closing behind her.

Venus reached down and switched her vibrator on again. It took her a while to get back to the same state as she had been in when she'd had to stop, but once back there, she guided the rounded end of the vibrator down onto her clitoris and rejoiced as she came, mightily, wondrously, groaning with the pleasure of her orgasms.

She rode them, thrusting the buzzing little machine as deep inside herself as its length would allow, and she made herself come again. When it was all over, she felt much better than she had before. Completely relaxed. But still ready for the sex session that she knew she would indulge herself in the moment she got home. She looked at her watch. Only twenty minutes to go. She washed her hands, and her vibrator, and put the latter back in her bag. Back in her office, she signed her mail, tidied up her desk, and left. She hummed happily all the way home.

CHAPTER TWO

Product Test

Venus opened the door of the closet in which she kept her Aphrodite robots. They were all there perfectly legitimately: testing the product was part of her job. There were five men – including a black – and two women: a blonde and a redhead. The women were a new development. They had both been experimentally programmed to perform lesbian sex acts. It had taken Venus a while to get the board to agree to the trial, but she had finally succeeded.

'Why on earth not?' she had asked them. 'Research says there is almost certainly a big lesbian market for a suitable product. Why shouldn't lesbian women have the benefit of our designs? We've had gay male products for years. They're approximately twenty per cent of our turnover right now. And these will go like hot cakes, with our projected rental business. Men will hire them in pairs to give lesbian demonstrations at parties, and then queue up to fuck them.'

The female robots, like all Aphrodite's women simulacra,

came in European, Asian, Chinese, Afro-Caribbean, and American body shapes, as well as in the body shapes of famous women. Venus looked at the redhead. As she looked, she was surprised to feel her pussy positively twitch. *A reminder of the action with my vibrator*, she thought, reaching down and pressing her hand over it, reassuring herself that all was well down there. She felt seriously raunchy.

Despite the fact that the two model girls' lesbian libidos were a microchip copy of Venus's own simulated lesbian sex play, Venus herself had never tested them out. Not being a seriously practising lesbian – she *had* enjoyed lesbian affairs, but not recently – she had left that to the company's professional female product testers. But she realized suddenly that she really fancied the redhead. She took off the girl's jacket, reached down the back of her blouse, and lifted the concealed flap between the girl's shoulders. She checked the level of the lithium battery, which indicated that it was fully charged, and activated the robot's electronics. She dialled various combinations of numbers, pressed a button and closed the flap. She then replaced the girl's jacket and stepped back.

Every Aphrodite robot, male and female, possessed an extensive range of variable controls, including choice of the degree of active sexuality and the level of the strength of sexual language employed by the machines. The active sexuality spectrum ran from 'gentle' through 'overt' to 'strong,' and ended with 'obscenely powerful.' Similarly, the strength-of-language scale concluded with 'grossly

Voluptuous Venus

salacious.' Venus, feeling pretty obscenely raunchy herself, had dialled both extremes.

After a set fifteen seconds' delay, the redhead came to life, turned her head, and looked at Venus. 'Hey, babe,' it said, its voice deeply husky, 'Do you like chicks? Are you into girls?' Venus hesitated for a moment. The robot put an arm around her waist, placed a hand behind her head, and pulled her head forward. She then kissed Venus strongly on the mouth, inserting her tongue into Venus's mouth in a long, sexy, exploratory kiss. After just another second's hesitation, Venus began to kiss her back.

The girl continued kissing Venus, but now she slipped a hand down between Venus's legs and began to stroke her pussy through her skirt. Venus opened her legs, affording the girl better access. The girl slowly, and somewhat reluctantly, pulled her mouth off Venus's. 'I guess you've answered my question,' she said. 'You obviously *do* like girls. I'm going to suck your pussy for you now. I love to suck pussy. Most women say I'm the best cunt lapper they've ever had. Shall I undress you, or would you rather undress yourself?'

'You undress me, baby,' said Venus. 'I don't often have the opportunity.'

'I'll undress you any time you want, darling,' said the robot. 'What's your name?' Venus asked. 'Jane,' said the robot. 'But I'm not plain. I've got great tits, and a gorgeous arse, and legs up to my armpits. And you'll love my cunt. You'll see everything in a minute.'

She wasn't wasting any time. As she spoke, she gently undressed Venus, taking off her jacket, her blouse, and her skirt. Venus wasn't wearing a bra, which left her standing there in her knickers and stay-up stockings. 'Pretty panties,' said Jane as she slipped them down Venus's legs and waited for her to step out of them. 'Shall we leave the stockings on? I love pretty stockinged legs around my neck. They're so sexy.'

'Sure,' said Venus. 'Whatever turns you on.'

'You turn me on,' the girl said. She leaned forward and kissed Venus's outer labia. 'And *I'm* going to turn *you* on, baby. I see your pussy's all wet,' she murmured. She picked up Venus's right hand and sniffed her fingers. 'Naughty girl,' she said. 'You've been playing with your pussy, haven't you? You've been having a sneaky wank. Come on now. Admit it.'

Venus laughed. 'Actually,' she told the girl, 'I've been wanking myself with a vibrator. In the office, this afternoon. It was lovely. I came and came and came.'

While Venus was confessing her masturbatory exploits, Jane was slipping out of her clothes. She did have a great body, as she had said. All the Aphrodite robots did, as a matter of course. Venus cast a professional eye over this one. Her breasts were firm, but soft. Her nipples looked good. Nicely brown and well shaped. They looked eminently suckable. Venus leaned forward, tweaked one a couple of times, and pulled on it. It became erect in her fingers. The girl's long auburn pubic hair exactly matched the hair on her head.

'You're a sexy little cow, aren't you?' said the girl. 'You can't wait to get at me, can you? But just you wait until *I* get at *you*.'

Voluptuous Venus

Jane was down to her stockings and undies now. She was wearing black thong-style knickers, over which she wore an old-fashioned tiny suspender belt that held up her black seamed nylon stockings. There was a damp, darker patch at the centre of the tiny scrap covering her vagina. 'Shall I keep these on for now?' she asked. 'They're pretty, aren't they?'

'Yes, they are,' said Venus. 'And do. I like them.'

'Where's the bedroom, sweetheart,' the girl asked. 'Or do you want me to suck you here, on the floor? I'll do it anywhere you like. I'm easy.'

I'll bet you are, thought Venus. *It's all in your program.* 'No, let's go to bed,' she replied. We may as well be comfortable. It's this way.' For a moment she felt quite excited at the prospect of being sexually serviced on the carpet by this woman. *Almost like being raped*, she thought. That could be provided, too, of course, she realized, with the right software.

She led the way to her bedroom. It was a pretty room. All whites and pale blues. The double bed was in the centre of the far wall, opposite the large window. She turned down the coverlet and lay down on the bed. Jane used her hands to spread Venus's legs. Then she knelt between them and put her face down, level with Venus's pussy. 'Mmmm,' she said. 'It smells nice.' She leaned down and licked it, slowly, from top to bottom. 'Tastes good, too,' she said. With which she started work on it. Not surprisingly, she was something of an expert.

It amused Venus to remember that this oral sex programme was based on her own actions. She was sucking

Eva Linczy

her own pussy, if she cared to think of it that way. Jane was sucking and slurping, tonguing and licking, kissing and sucking. She quickly brought Venus to her first orgasm. Venus reached down and held Jane's head as she came, bucking her hips and pressing her sex against the robot's mouth.

It was, as Jane had said earlier, the best oral sex she had ever had. Jane kept at her task, and Venus slowly worked herself up to what became almost a permanent non-stop multiple orgasm. 'Ooohh, that's nice,' she murmured to Jane. 'That's lovely. Please don't stop.'

Jane lifted up her head, just for a second. 'Don't worry, darling,' she said. 'I can go on forever.' And she set about Venus's sex once more, using her mouth to provide the pleasures that Venus was so much enjoying. Eventually, Venus had to ask her to stop. 'I'm sorry, but I'm exhausted,' she told the robot. 'Give me a little breathing space. Please?'

'Of course, darling,' said the girl, and she sat back on her heels as Venus lay there, her legs still spread, panting with the exertion of her orgasms. 'What you would like next?' Jane asked. 'I can go on doing what I've been doing to you. Or I can do it with my fingers.'

Venus was silent for a while. Then she remembered two things. One was that when she was still back in the office she had been dying for a fuck. And while there was no way that she could currently describe herself as frustrated, she still felt an excited tingle in her pussy at the idea of it being invaded by a male member. And the other thing that she suddenly remembered was that some-

Voluptuous Venus

where – where? – she had a dildo. A proper, strap-on, double-ended lesbian dildo. A hangover from her student days, when she had been more into other girls than she was now.

'I know what, Jane,' she said. She pulled herself up into a sitting position on the bed. 'I've got a dildo somewhere, if I can only find it. You know a double-ended one? We could *both* enjoy that.'

'Dirty little cow,' said Jane. 'I knew it the moment I saw you. I'm going to end up fucking that with a great big dildo, I said to myself. A huge, over-sized dildo that will stretch her cunt until she screams. And now you tell me exactly that. I knew it. Dirty cow. Where is it?'

Venus got up off the bed and went over to a chest of drawers at the other end of the bedroom. She pulled out the drawers, one after the other, and scrabbled amongst their contents. The third one down was the one. 'Ah,' she said triumphantly, holding up a frighteningly large dildo. 'I knew I had it somewhere.'

She looked over at Jane who had stood up, off the bed. She was a magnificent figure, still clad in her black knickers, black stockings, and little black suspender belt. For a moment or two Venus wondered whether or not she should return the oral compliments that Jane had just paid her, as she would have done with any human lover. But the thought of being polite to a machine suddenly struck her as ridiculous. Jane didn't have feelings. Anything that appeared as feelings (like the now much damper patch at her knicker crotch) was as a result of expert electronic programming.

'I'll just go and get some lubricant,' said Venus, and took herself off to the adjoining bathroom for that purpose. She found what she was looking for in the bathroom cabinet. Back in the bedroom, Jane held out her hand. 'Let me rub that in for you, my darling,' she said. Venus gave her the tube of lubricant and lay on the edge of the bed, her legs apart, for Jane to grease her sex prior to inserting the huge dildo.

Venus still held the dildo in her other hand. She looked at it, trying to remember with whom she had last used it. It was made from moulded rubber, and was attached to a leather adjustable harness. The rubber was very clean. She had obviously remembered to wash it after its last use. But the leather was beginning to show signs of wear and tear. And then it came to her. Suddenly. She had last used it with Tina, that blonde, tarty little student from university. She hadn't been in love. Absolutely not. In lust, maybe. It was just that Tina had worshipped her, and it had amused Venus, at the time, to allow the girl to make love to her. It seemed to Venus that Jane was being slightly over-diligent with the lubricant, but then, that was probably par for the course. When Jane said, 'Turn over, darling,' Venus did so, without really giving any thought to the whys and wherefores. Then, when she suddenly felt Jane's greased finger inserted into her rectum, realization dawned. She looked over her shoulder to see Jane smiling down at her.

'I know, sweetie,' said Jane. 'You didn't say anything about getting fucked anally. It's just that I love sticking my fingers up other girls' tight little arseholes. But you never

Voluptuous Venus

know, do you? If you should decide, later on, that you want it up your arse, we won't have to stop in mid-fuck to grease you, now will we?' Venus had to agree reluctantly that, yes, it probably did make sense.

When Jane had greased Venus's rectal passage to her complete satisfaction, she set about greasing the business end of the dildo. When that too was done, Venus said, holding out her hand for the tube of lubricant, 'Here, Jane. Get your knickers round your ankles, and let me grease your pussy for you.' Jane smiled, and did a mock little curtsey. 'Why, thank you, ma'am,' she said. 'What a pleasant surprise.'

She bent over and pulled her knickers down, finally stepping out of them. 'Oh, dear,' she said, almost laughing as she looked at her dripping wet knicker crotch. 'I've wet my knickers again. What will my mummy say? She'll probably spank my bottom.' She dropped them on the floor, unhooked her suspender belt, unclipped the suspenders, dropped that onto the floor also, and peeled off her stockings.

Venus bent down and picked up the tiny black knickers and then she did what she had seen a number of men do with *her* knickers when she had just taken them off immediately prior to sex. She buried her nose in them and inhaled, deeply. The scent of warm, wet pussy filled her nostrils and she was thrilled. Not because she was turned on sexually by it – which she was – but because she was excited by the smell, supplied (if you thought about it) entirely by Aphrodite's chemical expertise.

Jane was completely naked now. She sat on the edge of

the bed, opened her legs and raised her bottom up off it. She smiled at Venus. 'I'm ready now, baby,' she exclaimed.

Venus picked up the tube of lubricant, squeezed a goodly dollop of it onto her forefinger, and began to rub it into Jane's pussy. The girl's inner and outer cunt lips were swollen now, by her passion, and Venus marvelled at the reality of what was actually plastic. Specially formed, totally flesh-like plastic, but plastic for all that. As she moved her finger around inside the girl's pussy, Jane groaned. Venus hoped she was groaning with pleasure, rather than because she was in pain. But she wasn't left in doubt for long.

'Oh, baby,' said Jane. 'Frig me. Please. Wank me with your finger. Play with my clitty. Make me come. Play with my little wet pussy. Please, darling.' She lay down on her back on the bed, and spread her legs even wider. Venus felt herself getting excited at the thought of what she was being asked to do. She felt around inside Jane's vagina until she found the erect nub of the girl's clitoris. She began to massage it.

'Oh yes,' said Jane. 'Oh, Jesus. Yes. That's lovely. You're playing with my pussy, and I'm going to come. You're *so* naughty. I'm coming now. NOW. YeeeEEESSS. Oh. Yes. Thank you. Oh, God. Lovely.' She sat up and smiled her sexiest smile at Venus. 'I guess you're ready for me to fuck you now?' she said. Venus was, and she said so.

Jane picked up the dildo and slowly eased the receiving end into herself, grimacing slightly as she so did and then smiling again, once it was in place. She stood up, and arranged the straps around her waist and thighs. 'Would

Voluptuous Venus

you like to do the buckles up for me, darling?' she asked. 'It'll save me fiddling about with them.' Venus did as she was bid, adjusting the dildo's straps until it stood out firmly in position, like the obscene phallus that it was. 'Where do you want it, honey?' Jane asked. 'Front or back? Or both, in which case, which first?' 'Front, please,' Venus answered.

She lay down on the bed and opened her legs. Her vulva glistened from the lubricant that Jane had anointed her with. Jane climbed onto her and, taking the dildo in her hand, she guided it into Venus's waiting pussy. 'Ooooh,' said Venus. 'I'd forgotten how big it was.' Jane leaned forward and, placing her hands on Venus's shoulders, began to fuck her. 'Like they say, darling,' she said, 'a good big 'un will always beat a good little 'un.' And then, 'Shall I suck your tits while I fuck you?' Jane asked. 'Oh, please,' Venus said. 'I'd like that.'

Jane leaned down and took one of Venus's nipples into her mouth. She sucked and tongued it until it was rigid, and then did the same to the other one. When they were both fully erect, she took her hands off Venus's shoulders and pulled and twisted at her nipples with her fingers. It was rather painful but intensely erotic and that, combined with the thrusting of the hard rubber phallus into her vagina, began to bring her to orgasm. She shut her eyes and concentrated on the sensations brought about by the rubber cock inside her pussy. 'Fuck me harder, darling,' she asked. 'I'm ready to come. Make me come now.'

Jane increased her rhythm, and Venus's clitoris responded by triggering the first of a whole series of orgasms which built up to a crescendo and almost had Venus screaming, and which then slowly faded away until finally it was all over. 'Oh, yes. Thank you, Jane,' she said. 'That was lovely. I really enjoyed that.'

'So did I,' Jane said as she backed away from Venus, pulling the dildo out of her. She backed off the bed and stood up and Venus followed her. She then put her arms around Jane, pulled the robot towards her, and kissed her firmly on the mouth. 'That was great,' she said. 'It was the best fuck for a long time.' As Jane smiled back at her, Venus reached around between her shoulder blades, found the hidden flap, and switched her off. It was uncanny to see Jane transformed from what had appeared to be a living, breathing, human being back into a rigid, insensible, mindless machine.

Jesus, now I really am fucked, Venus thought, as she busied herself unstrapping the dildo. She next dialled Jane's self-cleaning mode and took the dildo into the bathroom to wash it. As she dried it, she became fascinated by its moulded veins, its frenum, and its whole phallic appearance. She put it in her mouth for a moment. It didn't taste right, but the feel of the shape made her pussy respond to its presence. The cocks on the male Aphrodite robots were much better, in that they were totally realistic. By comparison, the dildo was a crude imitation.

Venus realized that it was a while since she had sucked a real cock and relished the spurt of warm semen jetting down her throat. For a moment she considered using one of the male Aphrodite robots in that way, but decided that, what with her vibrator in the office and then Jane's efforts

Voluptuous Venus

at home, she had probably indulged herself sexually quite enough for one evening. She put everything away, showered, and went to bed. Her pussy was still making its presence known as she got into bed, and she eventually fell asleep as she masturbated herself happily into temporary oblivion. Her fingers were still in her moist pussy when she awoke the following morning, so she took an immediate decision to start the day the same way as she had finished the previous evening.

Back in the office later that morning, she dialled the internal number for Mark, the sales director. He picked it up straight away. 'Good morning, Mark,' she said. 'What news?'

'Not good, I'm afraid,' Mark replied. 'According to the overnight test reports, the whole batch of multiple orgasm microchips are duff. I've slung the entire production and I'm having the loss made up as quickly as possible, starting right now. I'm seeing the production of this lot all the way through myself, together with the production director. There should be a complete new batch by the end of the day. Starting again from scratch is the only way we can be certain that we won't have a failure with the media launch robots.'

'Terrific,' Venus told him. 'I'll see you later.'

For the rest of the morning she concentrated on finishing off a report that she was preparing for the board of directors, on the ways in which the company could develop its projected new hire business. She was initially suggesting approaching the larger hotel chains and demonstrating the range of Aphrodite products to their management. This would be in order to encourage them to either purchase or rent male and female robots, either for hire to their guests or simply to supply on request, as part of the hotels' overall service. It should help to resolve the constant problem, in some hotels, of prostitutes visiting guests.

And now that many of the airlines, with the bigger planes of the twenty-first century, had gone back to the sleeping cabins system of the 1930s, Venus was suggesting too that Aphrodite should approach the airlines' management about their first-class passengers. Given a choice of the finest-quality sexual activity of their choice with beautiful women or attractive men, watching an in-flight movie didn't seem to pose much of a contest, to Venus's mind. She knew which of the two she would prefer. One problem that kept rearing its head in Venus's mind was how to advise the hotels and airlines on coping with homosexual men and women who requested same-sex robots. Whilst there was no question of any kind of a legal problem, there *was* the question of taste, and of the possible reluctance of hotel and airline staff to deal with that particular situation. The problem would probably resolve itself, in time. It would, of course, apply just as much to the rental shops.

It made Venus laugh as she pondered the question of same-sex customer requests, remembering suddenly, as she did, that she had been very much involved in same-sex screwing herself for a long period the previous evening. *Well, what the hell,* she thought. *Decisions, decisions.* She wrote a couple of paragraphs into her report, suggesting that same-sex requests be treated in exactly the same manner as heterosexual requests. It made her feel much better about the whole project. Her second major item in the report that she was drafting was – at least in Venus's opinion – an even better idea. Accepting that the Aphrodite robots were manufactured to such standards that few people could tell them from real, live, human beings once they were activated, she was suggesting that the company set up a pornographic film production company in the United States, where hard-core blue movies had been legal for almost a century. Certainly since the early 1970s. Parliamentary advisors to Aphrodite forecast, privately, that British laws were soon to change and would make the public showing of pornographic movies legal in Britain too. *Not before time*, Venus thought. Pornographic videos had been freely available legally in the other nations of the European community for many years. It seemed a sound financial proposition.

Venus's idea was that, by using the robots to star in the films, the company would save a fortune in porno movie-star salaries, thus making their films even more profitable than those of the competition. In addition to which, there would never, ever be any production hold-ups due to a male star's inability to get it up. Aphrodite's male robots could be programmed to have permanent erections, while the company's technical expertise would be able to guarantee the all-important ejaculatory come shots in which the male actors withdrew as they were about to ejaculate and shot their load of semen over the nearest part of the female star's anatomy. Preferably her face. This was to prove, to the audience's satisfaction, that the male star really had been fucking or sodomizing or being sucked off by or masturbated by the female star.

Venus struck the final key, the one to end her report, with a flourish. It was, she knew, controversial, and she was aware that some members of the board were seriously concerned at the way in which the company was developing. What had started out as a small private company, producing high-class, expensively produced – and expensive to buy – sex toys for the very rich, was becoming – largely through Venus's efforts – little better than a massive brothel system.

The concept of robot-renting had brought the products within the financial range of most people. During which time profits had quadrupled, and the organization had gone public. At the end of the day, money was the name of the game. *Fuck it*, Venus thought. If they didn't want to know about these ideas, she'd take them away, find some financial backing, and set up on her own. There was nothing wrong with the ideas. Sex was their business. It always had been. Nothing altered, morally, just because they were making their products more available than they had been. Like they said, if you didn't like the heat, then don't go into the bloody kitchen.

Venus pressed the right buttons to set her printer up to produce the fifteen copies that she would need and left her office. She took herself off downstairs to product testing where she found Mark, this time with a different male tester, and the production director, Peter, all three of them gathered around a test bed on which lay a female robot. It was, Venus noticed, another red-headed Jane model. For just a moment she remembered, pleasantly, her sexual excesses of the previous evening, and then she banished them from her mind.

'Hi, Venus,' said Mark. 'You're just in time. Charles here is just about to fuck-test one of our new batch of multiple-orgasm microchips, from today's production run. All the electronic tests check out. He's just about to get onto the job here.'

Venus looked across at Charles. 'Hello, Charles,' she said. He nodded back at her. 'If you don't mind, sir,' he said to Mark, 'I'll take her without the voice mode. I know them off by heart now. To tell you the truth, they get on my bloody nerves.'

Mark laughed. 'As far as I'm concerned, you can have her any way you want her,' he said. 'If tying her up and beating the shit out of her is your bag, that's fine by me. All I need to know is whether her multiple-orgasm mode is functioning properly. How you get her there is your problem. OK?'

'Thank you, sir,' said the tester. He looked at the three of them. 'And now, if you'll excuse me . . .' They took the hint and withdrew.

'Funny, that,' said Peter. 'Most of them love an audience.'

'He's fairly new,' Mark said. 'I checked him out with human resources before he came down here. I wanted to make sure that he didn't have any kind of problems. He probably isn't quite as blasé yet about fucking dolls in public as the others seem to be.'

Eva Linczy

'He's probably got nasty habits,' said Peter. 'Last week I found one of them stealing all the female robot's dirty knickers from the laundry bag. I fired him, of course. But it's strange to think, isn't it, that, while I accept that sniffing girls' dirty knickers is a fairly common fetish and that men who steal girls' dirty knickers are hardly a rarity, this guy must have known that what he was sniffing actually came, originally, out of a bottle and was manufactured in our laboratories. It smells authentic, that's for sure, but we all know that it isn't real. Don't we?'

'Well, I suppose that's a sort of a backhanded compliment, really, isn't it?' said Venus. She was thinking, rather guiltily, of her own knicker-sniffing of the previous evening, and she wondered if Mark and Peter knew that, whatever the errant product-testing knicker-sniffer thought he was sniffing, the smell was actually a chemical reproduction of Venus's own strongly scented sexual effluent. She could feel her own knickers getting moist at the crotch at the recollection of what she had been doing the previous evening. She wondered what the others would say if she was to raise the question of what the company's female sexual aroma was based on, and if she then told them exactly what it *was* derived from.

She fantasized, for a brief spell, of pulling down her knickers and pressing the moist gusset against one or other of the two men's noses, saying, 'Sniff that, darling. Do you like it? That's the smell of my cunt that you're inhaling. And that's what all Aphrodite's female robots' knickers smell of. My hot, wet, juicy cunt. Would you like an opportunity to sniff the real thing?'

Voluptuous Venus

What a strange pastime, she thought. Knicker-sniffing. She had never heard of women sniffing men's worn underpants. She had certainly never indulged in sniffing men's underpants herself. The idea didn't begin to excite her. But then she suddenly remembered that she adored the smell of fruity cock. It could well be that the crotches of men's underpants harboured exactly that same odour. She would try to remember to test it out, the next time she was in a position so to do.

A technician had gone into the test bedroom as the three of them had come out, and he too now emerged, closing the door behind him. He greeted them by their first names. 'He's all set up now,' he volunteered. 'We'll soon know whether or not the new batch of microchips is up to standard. Personally, I don't think there's a problem. I think we must have had a glitch of some sort in the run for the last batch. But time will tell.' He looked at his watch. 'You know where to get me if you need me,' he said to Peter. 'But I sincerely hope you won't.'

'So do I,' Peter said. 'Cheers for now.' The man left. The three of them chatted for the next fifteen minutes, with much stealthy checking of watches. But nobody actually said anything about the time being taken by the male tester. It seemed an inordinately long period to all three of them, but they acknowledged that they were considerably on edge.

'Oh, come on,' said Venus eventually, under her breath. At that very moment the tester emerged from the test cubicle. He was smiling. 'No problems at all, sir,' he said to Peter. 'I'll fill out a full report right away, and give you all the readings, but I can assure you that her multiple orgasm mode is functioning perfectly.'

'Well, thank you,' Peter said. 'And thank God for that. Now we can all get on with the job. Thanks, Venus. Thanks, Mark. I'll see you.' He turned on his heel and left.

They said their goodbyes and made off for their respective offices. Venus looked at her diary when she got back to hers. She had what her staff facetiously called an 'audition' that afternoon. What it meant was that, in order to maintain a constant supply of male and female robots with attractive physiques, and particularly with attractive sexual organs Venus ran a series of advertisements in various publications, looking for suitable human models. Unless a robot was, by request, an exact copy of some famous person, they were normally an amalgamation, incorporating, for a female version say, the breasts from one model, the legs from another, the bottom from a third, and perhaps the sexual organs of a fourth. And, of course, the same process was used to assemble the male robots. This afternoon, Venus was scheduled to have a look at a variety of men and women, all of whom had already been passed by a selection committee as being suitable, subject to her final approval. It meant, in every case, seeing the prospective models naked.

Although she hadn't ever admitted it to any of her colleagues, Venus actually quite enjoyed the task. From time to time she got very turned on by some of the men. And, just occasionally, by one or two of the women. She looked at her watch again. The 'audition' was scheduled to commence at two-thirty. It was almost one o'clock. She

Voluptuous Venus

decided that she would lunch today in the canteen, where the subsidized food provided by a benevolent employer was excellent.

An hour and a half later, having lunched abstemiously in the executive canteen on a crab salad and a single glass of white wine, Venus arrived at the suite of rooms built specially for the 'auditions.' They comprised a dozen individual changing rooms. These were rather larger than the usual kind of changing rooms found in stores, or even in sports clubs. Each room was furnished with a comfortable easy chair, a television set, and a selection of reading material. This was so that would-be models could relax at their ease while they waited. Surgical-style white gowns were issued to all the applicants.

The male and female sections were so arranged that the two sexes at no time bumped into one another – unless Venus, for whatever reason, wanted to mix the sexes in her viewing room, a large room at the far end of the unit with separate entrances for men and women. Security guards were immediately to hand, and could be summoned by a bell sited under Venus's desk and pressed by her foot, should it ever be necessary. It hadn't been, so far, but there were some strange people about and, being in the kind of business that it was, Aphrodite tended to attract more than its fair share of them. For obvious reasons.

Venus had established a system whereby she saw the women first, then the men. Each applicant was collected from his or her changing room by an assistant, along with a folder containing details of the individual, the part(s) of their anatomy that they were being considered for, and a selection of recent photographs.

The first woman had applied for employment as a breast model and had been approved by the committee (unbeknownst, as yet, to the woman herself) for this purpose. She was a nineteen-year-old with brown hair, a pretty but not beautiful face, and long, slim legs. Venus shook hands with her, and asked her to take her gown off. The girl did so. She seemed relaxed and completely unembarrassed. She certainly had beautiful breasts. They were a good size, without being over-large. They were firm and pointed, with pretty, average-sized nipples set in attractive areolae that were a dark, pinkish brown. The girl smiled at her. 'Do you like them?' she asked.

'Yes, I do,' Venus said. 'Very much.' She went over to a small refrigerator in one corner of the room, and took an ice cube out of a tray. 'Would you mind rubbing your nipples with this ice?' she asked, holding out the ice cube.

'Why don't you do it for me?' asked the girl, from beneath fluttering eyelids. 'That would be more fun. For both of us.'

Oh ho, thought Venus. *Careful, darling.* 'I'm sorry,' she said. 'I'd prefer that you do it yourself.'

'Please yourself,' the girl said, crossly, and she snatched the ice from Venus's outstretched hand. 'My mistake,' she said, sulkily. She rubbed first one nipple, then the other, and gave the fast-melting ice cube back to Venus, who dropped it in a wastepaper basket. The girl's nipples stood up erectly. She looked down at them and twirled them between her fingers so that they stood up even more

Voluptuous Venus

firmly. The girl's breasts were really fabulous.

'Mmmmm,' said Venus, wanting to give credit where credit was due. 'Very pretty. I think we'd very much like to use you. I'll get our human resources department to see you when you leave me. They'll explain our terms and conditions to you. If you're happy with those, then we can do business.'

As she spoke, Venus found herself in something of a quandary. One of the parts of the female body that Aphrodite was always short of pretty examples for was the vagina and its various appurtenances. Young pussy was always the prettiest pussy of all, and the chances were that *this* young girl's pussy would be in splendid – and very attractive – condition. But she was obviously, if not actually lesbian, then probably bisexual. Which was a matter of concern to Venus.

She suspected that the girl might misunderstand her reasons for asking to look at her vagina. Venus's advertisements avoided any mention of applicants' sexual organs, in order not to attract cranks. It was left to Venus to use her discretion in raising the subject with anyone whom she thought might be a possibility. *Oh, the hell with it*, she thought. *What have I got to lose? If she's a problem, I can always have her thrown out.*

Just then the girl said 'Oh, terrific. Thank you. I really need the money. Oh, I'm so pleased. Thank you. Thank you.' She smiled at Venus through brown eyes that were suddenly noticeably full of tears.

It made Venus's mind up for her. She smiled back at the girl. 'I'm so pleased that *you're* pleased,' she said. 'Now

Eva Linczy

look. Just listen to me for a minute. I most particularly don't want you to misunderstand what I'm going to say to you, so let me spell it out for you. Your sexual proclivities are your own business. Mine are mine. I see a lot of people here – men and women – and there are, as I'm sure you can imagine, many opportunities for personal sexual encounters. But that's not what I'm here for, and I don't take advantage of my position. Ever.' (It wasn't strictly true, but it sounded good). 'So please remember that. Now then. Back to business. From a purely professional point of view, I love your breasts. They're fantastic.'

The girl smiled at her. 'Thank you,' she said.

Venus continued. 'And for the same reasons that we pay people to base some of our models on their breasts, or their legs, or their bottoms, we also pay people to base some of our models on their sexual parts. In your case, your vagina. So don't misunderstand me, please, when I say will you let me look at your vagina, to judge whether or not I think we might be able to pay you to use it as a model? And for the record, let me tell you that we pay more for sexual organs as models than we do for any other part of the human body. What do you say?'

'Christ,' the girl said. 'You mean you might pay me to use my cunt as a model? Ooops. Sorry. My veg . . . Vag . . . Oh, hell. Whatever. Cunt. Yes?'

'Yes,' Venus said. 'If I like the look of it.'

'Feel free,' said the girl. 'Do whatever you like to it.'

'Thank you,' Venus said, feeling that enough was enough. 'Now, come and sit on this chair here, will you, please, and lean back and open your legs. As wide as you can.'

Voluptuous Venus

The girl did as she was told. Her brown pubic hair was soft and long. Venus reached out and parted it, quickly finding the girl's outer labia. They were neat and tidy, and quite small. Venus looked at her. 'I'm going to open you up now, to look at you inside,' she said. 'It's necessary, but do remember that, as far as I'm concerned, it's not in any way sexual.' She could feel the moisture dampening her knickers and giving the lie to her words.

She spread the girl's outer labia and revealed her tidy little inner lips. She parted these to expose a healthily pink vaginal opening. The girl wriggled as she did so, and smiled at Venus when she looked up at her. The girl's vagina was small, delightfully tight, and – to a connoisseur, which Venus was – really very pretty. It was also, like Venus's, decidedly moist. From where she was standing, with her head bent over the girl's pudenda, Venus could scent her female secretions. She smelt clean and pleasantly sexy. Almost reluctantly, Venus withdrew her fingers from the girl's pussy and went over to her desk to find a tissue on which to wipe them. She turned and faced the girl directly.

'Well,' she said, smiling herself. 'I think we're in business. As I said before, the human resources people will tell you all about how much we pay, and about royalties and so on. If you find those acceptable, then we'll use your breasts *and* your . . .' She hesitated. Then, 'Cunt,' she said, laughing out loud. The girl laughed with her.

'If it all works out,' Venus said, 'you'll be able to boast to your friends about being fucked – in replica, as it were –

Eva Linczy

by literally thousands of men. How does that appeal to you?' The girl giggled.

'As long as it's only one at a time,' she said. Venus warmed to her. Perhaps she'd misjudged her initially. She pressed her bell for her assistant to show the girl out.

'Thank you,' she said, as the girl left. 'I'm sure we'll do some nice things together.' The girl put out her hand, and Venus shook it. 'Thank you,' said the girl. 'I look forward to seeing you again. Goodbye now.'

The rest of the girls were fairly unremarkable, as pretty girls go. Venus approved one of them, for her gorgeous, slim, lovely, muscular long legs. And she approved another girl's lovely bottom. *Oh, to be a man*, she thought as she looked at the young girl's exquisite derrière. *If I had a cock*, she thought, *that's exactly where I would want to put it. Right up that girl's gorgeous, tight little arse.*

'Tell me,' she said to the girl, 'do you take it up your bottom? Cock, I mean. Do you like it up your bottom?'

'Love it,' the girl replied. 'It's my favourite thing. But how did you know?'

'I didn't,' Venus said. 'Your bottom told me.' They both laughed.

After the girls, the men were a welcome change. Venus was, by this time, well primed. Her knicker crotch was so wet that the lubricant emanating from her pussy was beginning to trickle down the insides of her naked thighs. She felt as randy as hell. *What I need, right now*, she told herself, *is a good fuck*. Chance would be a fine thing. The first man in was, purely visually, very good news. Venus looked at his file. He was there, as far as the application

Voluptuous Venus

papers were concerned, for the quality of his buttocks. He had applied for the possibility of Aphrodite using his bottom, but the selection committee had not approved.

'Hi,' Venus said, shaking his hand as he came through the door. 'Perhaps you'd like to drop your gown and let me see you naked.'

'Sure thing,' he said. And did exactly that. Venus could see why someone (probably a woman, she thought) on the initial selection committee had liked his bum. It *was* a pretty good bum, as bums went. But it wasn't quite perfect. And everything that Aphrodite put out (look-alikes excepted) had to be physically perfect. But he did have a very good-looking cock. It was at a sort of half-mast right now.

Venus guessed that he was turned on by the whole process and was excited by the thought of having a young woman look at his arse. These thoughts, it seemed, were being broadcast to the world in general, and to Venus in particular, by the semi-erection that the guy was exposing right now. She smiled at him. *Why not*, she thought.

'Hey,' she said. 'That's a good-looking cock you've got hidden away down there. It's a genuine pussy-wetter. Take it from me. I'm an expert. But you're here to show me your butt, aren't you?'

'Well, that's what I filled in the forms for,' he said. 'The advertisement didn't say anything about cocks.' He pronounced advertisement as advert*ize*ment, emphasizing the middle of it. 'But if you think you'd like to use my cock for one of your robots, you're more than welcome.'

'Well,' Venus said, 'let's have a closer look at both items

then. Turn round, spread your legs and bend over.' The man grinned and turned his back towards her. Then he bent down, tautening his buttocks as she looked at them. She could see his balls, and the tip of his cock, hanging down between his legs. His arse was very hairy.

'I'm sorry,' she said, 'but, while your butt is good, it isn't quite right for us. That's a purely subjective decision, so don't get uptight about it. No one is saying that it's no good. But let me have a better look at your cock. Do you mind?'

'Not in the least,' he said.

'Come and sit over here,' said Venus. He sat on the chair where she had indicated. 'I'm going to have to handle it,' she said. 'If we use it, much of that use will be while erect. So I'm just going to half toss you off. Is that OK?'

The man grinned at her. 'Perfectly,' he said. 'Feel free to go all the way, if that's what you want.'

She knelt on the floor in front of him, which brought her face down onto a level with his cock. It grew as she looked at it, and she knew he was looking at her mouth. She deliberately licked her lips. Slowly.

And then she reached out and took hold of his swelling penis. She began to masturbate him, pulling his foreskin down and then running her fingers all the way down to the base of his cock and, very slowly, all the way back up again. He began just the smallest sort of fucking motion with his hips as he sat on the chair.

'Ooooh,' he said. 'Nice. I like that. You've done it before, I can tell.'

She grinned up at him. 'Once or twice,' she said. His

Voluptuous Venus

cock responded magnificently. It really was an excellent example of an uncircumcised penis, and it was *very* large.

'Is it fully erect now?' she asked him. 'Is that it at full stretch, as it were?'

He looked down at it. 'Yep. That's it,' he said. 'What do you think?'

'I think we can use it,' Venus told him. 'In fact, let me say now, if our terms and conditions are to your satisfaction, we definitely *will* use it. It's a beauty.'

'Oh, terrific,' he said. 'Imagine coming here thinking that you might like to use my bum, and then you decide to use my cock. Far out.' Venus let go of his cock. 'Hey,' he said.

'What do you mean, "hey"?' she asked him.

He looked down at her. 'Well, surely you're not going to leave it like that, are you?' he asked. 'You wank me into a full erection, and then you just stop.'

'Well, what do you expect me to do?' she asked.

'Surely you can finish it off, for God's sake,' he said.

'I told you at the beginning,' she said to him, 'that I was going to *half* toss you off. "Half" being the operative word. If you want to finish it off yourself, be my guest.'

She walked over to her desk and pressed a switch. 'Now we're off the record,' she said. 'All the conversations with would-be sexual models are recorded. For reasons that you'll understand. Now I've switched the machine off.' She turned the keys in both the doors into her office. Then she walked over to another easy chair, opposite the one the man was sitting on, leaned over its back, pulled up her skirt, and pulled down her knickers to below her knees.

She spread her legs as best she could in that position. The man could see her pussy, surrounded by her cunt hair. She put her hands behind her and opened up her vaginal lips for him. He could see her wetness, shining pinkly at him. His cock throbbed as he stood up.

'Come and have a quickie,' she said. 'Looking at your lovely cock has made me as randy as hell. But don't take *too* long, or my assistant will wonder what's happening.'

He stood behind her and guided his cock up into her wetness. Then he put his arms around her front and grasped her breasts through her blouse. He began to fuck her.

'Do you like it doggy fashion?' she asked him.

'Love it,' he panted. 'You're all hot and wet, and you're lovely and tight. Will you marry me?'

She laughed. 'No chance,' she said. 'I'm not the marrying kind. Sorry. But you can leave me your home telephone number, if you like.'

'Thank you,' he said. 'I do like. Very much.' He was increasing his rhythm as he began to reach the beginning of his ejaculation. Venus had realized, when she leaned over the chair, that it was unlikely that she would achieve orgasm herself in this position. She had simply felt rather sorry for the man, and had done it almost entirely for his benefit rather than her own. She had also realized, from the state of his sexual excitement, that he wasn't going to last for any time at all, and in fact she didn't want him to. She'd said quickie, and that was what she'd meant. For these reasons, she put an arm down and, with her fingers between her legs, she massaged her clitoris to orgasm,

Voluptuous Venus

timed beautifully, just as the man began to spurt his semen up into her receptive pussy.

'Christ,' he gasped as he came. And then, 'Oh, Jesus.' Venus squeezed his cock with her pussy muscles, milking him of his ejaculate. He was very noisy.

She let him stay where he was for a little while, and then she gently began to stand up, which had the desired result of allowing his now-wilting penis to flop out of her. She pulled her knickers up, her skirt down, and went over to her desk. She winked at him, and switched on the recording device again.

'I guess that's all, then,' she said. 'Thanks a lot. I'll see you another day, after you've seen the human resources people and made your decision.' She handed him a piece of paper and a pen. She'd written 'Home phone number?' on the paper. He wrote it down, and also 'Thank *you*'. She rang the buzzer for her assistant to show him out, saying to the girl as she was leaving with him, 'I think I'll take a five-minute break right now, Sally. OK?'

'Of course,' said the girl. 'Buzz me when you're ready for the next applicant.'

'Will do,' said Venus. She took herself off into the private bathroom that was off the 'auditioning' room, sat down on the bidet, and washed her genitals thoroughly. What goes up must come down, her mother had always said when initiating her daughter into correct feminine hygiene. And how right she'd been, thought Venus, as she dried herself. It didn't matter how forcefully semen was jetted up your vagina, the greater part of it slowly ran down again, particularly if, as now, it happened during the day and you had to stand up and walk about after sex. It could make for unpleasantly sticky knicker gussets.

She sometimes wondered how any of the sperm ever got as far as a woman's womb, there to impregnate her. But get there they did. Thank God for the latest in a long line of contraceptive pills. As for naughty girls who let men fuck their bottoms, the damn stuff slid back down that passage even more relentlessly, she remembered. She tried to think when she had last allowed anyone to penetrate her anally, but she couldn't be sure about it. It was probably that Christopher, over the last Christmas break. He was very into anal sex, when he was allowed.

Venus tidied up her make-up and took herself back into her office. She took a cup of coffee from the dispenser, and sat down with it. She was getting very slack about her love life, she thought. It was, she supposed, an inevitable result of this job, with its emphasis on sex and the sexual opportunities that it offered. Like the one she had just experienced. The offering, mind you, had come *from* her, she realized. Not *to* her. Although the man had more or less asked. But she could quite properly have ignored his pleas. Or she could have satisfied him with a simple wank.

She tried to stop feeling guilty and made a mental note to do something about a regular man, one outside the office. And she promised to stop pretending that all the sex that she got through the job was in the interests of research. *Research be buggered*, she thought. She just liked fucking and being fucked. She decided that she would at least be honest about it, if only with herself. She wasn't quite sure where sex with the company's robots fitted into

Voluptuous Venus

this new scheme of things, but she decided that she'd worry about that another time. Thus refreshed, she rang for the next 'audition.'

When he arrived, she took an instant dislike to him, and she gave him very short shrift. He was there because someone had liked his hands. They didn't look anything particularly special to Venus. The suggestion from the selection committee was that they would be good hands for a composite model.

He could tell that she didn't like him, and it obviously irritated him. 'Would you like to see them in action?' he asked her. 'It might give you a better idea of their potential.' She wondered what he was going to suggest. Maybe he would like to massage her neck. But she certainly wasn't going to ask him. He was far more likely to suggest massaging her breasts. Or her buttocks, perhaps.

'Thanks a lot,' she said, 'but no, thank you. You'll get our decision through the post. I wish you luck, and I thank you for coming here.' She stood up, and pressed the buzzer for Sally.

'That's the lot, for today,' Sally said, as she held the door open for the man. 'Great,' said Venus. 'I'm off, then. See you next week. And thank you for your help today. Ciao.'

For her next task, Venus got down to finalizing the arrangements for the launch of the new Aphrodite model range to the world's media. With the world as her oyster, she had persuaded the company to launch the new range at the St Lucian Hotel, in St Lucia, West Indies.

St Lucia is one of the Windward Islands, at the bottom end of the Caribbean chain of islands, with Martinique to the north and St Vincent to the south. The hotel was an old Caribbean establishment, with gracious bedrooms surrounding a new block which contained the restaurant, bar, disco, cinema and hotel offices.

The rooms Venus had booked were all superior, air-conditioned rooms with private bathrooms and views out across the bay in which the hotel was situated, with its mile-long palm-fringed white sandy beach and its view of the eighteenth-century castle on the top of the hill on the other side of the bay. The castle had been built originally by the British to protect St Lucia from invasion by the French, and was now a land-mark for the visitors attracted by the island's flourishing tourist trade. The hotel's cuisine was excellent, and it supplied every possible kind of water sport facility (apart, Venus thought, from the sort of water sports that some of her customers delighted in) including water skiing, scuba diving, snorkelling, sailing and deep-sea fishing. The placid Caribbean ocean apart, there was, of course, a large hotel pool.

Venus had been out to the hotel some three weeks before, and had decided that there was no need to inform the hotel's management of the precise subject matter of her forthcoming media conference. They might very well not approve of being used as a test bed – literally – for a new range of sex robots. So long as she had the necessary conference facilities – which she did – she could arrange for the individually designed robots to be delivered to the

Voluptuous Venus

guests personally when they all arrived there.

Venus had sampled the food in the main restaurant, the beach restaurant and the three bars, and had found it all excellent. The staff were experienced and charming, and the service was first class. There was a minor water shortage problem from time to time, when the room showers dried up temporarily, but wasn't there that problem everywhere these days? There was a local group playing gentle, and faintly rude, local music in the main restaurant, and most nights there was cabaret in the beachside bar area, ranging from demonstrations of limbo dancing with delightful young St Lucian men and women in extremely brief costumes, to the equivalent of a St Lucian Top of the Pops, which inevitably included a whole series of bongo drummers, rap singers, and keyboard players. The volume of noise produced by these groups was only exceeded by the enthusiasm with which their performances were received by the tourists staying at the hotel. Venus loved it all it, and took part in everything.

During her stay on the island, Venus drove up to the local town, Scarborough, and visited the local markets as well as the botanical gardens. She patronized the various bars and restaurants situated around the St Lucian hotel, and bought herself a charming, almost scandalous bikini – at great expense – in one of the local shops. But the high point of her stay was the week-long affair that she had with the young American lawyer that she met in the hotel bar on her first evening out there. She had left Heathrow at nine that morning, British Summer Time, and arrived at the hotel at seven in the evening, local time – some five

Eva Linczy

hours on from BST – so she wasn't feeling at her freshest.

But the Caribbean sunshine, the tropical vegetation, the charm of the local people, her pleasant room, and the beauty of the bay in which the hotel was set, together with its exquisitely manicured grounds, had put her in a good mood as she sat at the bar and ordered herself an exotic local rum cocktail.

She was just taking her first sip when a young, extremely attractive American man came and stood at the bar beside her. 'That looks good, ma'am,' he said. 'May I ask what it's called?'

'Surely,' said Venus. 'It's called a St Lucian Special. It's got five different Caribbean rums in it. And a certain amount of fruit juices. But they don't seem strong on the fruit juice here. It tastes delicious. I strongly recommend it.'

'Why, thank you, ma'am,' he said. 'That sounds as if it is exactly what I need.' He waved at the barman and ordered one for himself and another for Venus. 'May I introduce myself?' he asked. 'I'm Harry. Harry Moss. I'm an attorney, down from New York to look after a case here in St Lucia for one of my clients. I've just arrived, and I have to tell you, I'm feeling no pain. No pain at all.' He raised his glass. 'Cheers,' he said. 'Happy holidays. But that assumes that you're here on vacation. Are you?'

'Well, no, actually,' said Venus, and she explained that she was here to set up the arrangements for a media seminar for one of her clients, and that she, too, had arrived that very day. It was to be a propitious meeting. Venus didn't tell Harry the subject matter of her media

Voluptuous Venus

conference, nor the name of her company, nor did she describe its products: she simply said that she was the research director, also responsible for marketing, for an international company based in London.

'From your accent, that has to be London, England?' Harry queried. As a typical Brit, Venus's response was, 'Yes, of course. There isn't a London anywhere else.'

'Oh, yes, there is,' Harry said. 'There's London, Ontario. In Canada. But then we Americans are probably more insular, in world terms, than you British. We always say Paris, France, for example.' Venus laughed. 'And why not?' she said.

From the bar, they moved into the hotel restaurant together, and over their meal they quickly became attracted to one another. Harry was fair, tall, tanned and somewhere in his early thirties. He was sophisticated, enjoyed both people and conversation – which he was good at – and that quickly attracted people to him. He was single, and had an expert eye for (and way with) pretty girls.

Venus, as we know, was now pushing twenty-four. Her fair hair was blonde, with a certain amount of help from her hairdresser, and her pale skin reflected the cold British climate. She too was tall. She was also long-legged, and slim, with pert, firm breasts, and a lean, tightly rounded bottom. She was, in fact, quite beautiful.

When the two of them had finished their leisurely dinner, they moved from the restaurant to the hotel disco that, to their mutual enjoyment, was playing the kind of slow, smoochy songs that lovers the world over like to dance to. As they held each other close and navigated the wooden floor, which was built out over the sea, with the moonlight lighting a silver path across the bay, Venus could feel the hard outline of Harry's growing erection through his thin, tropical-weight white slacks, and she leaned back and pressed herself against it, showing him that it was indeed most welcome.

Harry danced divinely, and he was enchanted – and encouraged – by this young English girl who seemed to be telling him, by her body language, that she was available to him, if he so wished. He'd not met many British girls, and he was impressed by the warmth emanating from this one. He had always believed that British girls were as cold as the climate in which they were raised. Perhaps, chameleon-like, they reacted to the weather. If that was so, certainly the Caribbean weather was having a good effect upon this one. He could smell her perfume, mixing with the scent of her body. It was fresh, and he found it sexually exciting.

As far as Venus was concerned, she couldn't wait to get that lovely hard cock that she could feel pressing against her properly in between her legs. Surely Harry fancied her? She was telling him, in every way she knew how – apart from actually spelling it out – that she wanted him to take her to bed. He couldn't possibly be gay. Not with that erection pressing against her. *Oh well*, she thought eventually. *Faint heart never won hard cock*. She nestled her cheek against his, ground her pelvis against him, and whispered into his ear, 'Why don't you take me to bed, Harry? I'm told that I give terrific head.'

Voluptuous Venus

Harry gulped. He was so taken aback that all he could think of to say was to make a joke out of her question. 'Thank God,' he said. 'I was beginning to think you'd never ask. Your place or mine?' And then, before she had time to answer, he said quickly, 'Let's make it mine, if that's all right with you. Since my company is paying, and eventually my client will reimburse the money for it, I've got a suite. It's overlooking the beach, and there's a fridge full of booze. How does that sound?'

'It sounds good,' she told him. She reached up and kissed his cheek.

'Let's go, then,' Harry said. They returned to their table, Harry signed the bill, and they walked, arm in arm, along the low elevated path that led all around the bay, about five or six feet above the white, sandy beach. They could hear the sound of the Caribbean waves, breaking gently along the shoreline, and see the white of the foam, turned silver by the moon's reflection. Looking up, the sky was ablaze with a million tiny stars. 'The Milky Way,' said Venus. 'Isn't it all just so romantic?'

They arrived at the steps off the path leading up to Harry's first-floor suite. The entire hotel complex was only two storeys high, so the first floor was also the top floor. Harry unlocked his door and opened it for Venus. The suite was large, comprising an enormous sitting room opening out onto a wide balcony facing the bay that ran along the whole length of the suite. It was air-conditioned, which was best at night in the sometimes steamy St Lucia climate, and there were also ceiling fans for use during the day when the sliding doors to the balcony were open.

Venus explored the whole suite to find a large bedroom with two double beds, in the American manner, and a luxuriously fitted en suite bathroom leading off. 'There's champagne in the fridge, honey,' Harry said. 'It might make a pleasant change, at this time of night, from all that rum. What do you say?'

'That would be lovely, Harry,' Venus said. 'Thank you.' She went and stood beside him as he opened the bottle, and watched him pour two glasses.

'To us,' said Harry.

'To us, Harry,' said Venus. They both drank, and then Venus put her glass down. She took Harry's glass from his hand and put it down beside hers, and then she took him in her arms. She put up her mouth to be kissed.

Harry wasted no time in putting his arms around her, and they kissed, passionately, for a long time. Still kissing, Venus disentangled one arm and, reaching down between Harry's legs, she stroked the length of his now full erection. She found his zip and eased it down. Reaching inside, she released his rigid cock, pulled it out of its prison, and grasped it firmly in her fingers. Harry stopped kissing her and gasped out loud as she did so.

Venus took the opportunity to kneel down in front of him. She looked at his cock, hungrily. Lovingly. It was big. Really big. She could feel her own sexual moisture dampening her knickers at the thought of what was about to happen.

She took him in her mouth. Just the head of his cock, to start with. She enveloped it with her lips, wetting it with her tongue, and she sucked on it gently as she slid her

Voluptuous Venus

fingers up and down the length of his shaft. Then she took his glans out of her mouth and blew on it, softly.

'That's just a sample,' she said to Harry, looking up at him. And then she stood up. 'Now let's go into the bedroom and get ourselves more comfortable before I give you the full treatment.' She smiled at him. 'And then you can fuck me,' she said.

Harry was speechless, partly with excitement, partly because the forthrightness of this young girl's sexuality was something he hadn't come across before. Most of the American girls he'd been to bed with (hookers apart) had played coy with him and insisted on putting the light out before sex. None of them had voluntarily offered to give him head and then actually pursued that objective. It was, for Harry, a whole new, tremendously erotic experience.

He followed Venus into the bedroom. As Harry divested himself of shirt, pants, shoes and socks, Venus stripped off her short evening dress, revealing herself braless, but wearing minuscule black, lacy panties, and, once she'd kicked off her high-heeled patent leather pumps, nothing else. She smiled.

'That's better,' she said. She looked around the room and walked over to an armchair. 'This will do us fine,' she said. 'Come and sit here, Harry.' She next walked over to a sofa against a far wall and removed a couple of cushions from it which she put onto the floor, in front of the armchair. She then went and closed the curtains along the length of the bedroom end of the balcony's sliding windows. 'Giving you head is one thing,' she said. 'Giving a public exhibition is something else.' Harry was by now sitting in the armchair, as instructed.

He couldn't take his eyes off the almost naked Venus, and what he was thinking about her body was reflected in his magnificently swollen erection. Venus went back to the armchair, and knelt gracefully upon the cushions that she had positioned in front of it. She took her small, firm breasts, one in each hand, leant forward, and enveloped Harry's cock in them. She looked up at him as she rubbed her breasts the length of his rampant prick.

'This is what tarts in London call a tit wank, Harry,' she said. 'Some men prefer it done by girls with really big breasts. But I haven't had any complaints, as yet. What do you think?' She giggled at his expression, which was divided somewhere between fascination, adoration, and being completely sexually overwhelmed.

He had his eyes shut as he said, 'No, I never had one of these before. We used to talk about them at college, and the boys there used to call them French necklaces. They were supposedly the speciality of Parisian hookers. But I like it. I like it.'

'But not as much as this, I suspect,' said Venus. Saying which, she let go of her breasts, leaned back slightly, and took him once more into her mouth. She started to stroke his shaft again, and she then took him out of her mouth and began, gently, to rub his perineum. Clear mucous liquid started to leak from the tip of his penis. She licked it off, and took him back into her mouth. This time, she took him as deeply into her mouth as she was able, and then she began to suck him. At the same time, she started to

Voluptuous Venus

bob her head up and down. She could feel the tip of his cock actually in her throat. Deep-throating him.

It was an art that took long practice, and she remembered Richard, the London Harley Street surgeon, fondly as she fellated Harry. It was Richard who had spent hours teaching her how to deep-throat him. She had only been eighteen at the time. At first she had gagged, and choked, and for a long time she had trouble breathing while she took his cock deep into her throat. But perseverance had paid off in the end, and it was now something that she enjoyed doing. She enjoyed experiencing the salacious pleasure, the sheer, sensual ecstasy that it gave to the men whom she deep-throated. And she adored the feel of the men's ejaculate as they pumped it, lustfully, groaning with male gratification, down her throat. The combination of the novelty of the experience, the sheer, carnal sexuality of it, and Venus's practised mastery of it soon had Harry grabbing her head and literally fucking her mouth, immediately prior to exploding his semen down her throat. As she swallowed, she kept on with her head-bobbing, finger-manipulating, deep-throated sucking until he was spent, at which she slowly drew him out of her throat, out of her mouth, and looked up at him, curious as to his reaction.

'Was that good for you, darling?' she asked him.

'Jesus, was it?' he said. 'The earth moved, I tell you. The fuckin' earth moved. It was too much.' He reached down and stroked her cheek. 'Thank you, baby. That was real good.' He lay back in the armchair, his eyes closed, and she thought that perhaps he was going to sleep. But after a moment or two he opened his eyes and looked down at her. 'Would you like me to suck your pussy for you now, baby?' he asked. 'Before I fuck you, I mean. Not instead of.'

'Yes, I'd like that,' she said. 'I like having my pussy sucked.'

'Let's have a glass of champagne before we start,' he suggested. 'You must be thirsty too. All that salty semen.' He got up out of the chair, went through to the other room, and came back, moments later, with their refilled glasses. He handed hers to her. 'Cheers, baby,' he said.

'Cheers, darling,' she replied. They drank deeply. 'I've never thought about swallowing semen making a girl thirsty,' she told him. 'The one problem with deep-throating is that, if you're doing it properly, the semen doesn't come anywhere near your taste buds. It's simply a sensation. One can feel it spurting into one's throat, and feel the warmth of it. But that's all. There's no discernible taste.'

'I'm sorry,' he said. 'I'll try and make up for that in a minute.' And he did. She went and lay on the bed, and the first thing that he did, very gently, was to prise her legs apart. He then rubbed and stroked her vulva through her moist knicker crotch, until it was even wetter. 'I love wet pussies,' he told her. 'It shows real appreciation.'

She grinned up at him. 'I guess it does,' she said. 'Mine's been getting wetter and wetter for hours now. It started in the bar. Got wetter in the restaurant. Ran like a damn stream when we were dancing. And got even wetter while I was sucking your cock. It's just as well that you *do* like

Voluptuous Venus

wet pussy. You could probably wring cunt juice out of my knickers if you tried.'

'What a lovely thought,' he said. He put his fingers in the waistband of her tiny thong-style black nylon knickers, and when she raised her hips up off the bed he pulled them down her long legs and off, over her feet. 'They're certainly wet, baby,' he said. 'I'm flattered.' He cradled them carefully in his hands and then, holding them over his champagne glass – which was still about a third full – he wrung them out, slowly, over the glass.

Venus's prophesy had been entirely accurate. As Harry twisted his hands, the one against the other, a thin stream of liquid was squeezed out of the cotton-lined gusset of Venus's knickers and down into Harry's glass. By the time he was finished, the glass was more than half full. 'My God,' he said. 'I wouldn't have believed it possible.' He picked up the glass and raised it towards Venus. 'I told you I loved pussy juice,' he said. 'Here's health.' And so saying, he lifted the glass to his lips, threw back his head, and drained it. He licked his lips lasciviously and smiled at her. 'Delicious,' he said. 'Absolutely delicious. A new champagne drink. There's a champagne cocktail, of course. With brandy and sugar and bitters. And then there's Buck's Fizz, with orange juice. And Black Velvet, with champagne and Guinness. And the Venetians do one with peach juice. What's it called? Ah, yes, a Bellini. So what shall we call this one?'

'A Pussycat,' said Venus, instantly. 'What else?' They both laughed at her suggested label.

'And now for some more of the real thing,' said Harry.

'This time undiluted.' He put his glass down and positioned himself so that his head was between Venus's thighs.

She drew her knees back up towards her head and opened her legs wide. Harry first fingered her labia, stroking them, parting them, and finally sliding a finger gently inside her. She wriggled her buttocks as she felt the welcome invasion of his finger. She was wanting him to fuck her, but she was enjoying what he was doing. Then he licked her, wetly, running his tongue the length of her open pussy lips. He worked away at her, probing, licking, stimulating her clitoris which rose erectly beneath his oral ministrations. Then she gasped as she felt his finger touching her anus, and then again as he thrust it right up her.

'Jesus,' she whispered. 'I'm going to come. I'm going to come now.' And then, as she climaxed, she raised her buttocks up in the air, right off the bed, as her orgasm racked her body. She bucked and writhed, and emitted a strange noise: a half-scream, half-growl, deep in her throat.

Harry pulled his finger out of her anus and, grasping both her buttocks, he pressed her vulva up against his mouth as she squirmed and moaned. 'Oh, God. Oh, Jesus. I'm coming. I'm coming,' she cried.

Harry kept sucking her clitoris as her orgasms rose to their climactic peak and then slowly ebbed away. At the end she lay there, exhausted by both his efforts and her own. He kept his head between her legs, his mouth on her sex, kissing and licking gently, until she put a hand down and began to stroke his head. 'Thank you, darling,' she said. 'That was something else. It really was.'

He raised his head, and grinned up at her. 'Then it's what you might call even Steven,' he said. 'How about another glass of bubbly, before we continue? Would you like that?'

'That's exactly what I need,' she said. 'A glass of champagne, and then a long, gentle, slow fuck.'

'Coming up,' he said, getting up from between her legs and going off into the other room. He was back in a couple of minutes, a glass in each hand.

As they drank, they talked quietly to each other, of life with a capital L. Of their hopes. Their ambitions. Their fears. Harry spoke of his career as an attorney in the hustle of New York City. His offices, he told Venus, were on Third Avenue, at 62nd Street. His firm specialized in corporate matters which, while they were hugely profitable, were seldom exciting. His plan, he said – when the time came – was to settle down, get married, and put up his shingle as a practising attorney in some small town in America's Midwest, which was where he had been born.

Venus – who by now trusted Harry completely – took this opportunity to tell him exactly what the company she worked for produced. He was, of course, aware of Aphrodite and its range of products. He was both fascinated and impressed to hear that she was the company's research director. She told him that she had no thought of marriage right now. She was, she felt, much too young. 'And in any case,' she said, looking him in the eye, 'I'm having too much fun.'

As she spoke, she wondered idly if perhaps Harry possessed one of her company's female robots, kept handy in his bedroom closet to fuck him in whatever manner he wished, whenever he felt like it. Well, what if he did? The company had sold millions of them since its inception. *Someone* had to own them. Why not Harry? It was perfectly legal.

They finished their champagne. Venus put down her glass and reached for Harry's cock. It was quite flaccid as she put her fingers around it, but it sprang almost instantly into throbbing life as she ran her fingers up and down its increasing length. He turned to face her, put his hands on her shoulders, and pressed her lightly down onto her back on the bed. She parted her thighs and, still holding onto his cock, guided it into her. She felt hot and wet to Harry, who thrust up her as hard as he could. She was so wet, he was instantly in her, all the way up to his balls, which slapped gently against her buttocks.

She began to work her vaginal muscles as he started to thrust in and out of her. He leaned down and covered her mouth with his, invading her with his tongue which, as she reciprocated, she became aware still tasted of her pussy. They were both soon sweating and panting and groaning, and they stopped eating each other's mouths in order the better to take in the breaths that their physical efforts were demanding.

He took his hands off her shoulders and took a nipple in each, pinching and pulling until she gasped with the pain and wriggled and moaned with the pleasure. She reached down between her legs and took his cock by its base into her fingers. She began to masturbate him, slowly, as he pumped in and out of her. She was on the verge of

Voluptuous Venus

orgasming again, and she wanted him to ejaculate into her, in order to bring her orgasm to its climax. Her action quickly brought him to the point of no return, and he thrust hard into her as he spurted his semen up her.

'Oh, yes,' she said, bucking against him, milking him with her muscles, squeezing him dry. 'That's it, baby. You're fucking me, and I'm coming. Oh, yes. I like it. Do it to me. Don't stop. Fuck me like there's no tomorrow.'

Her words encouraged him to attempt to do as she asked, and for a short moment or two he managed it. But, having completed his ejaculation, his cock rapidly lost its erection. 'I'm sorry, baby,' he said. 'The spirit is willing, but the flesh is weak.'

'Hey, there's nothing to apologize for, darling,' she said. 'That was fantastic. It's all been fantastic. I've loved every minute of it.' She lay there, breathing heavily, wondering how to put her next thought into words. *Just say it, baby*, she told herself. So she did. 'And as far as I'm concerned, if you want to, we can spend the whole of the next week – well, the nights, anyway – doing what we've been doing this evening. And anything else that you'd like to do,' she told him, looking at him sideways, archly, from beneath raised eyebrows.

He turned and looked at her. He was smiling. 'Sounds good to me, baby,' he said. 'I can't think of anything I'd rather do, or anyone I'd rather do it with.'

She giggled. 'I bet you say that to all the girls,' she said.

'Funnily enough, I don't,' he said.

'Perhaps you should have said "Or anyone I'd rather do it *to*,"' she suggested.

'No, with is OK,' he replied. 'Sex is a two-way thing in my book. I mean, so OK, if you give me head, that's something you're doing to me, if you like. But you need *me* to do it to, so we're doing it together. Yes? So you're doing it *with* me. Whatever. But tell me, what's this "Or anything else that you'd like to do" bit? I would have thought that we'd pretty much run through the book this evening. Or am I being naive? Or unimaginative?'

'Good Lord, no,' she said. 'But there are a couple of variations that I find fun, when I'm in the mood.'

'Like what?' he asked, curiously.

She was silent for a moment. 'Well, like lying together naked, masturbating each other to orgasm. Or having you masturbating me while I just lie here, listening to you talking dirty to me. That really turns me on. Having my lover frig me, while he talks dirty to me. Oh, wow. Or having you lie there, with me masturbating you, while *I* talk dirty to *you*. That's a big turn-on too.'

'That sounds terrific,' he said. 'What else?'

'What is this?' she asked. 'Am I supposed to be teaching you about sex, or what?'

'I don't know,' he said. 'I think perhaps you are, in some ways. And I love every minute of it. So what else?'

She looked at him, almost seriously. 'I don't know if I know you well enough,' she teased.

He laughed out loud. 'Jesus H. Christ,' he said. 'You don't know if you know me well enough! For God's sake, you've been sucking my cock and swallowing my spunk. I've been sucking your pussy, and drinking a mixture of your vaginal juices with my champagne. We've fucked

Voluptuous Venus

each other for about the last three hours. And you don't know if you know me well enough. How well would you need to know me, I have to ask, to tell me what you're thinking about?'

She stared at him silently, and then broke into a big smile. She took hold of him, and snuggled up against him. She put her mouth close to his ear, and whispered to him. 'Do you like fucking girls in the arse?' she asked. 'Do you like buggering girls? Would you like to bugger me? Fuck my tight little arsehole? I love it up my arse. I just adore being buggered. But it's not everyone's cup of tea. So is it yours? Would you like to force your huge, swollen prick up my tiny, tight little anus? Tell me. Would you?'

Actually, Harry didn't have to say anything. His suddenly hugely erect penis said it for him. But when he did speak, he said, 'It's not something I've ever done. But it's something I've fantasized about, ever since I was old enough to know that girls *had* tight little arseholes, as you so succinctly put it. So the answer has to be yes, I'd love to fuck your tiny little arsehole. As to the wanking each other off, and talking dirty, just try me.'

Venus kissed him, long and hard. 'If that's what you would like to do, my darling, then that is what we'll do. All of it. All day, and all night. But not right now, if you'll forgive me. Not to put too fine a point on it, I'm knackered. Sleep calls. But at least we've both got something to look forward to. Now then. Be serious for a moment. Do you want me to go back to my room for what's left of the night, or may I stay here with you? Be honest, please. Some people love sex, but prefer to actually sleep alone. But I'm not one of those.'

'Neither am I,' Harry told her. 'So that's settled. Do you need anything before you go to sleep?'

'I ought to have a shower and clean my teeth,' she said. 'But I can't be bothered. I'll do it all in the morning.' She cuddled down alongside him, and fell almost instantly asleep.

Harry stayed awake long enough to get out of bed, put the lights out, and partially draw back the curtains. The room was flooded with moonlight, and his last recollection, before he too fell asleep, was of Venus's face in the light from the moon, as serene as a baby's, a half-smile turning up the corners of her mouth. He kissed her gently. 'Goodnight, baby,' he whispered. Needless to say, there was no reply.

The following morning, Venus was awakened from a dreamless sleep by the warmth of the sun on her face. She looked at her watch to discover that it was almost midday. Harry was still sound asleep, snoring slightly, his nose twitching as he did so.

She got out of bed and showered at length, starting off with the water as hot as she could bear it, and then turning it slowly colder and colder, until she was shivering beneath its needle points. She wondered if Harry would mind if she used his toothbrush, or whether she should wait until she got back to her own room, and then she suddenly realized how ridiculous such a thought was.

She dried her body and then her hair. One of the small

Voluptuous Venus

things that had attracted her to this particular hotel was the fact that every bedroom had a hair dryer. And Harry's suite was no different. Despite using it on its slowest speed, the noise awoke Harry. He sat up in bed, rubbing his eyes. He smiled across at her. 'So you *are* there,' he said. 'I thought perhaps it was all a dream. A nice dream, but still a dream. But now I can see that it wasn't. Come back to bed.'

She put down the dryer and went over and sat down on the bed beside Harry, and gave him a long kiss. 'There's nothing I'd like better, darling,' she said. 'But I've got a meeting with the events manager and his staff at half-past two, and it's a quarter to two now. I've still got to go back to my room and take off this evening dress.'

'Take it off here,' said Harry. 'Why wait?'

She laughed at him and got up from the bed, going back to finishing drying her hair. 'What are your plans for today?' she asked him.

'I thought that I'd go down to the beach for a quick swim when you've gone,' he said. 'And then back here for a shave and a shower, and into the bar for a couple, before a snack lunch down on the beach. Why don't you join me in the beach restaurant when you've finished your meeting? It's open all day. If I'm not in the restaurant, I'll be in the bar.'

'That will be nice,' she said, going over and kissing him. 'I'll see you there. My meeting should be over by three-ish. Then I'll just slip into something more suitable, and join you down there. Enjoy your swim.'

'Ciao, baby,' he said. Jesus, what a girl!

The two of them had a magical week. Harry turned out to be something of an experienced sailor, with his own small yacht, he told her, which he kept up in Sag Harbour, on Long Island, north of New York. It meant that they spent long, lazy afternoons, after the hottest part of the day had passed, sailing in one of the hotel's Sunfish sailing boats, exploring the coves and inlets around and about the bay.

It also meant that they could pull the boat up on tiny, deserted beaches, unreachable by road, where they could strip off their swimsuits to sunbathe and swim completely nude. Not unnaturally, this inevitably led to making love on the beach, and in the shallows, with the warm wavelets from the Caribbean breaking over them as they lay in each other's impassioned arms. They both quickly achieved the best tans that either of them had ever managed in their entire lives.

One morning they chartered a local fishing boat, and spent an exciting day deep-sea fishing. Venus didn't actually fish herself but spent the day watching Harry, who caught a largish sail fish and a decent-sized tuna. They returned the sail fish to the sea, after weighing it and taking the essential photographs, but the highly edible tuna was kept, as part of the captain's perks. He would either sell it when they returned to harbour at the end of the day or take it home to his family.

The captain was a charming, grizzled, grey-haired St Lucian of some sixty summers, whose local knowledge, sense of humour, and philosophy of life would have made their day, even had Harry not caught a single fish. The

Voluptuous Venus

captain knew his local waters, and guided the boat directly to where he said he could guarantee that Harry would hook a fish. But he only guaranteed the hooking. Whether Harry landed it was up to Harry. The captain kept his word, and Harry kept his cool. The two of them were delighted.

For the rest of the time, they bathed and sunbathed, explored the local bars and restaurants around the hotel, and danced the early evenings away, until their physical attraction for each other – fuelled, no doubt, by the strong rum drinks that they consumed to assuage the thirst brought about by their energetic dancing – overcame the pleasures of the dance floor, and they swapped them for the pleasures of Harry's bedroom. At that time on their second evening, Harry proposed that they make the bottle of champagne with which they had started their previous sexual encounter a traditional beginning to their late-night pleasures. So now they sat in his sitting room, drinking the champagne, healthily tired, but sexually excited by each other's presence, and by the thoughts of what they were soon going to do to each other.

'There are times,' Venus said, 'and this is one of them, when, even at my tender age, I could retire from the rat race. Just imagine spending the rest of one's life out here, doing what we're doing now.'

'I'm with you there,' Harry agreed. 'But it's the fact that neither of us could possibly afford to do it that makes the idea so attractive. That's what vacations are all about. But neither of us is actually on vacation, if you think about it. And, in any case, the grass is always greener . . . I bet, if you asked anyone who was both born here and still lived here – even someone quite wealthy, in local St Lucian terms – whether they would prefer to go on living here or whether they would swap their life here for either yours in London or mine in New York, I bet you they'd be on the next plane out.'

'I guess you're right,' Venus said. 'It's sad, isn't it? But let's not waste time feeling sorry for ourselves. We're here, and we're in love, and I need fucking. Are you going to fuck me, or shall I go look for someone who actually fancies me?'

Her smile gave the lie to her words. She stood up, went over to the radio in the corner of the room, and fiddled with the dial until she found some soft, romantic music. Then she unzipped her short black evening dress, slid it off her shoulders, dropped it down her long legs, and stepped out of it. This left her in just a small pair of white bikini panties, a startling contrast to her now well-tanned, almost native-coloured flesh.

She took her panties off and, with them still in her hand, she went over and sat on Harry's knee. She kissed him, long and hard, exploring his mouth with her tongue. And then she held the crotch of her panties just beneath his nose.

He inhaled, deeply. 'Mmmm,' he said. 'Nice. Sexy. And rather damp.'

'I thought that it might help to get you in the mood,' she said.

'I've been in the mood all afternoon, and all evening,' Harry told her.

Voluptuous Venus

'How lovely.' Venus said. 'Then if you'll come into the bedroom, I've got a present for you.' She got up off his knee and he followed her, bent over slightly, until he managed to adjust his erection into a position which enabled him to walk more easily.

In the bedroom, Venus found her tiny evening bag, opened it, and took out a small, gift-wrapped package that she gave to Harry. He unwrapped it carefully, to reveal a tube, about the size and shape of a medium toothpaste tube. He held it up, and read out aloud: '*Aphrodite Lubrication Cream. This cream is recommended with the use of all Aphrodite robot models. Despite the fact that all of our robots are self-lubricating, customers are advised, in the interests of sexual enjoyment, to use this cream on their genitals when indulging in the use of Aphrodite products.*'

He looked up at her, and then he suddenly remembered. 'My God,' he said, as he started tearing his clothes off. 'You weren't joking. Tonight is anal sex night. It's fuck-your-little-bottom night. Oh, Jesus.' He was naked in seconds. His penis was thrust out erectly in front of him, looking rather like the bowsprit on some eighteenth-century naval frigate. He put out a hand to Venus, who took it, and with the other hand he picked up the tube of lubricant. He led her over to the bed. 'Oh, my God,' he said, again.

She knelt up on the bed, her bottom towards him. 'The lubricant is more for my bottom than anything else, darling,' she told him. 'But you can rub it over your cock as well. It won't do any harm.'

Harry knelt down on the floor immediately in front of

Venus's bottom. He reached out with both his hands and stroked it, feeling her taut muscles. He squeezed her buttocks, and stared, longingly, at her small, brown sphincter. It looked, as she had jokingly told him, tiny.

It nestled in a thick muff of fluffy blonde anal hair. He reached out a tentative finger, and touched the very centre of her anus. He saw it instantly contract, and he took his finger away. He bent forward and kissed it, and he could smell its rich, pungent, almost tropical odour. He licked it, and found the taste to his liking. It was extremely sexually arousing.

Venus looked over her shoulder at him. 'No one's ever kissed my arsehole before,' she said. 'That's nice. And what a naughty boy you are. I may have to punish you later. But for now, I'd be grateful if you'd just grease me, before you start feeling me up, or whatever it is you're going to do to me next. Please?'

'Sure, honey,' he said. 'No problem.' He picked up the tube of lubricant and squeezed a thick worm of it out onto his forefinger. He then rubbed it all over the surround to her anus before squeezing out more and this time pressing his finger once more over the centre of her sphincter. It contracted, as it had before, but he kept pressing, and it immediately dilated, allowing his finger to slip inside. He rubbed her rectal passage slowly and carefully, as far as his finger would go up it. Then he pulled his finger down again, reanointed it with lubricant, and repeated the exercise.

Venus began to move her hips as he massaged the inside of her forbidden entrance. 'Ooohh,' she said. 'I like

Voluptuous Venus

it.' She looked back at him over her shoulder again. 'Just one thing, Harry,' she said.

'What's that, sweetheart?' he asked her.

'Despite what you might think, darling – I know that I told you last night that I love it up my arse, and that's true, I do – it's not something that I've done too often, and the last time was a while ago. So, please, take it gently, will you? Don't rush things. Take your time, And if I say stop, please stop. At once. OK?'

'OK, baby,' he said. 'Just tell me what's happening, and what you want me to do. I'll be very gentle. I promise you.'

'Thank you,' she said. 'I'm probably being over-cautious, but I have been hurt, in the past. And you *do* have a large cock.' She looked back at him once more. 'Thank God,' she said, grinning at him. 'Otherwise you wouldn't be here.'

She was almost as excited about the forthcoming anal sex as he was. She had grown – admittedly over a period of time – attracted to getting arse-fucked. She was fascinated by the sensations of a large, stiff prick thrusting up her arsehole, stretching it, expanding it, causing feelings in it that she hadn't known existed. Unlike many women, who claimed that the worst thing about anal sex was that it was an entirely selfish male activity which degraded women, who in any case could never achieve orgasm through being fucked in the arse, Venus came repeatedly – these days, anyway – when indulging in what was now an infrequent but favourite pastime for her. The ultimate, intense, passionate, sexual release, the one thing that never failed to bring her to an orgasmic high, was the

– to her – superlative sensation of sperm pumping hotly into her bowels as her lover came, deep into her fundament. She reached a hand behind her, feeling around for his prick. 'Let me put it in for you, darling,' she said. 'Since this is a first for you, I want it to be wonderful. Something you'll always remember, for the rest of your life.'

He stood up and, taking her hand, he guided it to where she could reach his cock. She gripped it firmly, and then, as he climbed up onto the bed immediately behind her, she parted her knees, opening up her bottom as much as possible. She wanted to make it as easy as she could for him.

She then guided his cock up against her anal aperture and pressed its head against her anus while she pushed firmly backwards with her hips and bottom. He watched, fascinated, as her sphincter opened up – quite easily – to accept his engorged member.

And suddenly he was realizing his ultimate fantasy. His cock was deep in the tight, tiny little arsehole of a really beautiful girl. She felt really hot, and really tight. Much tighter than any cunt he'd ever fucked. He could see the skin of her anus stretched tightly around the circumference of his cock, stretched so tightly that it looked like a transparent membrane. She was also well greased, thanks to her forethought and his careful application of the lubrication that she had supplied. She actually felt wet, rather than greasy. He was about to ask her if all was well or if she was in any pain when she said, 'That's wonderful, darling. That feels really good. Now fuck the arse off me. I'm ready.'

Voluptuous Venus

He began to move his hips, thrusting as deeply into her rectal passage as he could then slowly withdrawing. She began to move with him, thrusting backwards as he thrust forward, and using her anal muscles to squeeze him as hard as she knew how. He knew he wasn't going to be able to last any time at all. This was the ultimate fuck. It was fantastic. Beyond his wildest dreams. He could feel his semen gathering in his balls. Venus had dropped her head, and was bucking strongly backwards against him.

'Oh Harry,' she suddenly said, in a low, passionate sort of growl. 'Oh, Jesus, Harry. You're fucking my arsehole. Your huge cock is up my arsehole, and you're going to spurt your hot spunk up my anus. You're going to come in my arse. I love it. I love it up my arse. Promise me you'll always fuck me in my arse. Promise me, Harry. Oh, Jesus, Harry. I'm coming now, Harry.'

They actually came together. Harry had been trying, without much success, to hold his ejaculation back, but Venus's talking dirty to him destroyed any small amount of self-control that he might have had left. He gripped her waist as he thrust himself as far up into her bottom as he could go, and then he spurted his ejaculate into her in what seemed to him like a pulsing series of endless jets.

Venus's orgasm had started a fraction of a second before she felt Harry's hot semen spurting deeply inside her. But as it hit her innards she felt as if her bowels were on fire, and her climax turned into a seemingly unending, multiple, absolutely fantastic orgasm. The greatest orgasm that she had ever experienced. It seemed to go on forever, and they stayed in their position, the classic doggy-fashion position, with Harry clasping Venus's waist and the two of them screaming and panting and trying to get their breath. Eventually, Harry slowly pulled out his still semi-erect cock and subsided down onto the bed beside Venus.

They finally showered together in Harry's bathroom and then sat beside each other, closely entwined in each other's arms, both comfortably relaxed, on one of the sofas in Harry's sitting room. They finished the bottle of champagne, but both of them – without mentioning it to the other – seemed tacitly agreed that they had finished their sexual activity for that particular evening. They had done something that had reached a peak, a peak that it would take them some time to attain again.

The next day was Venus's last full day on St Lucia. She would leave early on the following morning. Unsurprisingly, she and Harry spent the entire day in bed, demonstrating and vowing everlasting love to each other.

They exchanged office telephone numbers, home televideo phone numbers and mobile phone numbers. They promised that they would commute between each other's countries, with the actual arrangements to be finalized when they were both back at their offices and knew more of their future work movements.

Sadly, Harry anticipated that the case for which he had come to St Lucia would be over well before Venus's media launch party on the island got under way. At the time, both of them believed everything that they were promising each other. It was more, they told each other, than a happy vacation romance. It had been the best fucking of both their lives. Harry travelled the two-and-a-half-hour journey to the airport, down in the south of the island, to see Venus off, taking a taxi back for the return journey. As the jet took off, he felt as if something had flown out of his life.

Venus, too, felt lonely on the flight back to London. She snapped the head off the man sitting next to her who had imagined that it was Christmas and Easter rolled together when he saw who his travelling companion was going to be. That night, Venus lay in her bed, her hands between her legs, thinking of Harry and the intense sexual pleasures of her stay in St Lucia. She fell asleep, only partially satisfied by her masturbatory orgasms, and dreamt that she was back in his bed, and in his arms.

CHAPTER THREE

On The Scent

Venus was pleased to be welcomed back warmly at the office the following morning, even allowing for the many barbed compliments about her deep tan and the comments that she looked far more as though she'd been away on holiday than on business for the company. They made her feel somewhat guilty. But she more than recovered from her guilt when she received a telephone call from Harry. He rang her at two in the afternoon, London time, which was nine a.m. his time, to tell her that he missed her. It made her day.

Her first meeting that morning had been with Jacques, the fragrance consultant, who was scheduled to deliver his various samples to her. She had not wanted to take any decisions about these artificially produced sexual aromas in isolation so, in order to speed things up, she had arranged for Mark, the sales director, Peter, the production director, and Sally, the girl who helped Venus with the 'auditions,' to join her.

Jacques had started the meeting by handing them each a mask into which could be inserted slides, a bit thicker than those used for examination under microscopes. The slides held cotton pads, each of which had been immersed in one or other of the various concoctions that produced the fragrances under discussion. The masks, Jacques explained, ensured that the wearer's ability to analyse a particular smell was not spoiled by any outside odours.

'Shall we start with the fragrance which you requested when we first met?' Jacques asked.

'Please,' said Venus. 'That was human breast milk, as I remember. But just before we sample it, Peter, you sent me a note recently telling me that there were no problems in producing robot nipples that will lactate when required. Can you confirm that?'

'Yes,' said Peter. 'I can. I've had three different female robots fitted with the new nipples, and all three have received one hundred per cent affirmative tests, for appearance, for ability to become erect – when stimulated in any way – and for an accurate, acceptable stream of liquid when either sucked or milked. The only thing missing is the actual milk itself. I used normal full-cream dairy milk in my tests.'

'Thank you, Peter,' said Venus. 'Is everyone ready now? OK, Jacques. Let's go.'

Jacques walked around the table, clipping a slide carefully into place in each of the four Aphrodite representatives' masks. The masks themselves were, for want of a better description, nose masks that left everyone's mouths free, thus enabling them both to inhale the sample and speak as well. There was silence for a few moments, broken only by the sound of inhalation. Venus was the first of the four to speak.

'Well,' she said, 'I'm no expert on the scent of mother's milk, but that aside, it smells spot on to me. Obviously we'll test it with a panel of nursing mothers, but I think this aroma is excellent. Very realistic.'

'Agreed,' said Mark. 'My kids are long past breast-feeding now, but that smells totally authentic to me.'

'And to me,' said Peter. 'Tell me, Jacques, in what form would you supply this fragrance to us?'

'In capsule form,' Jacques replied. 'Capsules that are slotted into the robot's interior, and which are activated when the correct setting is dialled by the owner.'

'How long would a capsule last?' Venus asked.

'Almost as long as you wanted it to,' Jacques said. 'It depends partly on how much room you have to spare in the robots' interior and, to a certain extent of course, on how often the facility is used. But we could easily supply a capsule that would last for six months, even if used every day. It really needs Peter and me to get together and look at the research figures. Once we've got approval for the fragrance itself, then that will take no time at all.'

'Great,' said Venus. 'Any other questions?'

'Just one,' Mark said. 'Can we include the new lactating nipple within the robot's self-cleaning circuit? That's an obvious necessity.'

'No problem,' said Peter. 'No problem at all.'

'Well, we're all agreed on that, then,' said Venus. 'Thank you, Jacques.' She made some notes on her pad. 'I'll minute the decisions that we're all agreed that the human milk sample is approved by us, and that it will now go to a nursing mothers' testing panel for final approval. I'll set that up. At the same time, Jacques and Peter will get together to finalize capsule size and positioning, and Peter will also plan the nipple hygiene programme. Agreed?' All three of her colleagues raised a hand in the air, signifying their approval. 'Right, Jacques. Next?'

'This, of course, is the big one,' Jacques said. 'I've read all your extremely comprehensive research material, and my recommendations are based entirely upon that. I accept that you have done amazingly well, so far, with but one odour to reproduce the smell of aroused female pussy. But I submit to you today that, first of all, your own research tells us that there are many more aromas that come from what my friend Venus here' (he bowed in Venus's direction) 'tells me to refer to as "cunt". Well, that makes it easier. At least we all know what we are talking about.'

His audience all laughed dutifully. He grinned at them and continued. 'Let me just run through some of the commoner variations for you. There is, of course, normal, clean, everyday European cunt. Then there is aroused European cunt. A very different scent. Much stronger. Much more complicated. There's black English cunt. And black American cunt. Or black African cunt. Three very distinctly different aromas. And flavours.

'Staying with the more common varieties, there's Middle European cunt. This includes Polish, Romanian, Bulgarian, Hungarian, German, Bosnian, Austrian, Swiss,

Voluptuous Venus

and so on. Not forgetting, going rather farther north, and east, Russian cunt. And then there's Norwegian, Swedish, Danish and Finnish cunt. There's Asian cunt. And Indian, Pakistani and Bangladeshi cunt. Loosely speaking, there's Mediterranean cunt, although that subdivides into God knows how many different varieties. French, Spanish, Italian, Greek, Turkish, Cypriot, Moroccan, Tunisian, Libyan, Egyptian, Lebanese, Syrian ... It's endless. Then there's Chinese. Japanese, of course. Korean. All totally different.

'But I think I've made my point. I'll ignore, for now, North and South America, Canada, Australia and New Zealand, and most of Africa. Indonesia, the Caribbean. Mexico. The Bahamas. It's never-ending. Now here's the good news. My company can provide you with – at extremely competitive prices – the vaginal scent *and flavour* of each and every country in the world. Each one in four versions: clean, unwashed, aroused and unaroused.'

Jacques paused for a moment. Almost as if he was expecting a round of applause. If he was, it didn't happen. 'We have done our own experiments,' he continued, 'with a number of your female robots, and we can manufacture the whole range for you. Both for use in-house and for sale to your customers, who will have to do nothing more than choose their desired scent and flavour of the evening and select the right options from their control pad. It will be as simple as that. We're offering you the ability to offer over four hundred variations on vaginal aroma and flavour. There'll be something for everyone. Literally.' He paused.

'Wow,' said Venus. 'That's quite something. I mean, if

we can offer that kind of variety, and at reasonable prices – which will also help us to show a healthy profit – then it's got to be good business. What do you think?' This last to her three colleagues.

Mark, the sales director, was the first to speak. 'It sounds terrific to me, Venus,' he said. 'It's obviously particularly appropriate to Sexational Unlimited. We're well ahead of the Japanese competition right now, and if we can offer this kind of choice to the rental clientele it will put us streets ahead of them. Perhaps permanently. I like it, Jacques,' he said. 'I really like it.'

Jacques was obviously pleased at the way his presentation was going. 'Thank you, Mark,' he said. 'Thank you.'

'But, of course, it's not only the rental business that will profit by it,' Mark continued. 'We've already got every kind of ethnic skin option available. And every kind of language in the world. At least,' (he hastily corrected himself) 'every kind of language from any of the races who are ever going to be able to afford to be customers of Aphrodite, that is. And in any case, we can always tailor robots to suit any request, however obscure, as long as the customer puts the cash up front.'

'Bon,' said Jacques. 'Très, très bon. So, ladies and gentlemen, we come now to the fragrance sampling. You are all familiar with the standard Aphrodite product to date. Am I right?'

He looked around the table at the four of them. They were all nodding. 'Yes,' they said.

'Bon,' said Jacques again. 'So I have brought you just three samples of the kind of thing that my company can

Voluptuous Venus

do. I have chosen them because they are all so completely different. All three. Different from each other. And from your standard product.

'If you will kindly put your masks on again, I shall insert the first slide.' They did as he had asked, and he inserted a slide into each mask. 'Now then,' he said. 'This is the scent of a young French woman, who is in the age bracket twenty-two to twenty-six. She is single, but is highly sexually experienced and she is, for the purposes of this sample, highly sexually *aroused*. It may or may not be of interest, but our chemists work in very subtle ways and to achieve this particular aroma the formulation is for that of a young woman who completed her menstrual cycle approximately three days previously, or so they tell me. This, they say, provides the slightly heavy, sensual fragrance behind the lighter, more superficial main fragrance. I will stop speaking now so that you may inhale, and come to your own conclusions.'

Venus breathed in, deeply. It was an exotic, highly erotic, intensely sexual odour that immediately brought to mind the mental image of the girl – woman – whom Jacques had just described. Venus shut her eyes and went on inhaling. She could see the woman. She had short black hair. She was naked, with heavy breasts, fat, erect nipples, and a luxuriantly hairy bush between her legs. As Venus looked at her, she opened her legs, and fully exposed her pussy. It was pinkly wet, and dribbling with vaginal mucus. Venus quickly opened her eyes. Jacques was looking at her. Expectantly.

'Tremendous, Jacques,' she said. 'Absolutely tremendous.

But I'd rather test all three, and then discuss them at the end. Is that all right with you?' she asked her colleagues. They all agreed that it was.

'OK,' said Jacques. He fitted the second slide into their four masks. 'This is a young Danish girl, of about nineteen to twenty-three,' he told them. 'She works in a sex shop in Copenhagen, and she is in an almost constant state of arousal. Here again, our chemists, who take this process – quite properly – very seriously indeed, tell me that this vaginal scent is based upon that of a young girl who masturbates frequently during the day, and who is sexually active almost every evening.' He laughed. 'I should be so lucky. But back to work. I am also instructed to tell you that this girl shaves her mound, for again, they tell me, this affects the overall bouquet. As before, I give you time to inhale and make notes before I give you the final slide.' Jacques got up from the table, went over to the window in Venus's office and looked out. There wasn't much to see, except other buildings.

Venus once more shut her eyes, and achieved a vision of the young Danish girl. She saw her in a lavatory, sitting on the lavatory seat but with the lid down. Her short black skirt was up around her waist, and her silky, lacy knickers were down around her thighs. The girl also had her eyes shut, and she had one hand on her pussy, frigging herself strenuously, while the other hand was slipped inside her open blouse, pinching and pulling at one of her nipples. Venus could see that the girl's knickers were wet at the crotch. She wondered whether it was juice from the girl's pussy or the sweat of arousal that was dampening the thin

Voluptuous Venus

material. She inhaled once more and got an even more intense scent than previously. It was part sweet, part acrid. Quite strong. And very personal. There was an underlying note of sweat beneath the covering of stronger notes which, Venus thought, gave a strongly sensual smell to the final odour. She took her mask off and looked across at Jacques.

'Interesting,' she said, 'Two down, one to go.' The other three continued to inhale and make notes. Venus wondered if Sally was ever going to say anything. Not that it mattered if she didn't. She was only there to be a female makeweight anyway. Finally, the other three were all finished with the Danish girl's sample, if that was the way to describe it. Jacques picked up the last slide and Venus put her mask back on. 'This last one is as different from the other two as they were from each other,' said Jacques, as he put the slides into position. Venus tried to guess the origin of the woman that this one represented. Her country, even. But she wasn't able to do so.

There was an overall, slightly musky essence to this one. A touch of ... what? Incense? Perhaps. She decided to await Jacques's description. He smiled at them. 'I'm tempted to ask you to guess the origin of this one,' he said. 'Except that I don't believe you'd get it. Not in a hundred years.' He paused. Silence. 'No takers, I see.' He laughed. 'Well, I can't say that I blame you. We produced this one in order to demonstrate to you the variety and the range of products that we are equipped to manufacture, and the lengths to which we can go when necessary. What you have on your slides right now is the vaginal effluent of a fifty-year-old virgin Italian woman. She is, in fact, a nun. I'm not suggesting for a moment that you will have a big demand for this particular concoction. It is here, as I said, simply to indicate our resourcefulness.'

Venus was relieved that, on this occasion, her imagination failed her and she didn't get a mental image of the source of the current slide as she had with the two previous ones. It was probably just as well, she reflected.

Jacques looked at the four of them around the table. He bowed once more in their general direction. 'That is the end of my presentation, ladies and gentlemen,' he said. 'I shall, of course, be happy to answer any questions that you have.' He sat down. Venus stood up.

'Before question time, Jacques, may I thank you, first of all personally and then on behalf of both my colleagues and my company for an excellent and compelling presentation.' She paused, and looked around the table. 'I'm sure my colleagues agree with me, in their position as our main product-sampling committee, that you have our complete approval.'

She looked at the other three again, and they nodded their heads in approval. 'Thank you, Mark, Peter, and Sally,' she said. 'That means that all we need to do now is to formalize our decision at the next board meeting. I will put in our report, signed and approved by the four of us. If I may, I would like to suggest to the board that Jacques should give them the same presentation that he has just given to us. It's probably not, strictly speaking, completely necessary, but I think it would be good for them – and for you, Jacques – if he did.'

'My pleasure,' said Jacques. 'Thank you, Venus.'

'I must say,' Venus continued, 'I found the aromas of the young French woman and of the young Danish girl with the shaved pudenda so convincing that I could shut my eyes and get a complete mental picture of them both.' Her three colleagues broke into Venus's speech, to agree with her. 'But although I found the Italian nun's fragrance convincing,' she continued, 'I didn't, in her case, get the same kind of mental picture.'

'That one will probably sell well in the Vatican,' Mark joked.

'Yes,' laughed Venus. 'But, seriously, Jacques, the moment we have final approval from the board, how long will it take from then to the first deliveries?'

Jacques thought for a moment. 'Not too long,' he said. 'With two provisos. One. That you let me have – within ten days – a list of the specific countries of whose women you want to offer sexual fragrances and flavours. I'll accept those on a subject-to-confirmation-by-the-board basis. And two, you let me know, within the same period, whether you want the four variations on each nationality that I mentioned earlier on. They were, basically, clean, dirty, normal, and sexually aroused. And if you don't want all four, then you must tell me what you *do* want.

'Cost depends largely, as ever, on quantities,' Jacques went on. He dug around in his briefcase and pulled out a sheaf of papers. 'I've got here some projected figures, at various levels,' he said, 'that will give you a pretty reasonable idea of costs. There's room for the usual two hundred per cent mark-up. I've assumed that you will want to get out your own package design, so I have included a costing for containers but not for actual pack design. With the conditions that I have outlined, and provided I get the information that I need, I shall be able to deliver sufficient quantities for you to launch exactly four weeks after the board's agreement.'

'That sounds tremendous,' Venus said. 'Are you happy with that, Peter? Will that give you enough time?'

'Yes,' Peter answered. 'That gives me sufficient time, thank you.'

'Good,' said Venus. 'Are there any other questions?'

'Just one from me,' Mark said. 'I'm still waiting for the final results of the research to be analysed, but when I get them, then they'll tell me whether or not our women customers want to have the same sort of facilities available on the male robots as we are now going to offer on the female products. In other words, the genuine smell and taste of a whole range of male sexuality. My guess is that the answer will be yes. If it is, will that cause you any problems, Jacques? And will that alter the delivery date for the female products?'

Jacques thought for a minute. 'Well, the answer to the first question is no, it won't cause any problems. And, if the answer to your research into your female customers' preferences *is* yes, that won't affect the delivery of the female products in any way. But you do realize, don't you, that I won't be able to get the male products out – assuming that you tell me that you want them – to coincide with the female products? I'll do the very best that I can for you, but there is bound to be a delay between delivery of the two separate ranges.'

Venus looked at Peter. 'Yes, of course,' Peter said. 'I appreciate that. Thank you. No more questions from me.'

Venus looked at Mark, then at Sally. Mark shook his head. 'Just one question,' Sally said. 'Assuming that the research says that yes, our women customers *do* want the same kind of scents and flavours that our male customers want, can I please be on the initial sampling committee, Venus?' She grinned, hugely. They all laughed.

'Yes, of course you can, Sally,' Venus said. 'Anybody else? No? I think that wraps it up, then. I'll e-mail the minutes later today. Thank you, Jacques. Thank you, everybody.'

Back in her own office, Venus mused over the outcome of the meeting. The one significant effect, as far as she was concerned (and assuming that the board endorsed her committee's decision, of course, but that was pretty much a foregone conclusion) would be that, from the date of the launch of the new scent and taste products, the vaginas of all Aphrodite's female robots, when operative, would cease to taste and smell uniquely of Venus's pussy, which had been the case up to now. She wondered whether perhaps, if she requested it, they might keep her vaginal odour and taste for just one of the four white European offers. She made a mental note to take it up – unofficially at first – with her colleagues, and see if any of them would have any objection. She couldn't imagine why any of them would.

She suddenly thought of Harry and realized that she was feeling horny. It wasn't surprising, really. She'd dropped down, in twenty-four hours, from getting fucked morning, noon and night, to not getting fucked at all. She'd have to do something about it, she thought. There were always the five Aphrodite male robots at home, of course. They gave as good a fuck as anyone. Better than many. That was probably the best thing, at least for the time being. She pushed the thought of personal sex to the back of her mind, as best she could, and tried to concentrate on dictating the minutes of the morning's meeting to her computer.

Back at home that evening, Venus poured herself a large Caribbean rum from the bottle she had purchased in the duty-free shop at St Lucia's airport, topped it up with coke, added some ice, and switched on the CNN television news. She sat back in her chair, half watching the dramas of the world unfolding before her, half wondering which of the five robots she should have fuck her, any minute now. She felt herself getting wet at the prospect. Well, this would be a good product test, she thought. What she really wanted was Harry. Aphrodite sold their products these days on an advertising platform which implied that, if you bought an Aphrodite robot, you would probably never need a sexual relationship with another human being again. She was about to find out if there was any truth in this expensively-sold supposition.

She quickly became bored with the world news. The revolution in China was so old hat now that she wondered why anyone still cared about its aftermath any more. It must be, what, ten years since the Chinese population had risen up, ousted those ageing impostors from their government and hanged them from the lamp-posts? Who cared any more if the new government was now squabbling among itself as to whether or not to invade the plethora of bankrupt individual states that were all that was left of the once all-powerful Russia? Let them all destroy each other. China didn't seem to have the intelligence to see that her real danger came from from the south. From what used to be called the Pacific Rim. From the thriving, financially strong and now militarily united countries of Thailand, Laos, Cambodia, Vietnam, Malaysia, Borneo, Sumatra, the Philippines, Indonesia, Java and Madura, and Papua New Guinea.

She switched her television off and wandered through to the closet in which she kept her robots. She had refilled her glass. Opening the door, she looked at the possibilities.

Don't let's fuck about, she thought. *I don't need to justify my choice. Who am I trying to impress*? She grabbed her favourite, and pulled him out of the closet. She had always called him Tony. He had been tailor-made to her own requirements. He was brown-haired, six foot six, and slim. He was muscular, but not over-developed (except perhaps in the genital area, but more of that in a moment). His accent was solid English middle class, and she had arranged for him to be programmed to French kiss, suck pussy, fuck strongly – both vaginally and anally – to masturbate both himself and Venus, and generally to know how to give a randy little bitch like her a good time in bed. Well, wasn't that exactly what Aphrodite robots were designed for?

Good old Tone, she thought, as she dragged him out of the cupboard. He was dressed in an exquisite Savile Row suit, with a Jermyn Street shirt and tie and handmade shoes from St James's. His underwear was from Ralph Lauren's Bond Street shop, selected personally by Venus, as were all his clothes. She checked that his batteries were fully charged – they were – and then she spent some considerable time programming him. He was the top-of-the-range, most sophisticated model that Aphrodite produced and, once switched on, anyone – including Venus – could believe that he was human. Finally, she was satisfied at last with her programme. She stood him up, switched him on, and closed the hidden panel between his shoulder blades.

He came to life after the automatic fifteen-second delay. 'Hey, Venus,' he said. 'Good to see you. How are you?'

'Good to see you, Tony, baby,' she said. 'I'm fine.' She stood in front of him and put her hand over his genital area. She felt him begin to swell. She slid his zip down and pulled his cock out of his trousers.

It was almost instantly fully erect. It throbbed beneath her fingers as she stroked it. Venus looked down at it, remembering specifying its various qualities. It was uncircumcised. At full stretch, it measured ten inches from swollen frenum to oversize testicles, and its girth was seven inches. She dropped to her knees and took its tumescent head in her mouth. It almost filled her mouth, stretching her lips. She took it out of her mouth and licked it, slowly, all over. It tasted just like real, horny, human male cock. She pulled back from it and, looking at it

Voluptuous Venus

closely, she ran her fingers up and down its shaft a few times, in a practised, erotic, masturbatory manner. It had the result she expected, and a clear blob of pre-come liquid exuded from its single eye. She licked it off, savouring its salty, slightly fishy taste. She looked up at him.

'I love your cock, Tony,' she said. 'I love to suck it. And wank it. And have it fuck me. Are you going to fuck me with your lovely cock, Tony darling? Please?' He looked down at her, and smiled.

'I'm going to do anything and everything to you that you want me to do,' he told her. 'If fucking you is on the list, then yes, of course I'm going to fuck you. I'll fuck you senseless, if that's what you want. I'll fuck you, suck you, frig you, bugger you, spank you. Anything. Just tell me what you want me to do, and I'll do it. You know that.'

'Thanks, Tony,' she said. 'But first of all, I'm going to suck you off. Very slowly. Until you come in my mouth and spurt your hot spunk down my throat. It feels so sexy. I love it. Will you like that?'

'Yes, of course I will,' he said. 'I'm ready when you are.'

'Let's go through to the bedroom,' she suggested. She held out a hand and he took it and followed her through to her bedroom. 'You undress,' she told him, 'and I'll do the same.'

She didn't do the sort of slow semi-strip that she had been doing for Harry out in the Caribbean, since in her heart of hearts she knew that, whatever Tony said, he was, in truth, only a very sophisticated piece of machinery. So trying to tease him was a complete waste of time.

Venus stripped off quickly. By the time she was naked,

so was he. She marvelled, as she always did, at the perfection of his body. His penis was still fully erect. 'Sit on the edge of the bed,' she told him. He went over and sat down. 'Now play with yourself until you're fully erect,' she commanded. He began to toss himself off, unhurriedly, his fingers sliding up and down his penis. It grew in circumference until it was so stiff, so rigid, that it looked as if it would break if she touched it.

'OK, Tony,' she said. 'Here I come.' She knelt on the floor in front of him and began to suck him off. She gave it her best try and whilst she told herself that this was good practice against the next time she sucked Harry's cock – or anyone else's, for that matter – what she really was enjoying as she was doing it was the taste and feel of Tony's cock in her mouth.

She sucked harder and began to wank him with her fingers until, suddenly, she felt his cock starting to twitch. And then there it was. What she was waiting for. His hot spunk, jetting down her throat. She sucked and swallowed, and sucked and swallowed again, feeling herself coming as she did so, the excitement of the sexual act that she was performing upon Tony bringing her to orgasm herself. 'Mmmmm,' she said when she had sucked him dry. 'Nice.'

'Thank you,' he said. Aphrodite robots were nothing if not polite, so long as you remembered to program them that way.

Venus got up off her knees and looked at Tony as he sat there. He looked exactly as he was supposed to look: like an attractive, fit young man, glowing with health, who had

Voluptuous Venus

just been satisfactorily – and enjoyably – given head by his female partner. His cock was flaccid, as any man's cock would be at that moment and in those circumstances.

Venus laid herself down on the bed. 'Come and fuck me, Tony,' she said. She had programmed him for maximum foreplay and for prolonged sexual activity. She was wet.

Tony turned around and clambered along the bed until he was alongside Venus. He took her in his arms and began to kiss her. As he kissed her, sensually, wetly, his hands were all over her. He stroked her neck, her shoulders, her breasts. He gently squeezed her nipples and pulled on them, carefully, until they were hard. He stroked her thighs, then half turned her on her side and massaged her flanks. He caressed her buttocks and ran his hand down her anal crevice, his fingers straying over her tightly held anus as he did so.

Next his hand just touched her mons veneris, as if by accident, and she felt herself gasp as he passed over it. Then he touched her softly behind her knees. Placing his hand between her legs and tenderly prising them open, he ran his hand slowly up her inner thighs, until – at last – he pressed it hard down, over her sex. All this time, his mouth and lips were everywhere. Exploring *her* mouth. Licking her breasts. Sucking at her nipples. Tonguing her umbilicus. Now he massaged her outer labia, rubbing them with the flat of his hand.

Venus lay back and opened her legs wider, drawing her knees up to facilitate his actions. He slid his middle finger inside her and parted her inner lips, feeling for her clitoris.

Venus groaned as he found it. 'Suck me now, Tony,' she said. 'Please suck me. I want your tongue up inside me.'

Tony arranged himself so that he was in a position to do exactly that. He began to kiss her vulva. Venus reached out and took his flaccid penis in her fingers. She began to play with him as he started to suck her properly, and his penis quickly swelled into full erection. She felt his tongue as it insinuated its way into her now even wetter pussy. His tongue was strong and forceful as it teased her clitoris, at first flicking across its engorged head, then running down its short length, tantalizing, exciting, tormenting, driving her wild with its probing.

She felt a sudden desire to invade him in some way. She let go of his cock and reached out to find his anus. When she found it, she forced her forefinger deeply inside it. It was warm and tightly closed. He groaned as she thrust her finger into him, and she watched in amusement as his prick once more began to jerk and then rhythmically pumped out his jism. His ejaculate spurted strongly out into the air, then fell onto the sheets between his knees. Venus reached out and caught some on her fingers. She sucked and licked it off them. It tasted exactly like the real thing, except perhaps – thinking of the recent, well-remembered taste of Harry's semen – it wasn't quite as salty.

Tony's ejaculation didn't in any way seem to detract him from his cunnilingual efforts (but then, why should it?) and Venus began to press her vulva up against his lips, as she felt her own orgasm gathering somewhere, way down in her womb. She rose up off the bed to press herself even

Voluptuous Venus

harder up against his mouth, grabbing his head and pulling it down upon herself, bucking against him, fucking his mouth with her sex.

She came strongly, enjoying the strength of her coming and revelling in the eruptions that racked her body. As they subsided, she rolled Tony over onto his back without pause, masturbated his spent cock quickly back once more into hard erection and climbed up onto it, impaling herself upon its stallion-like rigidity. She remembered that, when requesting the generous measurements for Tony's erect cock (when he was but a list of descriptions on an Aphrodite order form) the production assistant taking her order had said – slightly nervously, she recalled – that no such measurements existed in the department's stock of penile designs. The human male simply wasn't that well endowed, he had told her. She had told him that, in that case, he had better either find one or design one. Which of these two avenues he had explored, she didn't know.

But she rode the results of that instruction hard, enjoying the experience of ravishing herself upon what was still the largest cock in Aphrodite's selection of male appendages. She had recommended it to all her girlfriends, and those of them who had taken her advice still spoke in wonder of the pleasures to be obtained therefrom. She was moving quickly towards her orgasm now. She leaned down, and put her mouth beside Tony's ear. 'Talk dirty to me, Tony, darling,' she instructed him. 'Talk dirty, and make me come. I love it when you talk dirty to me.'

'I'm fucking you, Venus,' he said, obediently. 'I'm

fucking your tight little cunt with my huge cock, and I'm going to make you come. I'll do anything you like to make you come. Shall I spank you? Shall I spank your naughty little bottom, until it's all red and swollen? Or shall I turn you over and fuck you up your bottom? Would you like that? Would you like me to force my big prick up your tiny little bottom-hole, until you scream with pleasure? Or would you perhaps prefer my tongue up your arsehole? Licking you in your forbidden place, until your orgasm bursts upon you? Or would you like me to use my finger to frig you while I'm fucking you?' At this last suggestion (having been carefully programmed) he didn't wait for an answer, he just slipped a hand down between Venus's groin and his and inserted a finger into her pussy. He found her clitoris and began to massage it as she rode him, bouncing up and down upon him as hard as she could. It was exactly what she needed, what she wanted.

As she climaxed, she shouted out herself, with the sheer, unadulterated, physical joy of an enormous, multiple orgasm. She felt as if she were exploding, and her whole body shuddered with her orgasm's ramifications. 'Oh, Jesus, God,' she shouted. 'I'm coming. I'm coming now. Oh, shit. Oh, yes. Oh, Jesus.' She rode it out, enjoying every last moment of it until, finally, it was all over.

She climbed off the robot and slumped down onto the bed beside him. 'Thanks, Tony, old mate,' she said. 'Did I ever tell you that you were a great fuck?'

'Yes. Once or twice,' he replied. 'But thank you. It's always good to hear.'

When she had fully recovered from her – and Tony's –

Voluptuous Venus

sexual exertions, she switched the robot onto his self-cleaning hygienic program. When he had run that, some half an hour later, she switched him on again, just long enough for him to dress himself, before she finally switched him off, and put him away.

Back in the office the following morning, Venus decided to spend the day finalizing the arrangements for the forthcoming media launch in St Lucia. She started out by making a list of what she would include in the media kit. Each personally invited media representative would be given a male or female robot, tailored to each person's individual desires. These personal requests had already been received, and the manufacture of the models was well in hand. Their testing was about to commence.

The robots would be accompanied by a selection of different sexual programs – again individually selected by each recipient – prepared from descriptive material issued by Venus some months previously. The male and female robots would also be dressed according to journalists' individual wishes. Then there would be a user manual, a guarantee, and a service manual that would carry a list of service agents world-wide. With these items, she would need to include a comprehensive media release announcing – and describing in detail – the new range of robots, together with a price list. She would also need to describe the extensive new range of programs with which the new products were equipped. Plus either a selection of full-colour photographs, a colour video with commentary, or a taped radio soundbite (depending upon the type of media) of examples of the new range. To which she would have to add a second release, announcing the range of what Venus was beginning to call Aphrodite's 'Sniff and Taste' range of new sexual-effluent products. She could, she decided, finalize the actual name to be used at a later stage. But she would need to hurry, in order to allow time for package design and the production of promotional material for wholesalers and retailers. Then there would need to be a third release, describing the launch of Aphrodite's new rental company – Sexational Unlimited – together with an up-to-date list of the countries in which the chain would open its first branches, together with the managers' names and the addresses and telephone, facsimile, and Internet numbers, of each store.

To all this, she would need to add a list of the sexual acts obtainable with each rental model, together with the charges for each program, plus the credit references required and the insurance coverage necessary. Venus paused in her task, making notes as she went along. The user and service manuals were already drafted by the company's technical writers, and were currently going through a process of revision to make them rather more user friendly and generally easier to understand. The media releases were her own responsibility, and it was up to her to start drafting these.

She would need to check the question of credit references and deposit requirements with the company secretary, and with the accounts department. Photographs, video, and soundbites she needed to commission. She had a list of specialist commercial photographers,

Voluptuous Venus

video film-makers, radio consultants and technicians, all of whom were familiar both with Aphrodite and with the type of products that the company produced. She leaned back in her chair, and took a deep breath. There was still a lot to do.

She reminded herself that she needed to get together with the company's advertising agency fairly soon. She had briefed them before her trip to St Lucia and they should be coming back to her any day now with their recommendations for the advertising campaign to accompany the launch of the various new products. Whilst advertising agencies were celebrated for their penchant for doing everything at the very last moment, Venus was keen to get things moving. First and foremost she had to be happy with the campaign herself. Then she had to get it approved by her colleagues and, finally, accepted by the board. Advertising was the one thing that (as with most companies) everyone at Aphrodite believed they knew more about than the professionals.

Venus picked up the telephone and called Frank Brady, the account director for Aphrodite's business at Collins, Summers and Phillimore, their advertising agency. The secretary put her straight through.

'Venus, darling. How are you? I thought you were still sunning yourself in the Caribbean.' Frank was charm personified. He was also an extremely shrewd operator, and his agency had an excellent reputation for creative advertising that worked. That actually did increase sales.

'Frank, sweetheart,' she replied. 'And I thought that you were going to come out and join me for the weekend. What happened?' They had joked over an expensive lunch together, before she left for her trip, that he would fly out to join her for a sexy weekend. 'Darling,' he said. 'I'm desolate. But you know how it is. I'd got my secretary to organize the tickets. She'd booked the hotel, and I was all scheduled to arrive and surprise you. And what happens? We get yet another bloody new account. And who is told off by the board to fascinate the new client? Well, yours truly, of course. So I had to cancel everything. I was desolate, as you can imagine. I almost rang *your* secretary, to get her to send me an Aphrodite robot in your image, so that I could at least pretend that I was doing what we had both promised ourselves we would do!'

'Frank, baby,' she giggled at him. 'You're a wonderful liar. And there I was, lying in my lonely bed every night, playing with myself and thinking of you. I've a mind to recommend to my board that we fire you for neglect of duty.'

Frank was one of the few men in the world whom Venus seriously fancied, and he seemed totally unaware of the fact. They talked about sex all the time. Inevitably, really, bearing in mind the nature of the product that Venus's company sold. But that was as far as it ever went. Not because Venus didn't want it to go any further. She practically wet her knickers with excitement, every time she was with Frank. No. It was because Frank didn't seem to have any idea that she wanted to fuck his brains out. She might have wondered if he was gay had she not kept bumping into him in the West End over the years. In pubs and in restaurants, at the theatre and at concerts. And every time she saw him, he was with yet another gorgeous bit of fuckable crumpet, some girl who was always absolutely all over him, physically. It infuriated her. But she refused to give up. She'd get there, one day, if she died in the attempt.

'Darling,' he said. 'Playing with yourself. My God. Can I come and watch?'

'Any time, Frank,' she told him. 'Absolutely any time.'

'I tell you what,' he said. 'If you're free, why don't we have lunch together today? Then we can catch up on the gossip and start thinking about the new campaign. How does that sound?'

'That sounds nice,' she said. And she meant it.

'Terrific,' said Frank. 'How about Greens, in Duke Street? About one-ish?

'I don't know it, but I'll find it,' said Venus. 'I'll see you there. 'Bye, Frank.' *What fun*, she thought. *Lunch with Frank*.

When she got out of the taxi, it was to discover that Greens was an upmarket wine bar with a small restaurant, that described itself as an oyster bar and restaurant. Situated in Duke Street, St James's, off London's Jermyn Street, its prices matched its self-image, and it was popular with businessmen like Frank, who never spent their own money in restaurants if they could possibly avoid it. The oblong restaurant was small and intimate, with banquettes along the full length of one of the longest walls and rather cramped tables in the remaining area. The tablecloths, glass and silver were of good quality, and there were hunting prints upon the walls. The service was prompt and attentive, if a little lacking in style. It was hard to get good staff in the West End in the late twenty-first century.

The little restaurant was packed, but Venus was pretty enough to get the maître d's full attention. He greeted her like a long-lost friend, and when she gave him her name he ushered her to Frank's table, a secluded six-seater banquette in a quiet corner of the room. He was alone.

'Darling,' said Frank. He stood up, put an arm around her, and kissed her on the mouth. She kissed him back. 'Come and sit beside me,' he instructed. The maître d' hovered, and when Venus was seated beside Frank he shook open her carefully folded napkin and placed it across her knees. There was an open bottle of vintage Cristal champagne in an ice bucket beside the table.

The maître d' lifted the bottle out of the ice bucket. 'A glass of champagne for mademoiselle?' he suggested. 'Or would mademoiselle perhaps prefer something else? A cocktail, perhaps?'

Venus smiled at him. 'Champagne will be fine, thank you,' she told him. He poured a glass, topped up Frank's glass, gave them both menus, and left them to each other's company. Venus raised her glass. 'What a pleasant surprise,' she said. 'Cheers.'

Frank raised his glass. 'Cheers, baby,' he rejoined. 'Lovely to see you.' They drank. 'Let's decide what we're going to eat,' he suggested, 'and then we can get down to the serious gossip.'

Venus decided to start with a half-dozen oysters, but Frank talked her into a dozen. 'They're not fattening,

Voluptuous Venus

darling,' he said. 'And they're *so* good for you. Natives, of course. Those Pacific oysters aren't worth the bother.' He chose dressed crab to start with for himself. Venus finally decided on cold Scotch lobster with some new potatoes and a mixed salad as her main course. Frank went for the grilled sea bass with sauté potatoes and a green salad. He waved at the maître d' who almost came running to the table. Frank was obviously both a regular customer and a good tipper. He gave their order, and added a request for a bottle of white burgundy, a Macon-Villages, from the extensive wine list. 'What does mademoiselle like with her oysters?' the maître d' asked.

'Just lemon juice and pepper sauce, please,' she told him. 'But not Tabasco. Busha Browne's Jamaican pepper sauce, if you've got it, please.'

'Certainly, mademoiselle,' he said. 'No problem.'

'So, baby,' said Frank. 'I'm sorry about the cock-up with the trip to St Lucia. I was genuinely looking forward to it.'

'So was I,' Venus told him. 'I thought you were going to come and teach me how to fuck.'

Frank laughed out loud. 'Oh, baby,' he said. 'That'll be the day.' Venus almost blushed, both at the amount of noise his laughter was making – almost everyone in the small restaurant was looking at them – and at his slightly backhanded compliment.

'I tell you, baby, whatever we were going to do when we got there, I was looking forward to it. But a new client is a new client. There wasn't anything I could do about it. Except that I can apologize now.' He put an arm around her, pulled her to him, and kissed her cheek. She felt faintly irritated, not being able to separate his innate charm from his possible lies.

Did he really mean what he was saying? Would he really have joined her out in the Caribbean if he hadn't been prevented, by business? *Was* he really prevented by business? Did he really fancy her? Did he really want to fuck her? Did she care? Was she going to do anything about it? She was tempted to tell him about Harry. About the fact that Harry had fucked her, almost without stopping, for the entire time that she had been out there. That Harry had satisfied her more than any man that she had ever been to bed with in her entire life. That Harry had fucked her anally. She wriggled in her seat at the very thought of Harry's huge cock fucking her anally. Her panties were getting wet. Again.

'Let's call it quits, Frank,' she suggested. 'I wanted you. I *really* wanted you. You didn't arrive, and I had to make do without you. It's the story of my life. Don't worry about it.'

Right then a waiter brought their first courses, and the sight of the food caused them to drop that particular conversation. The restaurant provided the Jamaican pepper sauce that Venus had asked for. Frank was intrigued by it. 'So what's so good about this?' he asked her, picking up the bottle. 'Why is it better?'

'I didn't say that it was better,' Venus told him. 'But it's seriously hotter. If you like pepper sauce – and I do – then, in my entirely subjective opinion, that is the best pepper sauce made anywhere. I first came across it in Jamaica, some years ago. Now you can buy it most places here in the UK. Fortnum's. Tesco's. Wherever. It's made by a company owned by a lovely Jamaican man called Winston Stoner.'

Frank unscrewed the small bottle and sniffed it, carefully. Then he tipped the bottle, and allowed a tiny drop to fall onto the side of his plate. He picked up a fork, speared some of his dressed crabmeat, and dipped it into the pepper sauce. He ate it. 'Jesus,' he said. 'Man, that's HOT.'

Venus laughed. 'It sure is,' she agreed. 'But I did tell you.' Frank chewed silently.

Venus took the half-lemon, wrapped prettily in white muslin, that lay on the side of her plate and squeezed it over her oysters. She watched them as they each moved in silent protest, presumably at the pain she was causing them. It was the only way to prove that they were truly fresh. Alive. Then she picked them up, one at a time, by the shell and tipped both the oyster and the clear liquid in which it sat down her throat. She didn't chew them. 'Mmmmm,' she said, after she swallowed the first one. 'Delicious.'

'Good,' said Frank, 'Enjoy. That's what they're there for.'

'How's the crab?' Venus asked.

'It's good,' he told her. 'Really good. Just like it was when I was a kid down in Dorset, all those years ago. I was born, and used to live, in a place called Osmington Mills. It's a tiny little village, right beside the sea, just outside Weymouth. There's a pub there, down on the beach, called the Lobster Pot. It's still there, actually. I was down there not so long ago. They serve lobster and crab. Beautifully fresh. This tastes just as good.

'But tell me, Venus. How much money do you think Aphrodite are prepared to put behind this new product launch? I mean, it's got to be a tremendous help to me if I've got some idea of the budget.'

How like Frank to get right down to business, she thought. 'I've no idea, to be honest with you, Frank,' she said. 'That's a matter for the directors. But I don't think we've ever cut you back when you've put up a proposition. Have we?'

'No. No, you haven't, to be fair,' he said. 'But surely you can see that it's so much better – so much easier – for me to plan a good campaign if I know what the bottom line is.'

She grinned at him. 'I'm sorry, love,' she said. 'I can't help you. Truly. The only bottom line that I'm aware of is the one my knicker elastic causes when it shows through the material of my skirt.'

He laughed with her. 'Fair enough,' he said. 'So, that aside, let me see if I've got it right. There are three main component parts to the new campaign. One. New, improved models. With – not to put too fine a point on it – sensual new body smells and tastes. Two. A whole new range of exciting clip-on sexual variations. You can buy a package of whatever turns you on, and plug it into your own robot. S and M. Oral sex. Anal sex. Masturbatory sex. Group sex. Lesbian sex. Any kind of sex you want. The big difference between the old models, and the new models, being that, with the old models, you had to specify the kind of sex that you wanted up front, and have it built in to your robot, during the manufacturing stage. Now, all you have to do is buy the right package and plug it in. Am I right?'

Voluptuous Venus

'You're right,' Venus agreed.

'And finally – and, perhaps, most importantly as far as sales and profits are concerned,' Frank continued, 'there's the worldwide launch of Sexational Unlimited, the rental company. The company that is going to make the expensive sexual favours of Aphrodite robots affordable, and available, to the man – and the woman – in the street. Right again?'

'Right again,' said Venus. 'Absolutely spot on. On the button.'

'I think there's a danger of us all confusing ourselves here, if we're not careful,' Frank said. He scraped his fork around inside the shell of his dressed crab, making certain that he wasn't leaving any crabmeat hiding beneath it. 'From a strictly marketing point of view, the new models, and the new range of product packages, are completely separate from the announcement about the rental company. They're different markets altogether. A completely different audience. And we'll need to use different media to reach the different target audiences. I'm not even sure, thinking about it, which of the two should come first.'

'Well, I can save you time there,' Venus told him. 'The product launch of the new models and the new range of sexual goodies is already set up. Well, set up in public relations terms. That's what I was doing out in St Lucia.' She giggled to herself. *Well, one of the things I was doing out there,* she thought. 'That takes place in just over a month's time. But if we have to, I suppose we can always put an embargo on any publicity resulting from that launch. If you think that's necessary.'

Frank thought to himself. Then he said, 'I'm not certain, right now. It shouldn't be necessary. But if we have to, then we will. So, that answers one of the questions, anyway. If your editorial product launch is already set up, then we'll have to keep pace with that. It won't be a big problem.

'But I shall recommend to your board that we keep the launch of the rental chain for a later, quite separate date. You must have retail shop openings planned for specific dates, surely?' He refilled Venus's wine glass, and then his own, looked sadly at the empty bottle, and waved it at a passing waiter, indicating that the waiter should bring a replacement. 'Pronto,' he said, loudly. Frank wasn't used to being kept waiting. It was a tendency which didn't add a great deal of charm to his presence. Venus had become used to it, even if she didn't approve.

'I guess we do,' she said. 'But it's not one of my responsibilities. It's all being decided between the board, the sales director, and the production director.'

'Nothing wrong with that,' said Frank. 'But you'd think they would keep you informed of what was going on.'

'Oh, they do, to be fair,' Venus told him. 'I've not been back long enough yet to get through all my e-mail. I'm sure all the facts are there, waiting to be read. This morning was my first morning back in the office. I really shouldn't have come to lunch with you today. Like the song says, I'm just a girl who can't say no.' She smiled her most winning smile.

'I'm glad that you did,' he said. 'I really missed you.' The waiter brought the replacement bottle of wine and

Voluptuous Venus

opened it, topping up their glasses. He didn't ask Frank if he wanted to taste it.

'What do you think of the rental idea?' Venus asked him.

'I think it's tremendous,' Frank replied. 'Between you and me, I've done a bit of strictly illegal insider trading. I've bought a goodly chunk of shares in Aphrodite who, my brokers tell me, are the holding company for Sexational. Which means that if, in the fullness of time, Sexational is a success – which, incidentally, I truly believe that it will be – then Aphrodite will be the company actually creaming off the excess profits. And since much of their success will be bound up in the way that Collins, Summers, and Phillimore put it all across for them, in advertising terms, then I feel pretty confident about the final results. Is that very arrogant of me?' At least he smiled his charming smile as he asked the question.

'Yes, of course it's arrogant,' she told him. 'But it's well earned arrogance. I'm sure, too, that whatever your company comes up with, it will make the new products, and the new company, a great success. It's why we're with you, after all. But I hadn't thought about buying shares,' she mused, half to herself. 'I should probably do the same, shouldn't I?'

'Only you can decide that,' Frank said. 'It's your money. But it looks like a good risk to me.'

'Thank you, Frank,' she said. 'I will. I'll call my bank when I get back to the office. Thank you for telling me about your purchase. We'll get rich together. How can I thank you?' She uncrossed and then recrossed her legs. She could feel her knickers getting sticky, just sitting next to this marvellous man. She wondered if he was circumcised, or not. She preferred her men not to be. She just loved pulling that bit of loose skin up and down, and watching their cocks swelling as she did so. She mentally had Frank's cock in her fingers. She wondered what he would do if, under cover of the long tablecloth, she unzipped his fly, pulled his cock out of his trousers, and started to wank him.

Frank gave her a slightly quizzical look, and for a moment she wondered if her could read her thoughts. 'You know, the client/advertising agent relationship isn't really all it's cracked up to be,' Frank said.

Venus was somewhat taken aback. 'What do you mean, Frank?' she asked.

'Well,' he said. 'May I be completely honest?'

'Aren't you always?' she countered.

'No,' he said, laughing. 'It isn't always the right thing to be. Not if one wants to keep one's clients. Let me give you an example. I've got another client, called Lightbrook Plc. They make pens. My contact there, on a day-to-day level, is a man called Ben Whittaker. I can't stand him. He's a prat. A total prat. I cringe when he comes into the room. I want to punch him. But it's an excellent product. We do some really terrific work for his company, and we make a healthy profit out of it. So I'm not able to be honest with him. Not if I value my job. And I do.' He smiled at her. 'Now here comes the honest bit. I've wanted to fuck you, from the very first time that we met. There now. How's that for honesty?'

Venus opened her mouth and was about to say some-

Voluptuous Venus

thing, but he held up his hand. 'Hang on a sec. In for a penny, in for a pound. You can tell me to fuck off in just a moment. But let me finish. Let me say it all. Please don't misunderstand me. I'm not in love. I'm in lust. It's your body I'm after, not your mind. When I said that I was coming out to St Lucia to spend a weekend with you, I was serious. I really *did* have a ticket. But I lost my nerve. You see, although we always talk about getting together sexually, I've never been sure whether it was just chat as far as you were concerned. Simply an ongoing joke. And male vanity being what it is, I couldn't stand the thought of you laughing your head off at me when I arrived out there. So I backed out. But suddenly, being with you here today, having screwed up the only real opportunity I've ever had to get your knickers off, I just had to tell you.'

Venus reached out and patted his arm. 'So now you can tell me to fuck off,' he said, grinning rather self-consciously at her.

'Darling,' she said, squeezing his arm. 'Let's get a number of things straight, shall we? First of all, I've lusted after *your* body from the moment that we first met. I know we're always talking about sex, but that's mostly business, isn't it? It's the nature of the beast. That's what Aphrodite sells. But I've been wanting to give you my body for ever. When you take my knickers off – which I hope you're going to do immediately after we leave the restaurant today – you'll discover that they're wringing wet, because I've been fantasizing about you fucking me all through lunch. I've come in my knickers just thinking about your

123

cock. OK?' She looked at him, expectantly.

'Hey, OK,' he said. 'Fantastic.'

'Next,' she said, 'what you do with your client, Ben Whittaker, isn't dishonest. That's just diplomatic good manners. It's life. We can't go around telling people what we really think of them. Not when we don't like them. Life's too short.' She smiled sideways at him. 'So, young Frank. Will you take me to a hotel now, and fuck my brains out? Please?'

'Will I?' he said. He raised his hand at a passing waiter and asked for the bill. 'Not bloody half,' he said. 'Jesus!' The waiter brought the bill, and Frank paid it with a credit card. 'OK, baby,' he said. 'Here we go.'

They went to the Meridian in Piccadilly. The receptionist said that, yes, they did have a vacant suite. 'But you're lucky, if you don't mind my saying so, sir,' he said. 'One of our regular customers has just telephoned and cancelled this suite. Otherwise we were booked solid.' He rang for a bellboy. 'Suite twelve,' he told him, handing him the key. Neither the receptionist nor the bellboy mentioned their lack of luggage.

Venus could hardly keep her hands off Frank in the lift. As the bellboy pocketed his over-generous tip and closed the door, they took each other in their arms and kissed, passionately, for a long time. Then they broke apart and began to strip.

Frank remembered, while he was still dressed, to hang the 'Do Not Disturb' sign outside the door, and then he followed Venus back into the bedroom, and finished stripping off. His nakedness revealed his erect penis, standing out at an angle of forty-five degrees. Venus noticed that he wasn't circumcised.

'What a lovely cock,' she said. She was standing there, naked except for a tiny pair of lacy white knickers.

'I bet you say that to all the boys,' said Frank.

'Only when it's true,' she told him. She went over and took it in her hand. Then she knelt down and kissed the tip of it. It throbbed at her touch. She took it in her mouth and sucked it, lovingly. Then she took it out of her mouth, and stood up again. 'Let's not rush things,' she said. 'We've got all the time in the world. There's no hurry, is there?'

'None at all,' Frank said. He couldn't take his eyes off her. He took in her small, perfectly shaped breasts, with their pretty pink areolae, and her pert, taut little nipples. He couldn't wait to suck them. His eyes caressed her slim waist, her neat umbilicus, and travelled down over her flat stomach, to her lacily knickered crotch and her slightly bulging pudenda. His cock was so stiff it hurt. He wanted to do dirty things to her. All of her.

She watched him as he examined her. Then she smiled at him and, taking the waistband of her knickers in her hand, she pulled it down until it was level with her pussy. Then she stretched it out towards him, so that the effect was as if her pussy was being offered to him on a white, lacy tray. He could see the pink wetness of her nestling in the midst of her soft, fair pubic hair. He could also smell the rich sweetness of her sexual aroma as she held her knickers out away from her body. She looked down at herself, and then back up at him.

'See how wet they are,' she said. He knelt down in front

of her and kissed the sticky wetness of the cotton lining of her knickers.

'I love your wetness,' he told her. 'It is the very nicest of all the sexual compliments that a woman can produce for her man.'

He took the waistband of her knickers from her, pulled the slip of sodden white lacy material slowly down her legs and held it for her as she stepped out of it. He scrunched it up into a ball, and pressed his face into it, breathing deeply the musky odour that emanated from where it was wet. 'That's one more thing I've been wanting to do ever since we first met,' he told her. 'And here's another.'

He dropped the knickers on the floor and, putting his hands on her hips and pulling her towards him, he leant forward and licked her pussy, his tongue slurping wetly up the whole length of it, from the bottom to the top and then back down again. He hesitated at the centre of her, and thrust his tongue as deeply inside her as his position would permit. She tasted just as he had imagined that she would.

'Well, that's a move in the right direction,' she said. 'I've wanted you up my pussy for such a long time, and now I've got you there. We can work our way around to your cock later. Like you said earlier, there's no hurry.'

Frank tore himself away from between her thighs. Reluctantly. He stood up, took Venus by the hand, and led her over to the bed. He glanced at the windows, which looked out over Piccadilly. There were muslin curtains, as well as proper curtains (although these were drawn back, since it was daylight) to protect their privacy. There was also double glazing, keeping the traffic noise at bay. Frank went over to the fridge in the corner of the bedroom and opened the door. It was well stocked. 'Do you fancy a drink, Venus?' he asked.

'Mmmm,' she answered. 'Is there any champagne?'

'Sure,' said Frank. 'Straight or pink?'

'Oh. How lovely. Pink, please.'

The champagne was in quarter-bottles. Frank looked around for glasses, found them in a cupboard next to the fridge, and opened two of the bottles. It was Laurent-Perrier. 'Here's to you and me, baby,' he said, raising his glass.

She followed suit, and they drank. Frank couldn't keep his eyes off Venus's body. He had become accustomed to his seemingly permanent erection, and it no longer embarrassed him. But he was fascinated by her sex. It was so wet that her vaginal fluids were running down the inside of her thighs. A quarter-bottle of champagne is, at best, two glasses, depending upon the size and shape of the glass. The Meridian, as might be expected, supplied proper crystal champagne flutes, which allowed them two glasses each, but it was soon finished. Frank didn't offer – and Venus didn't ask for – a further bottle. They both wanted each other more than they needed another drink. Venus went and pulled back the covers on the king-size bed and laid herself down upon it.

Frank all but drained his glass, leaving perhaps just a couple of mouthfuls of champagne at the bottom. Taking it with him, he lay down beside Venus and, using his fingers to prise apart her labia, he poured half of the remaining pink champagne into her pussy.

'Ooohh,' she said. 'Fizzy pussy. That's a first.'

Frank put his head down between her legs and Venus raised her knees, the better to allow him access. He sucked away at her, lapping up the champagne, now flavoured by Venus's love juices. He swallowed with evident relish and then he looked up at her, grinning. 'We should bottle it, and sell it,' he said. 'We'd make a fortune. We could call it Pink Pussy.'

'Don't think it hasn't been suggested,' Venus told him. 'Because it has. But reproduced chemically, of course. Not the real thing. But I'm happy to volunteer, if you think it would work. All I would have to do would be to lie in bed all day, drinking pink champagne and getting fucked, in order to produce the goods. If you were fucking me, it would be a vintage year. What do you say, Frank?'

'I say "Yes, please",' Frank said. Then he started to pay serious attention to the cunnilingus at which he had been only half serious up to now, after draining off and drinking his last mouthful of pink champagne. His ministrations began to get through to Venus, who started to move her hips sensually in time with Frank's rhythm. She reached out, took hold of his magnificently erect cock, and began to masturbate him.

'Kneel over me, Frank,' she said, a few moments later. 'Then I can suck you while you suck me.'

He continued with his oral attentions but did as Venus suggested, moving around until he was in a position to kneel over her head, his rigid cock just inches away from her mouth. She took it in her fingers, guided it into her waiting, drooling mouth, and then began to fellate him.

Voluptuous Venus

They both came together, Venus's orgasm causing her to writhe and buck and squirm as Frank's semen exploded down her throat. She hit her peak rapidly, managing to hold it there for long, lovely, sexually rewarding moments, before it slowly faded and was – at least for the moment – all over. Frank's ejaculate issued in strong, thick spurts which she gulped down, thinking – incongruously – of the taste of Harry's semen, swallowed lovingly so many times during her stay in St Lucia.

They disentangled themselves and lay beside each other, their arms entwined, getting their breath back. Venus giggled. 'What's funny?' Frank queried.

'I was just thinking of the office,' Venus told him. 'Don't ask me why. I was imagining Sally asking me where I'd been, and me saying, "My lunch meeting with Frank Brady went on rather longer than I anticipated. But he's got some great ideas."' She giggled again. 'And so you have, my darling. Venus's bottled champagne-and-pussy-juice. Pink Pussy. As opposed to the Pink Panther, I suppose. It would have to be a winner. Let's go for it.'

'We could have fun with the packaging,' said Frank. 'Think about it. We could have plastic pubic hair around the neck of the bottle, to encourage the punters in the wine bars to drink it straight out of the bottleneck. And we could have elliptical, cunt-shaped bottle-necks. What else? We could produce mats – you know, like beer mats – for pubs and hotel bars, with "Pink Pussy" printed on them. They'd look like miniature sanitary towels, of course.'

He looked across at her. She was almost helpless with laughter. 'And the bottles could be wrapped in tissue paper

– you know, like some bottles of champagne are – that could be in the shape of a pair of panties. Or have pantie shapes printed on it. And we'd run scratch-and-sniff ads for it in all the glossies. Do you remember reading about how they used to do that, what, a hundred years ago? Back in the late 1970s, early 1980s. Scratch-and-sniff advertisements were very popular in the States in those days. They started off with perfume and aftershave ads, and progressed – eventually – through to the girlie magazines, who ran scratch-and-sniff centrefolds.' He looked sideways at her again. 'No, I'm serious, Venus. They did. Really they did.'

'I don't believe you,' she giggled. 'You're making it up.'

'I'm not,' he said. 'Honestly. But what else? I suppose we could have varying flavours. The main brand would be Pink Pussy. Champagne and pussy juice. But then we could have Golden Pussy. Champagne, and just a drop or two of high-quality female piss, to give it that extra-special flavour. For all those water sports specialists.'

Venus was still giggling softly to herself as she reached down between his thighs and took his soft cock in her hands. She rubbed it, slowly, sensually, back into its previously erect state and cuddled up against him, whispering into his ear, 'What shall we do now, Frank?'

'I don't know, darling,' he said, raising his hips up off the bed, so that she was now masturbating him properly. 'I'm enjoying this. What else did you have in mind?'

'I thought that you might fuck me,' she told him. 'Seeing as I'm lying here, stark naked, playing with your cock. I thought that you might perhaps do something useful with it instead of just lying there while I toss you off.'

He groaned a heavy mock groan. 'There's no peace for the wicked. No bloody peace at all,' he said. As he spoke, he rolled onto his side and then climbed on top of Venus. She obligingly spread her legs and put down a hand with which to unfold her pussy lips. Since she still had Frank's cock in her other hand, she then guided it up into herself. Frank shut his eyes, and groaned again, but this time genuinely, and with an excess of delight.

'Oh, Jesus,' he said, thrusting himself deeply inside her. 'Oh, God. That's wonderful. Just wonderful. So tight. So wet. It's like fucking a cunt made of satin.'

As he spoke, she started to squeeze his length with her vaginal muscles, clenching him as he thrust in and out of her, teasing him, stroking him, sucking him with her cunt. She reached out and grasped his buttocks, pulling him down onto her, revelling in the feel of his iron-hard penis, its head and shaft now swollen beyond description, filling her cunt, stretching her with his strokes, grinding joyfully against her clitoris. She could feel his cockhead thrusting at the entrance to her womb, and then – with immaculate timing – just as the greatest orgasm of all time rose up and overtook her with shuddering, climactic intensity, she could feel his penis throbbing as it pumped hot semen directly into her womb. She let out a strangulated half-cry, half-scream as she clutched him and ground her loins against his, succumbing to the body-racking convulsions of her orgasm.

He in turn held her hard as he jetted his jism into her. He could feel the round neck of her womb against his rigid cock, and he knew exactly where his semen was going. He crossed his mental fingers that she was on the pill, or had a coil, or whatever. But then, a woman of her experience, in her business particularly, would take all the necessary precautions. Wouldn't she? Or, if she didn't, she'd tell him – beforehand – to wear a condom. She wouldn't want to get pregnant. Not at her age. *Jesus*, he thought, in the seconds that he was shooting his semen into her. *Imagine ruining this fabulous fuck by having to wear a johnnie.*

He would not have been able to enjoy the soft, gently ribbed, velvet feel of her cunt as he fucked her, nor delight in the warm, flooded wetness of it, with all the feeling sensations in his dick strangulated in a bloody French letter.

She looked up at him, and smiled. 'If I wasn't on the pill, Frank darling,' she told him, 'I guarantee that we would have been making babies together then. It felt lovely, my darling. I came and came. You could probably feel me coming. Could you?'

'Yes, sweetheart. I most certainly could. It was the most unusual, most exciting, sexual sensation that I have ever experienced, feeling a woman that I'm making love with actually coming. It was quite unique. I was very deep inside you, as you know. My prick was banging away at the entrance to your womb. I could feel it.

'And then, when you started to come, it was as if your whole vagina was spasming. It was extremely physical. It was almost like a hand that suddenly came to life, and as you orgasmed the hand gripped my cock, and ...

Voluptuous Venus

manipulated me. Masturbated me. Made me come. *Squeezed* me, and brought me to my ejaculation. Previously, when making love, I'm compelled to say that I've made myself come, by the action of thrusting my cock in and out of the lady's cunt. That has always been what causes me to ejaculate. I thought that was what fucking was all about. But with you . . . It was completely different. *You* made *me* come. *You* brought about my ejaculation. It was your doing. Not mine.' He grinned at her. 'And I loved every minute of it. Thank you.' He leaned across and kissed her. 'We must do it again sometime.'

In fact, they did do it again. About ten minutes later. And then again. After a while, they looked at their watches and saw that the working day was drawing to a close. So they both telephoned their respective offices, telling their secretaries that their meeting was still going on (that was true!) and that they wouldn't be back that day. They were fortunate, in that no one of any import seemed to be looking for either of them. Since Frank had obviously booked the hotel suite for the night, they decided to stay there and take advantage of the hotel and its amenities.

Around about seven o'clock, Venus suggested that they take a break for food and drink. 'I don't know about you, darling,' she said to Frank, 'but I'm starving. Despite that lovely lunch. How about a drink, and then some supper?' She looked at him, almost shyly. 'I don't know what we'll find to do after that. But I'm sure we'll think of something.'

'Great idea,' he said. 'Where do you fancy?'

'Oh, anywhere, darling,' she said. 'You choose.'

'OK,' he said. 'They've got an excellent restaurant here.

It overlooks Piccadilly, from a sort of greenhouse-cum-atrium arrangement. It's very elegant, and the food is great. But I feel like a little English tradition. Let's go to the Ritz restaurant. Would you like that?'

'Oh, that would be lovely, darling,' she said. 'I've only ever been there on high days and holidays. You know ... uncles' birthdays. Daddy's and Mummy's silver wedding anniversary. That sort of thing. I've never been there with a boyfriend.' She looked down, fluttered her eyelids, and then looked up at him from beneath them. Positively coyly, he thought. 'Is it all right to call you that?' she asked. 'Are you a boyfriend?'

He laughed. 'I do hope so,' he told her. And then, sudenly all serious, because he realized that what she was asking was important to her. 'Of course I'm a boyfriend, sweetheart,' he said. 'And a lover. I hope.'

She kissed him and gave him a big hug. Frank telephoned the Ritz and booked them a table. Then they both showered, only just managing to get themselves clean without succumbing to their mutual physical attraction once more. 'I've never been fucked in a shower,' Venus said, rather plaintively. 'I thought that perhaps that was going to be the first time. A new experience.'

'Oh, sweetheart,' he said. 'I'm sorry. I didn't know. I'll fuck you in the shower when we come back, after dinner. I promise. OK?'

'OK,' she said.

The restaurant in the Ritz almost certainly hadn't altered in more than a hundred years. It was still furnished with circular tables, with pink tablecloths and napkins. It

Voluptuous Venus

still looked out over Green Park. The crystal chandeliers still gleamed, as did the crystal glasses and the silver cutlery upon the tables. The waiters all still wore tailcoats and white ties, and they still all looked a hundred years old. And they all still had the same old-fashioned charm and courtesy for which they were famous the world over.

'Would you like a dry martini?' Frank asked. 'They still know how to make a good one here.'

'Oh, that would be lovely. Thank you. What a great idea,' Venus said. Frank gave the waiter their drinks order and he handed them their menus. Their cocktails arrived shortly afterwards.

'I must tell you about the first time I ever came here,' Frank said. 'It was my birthday, and I was working in a different agency in those days. I had a colleague there called Gerrard Campbell. Lovely man. That particular day, he came into my office and asked if I was doing anything for lunch. I said no, I didn't have anything planned, but that, since it was my birthday, I'd be more than happy to celebrate it with him. "Wow," he said. "Your birthday. Fantastic.2 I should have told you that my birthday is in October. So Gerrard said "How about a nice grouse on your birthday?" I had to admit that I'd never had one, and it was then that Gerrard insisted that, in that case, it was about time that I did. "There's only one place for a chap to have his first grouse," Gerrard said. "And that's the Ritz." He consequently rang up the Ritz restaurant and booked us a table. But here's the amusing bit. At least, I thought that it was amusing, at the time. We were shown to our table, and Gerrard ordered a bottle of champagne to drink

135

while we decided what we wanted to eat. He was nothing if not a generous host. He also had a certain amount of family money, which helped.

'As we perused the menus, I saw something moving. Down on the carpet. Out of the corner of my eye. I looked at it, and saw it was a small mouse. It ran beneath the long tablecloth covering our table. I told Gerrard of this event. He peered under the tablecloth and saw the little mouse sitting there. "Damn me," he said. "You're absolutely right." He waved a languid hand at our waiter who came to see what was wanted. Gerrard told him of the mouse. "There's a mouse underneath our table," said Gerrard. The waiter lifted up the tablecloth and peered beneath. He stood up, releasing the cloth. "You're right, sir," he said. "You're absolutely right." And then he walked away. Gerrard and I laughed ourselves silly. True story.'

Venus laughed. Sitting in that delightful, rather otherworldly atmosphere, she could imagine it all happening. After all, what did we expect the waiter to do? He wasn't, after all, going to start chasing the mouse around the restaurant, if you think about it. The menu was a work of art. Obviously changed daily, for both lunch and dinner, it offered a range of delights not seen in too many restaurants in London's West End in these days. There was, of course, caviar. Well, there would be, wouldn't there? They offered two varieties: Sevruga and Beluga. There was also *foie gras*. Not *pâté de foie gras*. The real thing. It was, however, the wrong time of year for grouse or pheasant. But they offered wild Scotch salmon. And Welsh salmon trout. Venus decided on *Oeufs en Cocotte* to start with, mostly because she loved

Voluptuous Venus

them, and she hadn't seen them on a restaurant menu for simply ages. Fresh eggs, coddled in cream. Frank went for the devilled kidneys, for the same reason. They both settled for the salmon trout, with new potatoes and a simple green salad. When it came, the mayonnaise served with it was out of this world. They drank champagne throughout. Neither of them could manage a pudding, despite the mouth-watering possibilities.

By the time they got to the coffee, they both felt the need for a brandy, and in collusion with the wine waiter Frank ordered something expensively delicious. It was, after all, a celebration.

Frank leaned over towards Venus. 'Do you know what I'd like now?' he asked her.

'No,' she said, her eyes twinkling and belying her statement.

'Hot pussy,' said Frank, who was beginning to feel the effects of the champagne and the brandy. He smiled at Venus.

'Then hot pussy is what you shall have,' she told him. 'Will mine do, or did you have someone else in mind?'

He giggled at her. 'Yours was what I was thinking about, my darling,' he said. 'Is it hot to trot?'

'It most certainly is,' she told him. 'And it's wet, too. It's been thinking about you all the time that we've been sitting here. It's been thinking about that huge, thick, enormous cock of yours, and it's been getting itself ready to be fucked by it again. So it's very hot, very wet, and very ready to trot. Or anything else that you might have in mind for it.'

'How lovely,' said Frank. He waved at the waiter and made the international sign for wanting the bill – the hand-signing-a-receipt one. He settled the bill when it came, and they walked out into the evening.

They had taken their time over their meal, and it was now nearly eleven. They crossed over to the north side of Piccadilly at the lights and began to walk slowly along the pavements, looking at the shop windows as they did so. A couple of hundred yards along the way they came to a new nightclub. It was called Cymbals. Neither of them had been there, but they had both read about its launch party, some three or four weeks previously. It had received good reviews in most of the media. There were photographs of the interior outside. It looked extremely attractive.

On impulse, Frank said, 'Why don't we drop in there for a drink and have a look at it? Do you fancy it?'

'Oh, that would be fun,' said Venus. 'Yes, thank you. I'd love to.'

They went down the stairs. Frank paid an exorbitant entrance fee for the two of them. It made him a temporary member. They went inside.

It was an attractively decorated, fairly large room. It was all done out in a sort of peacock blue and silver, with black marble touches here and there. There was a small dance floor, and a seven-piece band that was playing romantic, smoochy music to the dozen or so couples already on the dance floor.

The maître d' showed them to a table, not too far from the stage upon which the band was sitting, and asked them

Voluptuous Venus

what they would like to order. 'Champagne?' Frank asked Venus.

'That would be lovely, darling,' she said.

Frank sensibly ordered a non-vintage bottle. After the amount that they had already drunk that evening, anything else would have been a waste of money. Particularly at the nightclub's prices. The waiter went off to get their order.

They looked around. Little cards on the table announced a cabaret at midnight. From the illustration on the card, it looked like the usual West End of London nightclub type of show, with pretty girl dancers in minimal costumes. One or two of the girls were topless. 'Pretty exciting stuff,' Venus said. 'Do you think your blood pressure's up to it?'

Frank took the card from her and looked at the picture. 'Hmmm,' he said. 'I'll take a chance.' He smiled at her. 'Would you like to dance?' he asked.

'I'd love to, darling,' she said. 'Thank you.' She stood up, and Frank took her by the hand and led her out onto the dance floor. The band was playing what would have been described, years ago, as a quickstep. It was funny how the old tunes lasted. They copied the other couples on the floor, and danced together in the old-fashioned way.

'You smell delightful,' Frank said. 'I'm not good at scents. What is it?' 'It's L'Air du Temps,' Venus told him. 'That, and hot, wet knickers. I guess the one aroma is mingling with the other. I'm sorry if it's embarrassing, but my pussy's so wet there's not a lot I can do about it.'

'It's not embarrassing. I love it,' he told her. 'It's a lovely, exciting scent.'

She could feel his cock pressing against her groin as they danced, which was probably going to make her even wetter. *What the hell*, she thought. *I can always go into the ladies and mop myself up.* She was determined to relax and enjoy her time with Frank. She hadn't been so happy for a long time. She realized now that, much as she had enjoyed her time in St Lucia with Harry, and though he was charming and sexually appealing, much of the attraction had been to do with their exotic Caribbean surroundings. The warm, balmy temperatures, the soft white sand, and the azure blue seas had brought about an aura of well-being that had been well-nigh irresistible. Venus nestled her cheek into Frank's shoulder, and held him closely. As if on cue, the band launched into 'Isn't It Romantic?' Venus sighed, deeply.

'That's a big sigh,' Frank said. 'What's the problem?'

'No problem, darling,' she said. 'That's a sigh of utter contentment. I can't ever remember being as happy as this. How about you?'

'I have to admit,' said Frank, 'that when I said to you this afternoon, over lunch, that I wasn't in love with you, I was in lust with you, I meant what I said. At the time. But something's happened since then. Something very rare – in my life, anyway – and something very lovely. I don't know what it is, because I've never experienced it quite like this before. Is it love? Whatever it is, I don't ever want it to stop.' He held her, tightly, as he spoke, and gave her a big squeeze as he finished.

'That's very sweet of you, my darling,' Venus said. 'I'll happily settle for that. What more could a girl ask?'

Voluptuous Venus

Right then, the music came to an end and with a roll of drums, a dinner-jacketed master of ceremonies came on and announced the imminent commencement of the cabaret. Frank and Venus made their way back to their table. By now Cymbals was quite full, and there was an air of expectation as the audience waited for the show to start. Then the band played an up-tempo introduction, the lights went down, coloured spotlights came on, and the star of the show, a young, extremely attractive long-legged redhead, came on stage, accompanied by a chorus line of eight of the prettiest young dancers that either Frank or Venus had seen anywhere.

The redhead wore the classic nightclub cabaret gear of glitzy black tailcoat trimmed with silver, tight white blouse, black fishnet stockings, and very brief tightly fitting black silver-trimmed shorts. The chorus girls' outfits were considerably briefer, comprising completely transparent gauzy brassieres and tiny G-strings that left very little to the imagination, particularly when the girls went into a high-kicking routine.

Venus looked at Frank. He was looking lustfully at the girls, as they kicked their long legs into the air with professional precision. 'Pretty girls,' Venus said.

'I'll say,' agreed Frank. 'It's enough to give a chap a hard-on.'

'If you could fuck just one of those eight girls,' Venus asked him, 'which one would you choose?'

Frank looked at her, grinned, and returned his full attention to the row of dancers. They had just gone into a reprise of the high-kicking part of their act.

'Difficult question,' he said. 'To be perfectly honest, as a normal, reasonably red-blooded male, I'd fuck all and any of them, given the opportunity.' He glanced around at her as she sat beside him. 'That's not to say that I wouldn't rather fuck you,' he said. 'But that's the nature of the beast. It's part of what being a man is about. We respond to sexual attraction. And those girls, and what they are doing right now, is intended to be – and, as far as I'm concerned, is succeeding in being – extremely sexually attractive.'

'But you still haven't answered my question,' Venus said. 'If you could only have one of them, which one would you choose?'

Frank concentrated. And then, 'I think the third one from the left. That little blonde one with the long legs.'

Venus looked carefully at the one he had, theoretically, selected. She was by no means the prettiest of the eight, but then none of them were exactly dogs. But on examination, she certainly had something that separated her from the other seven. She could have been the youngest. That was something that they would probably never know. She certainly appeared to have the longest legs. They were the kind that went all the way up to her bottom. And most of *that* (in common with those of the other seven girls) was on display, as could be seen when they turned their backs, provokingly, towards the audience. She had a lovely arse, Venus thought. Tight, firm, rounded little buttocks. She wondered if Frank would like to get his cock up in between them.

What else? The girl's face was perhaps her best single attribute. Whilst not a raving beauty, she had a pert, cheeky, impudent look about her. And lips that could only be described as being made for one thing. Sucking cock. Charisma. That was what she had, Venus decided. That, and the kind of body that most men would give their right arm to fuck. And then use their left arm to jack themselves off, thinking about it afterwards, Venus thought.

Her tits – which could be seen in their full glory through the gauzy material of her bra – were perfection itself, Venus had to admit. *Although*, she thought, *mine are still just about as good as that. And I can give her a couple of years, at least. Perhaps more.* But that didn't prevent her from admitting that they *were* great tits. *Insolent* tits, she thought. Full, firm, prettily rounded – although small in overall size – with comparatively large brown nipples set erectly on generous brown areolae. Asking to be sucked. And all of it, the entire package, asking to be fucked. Yes, she thought. Frank had probably picked the right one there.

She accepted that the girl was projecting an aura of sexual attraction – and sexual availability – that was simply part of her job. One of the things she got paid for. But she did it completely naturally. It was patently second nature to her.

'Mmmm,' Venus said. 'After due consideration, I think you're right. I reckon she's probably a right little goer. But what single thing about her attracted you to her in the first place? *Was* it any one single thing? Or was it just the overall picture I mean, she's sure as hell sexy. But then they all are. Aren't they?'

Frank turned towards her, looking, she thought,

perhaps just slightly abashed. 'Honest answer?' he asked.

'Of course,' she told him.

Frank cleared his throat. 'Well. I like the overall look, of course. But then, as you so rightly say, they're all lookers. But if you check out that tiny piece of flimsy material that is just about covering her pussy, you'll notice that it is much darker than that worn by all the other seven girls.

'I'm guessing, of course, because I can't be absolutely certain. But I think that it's darker because it's actually wet. And if I'm right, and it *is* wet, it can only be for one of two reasons. One, she's pissed herself. And I don't think that's very likely. Or two, she is so sexually excited by what she is doing up there, showing off her parts to all and sundry, that her sexual fluids are flowing to the extent that they've made her little G-string wet. And if I'm right about that, she's got to be the sexiest little tart of all eight of them. Do you agree?'

Venus laughed out loud. 'Oh, fantastic,' she said. 'Abso-bloody-lutely fantastic.' She peered at the girl's pubis, trying to catch a moment when the spotlight lit up her groin sufficiently for her to make an informed decision. 'It's difficult to see, isn't it?' she said. 'But it *does* look wet, I must say. Was that all? Just the fact that she has a wet pussy? *I've* got a wet pussy. But I hope that's not the only reason you're attracted to me.'

'Oh, come on, darling,' Frank said. 'Let's not allow the conversation to deteriorate down to that level, for God's sake. You asked me, were I was given the opportunity, which of those chorus girls would I like to fuck. It was your thought. Not mine. I answered your question, as best

Voluptuous Venus

I could. And now you're trying to make out that it was *my* idea. Well, it wasn't. OK?'

Venus slipped her arm through his and pulled him towards her. 'Oh, don't be silly, Frank, darling,' she said. 'I was only joking. As far as I'm concerned, you can fuck all of them. One after the other.' She looked at him, and grinned. 'But only if I can watch.'

He laughed with her. 'Right now,' he said, 'I only want to fuck you. OK?'

'OK,' she said. Right then, the chanteuse finished her spot, and she and the eight-girl chorus tripped off the stage to enthusiastic applause from the audience.

They were followed by a comedian. He was good, but neither Venus nor Frank were in the mood for his particular brand of material, all of which was hung on the peg of the man's obvious homosexuality. He was very funny, and in different circumstances they might well have enjoyed his act. Right now, they just wanted to go back to the hotel and fuck.

Frank called for the bill, paid it, and they left. 'That was fun, darling,' Venus said. 'Tremendous fun. I haven't had an evening out like that for longer than I can remember.' She squeezed his arm.

They continued their walk back along Piccadilly to their hotel, picked up their key in reception and took the lift up to their suite. Venus looked at her watch. It was nearly one in the morning.

She went through to the bedroom, tore her clothes off, dropped them where she stood and climbed onto the bed. She then lay on her back and opened her legs. Wide. Then she pulled her pussy lips apart, and held them in that position with her fingers.

'Come and fuck my wet cunt, lover,' she said, her voice low and husky from sheer sexual passion. 'Come and fuck me. I'm ready for you. More than ready for you. I've been wanting you all evening. Ever since we left the Ritz. Shut your eyes, and pretend that I'm that little eighteen-year-old chorus girl. Take me any way you want me and pretend I'm her. If you want her to suck you off, just shut your eyes and you'll never know the difference.'

Frank was stripping off as she was issuing her invitation and his cock grew steadily more and more erect at the mental images that Venus's intentionally dirty talk produced.

He went over to her, on the bed, took her in his arms and kissed her. Passionately. Wetly. His tongue exploring her mouth. 'Dirty cow,' he said. 'My own lovely personal dirty cow.'

'Oooh,' said Venus, pulling back from him. 'That reminds me. That chorus girl – you remember? the one you wanted to fuck? – she had the most exquisite arse. Among other things. She had great tits and wonderful legs. And an exquisite arse. The only thing we couldn't quite see was her cunt. But she probably has an exquisite cunt, too. What do you think, Frank?'

'I guess she probably has,' Frank replied. 'I can tell you one thing about her cunt, though,' he said, looking at her mischievously.

'Oh, and what's that?' Venus asked.

'She is almost certainly totally clean-shaven down

there,' Frank said. 'Like all of those dancers. Shaved pussy. There's no way that they can wear those tiny G-strings without showing their pubes, unless they shave them off. Most girls who trim their pubes end up shaving them off completely,' he told Venus. 'So I'm told.'

'Does that turn you on?' Venus asked him.

'Yeah. Sometimes,' he told her. 'There are times when shaved cunt turns me on and times when thick, hairy cunt turns me on. But I'll tell you a secret,' he said, conspiratorially. 'It's just plain cunt that turns me on. Square cut, or pear-shaped, those cunts don't lose their shape. Pussies are a man's best friend. Wasn't that what Marilyn sang?'

Venus laughed, partly at his appallingly bad rhyme and partly at his delightful – to her – mild drunkenness. 'Well ... something like that,' she told him. 'But there you go. Whatever turns you on.'

'*You* turn me on,' he told her.

'Ah,' she said. 'That reminds me. I was going to ask you something.'

'Ask away,' he said.

'What I was going to ask you,' she said, 'was – thinking about that little chorus girl's lovely arse – are you into buggery? Do you like to fuck girls' arses? Would you have liked to fuck that chorus girl up her undoubtedly tight little arsehole?'

'Oh, baby,' he said. 'Now you're talking. Do I like to fuck girls up their arseholes? Oh, sweetheart. Turn over, and I'll happily demonstrate the answer to your question.' He put his hand around her waist and pulled her, turning her over until she was lying on her stomach. He spread her legs, and ran his fingers down along her anal cleavage. He next found her anus with his middle finger and pressed it roughly down inside it.

Venus half screamed, half moaned with pleasure. Inside that forbidden place, she felt hot. And wetly sticky. He thrust his finger as far up her as it would go, and reamed her arsehole.

'Oh, darling,' she said, her breath coming painfully. 'Fuck me there. Fuck my arsehole. Bugger me. Please. Now. I want it. I love it up my arse. Give me your cock. Your big, stiff cock.' Frank pulled his finger out of her, and looked at it. It glistened wetly with her anal mucus.

'I haven't got any kind of lubricant,' he said. 'Have you?'

'No, darling,' she said. 'But don't worry about it. Spit on your fingers, and then rub it into me. That will do. Do it now. Please. Quickly. I want it. I *really* want it. Fuck me up my tiny arsehole.' She was almost painfully sexually excited.

Her pleadings fell upon entirely sympathetic ears. He looked down at her anus. Its wrinkled circle was the very same pink as her nipples. As her cunt lips. It was tiny, and tightly puckered. His cock was so stiff, waiting to force its way up into that forbidden heaven, that it actually hurt. He took a deep breath, spat a great gob of spittle onto his fingers, and began to rub it into her rectum.

'Oooh. Nice.' said Venus, wriggling her bottom against the thrust of his fingers. 'Cock next. Please.'

Don't worry, sweetheart, Frank thought to himself. *I'm going to fuck the arse off you, given a moment or two. Then, when I do, don't give me any of that 'Oh, no. Stop. Please stop, darling. You're hurting me,' fucking shit. You asked for it, and you're going to get it. Cock doesn't come a lot stiffer than this.* He pulled her buttocks apart, guided his rampant penis onto the very centre of her little pink arsehole, and pushed himself in. Hard. Her anus dilated as he sank slowly into it.

'Arrrrrgh,' moaned Venus. 'Oh, yes. Oh Jesus.'

As a sexual act, it didn't actually last very long. But they both enjoyed themselves immensely. Frank was so excited by it that he ejaculated almost instantly, shooting his sperm up Venus's rectal passage in long, concentrated spurts. Venus felt as if her very bowels were on fire, and then she came with him, shouting out her pleasure at the sensations that she was experiencing. She felt almost as if she was being consumed. Her orgasms kept her shuddering, her womb contracting, long after Frank's ejaculation was ended. He pulled out of her, rolled over, and lay down beside her. 'Oh, baby,' he said. 'The earth really moved for that one, I can tell you.'

'And for me,' she said. 'Thank you, darling. That was the best yet.'

They didn't sleep at all that night. They spent their time making love in every possible way. They drank rather a lot of champagne, which probably helped as a stimulant. They were so involved with each other that neither of them thought of sleep. At around eight in the morning they made love, urgently but slowly, lingeringly, for they knew it would be for the last time before they got themselves together to go off to work.

They had agreed, finally, that they either had time for breakfast or for that one last fuck session before it would be time to leave, and both plumped for love before food. They then washed away all traces of the night's excesses and swore undying love as they made their way down to the hotel lobby.

Frank settled their bill and they took off in different taxis, in different directions.

CHAPTER FOUR

Pressing Business

Venus wasn't at all sure exactly *how*, but everything came together and was actually ready – and on time – for the media launch. The new robot models, male and female. The packaging. The advertising campaign. The range of sexual variations. And the range of sexual scents and flavours. It had been a madhouse of what seemed like day-long panics, with days starting at eight and finishing anywhere between ten and midnight, followed by marathon, ecstatic nights spent with Frank. She lost almost a stone over the period (which she didn't mind at all. She had, prior to that, put on almost a stone, so she was pretty well back where she liked to be, in weight terms).

One of the more interesting aspects of that period, for Venus, was the day that Peter, the production director, and Mark, the sales director, called her down to Mark's office. They didn't explain what it was about when they spoke to her on her office telephone, so she was completely taken aback when she entered the room to be confronted by herself. It was, of course, the robot that had been requested for the media launch by the Australian tabloid journalist.

The robot smiled at Venus, stood up, and held out her/its hand. 'Hi, Venus,' it said. 'I'm Venus, too. How do you do.'

Venus, in a mild state of shock, held out her hand. 'How do you do, Venus,' she said. 'It's, er, good to meet you.'

Peter and Mark were killing themselves with laughter. Peter stepped forward, and switched off the robot's voice control. 'She's a great fuck, too, I'm pleased to be able to tell you,' he said.

'You haven't!' Venus said.

'He has,' said Mark. 'And so have I. I have to agree. You're a great lay.'

'You bastards,' said Venus, laughing with them.

'You never told us that you were into kinky sex,' Peter said.

'That's probably because I'm not. At least, not particularly,' retorted Venus.

Peter laughed again. 'You are now,' he said. 'As long as whoever's using you remembers to plug in the right sexual variation package. You were seriously into spanking, the afternoon that I spent with you. I remember it well. I made your pretty little bottom the most delightful shade of pink. You even cried. And it perked up your sexual performance no end. It was delightful.'

'All right, guys,' Venus said. 'You've had your fun now. But enough is enough. When I agreed to allow that Aussie prick to choose a robot that looked like me, I eventually changed my mind, and I finally, most particularly, did *not* agree to allow you to endow that robot with anything other than my personal scents and flavour. And that's something that has been common to all our female robots until this new range of scent-and-flavour products that we're just about to launch. I know – and you know – that no one here (or anywhere else, for that matter, apart from my actual lovers) knows anything about my sexual habits, my sexual preferences, or anything at all to do with my sex life. And while I can take a joke as well as the next person, I seriously don't want either of you two spreading untruths about this model here.

'Yes, it's a great joke. Yes, I'm amused. But it's a joke that I want kept strictly between the three of us. Do I make myself clear?'

'Let me answer for both of us,' said Mark. 'There's no problem. Of course it's a private joke. It was never going to be anything else. But you can surely understand that the temptation was too great for us to resist it? Just between us three? Far too great!'

'Well, yes. I suppose I can,' said Venus, albeit rather grudgingly. 'But that's that. OK?'

'Yes, of course,' said Peter and Mark, together. And that *was* that.

There was obviously a certain amount of joshing from Venus's colleagues once the fact of the Venus robot's existence became general knowledge. But it was all within the bounds of what passed for good taste in the Aphrodite organization. Less than a week later, Venus bid a fond adieu to Frank and took off, two weeks ahead of her fellow board of directors – who would be joining her out there – for the launch programme in St Lucia.

The robots being used for the launch had been airfreighted out the week before, accompanied by two of Aphrodite's top technicians, and they had already been assembled and tested by the time Venus arrived.

She already knew that Harry had completed his legal brief out there and returned home, for he had kept in touch with her until her feelings of guilt had forced her to tell him that she had fallen in love with someone else. She felt pangs of regret at so doing, but she got the impression that it was by no means the end of the world for Harry. She did, however, get a strong feeling of *déjà vu* on arrival once more at the St Lucian Hotel. Reasonably enough, she supposed.

The hotel staff greeted her pleasantly, and she got the impression that they were genuinely pleased to see her. 'But no Mr Harry,' said her favourite barman, her first evening there.

'Sadly, no,' Venus agreed. 'But who knows? Maybe by this time next week...'

The barman laughed a big, happy, Caribbean laugh, showing Venus a perfect set of beautiful teeth. 'Of course,' he agreed. 'Next week. Who knows... Maybe *another* Mr Harry.'

In fact, Venus was far too busy for the rest of that week to take much notice of her fellow guests. She finalized the arrangements for the media conference, wrote her introductory speech, and also a shorter, welcoming speech for the sales director. She identified and categorized the individual robots requested by the various media representatives. Aphrodite were giving away a fortune in the cost of these gifts, but it was just a fraction of the overall cost of the launch and advertising campaign. Aphrodite's board – with Venus's wholehearted agreement – believed that good, positive editorial coverage, in terms of real value, far outdid anything achieved by any paid advertisements, simply because the public accepted the implied editorial endorsement of the products. Frank, Venus reflected, would most certainly disagree with that philosophy.

Finally, everything at the hotel was ready, and for two whole days Venus was able to relax and enjoy her surroundings. She worked hard at topping up the tan she had gained on her previous visit that, inevitably, had faded somewhat during her more or less sunless sojourn in Britain.

When the media arrived, the full complement of twenty-six turned up on schedule. Basically, they split up into one TV reporter (with hand-held camera, not a full crew), one radio journalist, one newspaper reporter, and one magazine journalist, from six major cities: New York, San Francisco, Sydney, Berlin, Paris, and Moscow. Plus representatives from CNN News and Reuters.

Once the original invitations had been issued – an event that in itself had gained Aphrodite considerable publicity – they had been besieged with requests for invitations by media from the rest of the world. But they had stuck to their guns, believing that they would do better with what they were doing, which was to offer exclusive coverage of their launch to a small, select list of journalists rather than to ask along the world and his wife, in media terms.

They believed that most of the media representatives whom they had invited would in any case pass on the story and/or film, video, sound tape or photographs to other media for whom they were acting as stringers. And not forgetting that CNN and Reuters sold their stories all around the world anyway, which was why they had been invited. It was, to a certain extent, a gamble. But it was a calculated gamble.

On his arrival, despite an in-built inclination to dislike the Australian journalist who represented the *Sydney Morning Herald* (because of what she considered to be his vulgar original request, that his Aphrodite robot should be made in her image and have her full personal sexual characteristics) Venus actually couldn't help but like him when she met him. He was a typical, straightforward, upfront Oz, with an attractive, lived-in, weather-beaten face, a great sense of humour, and a fund of amusing stories, all of which he claimed were true.

He made a bee-line for Venus in the bar before dinner, that first evening, and she was delighted when he sat beside her during the meal. By the end of it, she felt he was an old friend and she didn't mind in the least bit when he suggested, much later, over their umpteenth drink in the bar after dinner, that he accompany her back to her bedroom. To be honest, she was actually quite pleased. He was far more sophisticated than his accent had led her

Voluptuous Venus

to believe, and she had sat there fancying him for most of the evening. She thought, briefly – and guiltily – about Frank, as she opened her legs to welcome her first-ever Australian male.

He had spent a considerable amount of time, and shown a great deal of expertise, in foreplay. He stroked her breasts, her inner thighs, and her pussy. He performed cunnilingus upon her for a long time, bringing her to orgasm after orgasm with a commanding skill, until she was almost screaming for him to fuck her. When he finally considered her to be ready for this act, it was an experience that she enjoyed sufficiently to repeat three more times before Neville – for such was his name – took himself off back to his own bedroom.

Before he left, she made him promise to return the following evening and fuck *her*, rather than the lookalike robot that he would by then have received. He swore, hand on heart, that it would be his pleasure so to do. Venus slept like a child.

The next morning broke, as do most mornings in the Caribbean at that time of year, with a pale blue cloudless sky. A golden sun was climbing up into it, and just the slightest of cool breezes was wafting gently in from the dark blue sea. It had rained heavily during the night, as it often does, and as the sun dried the leaves, the birds sang, the insects hummed, and the humans walked about their business slowly. There was no point in getting up a sweat this early in the day.

Venus breakfasted in her room. She went over her

speech just one more time as she drank her freshly squeezed orange juice and ate her chilled paw paw, with lime juice squeezed over it, followed by some exquisitely made pale local scrambled eggs and bacon. She followed that with toast and Jamaican orange marmalade.

The conference was scheduled for ten o'clock. Venus was down in the conference room, in the older part of the hotel close by the beach, by nine-thirty. Her colleagues arrived singly, between nine-thirty and nine-forty-five, and the journalists arrived in a bunch, promptly at ten.

Venus introduced her managing director, Charles Manton, who welcomed the guests. Charles introduced Peter and Mark, who did a double act as they described the new products, majoring on the new robot models and running quickly over the additional new product ranges. They did a good job, bearing in mind that it had been agreed beforehand, back in London, weeks ago, that they would present simply with charts and video, and that Venus would close the conference by actually introducing the individual models, one by one, to their intended new owners.

As a publicity-getting gimmick, it had also been agreed that she would start off the handover of the models by presenting the Venus robot to Neville, the Australian journalist whose newspaper had requested it. When the time for that revelation came, Venus announced to everyone that she was about to introduce the first of the new models, a female robot from the new range, modelled upon herself, at the request of the *Sydney Morning Herald*. This brought a united cheer from the assembled journalists, not least – unsurprisingly – from Neville himself.

Venus had arranged for a screen to be placed at the back of the stage. As the applause died down, she disappeared behind the screen and switched on the robot of herself – which had been programmed especially for the occasion – so that it walked back out from the other side of the screen. Reasonably enough, the audience (apart from the Aphrodite people) assumed that this was still the real Venus, since she had ensured that the robot was wearing identical clothes and had had its blonde hair dressed exactly as hers was dressed. The effect was as if she had walked behind the screen to the audience's left and then re-emerged again, almost immediately, from their right.

The robot walked to the front of the small stage and then stood there, smiling at the audience. Venus waited behind the screen for about fifteen seconds, and then followed the robot out, at first to gasps of surprise and then to enthusiastic applause as she ended up standing – to all intents and purposes – beside herself.

She paused once more while the audience made their comparisons between the two. They could have been identical twins. Such was Aphrodite's technical expertise with plastics that it was absolutely impossible to tell the real from the representation.

'Ladies and gentlemen,' Venus said. 'And in particular, Neville Chapman from the *Sydney Morning Herald*. I am privileged this morning to introduce you to the first example of our new range of Aphrodite models. This one' (and here Venus paused, put an arm around the waist of the Venus robot who looked at Venus, smiled, and then put *her* arm around the real Venus's shoulder) 'is from our new female robot range, and she's called Venus.'

She stopped here and grinned, first at the robot and then at the audience. 'You can, perhaps, see why.' There was more applause, signifying the audience's approval. 'It's all down to Neville Chapman,' said Venus, 'because Venus was what he requested when we sent out our order forms. So, Venus is what he's got. Neville, come up here and say hello to her.'

Neville stood up to yet more cheers and laughter. Venus put up a hand, to stop him. 'Just one point before you get up here, Neville, if I may. Venus here is in her purely social mode. She will walk with you, talk with you. Eat and drink with you, if you wish. But she's not programmed for any sexual activity of any kind.' This announcement was greeted by a loud chorus of laughter, mixed with boos. Venus laughed back at them.

'But worry not,' she told Neville and the rest of them. 'All you have to do is to select the sexual program – or programs – of your desire. Select it or them from our full range – you'll see them all laid out on that table at the side of the room over there.' She pointed to where the new range was displayed. 'And follow the instructions that come with the package. It's simple, and absolutely straightforward. We hope, of course, that you'll take your Aphrodite somewhere appropriately private. We don't want anyone frightening the horses. If you have the slightest problem with any of the electronics – or in fact with anything – Harry and Ginger, our two top technicians, are here to help you.

Voluptuous Venus

'Harry and Ginger. Will you stand up, so that our friends can see you, please?' The two technicians stood up. 'Thank you,' said Venus. 'You'll find that these two gentleman can resolve any problem that you may come up with.' The two sat down again. 'If, after this conference is over, you should have any problems – at any time of the day or night – dialling the number 711 on the hotel telephone system will get you straight through to one or other of these two,' Venus told her audience. 'One or other of them will be permanently on duty, for the rest of your stay here. Right, Neville. Come and say hello to Venus here.'

Neville came up to the front of the room, and climbed up the steps to the small stage. He held out his hand.

'Hi, Venus,' he said. 'I've been looking forward to this for weeks.'

'Hello there, Neville,' said the Venus robot, smiling at him, and shaking his hand. 'So have I. I just know we're going to get to know each other really well.'

'I very much hope so,' Neville said, winking heavily at his friends in the audience. 'But for the moment, come and sit beside me, down there in the audience.' He took her arm, and helped her, politely, down the steps.

'Thank you, Neville,' she said.

The audience seemed completely mesmerized by the female robot's realistic qualities. She followed Neville back to his seat and sat down beside him. The two of them immediately became involved in an intense, whispered conversation.

The real Venus gave the couple a smile, and then went on to continue with her introductions. It had been agreed earlier that, after the presentation of the Venus robot to the audience, it would be followed by the presentation of a male robot to one of the women journalists.

Margaret Telford represented one of the national American TV networks, and was based in New York. She had not wanted a representation of anyone famous, but had asked for a standard male robot from the new Aphrodite range. Venus called him out and introduced him. He had been christened Jack. Margaret had her camera, with its integral lighting, at the ready and switched it on as Jack appeared. Venus marvelled at the small size of the TV journalist's video equipment. It was – like Aphrodite's models – a tribute to the recent twenty-first century advances in microchip techniques and in camera lens miniaturization.

'Ladies and gentlemen, and this time, most particularly, Margaret Telford,' said Venus, 'I'd like to introduce Jack. Jack, come and take a bow.' Jack did exactly that.

'Jack is our basic model,' Venus told them. 'But he's only basic in that his appearance is that of one of our stock designs. He's not manufactured to look like anyone in particular. But he *is* manufactured to look attractive, and sexy,' she said.

Jack had been programmed to take another, apparently unrehearsed bow at that particular moment. It brought the expected round of laughter, and applause.

'Thank you, Jack,' Venus continued. 'But in every other way, he's exactly the same as all the new robots in this exciting new range. He'll take all the new sexual programs. His penis size is our standard male-organ size, since

Margaret didn't specify any personal requirements at all. For the record, that's ten inches long, with a circumference of five inches. Erect, of course. We can supply them larger or smaller,' Venus said.

'Jesus,' called out one of the men in the audience. 'Do you get many requests for larger ones than that?'

'As a matter of fact, yes, we do,' Venus told him, over the wave of laughter. She could have told him that the requests for large cocks usually came from sexually frustrated married women, but she thought that she'd probably do better to get right off that particular subject.

'All those kind of statistics are available from our library back in London,' she told the man who had asked the question. 'You'll find the fax number on our media release paper. And all the figures are provided for us by a completely independent research company, and validated by our industry's professional body.'

Jack was standing there patiently, looking pleasantly relaxed. He had well-cut, darkish brown hair and a good physique, without being over-developed in any way. He was exactly six feet tall. His eyes were blue, and he had attractively long lashes. His skin was lightly tanned and he was wearing a tailored dark grey Savile Row suit, a pale blue handmade shirt, handmade shoes, and a gold Omega wrist-watch.

Margaret looked both genuinely interested and excited. She must have been somewhere around the late thirties, whereas Jack was specifically twenty-four. His documentation said so. Margaret's lustful enthusiasm, Venus guessed, was probably as much for his generous penile measurements as for his attractive appearance. She wasn't exactly ugly, but she was no raving beauty either. If Jack had been real, she would have been a very fortunate woman indeed. But that, essentially, was the greatest attraction – and the strongest selling point – of these Aphrodite robots.

Venus repeated her short speech about the fact that Jack was operating on his limited social module, and reminded Margaret that she would need to choose, and plug in to, whatever micro-chip package from the available range she wanted before he would perform sexually.

Margaret took Jack off immediately. There was no question of sitting in the audience for the rest of the conference. She led him to the table displaying the range of sexual packages (which were all on offer, gratis and in their entirety, to the media representatives) where Venus noticed that she took one of everything. She then disappeared with him out of the conference room. Back to her bedroom, Venus assumed.

She felt her panties beginning to get damp at the thought of all the impending sexual activity for which she and her company were shortly going to be responsible. She became even stickier between her legs as she remembered that she had been one of the first to audition Jack, straight off the production line. From memory, she had actually been the very first woman to fuck-test him. And he'd come through (*forgive the pun*, she thought, with a little giggle) with flying colours.

She'd run him, first of all, on his oral sex program. He had given her some fantastic head. She had made a mental

Voluptuous Venus

note at the time to ask Sally to dig out the name and address of whoever had been the man upon whose oral activities his programme had been put together. She would love to have him service her personally. *God*, she thought. *I need a fuck. Or, at worst, a quick wank. Shall I drop my knickers and let one of the other male robots fuck me. A product demonstration?* No. Sadly. That simply was not on. She wondered next whether she could rely upon Neville to come and do his raunchy Oz thing with her again this evening, or whether he would be too busy fucking his Venus robot? Why should he waste his time with a real person, and all that entailed, when he could fuck himself stupid with a robot who would accede to his every whim? Not, she thought, to be fair, that she hadn't acceded to his every whim herself, last night.

This won't do, she said to herself. 'And next, ladies and gentlemen,' she announced, 'I'm going to ask Peter Jennings, our sales director, to take over from me and introduce you to our next model.' She stood there, holding out the microphone to a slightly surprised Peter who wasn't expecting this unrehearsed happening.

'Sorry, love,' she whispered to him, when he arrived on stage, her hand over the microphone. 'Emergency. I've suddenly got the runs. Must go to the loo.' She smiled at him.

'Oh, surely, Venus,' he said, taking the microphone from her. 'No problem.' She left him there as he was introducing a Grace Kelly (in her pre-Monaco era) lookalike robot to a fat, overexcited journalist from Russian TV, based in Moscow.

She came out of the conference suite and turned left, past the hotel's shopping centre with its bridge across a goldfish-stocked pool and fountains surrounded by an ice-cream parlour, a newsagent-cum-off-licence, a hairdresser's, and two fashion shops selling locally-made swimwear, evening dresses, beach clothes, and the like. There was also an information centre, offering tours of the island, visits to its rain forest, deep-sea fishing, sailing trips, and car hire. She saw a notice in the information centre announcing that the film for the evening would be shown in the conference suite, which doubled as a cinema in the evenings. She finally found the nearest ladies' rest room in the corridor, just outside the most expensive of the hotel's three (four, if you counted the beach snack bar) restaurants.

She realized with regret, once she got inside the lavatory and into a cubicle that, despite the fact that she had remembered to bring her handbag with her, she had totally forgotten, on leaving England, to bring her small travelling vibrator with her. *Oh well*, she thought. *It's naughty fingers again*. It wouldn't be the first time, for God's sake.

She lifted up her skirt, tucked it out of the way around her waist, and pulled her knickers down around her ankles. They were, as she knew, very moist at the crotch. She slipped her fingers inside herself. She was really wet, and although she was quite tight, they slid in with no trouble at all. Once inside, her fingers felt good.

She shut her eyes and drummed up a mental image of the male robot Jack's ten-inch – five inches in circumference – erect cock. She remembered, during her fuck-test of him, taking it in her mouth. Her fingers busied themselves at her clitoris as she called to mind the way in which he was programmed to spurt real-tasting come into her waiting, receptive mouth as she finally sucked him off. It had tasted exactly like the real thing, and she had swallowed every drop of it.

She remembered, in passing, that after that she had suggested to the new-product committee that they consider producing a special version of his ejaculating microchip, which extended his orgasm for far longer than any man in real life and which spurted greater quantities of reproduction come for much longer than was normal, simply for the pleasure that such an option would give to a lot of women customers. Sadly – at least for her, she thought – her suggestion had, so far, come to naught. She made a mental note to bring it up again at the next new-product committee meeting.

She was frigging herself really fast now. She could feel a good, solid orgasm not too far away, and she searched her mind for a hard sexual image to bring it scurrying to the surface. She suddenly hit on a hot memory of Frank's cock, embedded deeply in her fundament that wonderful evening, and the feelings it had produced in her as he had jetted his hot, creamy sperm up her rectal passage. She concentrated on remembering that feeling, and as her fingers frigged furiously at her clitoris she exploded into a tremendous orgasm, one that had her shouting out aloud as she came.

With her orgasm came much-needed sexual relief, the

yearning for which had been growing ever since she had got up that morning. The tensions involved in ensuring that everything was ready for the long-awaited media launch, and the stress of introducing a female robot that was her double, had combined to produce the reason for her sudden rapid departure to the ladies' room, there to indulge in a short session of good old-fashioned self-relief. *There is nothing like a frig*, she hummed to herself to the tune of 'There Is Nothing Like a Dame' as she cleaned herself up with some bathroom tissue, pulled up her knickers, and, pulling the lavatory chain behind her, exited from the cubicle. She then spent five minutes tidying her make-up and her hair before returning to the conference suite.

When she got back, she found that Peter had done a valiant job in introducing the remainder of the male and female robots. The only people left in the room were the Aphrodite directors and technicians.

The journalists had all departed with their robots, whether to begin what Venus liked to refer to as the 'road-testing' of the sex machines or whether simply to take them back to their rooms and then make their way down to the bar for a pre-lunch drink she didn't much care. She thanked Peter for taking over from her in her hour of need, and her managing director – and, in fact, everyone else – congratulated her on the efforts that she had made to ensure that this morning's launch worked.

'Well, done, Venus,' said the MD. 'That was an enormous success. All the television people have set up interviews. Some with me, and some with either Peter or

Voluptuous Venus

Mark. A number have been asking for you. Including that Aussie fella. What's his name?'

'Neville?' she suggested. 'Neville Chapman, from the *Sydney Morning Herald*?'

'Yes. That's the chap,' he agreed. 'And we've set up motorcycle couriers to deliver film to the airport for those people who need one. And the hotel has a modem for anyone who's using that method of transferring pictures or copy. The New York network woman has her own satellite transponder. I think we've done everything that we can do, at this stage. Let's break out the champagne.'

They made their way through to the main hotel bar where the managing director ordered bottles of vintage Perrier Jouet. A group of journalists were there before them and were invited to join up with the Aphrodite party.

Among the group was Neville who came and stood beside Venus. 'Very impressive' he said. 'That was one of the better product launches.'

'Thank you, kind sir,' she said, bending a knee in a mock curtsey. 'Well, we do have a rather more interesting product than most.'

'You can say that again,' he agreed. 'When I got my Venus robot up to my room, I couldn't wait to fuck her.' He grinned his wicked Oz grin at her. 'But I could see that there wasn't really time, not before lunch. Not to enjoy her properly. I mean, I *do* have to write a feature about it. It's not just a quick shag, you know.'

She couldn't resist it. 'Like last night's, you mean?' she whispered into his ear.

'No. Not at all like last night's,' he told her. 'But let me

169

finish. I read the instructions, chose the right microchip package, and had her fellate me. I just sat in the chair, and she came and unzipped my fly, hauled out my John Thomas, and sucked me off. Very slowly, very professionally, and very enjoyably.' He grinned his grin again. 'I think I've fallen in love with her,' he said.

Venus grinned back at him. 'You wouldn't be the first,' she said. 'Seriously. Did you read that piece in the *Guardian* the other week, reporting a divorce case in Canada where the wife has cited her husband's Aphrodite robot?'

'Christ, no, I didn't,' said Neville. 'Can you remember the date of the story? I'd love to refer to it in my piece.'

'No, I can't,' Venus said. 'But what I can do is to get the London office to fax a copy of it over here this afternoon. OK?'

'Oh, terrific,' said Neville. 'Thank you. But going back to my robot. That's amazingly sophisticated software, isn't it? I mean, first of all, she's real. Honestly, there's no question of her being a plastic model. She's *real*, Goddammit. She looks real, feels real, smells real, tastes real. She talks to me. After she'd fellated me, I told her to stand up and spread her legs. She did, and I gave her a quick feel. I slipped my hand up underneath her pretty knickers and felt her pussy. It felt so real, I pulled her knickers down and had a close look at it. Man, that's *real* pussy. Number one, high-quality, seriously good pussy.'

Venus laughed, out loud. Neville looked at her, suspiciously. 'What are you laughing at?' he asked her.

'Forgive me,' she replied. 'I'm laughing because that's

my pussy you're talking about. Your Venus robot is *me*. That's what you asked for. Everything about her is me. Except for her sexual programs. What kind of pussy do you expect? Like in a blow-up rubber doll?'

Neville looked startled for a moment. Then he relaxed and laughed with Venus. 'Of course,' he said. 'I was forgetting.' He ruminated for a moment. 'But what I'm still trying to tell you is that, your pussy or not, it's Goddamn *real* pussy. Do you see what I mean? If the thing was badly produced, it might *look* like real pussy. But it wouldn't feel like one. Or smell like one. Or taste like one. Don't you see what I'm trying to say? I'm probably not putting it very well, and I think you're selling me short because all you think about is that it's a reproduction of you. But what I'm trying to say is that, whoever it's modelled on, it's *believably real*. Now do you understand?'

'Yes, of course I do,' she told him. 'And thank you for the compliments. We've sunk a considerable fortune into the research and development that has enabled us to produce this new model range, and we obviously want it to work. *Need* it to work. But sometimes I wonder if we aren't maybe perhaps a bit *too* realistic. Even before this new range, people were suggesting that Aphrodite, as a company, might become responsible for the end of marriage, or even the end of people living together – cohabiting, as we know it – in the real world.'

'How's that?' Neville asked. 'That sounds a little far-fetched to me.'

'Not if you think about it seriously,' she said. 'Take any normal heterosexual man who chooses to either live with or marry (and then of course live with) a woman he loves. At the beginning of their relationship, they're sexually attracted and they love each other. It's roses, roses, all the way. But after a while – it might be years, it might be months – things begin to change.

'They both work. They are getting used to each other. They don't always want sex at the same time any more. She has a headache. He's late back from the office, and he's been drinking with the boys. At that stage, they'll either have to start working extremely hard at making their marriage survive, or they'll break up. And start in on the old vicious circle again. But this time with a different partner. And what's it all about? What's it all *really* about? Deep down?' Venus didn't give Neville an opportunity to reply, but carried straight on. 'It's about sex. That's what it's about. It's about sex, with someone you love, who is always available. Someone who is always ready for sex, at any time of the day or night. Always ready to do whatever naughty little things it is that turn you on. Who isn't put off sex by headaches, periods, tiredness, or sheer bloody-mindedness.

'In real life, people like that are very few and far between. But tell me, Neville, who *is* like that all the time? Who's up for sex any time you want it? Who will perform any sexual act – with both pleasure and expertise – whenever you wish? Who never nags you, never says "But you haven't said you love me," never accuses you of being selfish, never criticizes *your* sexual performance? Damn' right. An Aphrodite sex robot. So who needs marriage? Who needs a live-in sexual partner? Who needs the hassle, the angst, the expense? Forget it. Buy an Aphrodite robot for sex, and stay single. Enjoy all the options of being single. You'll *never* be short of a fuck. You'll never be short of any kind of sex. Full stop. Surely that's got to be a better arrangement?'

Neville scratched his head. 'I dunno, Venus,' he said. 'A flesh-and-blood Sheila's a Sheila, when you get down to it. At best, these Aphrodite robots are great at sex. But actually living with a robot – surely a guy will miss the love? the affection? Even – on occasion – the headaches? Surely a relationship between two people is more than just sex? Sex is vital, agreed. But it's only a *part* of the whole. There's respect. There are common interests. There may be children, in the fullness of time. There's love and affection, like I just said. And then there's companionship. Companionship is vital, to my mind. So what about all those things? Sex with a machine, when you really get down to it, is simply another form of masturbation. Mind you, don't misunderstand me. I'm not against a good wank occasionally. I don't know one man who doesn't enjoy a crafty wank now and again. But surely just plain sex – however good, however varied – isn't the be-all and end-all of life with another person. Is it?'

Just then, Venus's managing director came around with yet another bottle of Perrier Jouet, topping up people's glasses. Neville and Venus held theirs out gratefully.

When he'd moved on, Venus tried to answer Neville's question. 'Well, you say that. And I don't actually know what the honest answer is. But more relationships, among couples that I know, eventually fail for sexual reasons than for any other. They get bored with each other; or maybe just one of them gets bored. Or one of them meets someone new who attracts them, sexually, away from their partner. Or the sex just dies. Slowly. Until there isn't any left. But if – just for the sake of argument, and I appreciate here that I'm perhaps moving the goalposts a little, but never mind that – if, for the sake of the argument, you take a couple. It doesn't really matter, for our purposes, whether they are married or just living together.

'They love each other, and they have great sex, and all those lovely things. Now, if, when they got married, they each bought their partner an Aphrodite sex robot, with the complete range of programs, whatever else they had rows about, I doubt they'd ever need to have a row about sex. Or about the lack of it.'

'How can you say that?' Neville asked. 'What makes you so sure? And in any case, surely the very last thing that two people are going to buy each other, as they start a new relationship, is a sex robot?'

'Ah, well, you say that,' Venus said. 'But let me take that last point first. I do agree that it might need a bit of a rethink, for people to consider sex robots as wedding presents. Or whatever. But I don't see anything wrong with a rethink, if it's going to avoid a disaster. So assume, for the moment, that it becomes totally acceptable for that to happen.

'Then, whenever any of the little sexual disasters that we have already run through and listed pretty thoroughly begin to happen, the aggrieved partner (for want of a better description) could – obviously with the full knowledge and consent of the other partner – take his or her sexual grievance out, so to speak, on their robot. So no other human would be involved. So that there would be no unfaithfulness. No indiscretion. Purely – as you so succinctly put it just now – a little entirely mechanical masturbation. Now who could possibly take offence at that? And so, the end result would be that, instead of these journalists and broadcasters describing Aphrodite as a company responsible for the breakdown of marriages and heterosexual relationships as we know them, quite the reverse would be true, wouldn't it? Aphrodite, through its range of products, would become a major contributor to the encouragement of longer, happier, sexually more gratifying marriages than ever before.'

'Bravo,' said Neville, clapping his hands. 'I certainly can't argue with any of that. And I wouldn't want to, anyway. I simply hadn't thought of that particular approach. I shall most certainly use it in my feature. Thank you, sweetheart.'

Venus's MD chose that moment to bang a glass on the top of the bar counter and suggest to everyone that they might well now all go through into the restaurant for lunch. Neville stayed with Venus, and it was he who chose to raise with their table companions the subject that he and Venus had been discussing earlier. To Venus's surprise, they all, in fact, agreed with her submission. They also agreed with Neville's belief that accepting sex robots as suitable wedding or partnership gifts would take a little getting used to. But they all agreed that, once that hurdle had been crossed, the improvement in marriages and relationships that Venus suggested would quickly become established. Venus was hugely delighted with their complete agreement.

By the end of that day, the conference was pretty much over. Those of the media working to short deadlines had already submitted their stories, words, pictures, and/or film. Those working to longer deadlines – the weekly newspaper and magazine journalists, by and large – wouldn't complete theirs until they returned to their offices. A number had left already, and the residue were leaving the following morning, as were Venus, her directors, and the two Aphrodite technicians.

The general consensus among Venus's colleagues was that the launch had been an unqualified success. Media results were being monitored back in London, and the office was in contact with St Lucia almost hourly with news of this, that, or the other enthusiastic coverage from the various countries around the world. Aphrodite's board's decision to invite only a select few media seemed to have paid off, for the coverage of the new range was in far more media outlets than were directly represented by the journalists whom they had invited. And all of it was extensive, and good.

To her delight, Venus had no problems in attracting Neville into her bed that evening. It was more a question of fighting him off until she was ready for bed herself.

'Have you fucked your other Venus yet?' she teased him in the bar, before dinner.

Voluptuous Venus

'No, darling, I haven't,' he said. 'But I'm taking her home with me, remember? We're both leaving in the morning. It's no contest. Actually, let me rephrase that. There's no contest anyway. These products of yours are excellent, but they don't compare with the real thing. Nothing ever really compares with the real thing, does it?'

Venus told him that she had to agree with him. The more so because he was comparing her with a plastics-and-electronics model of herself. So they started off their last night together in a state of high sexual excitement. They knew each other well enough by now to realize that they were a well-matched couple, both sexually and in life experience, and they were both looking forward to a long, hard, rewarding night.

Venus had been rather touched by a conversation that they had had as soon as they were in her bedroom. They were undressing when Neville had asked her if he might beg a small favour from her.

'Surely, sweetheart,' she said. 'What is it?'

'Well, I ought to be embarrassed, but I'm not,' he said. 'Would you keep your knickers on when you are undressed, masturbate into them and make them really wet with your juices, and then give them to me? Why I'd like to have them is so that, when I'm back in Australia and fucking my Venus robot, wishing she was really you, I'll have a small part of the real you to remind me of these wonderful nights that we've had here. Then I can pull my Venus robot's knickers down, sniff them, smell the real scent of your pussy, shut my eyes and pretend she's you. Will you do that for me? Please?'

Venus was actually rather moved emotionally by his request . . . She was wearing a pair of abbreviated, coffee-coloured briefs by La Perla, which she kept on.

'You start me off, darling,' she suggested, lying back and opening her legs. He was pleased to do so and began rubbing her pussy through the soft, silky material of her briefs. She soon began to get wet, visibly, and after a while she said, 'Shall I take over now, Neville, sweetheart?'

He took his hand away and she replaced his fingers with hers, rubbing and delving, until she pushed one silk-encased finger deeply inside herself, on to her clitoris, and brought herself off to an enjoyable orgasm.

'Ooooh,' she said, when she had finished. 'Naughty. But nice.' She looked down at her panties, stood up and peeled them off. She sniffed, delicately, at the sodden crotch. 'Hmmmm,' she said. 'Wet pussy. My wet pussy.' She threw the knickers across to Neville. 'To you. With my love,' she said. 'To remind you of my cunt.'

'They will, darling,' Neville said.

Neville was sitting naked on the edge of Venus's bed, his legs apart, and Venus was kneeling on the floor in front of him. She had just taken his cockhead completely into her warm, wet mouth for the first time – after a delicious, tantalizing period of foreplay in which she had carefully peeled down his foreskin, licked his frenum, and masturbated the full length of his rigidity – when her telephone rang. She took his cock out of her mouth. 'Shit,' they said, in unison. They both laughed.

Venus picked up the telephone. She put her hand over

Voluptuous Venus

the mouthpiece. 'All we need now is for it to be a wrong number,' she said. Neville giggled, despite his frustration.

It turned out to be one of the two Aphrodite technicians. 'I'm terribly sorry to wake you at this time of night, Miss Venus,' he said. Venus looked at her watch. It was just after one o'clock.

'That's OK, Freddie,' she told him. 'What's the problem?'

'Well, you're not going to believe this, miss,' he said. 'But I was on duty – although I must admit that I was fast asleep in my room at the time. You see, I didn't really expect any problems on this last night. I was fully dressed, of course. And then I got called down to the conference suite by one of the male American journalists. He said they'd blown a fuse. Well, I got down there and there was about a dozen of them. Men, mostly, but there were a few women. And they'd all got their robots with them. And, like I said, miss, you're not going to believe this. But they were having an *orgy*.'

'Sounds like fun,' Venus said. 'I mean, what's wrong with that, if that's what you want to do?'

'I don't think I'm making myself clear, miss,' Freddie said. 'It wasn't just the humans. Or, er, humans, er, doing things with the robots. They had the *robots* doing things to each other. You know? Sexy things.'

'You mean fucking?' Venus asked. 'They had the robots *fucking* each other?'

'Er, yes, miss,' Freddie said. 'That's it. You've got it. And one of the male robots had blown a fuse. It wasn't fair. He was overloaded. I mean, they had him with *three* of the female robots. It was just too much for him. It's basic misuse. It's in the handbook. He was er, fucking one of the female robots. And they had another one sitting on his face. You know, miss?'

'Yes,' said Venus. 'I know. How lovely.'

Freddie cleared his throat. He obviously disapproved of the whole performance. (It was a strange fact of life that the technicians who worked for Aphrodite, who were, Venus supposed, probably the last remaining descendants of what used to be called, a hundred and more years ago, blue-collar workers, were almost the only employees left who actually seriously disapproved of what the company did. Or pretended so to do. She was never sure which.) 'And the third female robot was using a rubber dildo up his ... er ... bottom,' finished Freddie, clearly embarrassed.

'Wow,' said Venus. 'No wonder he blew a fuse.' She laughed. 'But whatever were they doing in the conference suite anyway?' she asked him. 'I mean, it closed down at lunch time.'

'I gather it was the only place that they felt was big enough, and where they wouldn't be bothered by the other guests,' Freddie said. 'I mean, they couldn't have done it in any of the bars. Or on the disco dance floor. I mean, could they?'

'I suppose not,' agreed Venus, still amused at the idea of the orgy. 'So what then? I mean, presumably you repaired the blown fuse?'

'Oh, yes, miss,' Freddie said. 'Of course I did. I got a big cheer for that. But then I had to almost physically

Voluptuous Venus

prevent them from setting up the robot to do the same thing again. It took me a while to persuade them that you actually can't overload them. They're simply not built for it. And then they wanted me to do other things that just aren't on. Mostly to the female robots. They wanted me to double the speed at which the female robots, er . . . move their hips, when they, er . . . indulge in sexual intercourse.'

Venus suppressed a giggle.

'Great,' she said. 'But not very practical. What else?'

'Well,' Freddie said, 'just before I left the room to telephone you, the last request that I had was to double the suction ratio with which the male robots, er . . . suck. You know. Er . . . down there.'

'Pussy?' Venus asked, smiling at the telephone.

'That's it, miss,' Freddie said. 'Yes. You've got it. Pussy.'

I have, too, Venus thought. *I wonder if you'd like to see it. Suck it. Fuck it. But that's not why you're calling me up.* 'So what do you want me to do, then?' she asked him.

'I want you to come down here, miss, and tell these people that our robots aren't designed for that. They won't take no for an answer, from me. They've all had far too much to drink, in my opinion, and things are getting seriously out of hand. Will you come down here? Now? Please?'

Venus looked at Neville, shrugged her mental shoulders, and said, 'OK, Freddie. I'll be down there as soon as I can get dressed. Don't worry. OK?'

'All right, miss,' he said. 'And thank you.'

She put the phone down and explained to Neville what was going on while she got dressed.

'Wow,' he said, pulling on his clothes. 'I'll come down with you, if I may. Admittedly I'd rather be staying up here, doing what we were doing. Or, at least, having you doing to me what you were doing to me. But that sounds like a pretty good party.'

When they got down to the conference suite, they weren't too sure, at first, whether it was a good party or not. Venus and Neville's arrival went largely unnoticed. Venus saw that the microphone was still up on the stage, so she got up there and tested it. It was still working. She switched it on.

'Hi, folks,' she said. 'It looks as if you're having a lot of fun, right now. But do me a favour, and hold it for a moment. Will you, please?'

Everyone stopped in their tracks. Well, almost everyone. As the room became rather quieter, Venus could see a group over in one corner who were still completely unaware of her. And of her request for quiet. At the centre, they had conjoined one of the male Aphrodite robots with the female Grace Kelly lookalike robot. Put bluntly, they were fucking each other. As Venus watched, it quickly became apparent that the small group gathered around watching the robots were betting on which of the two would be the first to blow its fuse.

In another corner, two of the female robots had been programmed to have sex together and were engaged in the classic – on this occasion lesbian – *soixante-neuf* position. Venus tried hard not to laugh out loud. Freddie was sitting on a chair at the far end of the room, his head in his hands.

Voluptuous Venus

'Now then, boys and girls,' Venus said, grinning hugely at them. 'Whatever you get up to sexually – with or without your Aphrodite robots – is entirely your affair. It's none of my concern. I am only here because Freddie over there,' she waved at Freddie, who waved back in a more-in-sorrow-than-in-anger kind of manner, 'is concerned that you are asking for certain adjustments to the models that are mostly, quite frankly, beyond the models' capabilities.'

There were jocular cries of 'Shame,' and one or two boos. Venus addressed herself to the group around the Grace Kelly lookalike robot and its plastic partner. 'As to the bet going on over there,' she said. 'I don't want to spoil your fun but provided that both of those models are properly programmed and that no unauthorized alterations have been made, neither of them is going to blow up. The only thing that is likely to happen, if you leave them doing what they're doing right now for about another twenty-four hours, non-stop, is that, sooner or later, their batteries will run down and – if you'll forgive the expression – they'll grind to a halt.'

This at least brought a round of laughter from the assembled crowd. 'Forgive me,' she continued, 'if I appear to be taking the edge off your party. It's not my intention. I only want your robots to stay in good condition so that they may continue to service you and your pleasures long after we have all left St Lucia. Thank you.'

There was a light scattering of applause and one of the American journalists shouted out, 'Hey, no problem. Come over here and join us.'

Venus did exactly that, joined on the way across the

room by Neville. The American was called Hank. 'Hi,' he said to Neville, after he had greeted Venus with a friendly kiss. 'You're the guy who ordered a robot in the form of the lovely Venus here, aren't you?'

'That's right, mate,' said Neville.

'So come on, buddy,' said the American. 'Tell us all about it. Is she a great fuck? Does she give good head? Will she do naughty things for you? Have you any complaints?'

'That's a lot of questions,' laughed Neville. 'But my lips are sealed. At least until all has been revealed to my readers. You'll understand that, won't you?'

'Oh, sure,' said the Yank. 'But surely you can give us some kind of an idea. I mean, here we are with the lovely lady here in person, beside us, and *you* know all her darkest sexual secrets. You can surely understand our curiosity, can't you?'

'Yes, of course I can,' Neville replied. 'But since she's here with us, why don't you ask her? Then you'd have it straight from the horse's mouth, as it were.'

Venus laughed good naturedly. 'Well, I must say, I've never been compared to a horse before,' she said. 'I suppose there's always a first time.'

'Hey, that's a good suggestion,' the American said to Neville. He turned to Venus. 'Let me run those questions past you this time, ma'am. Are you a great fuck? Do you give good head? And do you do naughty things for people? Men in particular, of course?'

The others gathered around laughed at the Yank's forwardness. Venus smiled back at him.

Voluptuous Venus

'I can't answer for the Venus robot,' she told him. 'You'll appreciate that I'm the wrong gender to have tested her, back at the factory. And I have no intention of answering on my own behalf because that's not what I'm here for. Aphrodite isn't selling *my* sexual capabilities. But before you say it, yes, you're quite right. Neville here did originally *ask* for a robot with both my appearance, *and* with my sexual proclivities. We agreed to his first request. But not to the second. As to the sexual performance of the Venus robot, well, Neville here is the person to ask. It's programmed to his sexual preferences.' She grinned cheekily at Hank. 'But tell me. Just for the record. What's naughty, in sex? You asked if Neville's robot did naughty things. What kind of naughty things did you have in mind?'

He looked at her lasciviously. 'I guess I've just got a dirty mind, ma'am,' he said. 'I didn't have anything particular in mind. It's just that I thought Neville here might tell us about some of the sexual delights of his robot and reveal all manner of naughtinesses. The kind of sexual things that the likes of us lesser mortals have probably never come across. But since you ask, I guess that if you told me that you took it up your pretty little ass I would think that was pretty naughty. Pretty. And naughty.'

They all laughed again, including Venus. She found it hard to be offended by his frankness. And he *had* been drinking for rather a long time. 'Well, thank you,' she said. 'But that makes it easy for me to answer at least one of your questions, Hank. The Venus robot will, as you so succinctly put it, take it up her pretty little ass. All the female robots will, provided you select the right program from the new range. Including yours.' She remembered that Hank had requested a Marilyn Monroe lookalike robot. 'All you have to do is ask her nicely.'

She thought for a moment. 'No. Let me get that absolutely right. I don't want you to misunderstand me. You don't even have to ask her. Just plug in the anal sex microchip program, switch her on, and you're instantly in business.'

'Wow,' said Hank. 'Do you know, I hadn't thought of that?' They all laughed.

'If you haven't, you're possibly the only red-blooded male here who hasn't,' Venus told him. 'And for the record, the male robots take the same program, should you want them to. There's no prejudice at Aphrodite. But if you haven't read through your instruction manual yet, or read any of the program literature, all these new models can be programmed for oral sex, anal sex, genital sex, and manual sex. In almost all of their many variations. You can deep-throat them. Spank them. Cane them. Tie them up. They'll spank or cane you, of course, if that's your bag. There's a water sports speciality programme. They'll take enemas, for example. All those things. Anything.'

Hank looked amazed. 'Jesus,' he said. 'What in God's name am I doing wasting my time down here?' He picked up his glass and drained it. 'I thought these robots were just fuck machines. I didn't know that you could fall in love with them. Why didn't somebody tell me?' He looked around, as if appealing for some kind of comment. None came. Was he going to rush off upstairs to his bedroom and fall in love? Apparently not.

Voluptuous Venus

'Oh, fuck it,' he said. 'What's the problem? Let's have another drink and go on talking dirty. This sure beats covering war stories.'

Venus's presence had achieved the result that Freddie had hoped it would when he had telephoned her, a while back now, in a panic about the way the all-night party was going. The level of consumption of alcohol had dropped. The intense, sometimes competitive feelings about what was going on had evaporated. And the misuse of the sexual robots had ceased altogether. After a while, people started bidding each other good night and drifting off into the night in ones and twos. The 'twos' frequently featuring an Aphrodite robot. Venus stayed until the end and Neville stayed with her until, finally, they were the only two there.

'Let's try again,' Neville suggested.

'Good idea,' said Venus. They made their way back to her bedroom. When they were naked once more, they took up the positions that they had been in when the telephone had rung some hours back.

Venus kissed Neville's quickly responsive cock back into its previously erect state and then held it in her fingers. Just before she took it once more in her mouth, she looked up at him and said, 'If the Goddamn 'phone goes again, this time we'll ignore it. OK?'

'OK,' said Neville. 'Agreed.' In fact, it didn't ring again, and they had a long, self-indulgent and mutually enjoyable night together. Hank would have been fascinated (and probably very jealous) had he been able to watch them at their lovemaking, for they worked their way through all the activities about which he had been so intensely curious. He would have been able to see that the answer to *all* of his questions was a resounding 'yes.'

Venus awoke as the sun came up the following morning, at just after six-thirty. Neville was still with her, lying on his back beside her sound asleep, his cock resting warmly, flaccidly in her fingers. She began to fondle it, her fingers caressing it lightly, until her tactile efforts penetrated to Neville's brain. As he awoke, his penis became engorged with blood and his mind was aflame with desire.

'Oh, Jesus, Venus,' he croaked, his voice not yet as awake as the rest of him. 'Just lie there while I have one last shag to remember you by, will ya? The folks at home will never believe this.'

Venus did as she was instructed, although the invasion, once more, of her welcoming pussy by this giant of an Australian cock urged her to move her hips and thighs in time with its thrusting intrusion into her most intimate, most sensitive place. She hoped that the folks back home would not, in fact, hear of her sexual adventures with this newspaper man. Or not too much about them. In her book, they were between him and her. Private.

She felt his hands clasp her buttocks firmly as he half lifted her up, the better to thrust more deeply into her, and she rightly interpreted this as an indication that he was about to ejaculate into her. She slipped a finger down between his stomach and hers, and then down between her legs, to find her clitoris which she then rubbed to an almost instant climax, just at the moment that she felt the wet warmth of his ejaculate pulsing deep into her womb.

'Oh, Jesus,' he moaned. 'Oh, Christ. Oh, darling.'

She giggled gently to herself. His words weren't his strong point. Not when he was fucking her, anyway. But his cock was what it was all about. And she had no quarrel with that. No sir!

'Thank you, Neville, darling,' she said, when it was all over and they had both recovered themselves. 'I didn't think you had anything left in you!'

'Neither did I, sport,' Neville said. 'It's a compliment, if you think about it. You could give the Pope a hard-on. I should bloody say so.'

After that, everything went very quickly. The two technicians were staying on for a couple of days, at Venus's suggestion, as a 'thank you' from the company for the stout work that they had put in, both in preparation for and at the product launch. So they would be tidying up the conference room, and arranging for the shipping back to England of the various bits and pieces.

So, after a final dash down to the beach for a last swim in the magic of the warm Caribbean sea, a shower, and getting dressed for the journey, all Venus had to do was pack, sign her bill for onward transmission to company headquarters (along with all the other room bills, and the expenses incurred by the guests, by herself, and by her colleagues from the company) and that was that. She surrendered her keys, asked the hall porter to have her bags brought down, and went into the bar for a drink while waiting for her taxi to take her to the airport.

Her favourite barman was on duty. He could tell from her clothes that she was departing. 'So,' he said, as he poured her drink, 'Was there another Mr Harry?' His smile exposed those marvellous white teeth again.

Venus laughed. 'You could say that,' she told him. 'You could certainly say that. Cheers.'

CHAPTER FIVE

Home Base

The journey home was as uneventful as an efficient supersonic flight should be. The rail helishuttle from Heathrow to Oxford Circus was as efficient as ever, and Venus amused herself on the fifteen-minute journey looking at the archaic black-and-white photographs mounted on the helishuttle's cabin walls. They all depicted road travel in the days when the only way to get from London Airport into London itself was either by road along the old M4 (which, judging by the detail in the pictures, was almost permanently clogged by traffic) or in those awful, claustrophobic, unhygienic travelling metal tubes which rejoiced in the unimaginative – but highly appropriate – name of the London Underground. How human beings could have willingly subjected themselves to such an appalling method of travel, she would never understand.

Venus decided to go directly to the office, rather than via her flat. Her secretary and assistant, Sally, welcomed her back with a big smile and an even bigger collection of mail and e-mail. She had, however, divided it into two categories.

'Anything that you didn't need to see, I've dealt with,' she told Venus. 'Where appropriate, I've copied you in on my actions. Then these you need to see and action yourself. This other lot you need to read, but not now. They're not urgent.'

Venus thanked her. She really was an efficient girl.

'So, tell me all,' Sally said. 'I gather the product launch went well. I've seen the results, and I've kept them all for you. There are cuttings, transcripts and videos of everything that has appeared, from all around the world. But did you fall in love? Were you swept off your feet? Or was it all just plain hard work?'

Venus grinned at her. 'Come on, Sally darling,' she said. 'Now, tell me. Do I look happy?'

Sally looked at her. 'Mmmm. Yes. I'd say you looked happy,' she replied.

'Right,' Venus said. 'What, then, can you reasonably deduce from the fact that, while I have been away from London for just over ten days, away from home and away from any regular source of sex, I still look happy?'

Sally's face broke into a great big smile. 'That you've been getting lots of lovely, hard cock,' she suggested.

'Absolutely right,' Venus said. 'Lovely, regular, hard *Australian* cock. All the way from Sydney, Australia.'

'Chapman,' Sally said. 'Neville Chapman, from the *Sydney Morning Herald*. It must have been him.'

'Absolutely right again, Sally darling,' Venus said.

Voluptuous Venus

'There's a copy of the story he filed his paper among the stuff on your desk,' Sally said. 'It came in this morning. It came via a satellite dish on the stratojet that he was flying in back to Australia. I read it. It's terrific. I'll dig it out for you.' She riffled through the top pile of paper, and came up with four sheets of air facsimile paper. 'Here you are,' she said. 'Now I understand some of the comments he makes.'

'What do you mean?' Venus asked.

'You'll see when you read it,' Sally said, handing it over. 'Would you like some coffee?'

'Please,' Venus replied.

It was a laudatory piece, written in the style and language with which she had become familiar while spending so much time in Neville's company. It was light, amusing, full of essential facts, and extremely complimentary. Venus read it through quickly, once, and then read it through again. Rather more slowly the second time.

What Neville said, basically, was that the Aphrodite Venus robot, as tested by him, was the best fuck he had ever had, in a life that had not exactly been devoid of good sex. He began by saying that he had asked for the robot to be made in the image of Aphrodite's research director and that, having now met the lady concerned, he was impressed with the company's ability to produce lifelike reproductions of individual people to order. He challenged anyone to tell his robot from the real person, and reproduced a photograph of Venus, standing beside herself, at the launch. Identical twins, he suggested.

He described, intimately and humorously, and with just

sufficient erotic emphasis, the robot's ability to perform the entire gamut of sexual acts. Here and there, throughout his copy, he referred to what he called 'a growing, uncanny feeling' that he had been to bed with this woman prior to the test. Not possible, he said. But increasingly, he continued, this eerie feeling heightened, until it began to become something of an obsession.

'There was even an occasion,' he wrote, 'when removing the robot's brief, coffee-coloured La Perla knickers (for Aphrodite are nothing if not both generous, and erotically sensual, in the selection and supply of lingerie with these robots) that I imagined that I could actually recognize the scent of juicy, aroused, wet female sex that floated up to my nostrils, released by the removal of those sexy panties from between the robot's legs. I believed that I was being reminded of one of the most memorable, most exciting sexual encounters of my entire life.'

He went on to detail the new range of vaginal scents and tastes launched alongside the new model robots, as well as describing the range of sexual-activity packages available. Venus felt her present knickers getting damp at the memory of how Neville had asked her to masturbate while wearing those coffee-coloured La Perla knickers, and to give them to him, to breathe some life into his intended future fucks with the Venus robot.

She drained the last of the coffee that Sally had brought to her while she had been reading. She sighed and put down the facsimile of Neville's article. Such happy memories. *But this won't do*, she thought. *It's time to get back to work.* She took a quick glance through the pile that Sally had said was material needing her action. Only two of the items were of any real interest. There was an e-mail memo from the maintenance department asking for a meeting soonest, to discuss the current fuck-test programme. While all looked well superficially, the author wrote, an increasing number of models were coming back to the factory with maintenance problems while still under guarantee. Problems which – in his respectful opinion – should, or could, have been discovered during the fuck-testing process.

The second item of interest was a handwritten envelope addressed to Venus and marked personal. She recognized that it was Frank's handwriting. She tore it open.

'My darling Venus,' it began. 'I don't know how to tell you this. Two weeks ago, I would not have thought it possible. But during your absence in the Caribbean, I have fallen in love again. With someone else. I know that doesn't sound credible. I wouldn't have thought that it was. But I have. I'm so sorry, sweetheart. I shall remember our short time together forever. Please accept my apologies. If you want me taken off your account in favour of someone else, I shall, of course, understand. With love, and fond memories. Yours, Frank.'

Strangely, she thought, it actually didn't matter. Maybe it was something to do with the fact that she had been being fucked rotten all the time that she had been away in St Lucia. Ah, well! So much for true love.

She slid her hand up underneath her knicker leg and began to stroke her clitoris while she pondered the e-mail from the man in maintenance. Since she was in fact in charge of the product-testing programme (to give it its correct title) the memo had obvious implications. She noted that it had been copied to all the other directors.

There was nothing particularly significant in that. It was fairly common practice. But it did mean that she should at least make certain that she discussed the issue, and took whatever action – if any – was necessary. She speeded up her masturbatory incursion, came happily, dried her fingers on a tissue, and then rang through to the author of the note.

'Arthur Harmsworth,' he said when he picked up the internal phone.

'Oh, Arthur,' she said. 'It's Venus. I'm back from the new product launch and I've just seen your e-mail. You remember? The one about the new product testing?'

Yes, he remembered, he said.

'When are you free? Now? Oh, excellent. I'll pop along, if I may. OK? Terrific. Thanks.' She walked down the corridor and was told by Babs, Arthur's secretary, to please go straight through.

After the greetings, and the expected chatter about her trip to St Lucia, they eventually got down to business.

'So what's the problem, Arthur?' she asked.

'I don't actually know,' he answered. 'But I've got far too many robots coming back, well within the guarantee time, with quite serious faults. The percentage of those coming back with anything at all serious has gone up considerably. From just under three per cent last year to – so far, this year – almost ten per cent. It's just too many. I really don't know what the problem is, except that it isn't any one particular thing. It's a whole slew of different things. But all quite serious. All beyond the capabilities of the local dealers to cope with. It could soon get us a bad reputation, if we don't do something about it. And quickly. I wanted to start an investigation while you were away, but I was told to wait until you got back. Which I understand. But now that you're here, do you think you could possibly get stuck into it right away, Venus? Please?' He looked positively anxious.

'Of course, Arthur,' she told him. 'I'll get onto it right away. I'll be in touch the moment there's anything to report.'

She made her way back to her office and called Sally in. Between the two of them, they cancelled all her existing appointments and they organized, for Venus, an examination of all the product-testing appointments scheduled, beginning the following morning.

That night, when she got home, she unpacked her bags, bathed, and fell into bed. She was asleep within seconds, despite not having eaten. She was bushed. It wasn't surprising, really. Not if you thought about it. She awoke the following morning feeling as fresh as a daisy. She ate a huge breakfast in an early-morning café on the way to work, and arrived at the office feeling relaxed and completely in control of herself once more.

The first product test was of a batch of five female robots. They had been assembled, tested technically, and were due this morning for their sexual-activities tests by two of the regular testing staff. Venus knew quite a number of the sex-testing staff, but these two were new to her. She had decided that she wasn't going to tell them that there was a problem. That, in itself, could cause lack of confidence, with the resulting loss of human performance, that could of course affect the robot's performance too. But she would tell them that she would like to be present, at least for part of their tests. That was normal, and an agreed part of their job specification. It was something that she did from time to time, so they shouldn't be too disturbed by her presence. The first tester was called Brian. Brian Woods.

He looked pleasant enough. About twenty-two or twenty-three. Brown hair. Brown eyes. Good physique. His human-resource folder included a nude photograph of him. His unerect cock was of a good size, as far as she could tell. There was, she had quickly discovered, no way of knowing how much a flaccid cock would grow when erect. It certainly wasn't proportionate. Sometimes quite small flaccid ones grew impressively. Sometimes quite large flaccid ones were very disappointing when erect.

When Brian came into her office, he was stripped and wearing a white towelling dressing gown. He seemed relaxed and unperturbed by her impending presence during his test. Which was right and proper. Despite the intimate aspects of these tests, the testers should be – and usually were – as unfazed as a technician or a mechanic would be in similar circumstances.

'Is there anything that you especially want me to do?' he asked. 'Or not do?'

'Not that I can think of, right now,' she told him. 'But if

Voluptuous Venus

anything comes to mind, I'll let you know. OK?'

'Absolutely OK,' he said. Prior to leaving her office, he held out his hand, which she shook. It was firm, warm, and dry.

Which was more than Venus could say for her pussy, which was soft, warm, and wet. She always got sexually excited when she was going to be present at these sex tests. Their very nature had her gagging for a shag, as the old, rather vulgar expression had it. Her brief masturbatory session earlier, immediately prior to her short meeting with Arthur, had given her some temporary relief, but long-term had only increased her need. The dampness of her crotch was a constant reminder of that which she lusted after. A serious fuck. She tried to banish the thought, and went off to the product-testing section.

Brian was already there. He greeted her, and told her that he had asked for the first robot – a specially ordered Jayne Mansfield lookalike – to be delivered wearing only her lingerie.

'I thought I'd spend some time in foreplay,' he told Venus. 'Ending up with my performing cunnilingus upon her. So that we can test both her nipple erection, and her vaginal lubrication, together with her vaginal odour and flavour, and of course her vaginal texture. Then I thought that I'd go on to have her fellate me for a while, to check her salivation ability, her tongue elasticity, and her lip agility. And then I thought I'd fuck her. There's a lot more to come after that, naturally. But that's as far as I've got planned. Does that sound all right to you?'

'It sounds very thorough, Brian,' Venus said. 'Thanks.'

Right then, two technicians wheeled in a trolley upon which sat an unbelievably realistic Jayne Mansfield lookalike. Neither Venus nor Brian had ever seen her in the flesh – she'd been dead for, what, about a hundred and twenty years, Venus reckoned. But there couldn't be anyone alive with some kind of interest in the history of what used to be called the cinema who hadn't seen either film or video or photographs of this gorgeous Hollywood lady. The star of *The Girl Can't Help It*, among other historic movies. Her hair colour was an exquisite oddly natural-looking platinum blonde, and it was set in a style that was, in fact, also reminiscent in its look, Venus thought, (remembering the old photographs) of Veronica Lake's long, blonde 'peek-a-boo' hair. The lovely robot's ample bosom was well-nigh overflowing the transparent lavender-coloured gauzy brassiere which, together with her briefly cut high-sided matching knickers and sheer black silk stockings held up by frilly lavender garters, was all that she was wearing.

One of the technicians reached between her shoulder blades and activated her. She stood up, off the trolley, took a step towards Brian and Venus, and held out a hand.

'Hi,' she said, smiling, her lips glistening, looking almost wet with their heavy 1950s coating of glossy lipstick. 'I'm Jayne.'

They both shook her hand and introduced themselves. Then Brian walked behind her and, opening up her control panel, deactivated her voice control. 'If you've no objection, Venus, I'll switch her voice off until I need to test it, right at the end,' he said. 'I find that it tends to

Voluptuous Venus

distract me if I'm trying to assess some particular reaction, and they start chattering or moaning or talking dirty.'

'I quite understand,' Venus said. 'It's not a problem.'

Brian looked as if he was about to continue speaking when Venus suddenly remembered something that she had completely forgotten. Something that would make all the difference to her needing a fuck. That would, in fact, enable her to have one. *Jesus*, she thought. *How could I be so stupid?*

'You're reasonably new to us here, aren't you, Brian?' she asked him.

'Yes, Venus,' he replied. 'I actually only finished my training course last month. I've been operative for about four weeks now.'

'Then you probably haven't yet had your first experience of a personal supervisory test since you started. From someone of senior inspector status, I mean,' she asked him.

'No, I haven't,' he told her.

She thought she detected just the slightest hint of a blush on his cheeks. 'As research director, I automatically have the status of a senior inspector, for the purposes of product testing,' she told him. 'I will, if you have no objection, instigate a personal supervisory test with you. Commencing now. Is that all right with you?' She smiled at him.

Personal supervisory tests were where the testers themselves were tested. It was a regular part of the Aphrodite system of product testing, undertaken on the principle that in order to be able to test the sex robots efficiently the testers needed to be tested regularly themselves, so as to maintain the highest possible standards. In practice, it probably happened to each tester about once every two months. Testers were given the opportunity to turn down one of these randomly applied tests, on the grounds that they might be feeling overly tired, due perhaps to a strenuous testing programme. If they *did* decline such a test, they had to report two days later for an obligatory test. Unofficially, it was not considered a good career choice to refuse a random test.

'Yes, of course,' Brian replied to her question. 'But is there any special reason why you feel it to be necessary?'

'As a matter of fact, yes, there is,' Venus told him. 'I've had a report from the maintenance department claiming that too many robots are coming in with faults while still under guarantee. Serious faults. Faults that are beyond the technical abilities of our dealers. They're asking me, as the director responsible for product testing, if our testing standards are being properly sustained. It's nothing personal.'

Venus walked over and closed the door to the testing cubicle. 'In fact, you may even enjoy it.' She smiled at him. As she spoke, she took off her jacket. 'We'll keep Jayne here with us. She might come in useful,' she said. 'Will you take off your robe now, please?' she asked him. She indicated the watch that she was wearing, which included a stopwatch facility. 'I'd like to time your erection.'

Brian took off his robe. He had a decent-sized cock that hung pendulously down over his scrotum. *But then, he would, wouldn't he?* she thought. He wouldn't be here if he hadn't. He was circumcised, she saw.

She undressed – clicking the stopwatch function as she began – down to her white, semi-transparent knickers. As was usual, she wasn't wearing a bra. Her nipples were tautly erect. She saw Brian looking at them. 'It's the air-conditioning,' she lied. 'It always makes my nipples hard.' She was glad that she had decided, that morning, to wear black lacy-topped silk hold-up stockings. She watched as his erection literally sprang to life. It was one of the fastest erections that she had ever witnessed. Which was a lot, she realized.

She judged it finely and stopped the stopwatch. 'Fantastic,' she told him. 'That's certainly a company record.' *And I haven't even taken my knickers off yet*, she thought. *Maybe he actually fancies me*. She went over and took his penis in her hand. It throbbed with energy as she held it. She tried to keep her voice level. 'That's an excellent erection,' she told him. 'It's really hard.'

'I know,' he said, smiling at her for the first time. 'It always is when a pretty girl takes hold of it.'

She smiled back at him. 'Well, thank you, kind sir,' she said. 'We're going to get on, I can tell.'

'I do hope so,' he said. 'I wanted to fuck you from the moment I walked in here. You can keep my share of Jayne Mansfield over there. May I pull your knickers down now?'

She laughed. He was fun, this one. She was going to enjoy herself, she knew. *And she would be well fucked.* 'Soon, sweetheart,' she said. 'But first we have to do the premature ejaculation test. Didn't they tell you about that?'

'Oh, yes,' he said. 'They did. I forgot. I was concentrating on pulling your knickers down, and thinking about what I would find underneath them. I can see your lovely long blonde pubic hair, showing through your knickers. And I can see a little damp patch, where you're wetting your knickers with your pussy juice. But I can't actually see anything of your pussy through those little white knickers.' He looked at her, eye to eye. 'But I can smell it,' he said. 'It smells lovely. I can't wait to taste it. Let's do the premature ejaculation test, and then we can get on with it. Is that all right with you? Tell me.'

'It's fine,' she said. 'So just sit on the edge of the bed, will you?'

He did as she asked and she stood in front of him. Taking his swollen cock in her fingers, she began to masturbate him. He looked up at her.

'That's nice,' he said. 'I like that. But could you do it a little faster, please?'

She increased her rhythm. Most men that she knew, on a first fuck – as this in fact was – would have ejaculated by now. She stopped what she was doing. 'I think we can say that you've passed *that* test with flying colours,' she said.

'Oh, thank you,' he said. 'But do you really have to stop? I thought that you were going to toss me off.'

She looked at him quizzically. 'Well, it's up to you, Brian,' she said. 'I don't mind tossing you off, if that's what you want me to do. But do remember that you're going to be judged on your fucking ability quite soon, among a number of other sexually quite gruelling exercises. Your ability to maintain a first-class hard erection while fucking will be part of that. And the time that it takes you to regain

Voluptuous Venus

your erection after ejaculation is another. If, of course, I *do* toss you off, and then you pass all the subsequent tests with flying colours, well, that, naturally, will increase your pass rate. Like I said at the very beginning, it's up to you.'

He smiled up at her again. 'In that case, Venus,' he said. 'Toss me off. Please. And can I put my hand up your knickers while you're doing it, and feel you?'

She had to laugh again. He was a right little goer, this one. 'Cheeky boy,' she said. 'You can do anything to me that you want.' *Including sucking my cunt*, she thought. *As you like, darling. How about now?*

She began masturbating him again, really working at it. She wanted him to enjoy himself. He put both his hands around behind her and pulled her towards him. Then he took her plump, firm buttocks in his hands and squeezed them, feeling them, kneading them. Next he slipped his hands up underneath her knicker legs at the back and did the same thing again, but this time his hands were on her smooth, naked flesh. She felt her juices trickling down between her legs. Then he pulled her buttocks apart, and ran the fingers of his right hand slowly down her anal crevice, gently fingering her tightly closed little anus on the way.

'That's naughty,' she said. She was jacking him off quickly now, carried away herself by his imminent ejaculation.

'But did you like it?' he asked.

She paused before answering him. This so-called personal supervisory test was becoming more of a straightforward sex session. But what the hell. That was

what she had wanted, right from the very start, wasn't it?
'Yes,' she said. 'I loved it. It's so sexy. It makes me come. Push your finger right up inside me. Please.'

He was quick to do as she asked and as he did so his ejaculate spurted hotly up out of his swollen penis, splashing warmly over her breasts. She let out a moan. A moan of sheer pleasure. She wished she had been sucking him off, rather than using her hand, but it was her hand that he had seemed to want. She continued masturbating him, until finally there was no semen left. She let go of his cock and stood back, the movement necessitating him removing his finger from her anus. She put her hands to her breasts and slowly and carefully rubbed his semen into them.

'Oh, Jesus,' he said, as he watched, fascinated. 'Thank you. That was fantastic. Lovely. You've done it before, I can tell.' He grinned at her. 'And with any luck, you might do it again. I love it.'

She looked at him, perhaps a little crossly. 'Let's get one thing straight right now, Brian,' she said. 'You and I both know that what's going on in here is far removed from a normal personal supervisory test. Frankly, I'm enjoying myself. I hope you are.'

'So far, so good,' he commented wryly.

'Shut up,' she said. 'But don't get any strange ideas about me, and your work relationship with me. That stays exactly where it always was. Totally separate. If both of us should decide that we would like to repeat this exercise, either inside or outside the office, then that's between the two of us. But our working relationship stays exactly as it is. That's with me as a director, and you as a product tester. Do I make myself clear?'

'Perfectly clear,' he said. 'Shall I suck your pussy now?'

Much as she would have liked to say yes, Venus felt that she needed to impose just a tiny bit of authority at this particular moment. 'That will come later,' she promised. 'Right now, I want you to do a little test for me. After all, don't forget that, whatever else happens, I'm still going to have to put in a test report on you.'

'Mmmm,' he mused. 'I must admit I hadn't thought about that.'

'Well, think about it now,' she suggested. 'I want to watch you run through the foreplay actions that you described earlier on with Jayne Mansfield here. *And* with her voice mode on. OK?'

'Sure,' he said. 'But that makes you a voyeur, in my book.'

'I don't give a fuck what it makes me in your book,' Venus told him. 'Just get yourself together and see what you can make yourself in *my* book. My report book. Now get on with it.'

'Yes, ma'am,' he said. He went over to Jayne, found her control plate, opened it up, and switched her voice mode on.

'Go and stand by the bed, Jayne, will you, please?' he said to her.

'Sure,' she said. 'I hope you're going to come and join me.'

'I most certainly am,' he told her. He followed her over to where she stood beside the cubicle test bed. He went behind her, undid her lavender brassiere and slipped it off, dropping the straps over her shoulders, then down her arms. He stood behind her and put his arms around her, and started to nuzzle her neck.

'Nice,' Jayne said.

He took a nipple in each hand and slowly teased them into rigidity.

'That's nice, too,' said Jayne. 'It's making me get my panties wet.' She paused, but wriggled her upper body beneath his fingers. 'Does that excite you?' she asked.

'I guess it does,' he said. He let go of one breast, and, taking her right hand in his, he pulled it gently behind her, so that it was between the two of them, and out of Venus's sight. 'What does that feel like?' he asked.

'Oooh, you poor boy,' said Jayne. 'You've got a great big swollen thingy. Whatever can we do to make it go back down again?' She giggled, and cast a glance over her shoulder. Venus couldn't believe it.

The robot really did have the almost coy mannerisms of over a hundred years ago. 'Don't you worry about me,' Brian said. 'Nipple erection excellent,' he added, as an aside to Venus. 'Now then, Jayne darling,' he said to the robot. 'Come and lie down on the bed, will you?'

'Oooh, yes please,' she said, and did as she was asked. Brian lay down alongside her, and began to stroke her beautiful long legs. She was still wearing her black silk stockings, together with her lavender garters. He ran his hand up and down her legs, each time getting nearer and nearer to her knicker-covered crotch at the top of each stroke. She wriggled, this time with her whole body.

Voluptuous Venus

'Oooh,' she said again. 'Is naughty Brian going to do naughty things to poor little Jayne?'

'Yes,' Brian said. 'Naughty Brian's going to fuck naughty little Jayne's brains out in a minute.'

'Oooh,' Jayne said. 'How lovely.'

He looked across at Venus. 'Sorry,' he said. 'Strike that from the record. Whoever ordered this particular package is obviously obsessed with early twentieth century boop-boop-de-do girls. Dumb blondes. Whatever.' He put out his hand, spread the flat of it entirely over Jayne's pudenda and began to rub the material that covered it, very slowly.

'Nice,' she said again.

'Tell me about it,' he said, half-jokingly.

She turned her head to look at him, sideways. 'Well, where your hand is, underneath my panties, is where my, er . . . little . . . *thing* is,' she said. '*You* know? My . . . er . . . *down there*.' She giggled again, furiously this time.

Venus could swear that the robot was actually blushing. 'Jesus,' Venus said.

Brian had patently reached the end of his patience. 'Look, darling,' he said to Jayne. 'Let's not fuck about. What we're discussing here is your pussy. Your cunt. Your twat. Let's not be all girlish about it. We're here to fuck. Right?'

Jayne paused for a moment or two, and then she said, 'Yes, Brian,' her voice quiet and all little-girlish. 'I'm sorry. I didn't mean to make you cross. My cunt. OK?'

'OK,' Brian said. 'That's more like it. Now lift your arse up off the bed for me, will you?'

Jayne did as he asked, and he pulled her silky little

lavender knickers down her long, shapely legs, still adorned with her sexy black silk stockings. When she got her feet out of the knickers, he dropped them onto the floor beside the bed. 'Good,' he said. 'Now then. Get your knees up around your ears, and spread your legs. Wide.'

Jayne pulled her legs back as far as she could and obediently opened them as wide as she could in that position. She looked quite obscene, Venus thought. The posture exposed her thick bush of curly blonde pubic hair, looking like golden moss. Down its centre ran her closed pink outer labia. Brian was the only one of the two humans near enough to see the tiny trickle of colourless liquid that was oozing slowly out of it and down into her blonde thicket. 'Naughty Jayne's thinking naughty thoughts,' he teased, whispering into her ear. 'And they're making Jayne's pussy all wet.'

'Yes,' she admitted softly, so that only Brian could hear.

'Right,' Brian said in his normal voice. 'Now I'm going to suck your pretty pussy. OK?'

'Yes, please,' Jayne said, meekly. 'I'd like that.'

Brian used his fingers to open up the female robot's vagina, spreading first her outer, then her inner labia. Inside, she was a dark pink colour, shading into purple the further in you went. Her membranes shone wetly with the mucus that she was producing in generous quantities.

Brian slipped a finger deeply inside her. 'Vaginal texture excellent,' he reported. 'Clitoris in place, and swelling.' He knelt down now and began his task of performing cunnilingus upon the robot. It didn't look as if he was in any pain, Venus thought. He was obviously enjoying

Voluptuous Venus

himself. Making a meal of it would be a good description. *I'm jealous*, she admitted. After a short while, Jayne began to writhe her hips, and she started moaning, indicating her approaching orgasm.

Brian took his mouth off her and looked across the room at Venus. 'Excellent production of vaginal lubricant,' he said, 'and both first-class scent and first-class flavour. Absolutely full marks, so far.'

He got back down to the job again, and in double quick time he had brought Jayne to an obviously enjoyable climax. He kept at it until she had finished and as her last shudder died away he stood up. His erection was rampant, but it didn't seem to embarrass him at all.

'I can't fault her in any way, in the oral sex examination,' he said. 'She was perfect.'

'Great,' Venus said. 'Pity about her vocabulary.'

'I understand that's all at the request of the customer,' Brian said. 'Apparently he's into the period in a big way. It really turns him on. I'll make sure she's tested, and any necessary verbal adjustments made to her vocals when I've finished her fuck test.'

'Fine,' Venus said. 'I haven't noticed you kiss her yet,' she said next. 'We need to assess her lip and tongue synchronization at some stage. I think I'd like to see her perform fellatio on you. Do you fancy a blow job? If I was a man, I'd love those soft, wet, thickly lipsticked lips around my cock.'

Brian gave her a bit of an old-fashioned look. 'I'd rather have *you* suck me off,' he said. 'But I'm here to do a job. If that's what you want me to do, then that's what I'll do.' He sat on the edge of the bed, his penis like a small pole between his legs. He looked back at Jayne, who was still lying on the bed behind him.

'Come and suck me off, sweetheart,' he said. The robot got up off the bed obediently, came around and knelt down on the floor between Brian's open legs. She reached out and took hold of his cock and then, looking up at him and maintaining eye contact as she did so, she took the end of his circumcised cock slowly into her mouth and began to suck it. As she sucked, she used her tongue upon him, expertly.

Venus watched, enthralled. She found it surprisingly sexually exciting to sit back on a chair, totally relaxed, and watch Brian having his cock sucked by this beautiful woman. She wondered idly, as she sat there, which of her male colleagues had had the pleasure of auditioning the woman upon whose fellatio this particular robot's cocksucking program was based. She was getting randy again.

While she was thinking about what it would feel like to suck Brian's cock, he suddenly grabbed hold of the robot's head and thrust his cock way down into her mouth, deep-throating her as he pumped his semen into her.

'Oh, God,' he said. 'I needed that. But what I really need is a fuck. You kindly tossed me off. Since then, I've sucked Jayne here's pretty little pussy. And now I've just fucked her mouth, if you'll forgive the expression. But give me a couple of minutes, and I'd love a fuck. A *real* fuck. With a *real* woman. Are you ready yet?'

Voluptuous Venus

'God, you're a randy little sod, aren't you?' Venus said. 'Now then. One thing at a time. First, your assessment of Jayne's oral capabilities.'

Brian took a deep breath. 'Excellent lip and tongue surface texture,' he said. 'Perfect coordination. A really good oral program, as far as we went with it. Good deep-throat receptivity. I don't know whether this model has had its gagging reaction removed, at the customer's request. It may well have done. But it's in the standard microchip oral program, and if Jayne here hasn't had it removed, then it isn't working. As the original chauvinist pig, I rather like to feel a girl gagging when I first thrust my cock hard down her throat.'

Venus ignored his macho remarks but concentrated on the important content of his statement. 'Good point,' she said. 'That's just the sort of thing the maintenance department are complaining about. I'll make sure that it's checked out. As to wanting a fuck, you're not the only one, you know. But don't bloody forget you've ejaculated twice already this morning. I've tossed you off, and Jayne here's sucked you off. I haven't even had a bloody orgasm yet. And don't forget that you promised to suck *my* pussy. That's definitely the next item on the agenda. I claim directorial priority. After that, you can choose which of us two girls you screw first. Me or Jayne.'

'You,' Brian said, without a moment's hesitation. 'It's all I've been wanting to do, all morning.'

'Aaaaaah,' said Venus. 'You've obviously discovered that the way to a girl's heart is through her pussy.' She smiled at him. The more time she spent in his company, the more

213

she grew genuinely to like him. What she had originally seen as his slightly downmarket, intellectually unprepossessing character attracted her the more, the better she got to know him. He had a dry, quite wry sense of humour, and an ability to treat everything with just a touch of facetious drollery.

Venus looked at her watch. It was approaching lunch time. 'It's getting on for lunch time, Brian,' she said. 'Do you want to eat?'

He looked at her. 'Mmmmm,' he said.

'Shall I send out for something?' she asked. 'What do you fancy?'

'Pussy,' he said. 'Yours.'

'Oh,' she said. 'That kind of eating. How lovely. Let's skip lunch. I'm ready when you are.' She went over to the bed and lay down upon it. She still had on her white, semi-transparent bikini knickers (although the area around her crotch was more of a damp grey colour by now) and her black lacy-topped hold-up stockings. She opened her legs.

Brian came over to the bed and lay alongside her. He took her in his arms and kissed her on the mouth, his tongue exploring. She responded in the same manner. She could feel the pressure of his swollen erection pressing against her thigh. He pulled away from her mouth and moved down her body slightly, until he was in a position to take first one, then the other nipple into his mouth. He sucked and nibbled at them alternately, until Venus cried out aloud at the sensual, entirely pleasurable pain that he was causing her. Her nipples stiffened, like tiny helmets.

He lifted his head, and looked down at his handiwork. He laughed.

'What are you laughing at?' she asked.

'You remind me of that old schoolboy joke,' he said.

'Which old schoolboy joke?' she asked.

'You know the one,' he said. 'The one about the young girl swimming in the sea, down at Brighton. Her bikini is rather an old one, and as she's splashing about the strap to the bra bit breaks and her top falls off and is swept away. She's very embarrassed and as she wades back to the shore to get a spare costume out of her bag, she crosses her arms across her breasts to try and cover herself up. However, she has rather large breasts, and she isn't that successful at hiding her predicament. As she gets near to the shore, a small boy sees her coming. He looks up at her. He seems very taken aback for a moment, and then he says "Excuse me, miss, but if you're going to drown those puppies, I'll have that one with the pink nose."'

Venus giggled. She hadn't heard it before. Then Brian wriggled even further down and spread her legs with his hand.

But it was his mouth and nose, rather than his hand, that he buried between her legs, burrowing into the sticky confines of her moist knickers. He snuffled and sniffled, and then came up for air for a moment. 'Fantastic,' he said.

'What?' she asked.

'The smell of cunt,' he said. 'Hot, wet, randy cunt.' He buried his nose and mouth once more. Quite soon he stopped his imitation of a truffle hound and, putting his hands beneath Venus's bottom, he raised her up off the bed. Holding her there with one hand, he used the other one to pull her knickers roughly down around her thighs, from whence he used both hands to pull them quickly down her legs and off. She settled back down on the bed, spreading her legs in anticipation of what was to come.

He looked at her pussy almost as if it was the first one that he had ever seen. He touched her long golden pubic hair, as if it might fall out if he was too rough with it. She had oversize outer labia. They were darkish brown, almost black in colour, and the size of a large butterfly's wings. *Or a small bat's*, he thought. He'd never seen such large labia. They were beautiful. He used his fingers to spread them, carefully, to reveal her inner lips. These were the same colour, but a quite different shape. They were far smaller, and fat, like tiny swollen spaniel's ears.

The scent of Venus's aroused sex was strong. She smelt like a bitch on heat. *Not a bad description*, he thought. She was so wet that her juices were running down her inner thighs. He eased two fingers into her, more out of curiosity than anything else. She was much tighter than he would have guessed. Really tight. Wet and tight. He felt his prick throb at the feel of his fingers up inside her, and he wished that the cunnilingus was already over and done with, and that now he was about to ram his cock up her tight, gorgeously wet little cunt.

He bent down and licked her, running his tongue all the way up her, from the bottom of her vaginal aperture to the very top. And then back down again. She tasted marvellous. A tangy, sexy, slightly acrid taste. Of melons. Of over-ripe paw paws. Of limes. Mangoes. Lush, exotic,

Voluptuous Venus

tropical tastes. He began to suck and lick her with increased fervour. He thrust his tongue down into her as far as he could reach with it, relishing her taste, and titillated her clitoris. It responded quickly to his ministrations, by swelling and growing, until it was quickly as rigid as a third nipple.

He felt her beginning to respond to his tongue, moving her hips in a slowly increasing rhythm. Her breathing became heavier, almost stertorous. She began to make the small animal sounds that the Jayne robot had so uncannily reproduced a little while earlier.

He remembered her earlier request, while she had been masturbating him, so he next insinuated his right hand beneath her and, searching the length of her deep anal cleavage, found the puckered entrance to her rectal passage. He found its centre, and forced his finger quickly inside it.

She gasped as she felt the entry, and then she squirmed her buttocks down onto his finger, signifying her approval, and her hips began to increase their movement. Suddenly, he was finger-fucking her arsehole.

She began to mouth things that he couldn't hear. They sounded like obscenities. He increased the pressure that he was making with his mouth and lips, and increased the activity of his tongue. She matched his faster rhythm with her own, and her mouthings became louder. Then, suddenly, they were audible.

'Oh, shit,' she shouted. 'I'm going to come. You're sucking my cunt, and it's making me come. I'm going to come. Now. I like what you're doing to me. You've got your finger up my arsehole. It's so sexy. Oh, Jesus God. You're giving me a great big juicy come. Oh, God. Here it is. I'm coming. Now. NOW. I'M COMING NOW. OH, JESUS. OH, YES.' She bounced her bottom up and down off the bed so rapidly, as she gave in completely to the orgasm, that Brian found difficulty in keeping his mouth in place over her pussy. He kept at it until she was completely finished, and then he climbed up onto the bed, beside her. His cock was still fully erect.

'That was beautiful, darling,' Venus said, taking hold of his cock. 'Now you can do things to me with this. It's what you've been wanting to do all morning. Do you remember? That's what you said, earlier on.'

'Of course I do,' he replied. 'And I still do. But let's not forget what we're doing here. This is my personal assessment, as well as what I hope is going to be a good fuck. How do you assess me for cunnilingus? What are my marks for overall foreplay? Am I up to standard?'

She giggled and turned over on her side to put her arms around him. She kissed him, wetly, before she replied. Then, 'How about the best ever?' she asked. 'Will that do?'

He had to laugh. In actual fact he was getting back at her (or trying to) for her being what he considered snotty to him earlier on. When she'd made her rather pompous speech about her being a director and him being but a humble tester. But he had to admit that she'd obviously seen him coming from a long way off. *And close to, as well*, he thought, giggling silently at his own joke.

'Well, thank you, ma'am,' he said. 'A compliment indeed.'

Voluptuous Venus

'Oh, come on, Brian,' she said. 'Stop being so fucking pedestrian. And speaking of fucking, will you fuck *me* now, please. I need it.'

She turned over, onto her back, and parted her legs. He put his hand down between them and felt her pussy. It was gorgeously wet from the lip service that he had been paying to it. He got a leg across her and knelt up.

She took his rampant penis in her hand and guided it home. She gasped as it entered her. It felt like iron. 'Mmmmmm,' she said. 'That feels good.' She pulled her knees back and up, the better to allow him to penetrate her as deeply as possible. 'Oh, yes,' she said as he obligingly thrust up her. 'That's what I've been waiting for. Oh, yes. Do it to me. Harder. Harder. Please. Oh, yes.'

She felt good to him as he rode her, and he put everything that he had into it. He looked down at her. Her eyes were closed. He hadn't noticed before how long her pale blonde lashes were. Nor had he previously noticed the pale lavender mascara that adorned her eyelids. Her mouth was half open, and a tiny dribble of saliva trickled from one corner. Her lipstick was long since all kissed off, but her lips were still bright red and swollen with passion. Her small, prettily pointed breasts rose and fell as she breathed deeply, their nipples erect and slightly sore-looking from his earlier attentions.

But he was too tightly pressed against her to be able to see his penis entering and withdrawing from her. It was the reason why he loved fucking women doggy fashion. He loved to watch his cock as it shafted deeply up into them, forcing its way between their stretched vaginal membranes, their labia dilated by the thickness of his swollen tool, itself wet with their precious, intimate liquids. And, of course, the ability to look at that other, higher entrance. That tiny, brown, puckered, usually forbidden orifice.

Had she said, earlier, that she liked it up her arse? He couldn't remember. But this wasn't the time to worry about that particular question. This was the time to enjoy the tightness of her pussy, clenched, as it was, tautly around the length of his rigid cock, engulfing it, massaging it, her juices making its passage an easy, erotic, sensual journey. He grabbed her by her waist and pulled her to him more tightly, endeavouring to bury himself up her.

She responded by thrusting her buttocks hard back against him, and their joint efforts succeeded in making him penetrate her even more deeply. She groaned out loud as he sank into her, and then she began to increase the rhythm which, up until that moment, he had dictated. As their movements gathered pace, indicating her approaching orgasm, Brian too felt his ejaculation gathering momentum. Eventually, they reached orgasm together, as if already practised lovers, accustomed to each other's sensual patterns. They collapsed, exhausted, in each other's arms and were silent for a while. 'Jesus,' said Venus. 'That was too much. Can we do it again? Soon, please?'

Brian laughed. 'Yes, of course we can,' he told her. 'But give me a minute or two, sweetheart.'

As she lay there, she took hold of his flaccid cock and massaged it rapidly back into an appropriately rigid state, upon which she climbed on top of him and fed his rampant appendage into her eagerly awaiting pussy.

'Do you mind, darling?' she asked.

'Mind?' he said. 'I love it. There's nothing more enjoyable than lying back, letting someone else do all the work.'

'If this is work, all I can say is that I wish I were employed doing it full-time,' Venus said. 'Can you imagine getting paid to fuck?'

'Sure,' Brian said. 'Hookers do it.'

'Oh, yes,' Venus said. 'Of course they do. I was just thinking of you and me.'

'I'll happily pay you, if that's what you need to make you happy,' said Brian.

Venus laughed. 'What I need to make me happy is what I'm riding on right now,' she said. 'It's called cock. Stiff, long, fat, hard cock. Your cock, my darling.' She bent forward, and kissed him on the mouth. She then stuck her tongue into his mouth for a few exploratory excursions, after which she pulled it out and sat back upright. 'Will you do me a small favour?' she asked him. 'If I ask you nicely? Pretty please?'

'Of course I will,' he said. 'What is it?'

'Play with my tits,' she said. 'I love it when I'm on top, doing the fucking, and someone plays with my tits. It makes me come and come. Especially if you do it hard enough to hurt me.' She grinned down at him, as she bounced up and down on his cock. 'I like just a *little* bit of pain,' she said. 'Nothing serious. But you can spank me later on, if you like. Would that do anything for you? What would excite you? Give you a hard-on?'

He took a nipple in each hand, twisting them both between his fingers before he answered her. She grimaced at the unexpected pain, for all that she had asked for it. He pulled on them, stretching them, and then he squeezed and pinched them. Hard.

She squealed. 'Ooooh, yes,' she said. 'I love it. Hurt me. Hurt me again.'

He continued pinching and squeezing, as he began to answer her. 'I don't know about the spanking,' he said. 'I don't know if it would excite me. Or turn me on. It's not something that I have ever been asked to do before. It's certainly not anything that I've ever fantasized about. But I'm more than happy to give it a try, if that's what you like. I must admit that it sounds more interesting the more I think about it.'

She didn't say anything. He wasn't even sure that she was listening to him. She seemed totally involved in fucking him and in enjoying what he was doing to her nipples.

He continued to answer her. 'My fantasies are all the usual ones, I suppose. I fantasize about group sex. About me and a lot of women, all of them wanting me. About fucking one while I suck another one's pussy. That sort of thing. And I fantasize about the lesbian sex thing. You know, two girls, with the me-joining-in bit.

'I fantasize about anal sex. I've met a couple of girls who were into it. But most girls are very against it. They're usually either against it in fact, because the only time that they tried it, it physically hurt, simply because the man

Voluptuous Venus

with whom they were doing it didn't have any bloody common sense. Or simply didn't care. Or they're strongly against it on principle. It puts women down. Women don't get any sexual pleasure from it. It's for queers. That sort of thing. And of course, like most men I know, I fantasize about all that century-old antique lingerie stuff. Women wearing black silk stockings held up by suspender belts. Frilly, silky, French knickers. Basque corsets. Thick black cotton stockings on housemaids of *more* than a hundred years ago, rolled over at the top to make a kind of built-in garter. Looking like a rolled-up condom. I find those old-fashioned elastic belts for what they used to call sanitary towels very sexy too. But I think my favourite fetish, or fantasy, is that involved with anal sex. How about you?'

Having come at the very least three or four times – Brian wasn't sure which – whilst he was talking, Venus was now paying him her full attention. 'Oh, I don't know,' she said. 'Like I said, I'm very into spanking. I love everything involved with it. I love my knickers being pulled down, exposing my naked bottom. And then being put across someone's knee. One's pussy is almost rubbing on the sex of the man giving the spanking, if you think about it. The actual spanking itself makes me come, and makes me all wet between my legs, both of which are excellent preparations – as far as I'm concerned – for the fucking that inevitably follows the spanking. And I love the formal ceremony of it all. If I'm going to be caned – as opposed to just plain spanked – I love the ritual of being ordered to go and bring the dreaded implement (the cane or whip, the slipper or the paddle, whatever) from its everyday hiding place, and having to hand it over to the person who is going to administer the punishment. It's tantamount to having to say, "I've been a naughty girl. Please punish me. Please pull my knickers down and spank my bare bottom." It's also tantamount, of course, to saying, "And please fuck me afterwards. Or shall I suck your cock?"

'But you mention anal sex. You say it's your main fetish. Your biggest fantasy. Tremendous. We'll get on well, you and I. I *adore* anal sex. But I've told you that before now. Although not in any kind of detail. It's partly the *intimacy* of it. It's partly the fantastic feelings that it induces. One is being fucked deep in one's very bowels. It's so much sexier than straight vaginal sex. You talk about women who say that there is nothing in it for a woman. But that's arrant nonsense.

'First of all, I come every time that I am fucked in my arse. *Every* time. If that doesn't happen to all women, well, I'm sorry. But it is a very simple matter for the man who is fucking you in the arse to masturbate you at the same time. Or for you to do it for yourself. My problem has always been to find men who like to fuck girls up the arse. Most men think that it's perverted. Or that it's dirty. Or they just don't think of it at all. They're all so cunt-oriented. Or mouth-oriented. All men – without exception – want to fuck girls' mouths. Many, I think, given the opportunity, would rather fuck a girl in the mouth than in her cunt. Don't you agree? Which would *you* prefer, given a free vote?'

Brian thought for a moment. 'Difficult to answer,' he

Voluptuous Venus

said. 'I like both. I like every possible kind of sex between a man and a woman. I don't actually prefer any one over and above any other. But it depends, to an extent, how long it might have been since one last had a particular kind of sex. If one is in a relationship, and able to have sex regularly, and without worrying about the time factor, then both parties to the relationship should be able to satisfy their sexual desires fairly frequently, shouldn't they? Surely that's what relationships are all about? But maybe, say, a chap hasn't got his own place and his girlfriend shares with other girls. Or perhaps she still lives at home with her parents. So that it's difficult enough for them ever to get any real sex, and maybe they have to make do with feeling each other up in the back row of the local cinema, followed by a bit of mutual masturbation. Well, in those circumstances, then yes, possibly the man would give anything to be fellated, rather than get fucked. Who knows? But I think that availability has got a lot to do with it.'

'I suppose you're right,' Venus said. 'But I can feel my orgasm getting itself together. So enough of fantasies. At least for now. Just fuck my socks off, will you? Please?'

Remembering Venus's earlier delights, and her recently finished (at least for the moment) testament about the joys of anal sex, Brian reached up and, pulling her buttocks apart, found her rectum and thrust his middle finger deeply inside it. Venus gasped as she felt the invasion, and immediately began to orgasm.

'Oh, yes. That's it. Oh, my God. That's good. That's GOOD. I'm coming. I'M COMING.' She went on in a similar vein for a while as Brian caught up with her effortlessly and began to pump his ejaculate up into her in long, warm jets. This brought on another flood of long, intense, continual orgasms, until finally Venus lay back, replete. She then dragged herself off Brian's supine body and flopped down alongside him. She gave him a kiss.

'Thanks, baby,' she said. 'Please don't ask me what your marks are. I might cry.'

At least he had the grace to laugh. 'And full marks to you too, darling,' he said. 'That was the best day's work I've done for a long time.' She hit him. Gently.

They called it a day after that. As far as both sex and work were concerned. Brian suggested that Venus might like to join him for dinner later that evening, which invitation she accepted with alacrity. On condition, she said, that although he was more than welcome to share her bed after dinner, it would be solely for the purposes of cuddles and sleep. He agreed, willingly.

They dined at a new Chinese restaurant in Coventry Street that had recently been built on the site of the old Planet Hollywood hamburger joint. She found him pleasant and amusing company. He quietly displayed an up-to-date and extensive knowledge of the theatre and of the other arts that Venus would have found difficult to accept had anyone suggested to her prior to this day's events that he was that kind of person.

At the end of an excellent meal, he offered her the choice of his bed, as opposed to hers, which she gracefully turned down. They then returned to Venus's place, where, after two cups each of freshly brewed Jamaican Blue

Mountain coffee, and a large, carefully warmed, Hinc VSOP brandy each, they retired to bed, to fall soundly and happily asleep in each other's arms. The end of a perfect day.

CHAPTER SIX

Shop Front

Later that week Sally, Venus's secretary, came through on the telephone. 'I've got a Hank Sherman on the line from New York, Venus,' she said. 'He says he wants to talk to you about the new retail outlets. Shall I put him on?'

'Surely,' Venus said.

'Venus, hi,' said a pleasant American voice. 'I'm Hank Sherman, of the Hank Sherman Corporation in New York City. I read in the *Wall Street Journal* this morning of your new Aphrodite product range, and of your plans to open up a retailing network world-wide. My corporation would like to make an offer for the franchise of those outlets for the whole of the United States of America. We have the capital. We have the references. We have the staff. We even have the premises, because we are currently the States' biggest video-rental company, with outlets in every major American city. I reckon that your retail chain is going to put the sex-video business out of business, which is a big chunk of our profits. Why rent a video, when you can rent a sexy lady? One who'll do anything that you want her to? *And* stay within the law.'

Venus hadn't yet said more than hello. This man was a fast talker. But he was talking sense.

'Here's what I'd like to suggest,' Hank continued. 'I'll send our corporate jet over for you. Come stay in New York at our expense. Bring half a dozen of the sex robots with you, together with a technician. If I like the product – and I'm certain that I will – I'll send you back to your company, within the week, with a draft contract. To show that I'm genuinely interested, I'm prepared to deposit five million dollars into your company's account later today. All you need is your fellow directors' approval to come and have the conversation. Neither you, nor your company, are committed to anything until you approve the deal and sign the contract. You can't lose. What do you say?'

'It sounds like a fantastic offer, Hank,' Venus said. 'Leave it with me. I'll be back to you before the end of the day.'

'Great, baby,' said Hank. 'I look forward to meeting you.'

It took Venus just twenty minutes to get together an urgent board meeting. Fortunately no one was away. It took them only fifteen minutes to agree the trip in principle, subject to John Barton, the finance director, obtaining acceptable business references. These were completed by the middle of the afternoon. Venus got back to Hank at four p.m. Eleven a.m. New York time.

Hank was delighted. 'Fantastic,' he said, when she gave him the news. 'When can you be ready to leave?'

Voluptuous Venus

'How about any time tomorrow afternoon?' Venus suggested. 'I can have the products ready, together with all the necessary customs documentation, and down at Heathrow at lunch time. Say midday.'

'Terrific,' he agreed. 'I'll have the corporate jet there some time after midnight. If you'll give me the name of whoever my people should deal with over the telephone, we're in business.'

Venus thanked him. 'What's the weather like in New York?' she asked, wondering what sort of clothes she would need.

'Hot,' he said. 'Do you know New York at all?'

'Not well,' she told him. 'I've been there a couple of times on business, but never for longer than twenty-four hours.'

'Well, I guarantee that you'll know it better when you leave it this time,' Hank said. 'And don't forget that the heat is only in the streets. It's reaching a hundred and ten, right now. But the offices, the restaurants, the stores, the theatres, people's apartments, the cabs, everything, is air-conditioned. So you'll possibly need warmer clothes than you might think. Anything you want to know, just call me. The crew will let me know what time the plane gets in. I'll meet you at Kennedy. And I'll book your hotel. Don't worry about a thing. See you tomorrow, Venus. Look forward. Ciao.'

The next twenty-four hours were a blur. Along with selecting robots, briefing a technician, overseeing the documentation, arranging transport, and talking to her fellow directors about finance, franchise agreements, possible product delivery dates, legal requirements, servicing arrangements, and a million and one other things, she also had to get herself together. She needed to pack sufficient clothes for a week, find her passport, cancel her milk and newspaper deliveries, and make arrangements with her cleaning lady to look after things while she was away. She had the sense to give Sally a spare set of keys to her flat, in case she might have forgotten something vital. She remembered to turn the water-heater off and to throw away anything in her fridge that might not keep while she was away.

The Hank Sherman Corporation jet was the latest model Boeing executive rotorjet. A magnificently accoutred, luxuriously furbished ten-seater. White, with a gold HSC insignia on its slim fuselage. While the technician oversaw the loading of the robots, Venus was welcomed on board by a gorgeous, sun-tanned, blonde 'trolley dolly', who introduced herself as Dawn. She had luscious full red lips, of the kind that looked as if they were tailor-made for cocksucking. Venus wondered if giving head to the chief operating officer on transatlantic trips was part of her duties.

Dawn showed Venus how to operate the individual video with which each seat was fitted. She next handed her a menu that gave an amazing choice of dishes for lunch and that also listed a selection of available films. They were all current releases. Beneath the film list was another directory, headed *Adult Viewing*. This itemized various HSC videos under various categories, including

Voluptuous Venus

heterosexual, lesbian and fetishes.

'Tell me, Venus,' Dawn asked a few minutes later. 'I'm told there's another passenger joining us. A technician called Rodney Wates. Do you want him to sit next to you, or shall I put him further back, on the other side of the cabin? It's no problem, either way.'

Thinking of the opportunity to see some of HSC's sex videos, Venus asked Dawn to put the technician behind her. Dawn then departed and came back with a glass of champagne. Rodney came on board ten minutes later. Shortly after, the pilot announced take off and they were on their way.

The crossing took just under three hours. Less than the supersonic Concorde of all those years ago, although it was, in its day, the fastest commercial airliner in service. But three hours was sufficient time to watch two of the HSC videos, separated by the time that it took for Dawn to serve her two passengers with lunch. Venus chose a video from the 'heterosexual' category first. It was called *Tina's Turns*. Tina turned out to be an accommodating lady with a good body, rather large breasts (a common American male fetish) and a practised mouth. Not to mention practised pussy, hands, and arse. There wasn't much in the way of a believable story line, but the video was well-made, and the colour, film quality, and sound were all excellent. Tina spent almost all of the time with all three of her main orifices being filled – flooded, even – frequently and enthusiastically by a variety of exuberant male participants. There was never a dull moment. Venus was hugely impressed with the girl's energy.

She sucked a lot of cock. Since Tina was white, much of the cock inserted into her mouth was black, it apparently being the belief of pornographic video producers that this skin contrast adds to the general sexuality of the proceedings. In similar vein, much of the cock up Tina's cunt, and up Tina's arse, was also black. But not exclusively. To be fair to her, she seemed genuinely to be enjoying herself. So much so that one could not help but get the impression that she would have given her performances free had she not been being paid so to do. The relish with which she took seemingly endless about-to-ejaculate cocks out of her mouth and – uncut – sprayed the jets of spurting spunk over her face, showed a devotion to duty of which Lord Nelson himself would have been proud.

On one occasion, she was being fucked simultaneously in her mouth (as opposed to simply sucking cock), fucked vaginally, and fucked anally, and yet she still found time – and the stamina – to masturbate two more gentlemen, one in each hand. Golden Cock – the porno movie business's Oscars – stuff. She took the oral ejaculate on her face, the vaginal semen on her generous – if slightly pendulous – tits, and the anal outcome in the small of her back. She rubbed the results of both the masturbatory ejaculations into her buttocks. After all these years, Venus thought, blue movie producers still reckoned that the punters wouldn't believe that the girls were really getting fucked unless they could actually see the cocks withdrawn at the moment of ejaculation and the resultant sperm sprayed anywhere other than where God intended it to go. Come shots, they were called in the trade. What a strange world we live in, she thought.

Lunch was a gourmet experience. Venus chose Beluga caviar to start with. It came in a crystal bowl, surrounded with ice, and was served simply with toast – and a choice of either champagne or vodka – eschewing the separately chopped egg yolk, egg white and chopped onion often served with caviar in restaurants to eke out a less than generous amount of caviar. Venus chose the vodka, and drank it neat. The only way to drink genuine Russian vodka. It was ice cold, as it always should be.

She followed that with a steak Diane, something not often seen on menus these days. A thinly sliced sirloin steak, flambéed in butter, with Worcester sauce, shallots, and brandy. To her complete amazement, a properly white-trousered, blue-aproned and white-hatted chef wheeled a trolley down the aisle, and flambéed it beside her. She had asked for it rare, and rare it was. Hank obviously spared no expense when travelling. He patently liked his comfort and enjoyed his food.

Not to mention his wine. Venus had asked for red wine with the steak Diane, and Dawn opened and served a vintage Chateau Talbot. Venus knew that it would have cost her a month's wages from an off-licence back in London. And she wasn't underpaid. She finished the bottle.

She looked at the menu afresh when offered it once more, this time to select a dessert. It had been her original intention to forego pudding and simply end with espresso coffee. But when she saw freshly gathered *fraises du bois*, served with fresh clotted cream, she was unable to resist. They were delicious.

When invited, she ordered a cognac with her coffee and settled down to watch another dirty video. Watching Tina earlier had actually made her quite randy. She hadn't seen Brian since their *magnum opus*, and she hadn't used either a vibrator or even her fingers upon herself since then. Consequently, watching Tina's various salacious turns had revved Venus's sexual needs up considerably. She was raring to go. She ran through the list of possibilities, turning down a fleeting fancy that she might watch one of the homosexual videos to enjoy the guaranteed concentration of the camera upon the numerous giant-size cocks that would inevitably be featured, and finally settled for a video which came under the heading of Group Sex – General.

The film started with shots of what was obviously intended to be a smart party. There were about twenty partygoers, divided roughly half and half between the two sexes. Everyone was dressed as for an elegant, fairly formal evening party, with the girls in mostly very off-the-shoulder evening dresses, with a great deal of revealing décolletage, and many of the men in black tie. Those not in evening dress were in formal suits, collars and ties.

Cut to what a voice-over on the soundtrack informed the viewer were the party hosts. An attractive young man in his late twenties, and a very pretty redheaded girl – his girlfriend, Venus was informed – maybe a year or two younger. The guests had just arrived, and the hosts, having offered them all a glass of welcoming punch, were

Voluptuous Venus

now busy spiking the remainder of the huge bowl of drink. It wasn't possible to tell exactly what they were spiking the booze with, but their conversation told the viewer, mixed with a great deal of giggling, that whatever it was would have the whole room tearing each other's clothes off, and getting down to some fairly serious sex, within a few minutes.

And sure enough, in no time at all, the guests were kissing, touching each other up, shedding their clothes, and generally behaving like an orgy with nowhere to go. Our hosts, who presumably hadn't swallowed any of the magic elixir, were the only couple – at least for the time being – to retain their clothes. No one else seemed either to mind or even to notice this obvious disparity.

The two (Charlie and Jane by name) began to organize what could only be described as a variety of sexual party games. In the first the men were instructed to pick two teams of three girls each, from the total of around ten or so young ladies, to compete to see which of the teams could bring off the largest number of ejaculations in the shortest possible time. Despite their genuine enthusiasm, both teams of girls could have learned a great deal from watching Tina of the earlier video.

It didn't seem to occur to any of them – all now almost entirely naked – that each one of them was equipped to allow at least three men to fuck them at once – orally, vaginally and anally – while they could surely have managed to jack off at least one other man as this was going on, if not Tina's two. But no. There was too much concentration, for anyone taking the contest seriously,

237

upon cocksucking. All six girls in the two teams were seemingly skilled fellatrices, and they brought many a round of applause from the enthralled audience as they swallowed mouthful after mouthful of male ejaculate. In the end the winner, a rather scrawny brown-haired girl, led the field with a not particularly exciting score of seven ejaculations.

Her prize was to choose which of the assembled audience – male or female – should publicly perform cunnilingus upon her. To cheers from the men, she selected – surprise, surprise – a lithe, firm-breasted black girl, with fabulous legs and, as we soon saw, a quick and practised tongue and mouth. She sucked the white girl's pussy until the girl was screaming with delight, her body convincingly racked by multiple orgasms, to the unstinting and noisy applause of the rest of the group.

The cameraman was very professional, and at no time did he forget why he was making this film. In this particular scene, his close-up lens lingered fondly on shots of wet, pink pussy being lapped and sucked by a long pink tongue. In the six-girl competition of earlier, Venus had felt her knickers getting wetter and wetter as he had concentrated on close-up shots of swollen, hard cock penetrating mouths, pussies, and rectal openings. He was fond of taking long, lingering shots with what can only have been a macro lens of sections of throbbing, veined, stiffly erect penis, shining with wetness, sliding in and out of stretched, mucus-covered vaginal membrane.

The labia thus stretched, and filmed, showed an amazing range of skin colour, from the almost transparent

Voluptuous Venus

through varying hues of pink shading to a dark purple and then to pure black. The colour of the filmed cocks, although going from black to white, was far more limited in the middle ranges.

Venus finally became so frustrated that she first looked around the cabin to see who, if anyone, was around and, seeing no one other than Rodney Wates, the technician, who appeared to be asleep, she pulled up her skirt, tucked her hand down the front of her bikini panties, and began to masturbate herself. She was surprised, therefore, when she felt a gentle hand on her shoulder and looked up to see Dawn smiling down at her.

'Forgive me, Venus,' said Dawn, quietly. 'But I was passing by, and I couldn't help seeing you with your hand in your panties there. I thought that you might like to know that our ladies' restroom on this aircraft is equipped with a small selection of vibrators, in case of this kind of emergency. Or, if you prefer it, I could join you in there for a rather more personal service.' She continued smiling, as she waited for a reply. *Not just cocksucking lips*, Venus thought, *but pussy-sucking lips too. Why not?*

She took her hand out of her panties and stood up. 'A little personal service sounds very attractive, Dawn,' she said. 'Thank you.'

'Oh, how nice,' said Dawn. 'If you like to make your way to the restroom, I'll join you in there in a minute or so.' She turned and walked back through to the crew quarters, just behind the cockpit section of the aircraft.

Venus made her way to the back of the plane where both men's and women's restrooms were situated, one each side of the fuselage. She was surprised most of all by the restroom's size. It was large enough to contain a double bunk and two large, comfortable-looking easy chairs, as well as two lavatories, two washbasins, a bidet, and a shower. Luxurious quality towels and robes, soaps, scents, a hair-dryer, and hair-brushes, the latter sealed in sterilized packets, were all about the place. There seemed to be everything that a woman could need. *Except a man*, Venus thought.

At that moment Dawn came into the cabin, closing the door behind her. 'I'm really looking forward to this,' she said, smiling. She took off her flight uniform jacket, and began to peel off her skirt. She saw Venus watching. 'It's called stripping for action,' she said, grinning.

She hung her uniform up, carefully, on a hanger. She was wearing a white silk teddy that revealed her firm, full-breasted, small-waisted figure. She also wore black hold-up stockings. And nothing else. 'Now then,' she said, putting out her hand, 'let's get to know each other a little better, shall we?'

Venus put out her hand and, taking it, Dawn pulled her close, put her arms around her waist, and began to kiss her. It was a deep, wet, lovers' kiss. Venus kissed her back. She smelt nice. Some kind of light, flowery scent. And she tasted nice. Fresh. Clean. She certainly knew how to kiss. As she kissed, she slipped a hand down between Venus's legs and felt her pussy through her panties. 'How lovely,' she said, pulling away from Venus's mouth for a moment. 'Your pussy's all wet. That's very naughty.' And then, 'Let's get you ready,' she said, leading

Voluptuous Venus

Venus over to the bunk. Venus didn't resist.

Dawn undressed her quickly. It was obviously something that she had done many times before. When she got down to Venus's tiny panties, she pulled them rapidly down her legs and held them, almost impatiently, while Venus stepped out of them. When the knickers were finally free, in her hand, she held their wet crotch up to her nostrils and inhaled deeply.

'Mmmmm,' she said. 'It isn't just men who love the scent of pussy, you know. Yours smells beautiful. I'm going to enjoy kissing it. But there are a couple of things that I need to know before I start to do that.'

She put the knickers down. 'First of all, may I tell you that I'm bisexual? I love both men and women. Equally. But the lesbian part of me is serious, bull-dyke lesbian. I love to suck pussy. I like to strap on a cock and fuck girls. Particularly young, beautiful girls. Like you. And I love to have girls suck and fuck me. But I never want to impose anything upon anyone that might upset them. So I have to ask you, what do you want me to do to you?' She stopped, and smiled a happy smile. 'Do you want me to kiss and suck and lick your pretty pussy?'

'Yes, please,' said Venus, smiling back. 'Perhaps it will help if I tell you that I don't believe that I am truly bisexual, in that I prefer men. But there are certain women – and you are one of them – who attract me. If I am sufficiently attracted, I don't mind what they do to me.' She paused. 'Or what they want me to do to them. So feel free to do anything that you wish. You can fuck me with a dildo, and use a vibrator on me. Bugger me with anything that you

Eva Linczy

feel is appropriate. And I'll do all of those things to, and with, you. And enjoy all of them.'

'Oh, baby,' said Dawn. 'Oh, God. Lie down, Venus, and spread your legs wide. I'm going to fuck the living daylights out of you.'

Venus lay down on the bunk and spread her legs. Dawn knelt between her legs, bent down and kissed Venus's pussy. She fingered Venus's soft blonde pubic hair and stroked it. 'Pretty, pretty pubes,' she said. Her fingers separated Venus's outer labia. 'And what a pretty little cunt,' she said. She bent down again, and kissed the wet, pink slit that ran down the centre of Venus's parted pubes. And then she licked it. Her tongue traversed its full length, from top to bottom, slowly. Lasciviously. She sucked as she licked. Then she lifted her head and looked up at Venus, sighting a line up along her body. Over the flat stomach. Over the tip-tilted breasts and the erect nipples. All the way up to the exquisitely bone-structured face. 'God, that tastes good,' she said. 'It's my most favourite flavour. Young, fresh, fully aroused, succulent cunt.'

She buried her head back between Venus's legs and began to eat her pussy again. This time in earnest. There was no doubt about it, thought Venus, lying back and thinking not of England but of the skilled abilities of the woman whose mouth was bringing her such carnal pleasures. Venus had been sucked off by a number of girls over the years. But never one as adept as this one.

Just then, Dawn insinuated her hands beneath Venus's bottom and, holding her firm buttocks in them, she

Voluptuous Venus

squeezed and manipulated them as she tongued and sucked her new playmate to orgasm. *If this is how a self-confessed bull-dyke lesbian makes love*, Venus thought, *maybe I should give up men. I could put up with an awful lot of this.* She felt her first orgasm beginning to build, starting somewhere down in between her womb and her anus. She raised her hips up against Dawn's mouth as she started to come.

'Oh, yes, baby,' she cried. 'Oh, darling. That's wonderful. That's too much. I'm coming. Oh, yes.'

Dawn didn't stop her oral ministrations until Venus's multiple orgasm had finally subsided. At which point she stripped off her teddy and got up onto the bed beside Venus and kissed her, wetly, on her mouth.

'I can taste my pussy juices on your lips,' Venus told Dawn. 'That's very sexy.'

'I enjoyed that too,' Dawn said. 'It's nice to find a girl who knows when her pussy is being well sucked. There are so many amateurs about, these days.'

They lay there quietly for a while, each comfortable with the silence, their arms about each other. Then Venus took one of Dawn's nipples between her fingers and began to play with it, pulling it and twisting it. It rose, magnificently, beneath her fingers. After a while, she sat up and, leaning down, she took the nipple between her lips and started to suck on it and chew it.

Dawn groaned with pleasure. 'Oh, darling,' she said. 'That's really nice.' She was silent for a while, but her body was twisting and writhing as Venus continued sucking her breasts. Then, suddenly she could stand it no longer.

'Please kiss my cunt,' she pleaded. 'Please suck me. Please make me come. I want to feel your mouth, your lips, your tongue, in my cunt. Please? Now? And when you've made me come, I want us both to fuck each other with a huge double-ended dildo. I want to feel you inside me. Fucking me. Filling me.'

Venus obediently slid down Dawn's body until her mouth was positioned over the blonde's saturated pussy. She covered it with her mouth and used her tongue to tease and please. Dawn tasted good. A strongly piquant, gamey, erotically flavoured treat.

Venus settled down to attempting to provide the same kind of intense oral pleasure that Dawn's lovemaking had given to her. Once she got into her stride, she was rewarded, quite quickly, by Dawn's extremely vocal response to what was happening between her legs. Dawn came rapidly, repeatedly, and quite splendidly. Both girls enjoyed Dawn's orgasmic pleasure.

When it was finally all over, Dawn thanked Venus for the joyous sensations that she had provided. After a while, Dawn got off the bed and went over to a cupboard along the cabin wall. She opened the door and took something out which she brought back to the bunk to show to Venus.

It was, in fact, the double-ended dildo to which she had referred earlier. 'Do you fancy a little fun with this now, darling?' she asked.

Venus took it from her and examined it. It was a fairly standard-issue dildo, with the difference that the diameter of this particular cock-shaped toy was about twice as large – in Venus's experience – as was usual with these penile substitute devices. 'Mmmmm,' Venus said. 'It looks like a lot of fun. But it *is* rather large, isn't it?'

'It sure is,' Dawn said. 'And that's what the fun is all about. Shall I wear it, or will you?'

'What's the difference?' Venus asked. 'I'm not very experienced in these matters. I've used them before, of course, but I don't understand the significance of who wears what.'

'It's quite straightforward, really,' Dawn told her. 'The one who wears the dildo does the fucking. The one who doesn't wear it gets fucked.'

'Oh, no problem then, darling,' Venus replied. 'You wear it.'

Dawn giggled. 'My pleasure,' she said. She went over to the cupboard again, and this time she came back with a jar of lubricant. She rubbed both ends of the enormous dildo with the rather greasy-looking concoction, and then rubbed another generous helping into herself. She began to strap the harness around her waist, after which she said to Venus, 'If you'd like to take these thigh straps through between my legs and buckle them up for me at the back, it will save us both an awful lot of time.'

'Of course,' Venus said, taking hold of the straps and doing as she was asked. She helped Dawn to adjust the various straps and buckles until she was happy and comfortable with the fit.

Dawn stood there, the huge rubber cock standing up erectly in front of her. 'I guess you'd better use some of this lubricant yourself,' Dawn suggested to Venus, holding out the jar. Venus took it from her and, holding her pussy open with the fingers of one hand, she rubbed a couple of fingerfuls of the lubricant into herself with the other.

'How do you want it? *Where* do you want it?' Dawn asked.

Venus thought for a moment. 'Up my cunt, doggy fashion, from the back,' she replied. 'Does that suit you?'

'Sure does,' Dawn said.

Venus climbed back onto the bunk once more and squatted down on all fours, her arse towards Dawn. She spread her legs and waited. Looking over her shoulder at Dawn, she said, 'Come fuck me baby. I'm all yours.'

Dawn climbed up behind her and, holding Venus around her waist, she thrust the huge dildo in and up. It was so big that she needed a little help but, using both hands, and with Venus reaching down and holding her pussy lips open, she finally managed to get it at least partially inserted.

At first, only the tip was introduced. Dawn grabbed Venus's buttocks and, hauling on them and thrusting with all her might, she contrived to ram the obscene object all the way into Venus's greased pussy.

'Jesus,' Venus said. 'Wow. That feels good.'

'My end's quite jolly, too,' Dawn said, as she began to simulate fucking movements. As she did so, she leaned forward and took one of Venus's breasts in each hand, cupping them and then using her fingers to play with the nipples.

'Ooooh, nice,' said Venus.

As they were thus pleasantly engaged, they were startled to hear the pilot's voice over the aircraft's sound

Voluptuous Venus

system. 'Ladies and gentlemen, we are now on our approach to Kennedy Airport. We shall be landing in approximately ten minutes. Please take your seats, and fasten your seat belts. Will the cabin crew please take up their landing positions? Thank you.'

'Shit,' said Dawn. 'Can you come quickly?'

'Sure,' said Venus. She put her hand down between her legs and rubbed her clitoris as Dawn continued to fuck her from the rear. 'Now,' she said, moments later. 'Now. I'm coming now.'

'Me too,' Dawn said, her movements frenzied as she worked herself up to her climax. 'Me too. Oh ... Lovely.'

Anyone seeing them coming out of the ladies restroom slightly less than ten minutes later would never have believed what they had been doing with each other, both stark naked, only minutes previously. They were both once more dressed up to the nines. Their make-up was immaculate, their hair impeccable. Dawn held the cabin door open for Venus.

'Thank you, darling,' she said quietly as she passed through.

'My pleasure, sweetheart,' Dawn replied as she followed.

'Oh, there you are,' Rodney said as they passed his aisle. 'I was beginning to wonder where you were.'

'Oh, we were just tarting ourselves up, Rodney,' Venus said. 'A girl always wants to look her best when she arrives in New York, doesn't she?'

About a minute after they fastened their seat belts, the aircraft landed. The pilot's voice came over the sound system once more. 'Please keep your seat belts fastened until we're stationary,' he said. 'I hope you had a pleasant journey. Mr Sherman is waiting for you in the VIP Arrivals Lounge. He knows we've landed. You should be through Customs and Immigration in about fifteen minutes. The temperature here in New York is 110 degrees Fahrenheit. Have a nice day.'

Venus left Rodney to see the robots and their accompanying equipment off the plane and through customs. He was being met by a Hank Sherman Corporation van and driver, and was to deliver the goods to the HSC offices on Third Avenue, close by Fifty-fourth Street. As they came down the steps from the plane, the heat hit them like an iron fist.

Dawn smiled her charming smile, standing at the bottom of the steps. 'Goodbye, sweetheart,' she said. 'Have fun. I hope we'll meet again.'

'Me too,' said Venus. 'Goodbye now. And thank you.'

Hank was waiting just inside the entrance to the VIP Arrivals Lounge which, unlike the Customs and Immigration building, was fully air-conditioned. He was tall – about six two – and much younger than Venus had imagined from listening to his voice on the telephone. She put him somewhere in the middle to late thirties, at the very most.

He was dressed in a pale blue lightweight summer suit, a startlingly white shirt, and the kind of tie that only an American can wear. He came up to her. 'You must be Venus,' he said, holding out his hand. 'I recognize you from your picture in the *Wall Street Journal*. Hi. I'm Hank. Welcome to New York City. My limo's waiting just outside. Let me lead the way.'

Voluptuous Venus

He turned and walked ahead of Venus and out through the building's swing doors. As he emerged, the driver of the longest Cadillac stretch limousine that Venus had ever seen – either in real life or in an American movie – leapt out of the driver's seat, and opened the rear door. 'Hop in,' he said. She did.

There was room for six people, in unbelievably comfortable individual seats. There was more room in the back of the limo than in many people's bedrooms, Venus thought. There was a cocktail cabinet, a small refrigerator, a large screen television set, and a whole selection of cupboards, holding God knew what. Remembering the ladies' restroom on the company rotorjet (would she ever forget it?) she wondered if one of the cupboards held a selection of vibrators and dildos.

Hank opened the fridge door and took out a bottle of vintage Mumm. 'Champagne?' he asked.

'That would be nice,' she said.

He opened one of the cupboard doors and took out two lead-crystal champagne flutes. 'It's probably almost supper time for you, right now,' Hank said, looking at his watch. 'But since New York is five hours behind London, it's lunch time here. I thought we'd have something simple but delicious at the Four Seasons,' he said. 'Does that sound all right to you? If you're not overly hungry, you don't have to eat more than you want to. I shall quite understand.'

'That sounds delightful,' Venus told him. 'Thank you.' She accepted a glass of champagne. They toasted each other, and she drank deeply. She was thirsty. The Four Seasons. Wow. One of the world's great restaurants. She had never known anyone, on her previous brief trips to New York, who could afford to take her there.

When they arrived, the first thing that surprised her was the size of it. It was huge. Rather like an aircraft hangar, but with tables in sections at different levels, which broke up the overall area into more acceptable smaller units.

'Good morning, Mr Sherman, sir,' said the maître d' as they approached his desk. 'Your usual table is ready for you. And I've had the sommelier put a bottle of Mumm's on ice for you.'

'Thank you, Charles,' Hank said. A folded note passed, almost unnoticed, between them. Venus couldn't see what it was worth.

It had always seemed strange to her that all American dollar bills looked exactly the same at first glance. The only way in which they differed was in the amount of dollars that was printed on each note. What had changed hands – as far as she was concerned – could have been anything from a single dollar bill (which she doubted) up to a one hundred dollar bill (which she also doubted).

'Thank you, sir,' said the maître d' again. 'Allow me to show you to your table.' He led them to a table in a quiet corner high enough up to give them an uninterrupted view of the entire restaurant, spread out beneath them.

As they sat down, one of the floor waiters came straight over. 'Shall I open your champagne, Mr Sherman?' he asked.

'Please, Billy,' said Hank.

The waiter opened the bottle expertly, poured a little

Voluptuous Venus

for Hank to taste and, getting his approving nod, then filled both their glasses.

'Have you been here before?' Hank asked.

'No, never,' Venus told him. 'It's beautiful, isn't it? But why is it called the Four Seasons?'

'Oh, for the simplest of reasons,' Hank told her. 'They change the decor here four times a year, to coincide with the year's four seasons. Spring, summer, fall and winter. It's nothing dramatic. It's mostly a matter of flowers and paintings. If you look around, you'll see a lot of expensive summer flower arrangements, and a lot of pictures – most of them on loan from museums and galleries – reflecting the summer season. It's not so much famous for its decor as for its food, and its prices. It's probably the most expensive restaurant in New York, after Le Cirque de France. But let's order some food, and then we can talk. How hungry are you?'

'Despite an excellent lunch on your plane, I'm starving,' Venus told him. 'Travel must broaden my appetite.'

'Well, good,' Hank said. 'We're in the right place to deal with that. What do you fancy?'

After a long look at the menu, and three glasses of champagne, Venus ordered Clam Chowder to begin with. Manhattan style (as opposed to New England style). Hank had explained that Manhattan clam chowder had a tomato base, whilst New England clam chowder had a cream base. She was keen to eat American food, since she could eat French-style food any time, back home in London.

'Well, you can't get much more American – or much more New York – than Corned Beef Hash with Hash

Browns,' Hank suggested. He explained to her that it was a very typical all-American dish, consisting of minced corned beef (which had no connection with the tinned Argentinian product that most British people thought of as corned beef. The nearest one could get to it in Britain was probably the salt beef of Jewish cookery and of Soho sandwich bar fame). Corned Beef Hash was cooked in the oven and browned under the grill, with fried potatoes similarly treated.

'They make an authentic and really very good one here, although not too many people know that,' Hank said. 'I don't believe it's on the menu. You can have it straight, just like that, or you can maybe have a side salad, if you fancy one. A green salad, perhaps?'

Venus declined the salad. Hank had decided to join her in her choice of her main course, but he was going to start with soft-shelled crab. And he did order a side salad.

'So I guess we'd better have some American wine, then,' Hank suggested. 'You'll know, of course, about Californian wine. It's world class. Mind you, there is New York State wine. Even New York State champagne. But don't ever waste your money on any of it. It's all disgusting. Well, in my opinion it is, anyway. But Californian wine is terrific.'

He consulted with the wine waiter and they chose a half-bottle of Californian Chardonnay to go with the soup and a red Pinot Noir for the main course.

The chowder was a great success: plump Atlantic clams that had been pulverised and mixed into a strongly flavoured tomato-based liquid that combined deliciously. The chardonnay was light, fruity, and aromatic. When it

Voluptuous Venus

came, the corned beef hash was burnt on top and very well cooked below. Just as it should be, Hank said. The hash browns were crisp on the outside and succulent in the middle. The Pinot Noir was strongly flavoured, robust, and also fruity. And it was quite heavy. An excellent choice to accompany the piquant, powerfully-flavoured hash.

Venus enjoyed every mouthful, and complimented Hank upon his choice of both food and wine. Hank was patently pleased that she was pleased. Throughout the meal, he chatted away to her in a relaxed, comfortable way. He told her of his early struggle to build up HSC from a one-shop video-rental outfit in Manhattan over ten years ago to its present success. It had been achieved, so he said, on the back of the boom in renting sex videos. He had progressed from buying wholesale and selling and renting retail to producing his own products. The fact that HSC videos were that much stronger than those of his many competitors – 'we are often only half a step ahead of the law,' he said – had resulted in his becoming number one in the sex sales and rental video markets in the United States, and in some other countries.

'And that's what has kept me single,' he told Venus. 'I guess it must be the same for you, Venus. If you're in the business of selling sex, there's so much sex on offer, all day, every day, that you simply don't meet the kind of members of the opposite sex that you want either to marry or at least to settle down with. The girls who star in my video films fuck all day for a living and then, when they've spent the day doing that – not to mention every other form of sex known to man – then they fuck for fun, after work.

Often all night. So while I'm not short of sex, I *am* short of any kind of lasting relationship.'

He paused and looked at Venus. 'I'm not sure if I'm missing anything or not. I sure as hell get more sex than any of my men friends. But am I happy?' Another pause. Then, 'Yes, I guess I am. I'm rich. I'm successful. And I get to fuck a lot of pretty girls. What more could a white man want?'

Venus laughed. 'I can't imagine. But tell me, are you producing films all the time? I mean, is there one in production now? Here in New York?'

'There certainly is,' Hank said. 'As a matter of fact, I've got three on the go at this very moment. In three different locations, here in the city. Have you ever seen a movie being made? Have you ever seen a *dirty* movie being made?'

Venus had to admit that she hadn't. 'Well, if you would like to, you can come on set with me in the morning and have a look-see. Would that amuse you?' Hank asked.

'It certainly would,' Venus told him. 'I'd love to do that. May I?'

'You surely can,' he said. 'How about some dessert?' Staying with her wish to try anything and everything American that she was able to, Venus chose pecan pie, with a side order of ice-cream. She passed on the cheese. They both ordered espresso coffee.

'I've booked you into a suite at the Plaza,' Hank said, a little later on. 'I'll drop you off there after lunch. Please feel free to order absolutely anything that you desire there and charge it to my account. You'll find everything that

Voluptuous Venus

you need. If there's something that you want and they haven't got it, then they'll send out for it for you. So please feel free. First of all, it's my pleasure, and secondly, it's all tax-deductible anyway.' He laughed. A genuine, infectious laugh.

Venus thanked him. A suite at the Plaza, indeed. On Central Park South and 59th Street. Arguably one of Manhattan's best hotels.

'I thought that we'd leave any thought of business until tomorrow,' Hank said. 'That should give you time to get over your jet lag. So relax, and enjoy yourself. It would be my pleasure – unless you have other plans – to show you something of Manhattan at night, this evening. Would you like that?'

'I'd love it,' said Venus, completely honestly. Although she hadn't spent too much time with this youngish New York entrepreneur, she had warmed to him from their very first contact at the airport.

'Great,' Hank said. 'Oh, and by the way, I've arranged for your technician – Rodney, isn't it? – to be looked after. He's in a comfortable hotel, and will also see the sights this evening. I'm sure he'll enjoy himself.'

'That's good of you, Hank,' she said. 'And very thoughtful. Thank you.'

Despite New York's notoriously difficult parking problems, Hank's limo was waiting outside the Four Seasons when they finally emerged. The drive to the Plaza was quick and Hank came in with Venus to check at reception that all was well. It was. He bid her adieu, and they agreed that he would pick her up at six that evening.

A bellhop took Venus's bags up to the suite which was on the sixth floor, overlooking Central Park. She looked out at the summer crowds of tourists strolling along Central Park South, at the horses and carriages that plied for hire in the park, and at the tops of the elegant apartment blocks lining the east side of Fifth Avenue as it ran northwards, up towards East Harlem. Up and across the park, she could just make out the roofs of the zoo buildings. Afternoon sunshine illuminated the suite. Inspecting it, she found that there was a good-sized sitting room, an enormous bedroom, and a small dressing room with closet. It was tastefully, expensively and elegantly furnished in antique Empire style, with a great deal of silk and satin. The exquisite furniture was genuine, and in perfect condition. Everything in the bathroom was state-of-the-art contemporary.

Feeling her jet lag beginning to tell, she unpacked a minimum of clothes and toiletries, took a quick shower, called the telephonist for an alarm call at five p.m., and took to her bed. She was sound asleep in moments.

The telephone awoke her what seemed like five minutes later, but after a fresh shower, which she finished with ice-cold jets of water from the sophisticated shower unit, she felt like a million dollars. She completed her unpacking, hung up her clothes, rang the housekeeper to have a couple of things pressed, and spent the remaining time before six attending to her hair and applying her make-up. At six p.m. prompt, she was in the Plaza's Oak Room bar to find Hank waiting there for her. He rose to greet her,

Voluptuous Venus

and waved at a waiter at the same time. 'Hello, again,' he said. 'What'll it be?'

'What's typically American?' she asked him.

'I guess, even after all these years, a dry Martini is still about as American a cocktail as you can get,' he told her. 'Would you like one?'

'I'd love one. Thank you,' she said.

'Two dry Martinis, straight up, hold the olives, please, Charlie,' he said to the waiter.

'Coming up, Mr Sherman,' the waiter said, bustling back to the bar. He was back again five minutes later, with as dry a Martini as it had ever been Venus's privilege to drink.

'Wow,' she said. 'Fantastic.'

Hank grinned his pleasure. 'Now then,' he said. 'I spend a lot of time with visitors to New York who want to see the Staten Island Ferry, the Statue of Liberty, the Museum of Modern Art, the Guggenheim Museum, the Empire State Building, Carnegie Hall, the Lincoln Center, all that stuff. Which, if that's what you want to see, we can do, with pleasure. But I thought that being in the sex business, you'd like to see something of what is on offer sexually here. Am I right?'

'Absolutely spot on,' Venus said. 'That would be fun. And interesting.'

'Good,' Hank said. 'I thought we might start with dinner in Chinatown. Do you like Chinese food?'

'Love it,' she said.

'Great,' said Hank. 'Will eating this early bother you? They tell me that you eat late in London.'

'Eating now is fine,' she told him.

'I suggest that we have one more of these for the road,' he said. 'And then we'll take a cab down to Canal Street. I've sent the limo home. It's just impossible to park around town in the evenings. It's even worse than during the day.'

They enjoyed a second Martini, by which time Venus was feeling no pain. The Plaza doorman got them a cab which took them all the way down Manhattan Island to Chinatown, situated below Little Italy, which itself is just slightly below the Bowery.

Hank took them to a very ordinary-looking Chinese restaurant, just off East Broadway, where he was greeted like a long-lost friend by the proprietor. Hank asked Venus if she wanted to see the menu, or if there was any particular dish that she felt like. Or would she, he suggested, care to do what he always did and leave it all up to the owner? That she was happy to do, she said.

Whilst the decor and furnishings were unimpressive (if immaculately clean) the food itself was out of this world. It was delicious, and as different – in both taste and appearance – from the Chinese food obtainable in London's Chinatown as chalk from cheese. The two spent the meal getting to know each other a little better.

Without the formality of the Four Seasons at lunch time, they both relaxed more, and by the end of the Chinese meal they were chums. They made each other laugh, and Hank treated her as an equal, both in business acumen and experience which, while well-deserved, was a fairly unusual compliment.

As they finished their meal with repeated tiny glasses

Voluptuous Venus

of Chinese plum wine, compliments of the owner, Hank said, 'I thought that we might start at the bottom end of the market and work our way up. How does that sound?'

'It sounds interesting,' Venus said. 'What exactly *is* at the bottom end of the sex market in New York?'

'It's probably two or three different things,' Hank replied. 'Whatever it is, it's centred on the area around 42nd Street and Times Square. The worst parts are in the side streets, off the main Avenues. There are pornographic movie houses, live sex shows, emporiums that combine strip shows, sex shows, and girls performing personal sex acts in booths, where the customers pay by the minute.'

'You mean the kind of thing where men are looking through peep-holes at girls masturbating, while they masturbate themselves?' Venus interrupted.

'Exactly that,' Hank said. 'And then, that area is the lowest possible end of the market for hookers in New York. The city has some of the finest, most expensive, brothels anywhere in the world, with beautiful young girls who will perform any sexual act that you wish – and expertly – provided that you can afford it. But we also have the lowest of the low. Many of them are still young, but they're not at all attractive. They're mostly girls with heavy drug problems who'll fuck for ten dollars. Or give you a blow job for five. Without a condom. And it shows. They're mostly beaten-up losers, working for pimps. The pimps are usually, but not exclusively, black. The girls vary. About half black and half white. With every shade in between.'

'Jesus,' Venus said. 'That sounds revolting. I'm not sure that I want to see too much of that.'

'No, of course not,' Hank agreed. 'We'll get a cab and drive along a couple of the streets and you'll see more than enough. And maybe we'll pick up one sex show. Then we'll go to the other end of the market. That'll be a lot more fun, I promise you.'

They did as he suggested and picked up a cab. Hank explained to the driver what he wanted him to do, and then gave him a fifty-dollar bill. 'There's another of those for you when we finish, on top of the fare,' he said. 'But if I say go, I want you to go. OK? I don't want to do anything other than just look.'

'Sure, bud,' said the cab driver. 'Whatever you say.'

They drove off, uptown a little and westwards, over to the Lower West Side, and on to 42nd Street, close by the New York Port Authority Bus Terminal.

It was nearing eight o'clock, and the pavements were teeming with hookers of all sizes, shapes, colours, and ages. They all had two things in common: their garish outfits, consisting in the main of minuscule, obscenely short tight skirts, so short that they exposed the girls' pantie crotches, and whatever kind of almost non-existent top the wearers thought best showed off their otherwise naked breasts. And then their prices, which were absolutely rock bottom. The women were loudly vociferous in their plying for trade. Once they thought that the passengers in the cab might possibly be looking for sexual entertainment of some kind, they became even more noisily obstreperous.

Voluptuous Venus

'You want some prime pussy, man?' 'You wanna fuck?' 'You like me to suck your cock?' 'I take it up the ass, buster. You wanna fuck me in the ass?' 'You want the best fuck this side of Central Park? Here I am, man.'

Venus found that she had soon had enough of these sad women, close to. They were, on the whole, ugly. Their bodies showed the ravages of a short life spent selling those same bodies for enough money to inject heroin, in whatever form they preferred it. Not one of them looked as if they'd had a decent meal for weeks.

But even as Hank and Venus cruised the area, the girls were being picked up in their droves by what appeared to be ordinary, normal-looking businessmen. Salesmen, in New York to attend their company's annual sales conventions. Some married men, whose wives, for whatever reason, had long since stopped catering to their husbands' sexual needs. Other lonely men, unable to find a normal sexual relationship. A small percentage of perverts, whose only receptive partners were among those who sell their bodies, however cheaply, to feed unquenchable lusts of their own.

'I think that's enough of cheap hookers,' Venus said, after about ten minutes of cruising the streets. 'It's a pretty depressing sight, isn't it?'

'It certainly is,' said Hank. 'Shall we give the sex emporia a miss, perhaps? It's pretty much the same sort of thing as here, except that it's rather more organized. It's run by the Mafia, rather than by individual pimps or individual amateur hookers. It's even more sordid. But they make a fortune.'

'I've read about them,' Venus said. 'One of the main attractions, apart from the live sex shows apparently, is where you go into a booth with a peephole, drop a quarter into a slot, the peephole opens, and this live girl, standing on the other side of the wall, drops her panties. Then the slot closes, and the guy drops another quarter in, and she takes off her bra. This goes on, until – if the guy hasn't run out of quarters – the girl starts playing with herself. The man's been playing with himself all this time, so that when she starts, it brings him to his ejaculation. The insides of these booths, so I read, are almost ankle-deep in come. It sounds quite disgusting.'

'It is,' Hank said. 'But it's also highly profitable. The girls like it, because it's easy money and they don't actually have to fuck anybody. They don't even have to touch anyone. And it's steady. Guys actually stand in line to put their quarters in the slot machines for a girl who has a reputation for putting on a really raunchy show. The word gets around very quickly. But it's a short life, for obvious reasons. Now, how about dropping by one of New York's most exclusive brothels, for a change of scenery? We can have a drink there, and relax. The girls are amusing to talk to, and the madam is a personal friend of mine.' He spoke to the cab driver, through the bullet-proof division. 'Third and 49th, please,' he said.

The cab dropped them on the corner of Third Avenue and 49th Street, as Hank had requested, and Hank led them east along the street for a couple of hundred yards, stopping in front of a luxurious-looking apartment block. 'This is it,' he said. They walked into the entrance, which

Voluptuous Venus

opened out into an enormous atrium, with fountains, palm trees, flowers, and a whole desk of doormen.

'Good evening, sir,' said one of the doormen, as they approached.

'Good evening,' said Hank. 'Miss Jennifer Holmes is expecting us. My name is Sherman.'

'Thank you, sir,' said the doorman. 'If you'll kindly wait a moment.' He picked up a house phone and, looking at a list of residents, dialled a number. 'Oh, good evening, Miss Holmes,' he said. 'This is the front desk. There's a Mr Sherman here to see you, with a friend. Yes, of course, Miss Holmes. Thank you, miss.' He put the phone down. 'Will you go right up, please, sir' he said. 'It's the west elevator, over there. Miss Holmes's apartment is 21B, on the twenty-first floor. Thank you, sir.' He turned politely away.

The elevator was operated by yet another polite employee, who bid them both good evening as they entered his elevator.

'They've got great security here,' Hank said to Venus. 'I wish it was half as good in my apartment block.'

'Is it really necessary?' Venus asked.

Hank laughed. 'You'd better believe it,' he told her. 'Systematic armed robbery of apartment blocks in Manhattan is the fastest-growing crime in the city these days. It's almost impossible to get insurance, unless you're a long-established customer or you don't mind paying seriously over the odds.'

Just then the elevator stopped at the twenty-first floor and they got out. 21B was along the corridor to the left.

The corridor was luxuriously carpeted, and the walls were hung with good-quality reproduction prints of some of the better-known French Impressionists. They stopped outside the door to the apartment.

Hank pressed the buzzer. The door was opened almost immediately by a pretty young girl of about eighteen. She had black hair, was about five eight, and was dressed exquisitely in a classic French maid's uniform, even to the starched white apron and matching mob-cap. She curtsied. When she spoke, her accent was not French but strongly Brooklyn.

'Good evening, Mr Sherman. Good evening, miss. Miss Holmes is expecting you. She asks if you would like to go through to the bar? Shall I lead the way?'

The girl didn't wait for an answer, but as she turned away from the two of them, Venus was amazed – and delightedly amused – to see that, from the back, she was naked from the waist down. Her skirt was simply cut entirely away, and she wore neither petticoat nor knickers. Just black silk stockings, held up by garters. Her bottom was something else. Twin globes of firm, tanned, muscled flesh. As she walked along the passage, ahead of Hank and Venus, her buttocks moved elegantly. Attractively. Excitingly. They were so perfect, Venus wanted to reach out and stroke them. Feel them. Squeeze them. She'd have bet a great deal of money that Hank wanted to as well. Probably rather more so, she thought. She wondered if he patronized the girls from this brothel, or whether he really was just a friend of the owner.

At the end of the corridor the maid turned right and

Voluptuous Venus

held open the door for Venus and Hank to enter. Venus thanked her as she passed through. The girl smiled, but didn't say anything.

The bar was furnished in contemporary style, apart from the bar itself, which had probably started life, Hank told her later, as part of one of the old Irish bars that New York had been full of back in the middle and late parts of the twentieth century. It was solid mahogany and beautifully polished, with carved panels and brass fittings.

There were three expensively dressed men at the bar, and Venus counted five girls and one slightly older woman, whom she correctly assumed to be Hank's friend Jennifer and the owner of the establishment.

The woman got up off her bar stool and came over to greet them. 'Hank,' she said. 'Hi. Good to see you.' They kissed affectionately and, seemingly, genuinely.

'Jenny, I'd like you to meet a business associate of mine, Venus,' Hank said. 'Venus, this is Jenny. Jenny is an old friend.' They shook hands.

'Hello, Venus,' Jenny said. 'Make yourself comfortable. You're very welcome here. Any friend of Hank's, as they say. What would you like to drink? It's on the house. How about a glass of champagne? You look very much like a champagne lady to me.'

Venus laughed. 'Well, thank you. That's quite a compliment. I'd love a glass of champagne.'

Jenny waved a languid hand at one of the other girls. 'Trudi. Come over and say hello to an old friend of mine. And a new friend.'

The girl came over and Jenny introduced her to Hank

and Venus. 'Trudi's new here,' Jenny explained. 'She's from Stuttgart, in Germany.'

Trudi was short – about five two – but everything else about her was on the generous side. She was blonde, with a big-lipped, generous mouth, a generous smile, and the largest, most generous breasts ever to be seen this side of a pair of Second World War British barrage balloons. Most of them were on display, over and around a tightly-fitting tank top. From what could be seen (about ninety per cent of the whole, Venus judged) they appeared to be in excellent shape. Big, but firm. Her nipples could also be seen, standing out through the thin knitted woollen material of her skinny top, and they too were on the more than generous side. They looked like miniature skittles.

Venus just about managed to suppress a giggle when the thought crossed her mind that, on the available evidence (all of it patently *extremely* available – at a price) the girl must also have an outsize cunt.

'Be a good girl, Trudi, will you, dear, and pour us each a glass of champagne? Please? And bring one for yourself. Thank you, darling.'

Trudi went off, behind the bar, to do as she was bid.

'I just can't believe those tits,' Jenny said. 'They're just out of this world. And I can tell you that they are in absolutely perfect condition. All my girls strip off when they audition for jobs here. Not a hint of sag, or droop, anywhere. I've never seen anything like it. She'll make us both a fortune.' She looked at Venus, and winked. 'Please God,' she added. 'So,' she continued. 'Hank tells me

Voluptuous Venus

that you're the young lady whose company is going to put me out of business. Tell me all about it.'

Just then Trudi came back with a tray, on which were the requisite four glasses of champagne. 'It's Dom Perignon,' Trudi said, handing the glasses around. 'Jenny tells me that's the only champagne she serves here.'

'I'll drink to that,' Hank said, picking up one of the glasses and handing another to Jenny. Venus already had hers. They drank.

'Well,' said Venus, answering Jenny's comment, 'I don't know about that.' She ran through the details of the projected tie-up with Hank, describing his wish to be the US franchisee for the Aphrodite rental models, subject to his approval of the actual robots, which he would see the following day after their early morning visit to Hank's blue movie film set.

'But we're not looking to compete with anyone,' she continued. 'We're looking to open up a whole new market. Although I do agree with Hank that we may well have an adverse effect on his blue movie/video business, in that we will offer what many people might well see as a better alternative. Instead of first having to find a cooperative sexual partner, and then renting a blue movie or video to watch, or subscribing to a blue TV channel to get themselves good and horny, they will be able to rent a male or female robot that is virtually indistinguishable from a human, who will tease them and stimulate them sexually as much as they like before actually providing the sex as well. Any kind of sex, for any length of time. With no taboos, no refusals, no getting tired. Or bored, or cross, or wanting to do the crossword. In fact, never a cross word! Forgive the pun.'

Jenny laughed. 'Well, I must admit that these robots sound fantastic,' she said. 'But, not having seen one, I find it difficult to accept that they *are* indistinguishable from the real thing. I'll bet you anything you like that if you brought one up here and put it in amongst my girls, no one would be fooled. You'd never get one of my customers wanting to fuck it, or be given a blow job by it. No way. Not in a million years.'

Venus thought for a moment. 'I won't take your money, Jenny,' she said, eventually. 'It just wouldn't be a fair wager. But, with Hank's permission, I'll take you on.'

'I love it. No problem.' Hank said.

'However,' Venus continued, 'before we start, I'd like to make one thing absolutely clear. What you've said is that an Aphrodite robot wouldn't pass as human up here in this establishment, competing sexually with your girls. I'll happily have one brought up here within the next hour or so, and show you just how wrong you are, provided that you accept that there will be one major difference between the female robot that you'll see and the female robots that will be for rental.

'That difference is that the ones for rental have a fairly limited vocabulary. They can, and do, talk about any aspect of any sexual act, and they have a perfectly acceptable complete sexual vocabulary, together with the basic necessary social graces. But, while we have the technology to equip any of our models with the ability to talk comprehensively on any and every subject, it is far too expensive a facility to install into what are, basically, simply sex toys. Reasonably enough, I think, we brought over with us the facility to demonstrate to Hank the whole range of our capabilities, and to win this bet – and I emphasize again, if I may, that I'm not entering into any financial wagers – I'll obviously need to use that full conversational facility. With that, I'm confident that my robot will pull at least as many of your clients as any one of your girls, over an agreed period of time. What do you say?' She grinned at Jenny as she waited for her answer.

'You're on,' Jenny said. 'But we have to have *some* kind of wager. How about a bottle of Dom Perignon? Just to keep it interesting?'

'Oh sure,' Venus said. 'But of course the whole thing hangs on whether or not Hank here is able to get hold of Rodney, my technician. We need him to equip one of the robots with the total conversation microchip set-up, and to give it the complete range of sexual athletics. Is that a problem, Hank?'

Hank looked at his watch. 'I don't think so, Venus,' he said. 'I think I know where Peter Sangster, the guy who is looking after Rodney this evening, will be right now.'

He took a miniature radiophone out of his pocket and pressed in a number. He got through to it. 'Hi,' he said. 'Is Pete Sangster there, please? He is? Oh, terrific. Tell him it's Hank Sherman, will you, please? Thanks. I'll hold.' He looked across at Venus. 'He's there,' he said, rather unnecessarily.

When Pete came to the phone, Hank explained what was needed and asked if he and Rodney could get it together and organize the robot, or whether they needed any extra help. Pete went off to consult with Rodney, who then came to the phone and spoke to Venus, after which she reported that the two felt competent to produce the correctly programmed robot. They anticipated bringing it up to Jenny's address in about an hour's time, give or take.

That hour passed pleasantly. Jenny introduced Venus individually to all of her girls and told each of them a cover story that she and Venus had agreed beforehand, namely, that Venus was a film producer who was researching a story for a projected film, and that her scriptwriter had asked if she could spend an evening as a prostitute, in a brothel, in order to enable her to write true-to-life, believable dialogue. Any custom that the girl might take away from the brothel's regulars would be reimbursed, with a generous commission added. Jenny asked that the girls treat the newcomer as one of them, and act accordingly. Not surprisingly, the girls were more than happy to oblige.

To Venus's surprise, the girls were not only all extremely attractive, which was to be expected, but they also all appeared to be well educated, well bred and well spoken. They were dressed rather revealingly, but then what they were revealing was exactly what the customers of a brothel had come to buy. It was but window-dressing. They were all very young. Aged between about eighteen and twenty-five, Venus guessed. She wondered if they enjoyed their work, or if it was simply a means to an end. She felt, probably correctly, that it would have been extremely gauche to have asked any of them that particular question.

Voluptuous Venus

All of the girls seemed to know Hank, and Venus wondered again if he actually fucked them or just knew them because he brought some of his customers here. But after listening to his conversation with the girls, it suddenly became apparent to her that a number of them had starred in his blue movies. Obvious, when you thought about it, but it still didn't answer her question.

And then, finally, the robot arrived. Rodney had called fifteen minutes earlier to say that they were about to put her into a cab, and that her name was Angela. When she arrived, Jenny went out to meet her in the hall, so that she could bring her into the bar and introduce her around.

Jenny admitted later that she knew she had lost her bet the moment that Angela had walked through the apartment door. She was an absolutely standard basic Aphrodite female robot, but from the range newly and specially designed for the proposed rental business.

She had red hair, cut short in a currently fashionable style. She was overtly sexually attractive, with slightly larger breasts than the earlier standard range basic models, and she was intentionally dressed provocatively. She wore a skirt that, some 120 or so years ago, back in the so-called Swinging Sixties, had prompted the description 'pussy pelmet'. It came almost to the top of her thighs. Her top revealed almost as much of her ample breasts as did Trudi's. She had slightly longer legs than the other basic models, and her lips were fuller, her mouth poutier.

As Jenny introduced Angela around the room, Hank couldn't believe his eyes. 'Jesus,' he said to Venus. 'No one's going to fuck that thing before me. Excuse me. I'm just going over to tell Jenny that, before someone else gets there ahead of me.' He almost ran across the room. 'Hi, baby,' he said, with undue haste, as Jenny made the introduction. 'Let's get down to business, shall we?' He took Angela by the hand and led her away, out of the bar.

'Well,' said Jenny, inadvertently answering the question that Venus had been asking herself all evening. 'We all know Hank likes to get his rocks off, particularly whenever we take on a new girl, but I've never seen him move quite as quickly as *that* before.' As she spoke, one of the other men in the bar came over to talk to Jenny. (The original three men at the bar had disappeared, over a period of time, with various of the brothel's girls, but four more had arrived to take their places.) The upshot of his conversation was that he wanted to know in what specific sexual activities the new girl Angela specialized.

'The strange thing about Angela,' Jenny told her punter, 'is that she "specializes" in absolutely everything. She will do anything for you that you wish, with both skill and enthusiasm. But she doesn't actually specialize, as such, in anything. It's unusual, but that's what she's about. And she comes highly recommended.'

'Do you really mean *anything*?' the man asked. 'I mean, for the sake of the conversation, will she let me spank her? Tie her up and humiliate her? That sort of thing? Bondage and discipline?'

'She most certainly will,' said Jenny. 'And she'll love every minute of it.'

'Christ, I'm next,' said the man. 'Put me down for three

hours, will you? Shit,' he muttered to himself as he walked to the bar. 'Suddenly it's Christmas. And I'm Jewish.'

Down the corridor, in one of the brothel's large, comfortably furnished bedrooms, Hank was watching Angela undress. He still couldn't believe that this gorgeous creature standing before him, stripped down to the sexiest undies that he had seen for a very long time, was actually a machine. A product of plastics and cybergenics, and not a flesh-and-blood human being. He got up off the chair he had been sitting on, and went and stood in front of her. He put his hand between her legs, and felt her pussy through her silken knickers. She squirmed as he did so.

'Do you like that?' he asked her.

'I love it,' she answered. 'I love having my pussy felt. It makes it all wet, and ready for you.'

'Do you like to fuck?' he asked. He wasn't just into getting his rocks off. Or even into just talking dirty. He wanted to see and hear and – most of all – feel what his customers would get for their money, if he took on this sex-robot rental franchise.

'I adore to fuck,' Angela said. 'You can fuck me anywhere and everywhere. You can fuck my mouth, if that's what you would like.' She pouted her lips in the most unsubtle, sexually explicit manner, and made lascivious, extremely sexual, gobbling noises. She licked her lips. 'I'll deep-throat you, too, if you wish. Or you can fuck me anally, if that turns you on. I love it up my arse.'

Hank smiled to himself, enjoying his growing erection. He'd have to remember to get these Brits to alter the girl's pronunciation of *arse* – such a very British word – to the

American *ass*. *Arse or ass*, he thought, *what the hell. Who cares what she calls it, as long as it's available.*

'Drop your panties now, honey,' he told her. 'Let's get down to the action.'

'My pleasure,' she told him and, bending down, she slipped her knickers down her long legs and stepped out of them. Then she put her hands behind her back, undid her brassiere – a token, completely unnecessary, sexy little bra – and took it off. She fingered her nipples as she stood there and looked at him looking at her. Her nipples rapidly grew beneath her fingers, and became rigid. She really had a fantastic body.

Hank reached out and felt her breasts and nipples. He was, mostly, curious to see how real it all felt. It could have been real flesh. It was fantastic.

'What would you like me to do now?' she asked him, her voice a low, throaty, completely sexual invitation. 'Would you like me to suck your cock for a while? I can suck it until you're ready to do something to me with it. Put it up one of my three waiting holes. They're all warm and wet. And very willing. Or I can suck you off. All the way. I love to swallow men's come. Which would you prefer?'

'I think I'd like you to suck my cock, baby, since you ask,' he told her. 'But first, come here and let me have a look at your pussy.' He sat down on the edge of the king-size bed.

Angela walked over to him, stood in front of him, and spread her legs apart. Her pubic hair was red, as it should have been. It was long, soft, and wispy.

Voluptuous Venus

Hank knew that the models came with a variety of choice in the pubic hair department, from short, minimal hair, to long, flowing, hirsute hair, or tightly curled hair. Or they could be clean-shaven. He could also see that Angela's labia were slightly larger than average, and he remembered that they too came in a wide range, from hardly discernible labia to long, fat, fleshy pendulous lips.

Angela put her hands down to her pussy and pulled her outer labia wide apart. 'Would you like to see inside my cunt?' she asked. 'I know it excites some men to look up a girl's cunt. Mine's all wet, as you can see. My juices are running down my thighs. That's because you've got me all excited, and I'm wanting to fuck. But there's no hurry.'

She was very wet, as she had said. Inside, she was a deep, glistening pink, shading to a much darker pink the further in you looked. She pushed a finger deeply into her pussy, and wriggled it around. 'Ooh, naughty,' she said. She giggled. 'But nice.' She pulled her finger out. It was wet and sticky with her emanations. 'Would you like to taste my pussy?' she asked, holding her finger out.

Hank took her wrist and brought her finger to just beneath his nostrils. He sniffed. He could have sworn that she smelt of genuine hot, wet pussy. *Amazing*, he thought. Still holding her wrist, he sucked her finger clean. The taste was as authentic as the scent. It was extraordinary what they could do with chemicals these days. When he'd been a young lad, he and his male contemporaries had always joked that if anyone could produce and bottle the scent and flavour of hot pussy, they would make a fortune. Now they could. And – with luck – it was going to make *him* a fortune. 'Mmmmm,' he said, looking up at Angela. 'Delicious. Really nice. I like it. Now suck my cock, please, baby.'

He was still sitting on the edge of the bed. Angela came and knelt down upon the thick carpet in front of him and slowly unzipped his fly. She put a warm hand inside his trousers and carefully pulled out his erect penis. He was circumcised, and his glans was swollen and purple.

She made three or four slow masturbatory movements with her fingers, and then she leaned forward and licked the head of his cock, very deliberately. Her tongue was warm and wet, and felt exactly like any other girl's tongue felt, as it licked at him. Hank looked down at her and found that her eyes were fixed on his as she licked happily away. Lingeringly. Lovingly. Then, eyes still fixed upon his, she took him unhurriedly into her mouth.

Her lips were soft, and he felt himself swelling even further as his brain registered the glorious sensations that her mouth was producing in his cock. She managed to suck him, to tease his cock with her tongue, and to bob her head slowly up and down the full length of his shaft, all at the same time. Each of these three actions generated intense, increasing sexual pleasure.

Remembering Angela's earlier boast of her deep-throating abilities, Hank took her head between his two hands and, holding it firmly in position, began to fuck her mouth, forcing his cock further and further down her throat, enjoying the tightness of it, the feeling of ductile constriction around his swollen prick. It had to be akin to fucking a young virgin, he thought. How girls managed to

Voluptuous Venus

train themselves to accept an erect, tumescent penis, rammed hard down their throats, without choking, he would never understand. But that wasn't his problem, he thought, as he started to ejaculate his semen down Angela's throat in hot, pulsating, liquid spurts. Her eyes, he noticed, were still fixed upon his. He suddenly realized that in his mind he was thinking of Angela, and treating her, as if she was a real person. *That's it*, he thought, as he enjoyed the final contractions of his orgasm. *That's proof enough. If – with all the sexual experience that I've gotten – I can be lulled into thinking this machine is human, then it has to be a winner. I'll go for it.*

Angela continued to suck him until every last drop of his ejaculate had been extracted, after which she took him gently out of her mouth and stood up. 'Was that good, Hank?' she asked. 'Did the earth move for you?' She was smiling at him.

He chuckled. 'It was good, baby,' he said. 'You give great head. And like they say, one good turn deserves another. So I'm going to suck your pussy for you now. Does that sound good?'

'Anything that you want to do to me sounds good,' she said. 'Where would you like me? On the bed? In that chair? On the floor?'

Hank looked at the possibilities. The easy chair looked like as good a place as any. 'On the chair, I think, honey,' he said. 'Make yourself comfortable. Just lean back, and spread your legs. I'm going to eat you out.'

'Would you like me to wash my pussy first, or do you like sucking very wet pussy?' Angela asked. 'Mine's good and wet right now. It might taste a bit gamey.'

'Leave it as it is,' he told her. 'But what's gamey, for Christ's sake? That's some kind of British word, I guess. What does it mean?'

Angela paused. You could have been forgiven for believing that she was thinking, and in a way she was. It was simply that her microcomputer was processing the answer to an extremely obscure question from rather an obscure file.

'Oh,' she said, finally, 'I guess that's the equivalent of "strongly flavoured". Rich. You know? Like game. Venison. Hare. Grouse. That sort of thing.'

'I must remember that,' Hank said. 'Gamey pussy. Terrific.'

While they had been talking, Angela had settled herself down onto the easy chair. She lay back, her crotch at the front of the seat, and opened her legs. She reached down an idle hand and began to gently masturbate as she waited for Hank to get his act together. Her thighs glistened wetly as she spread them, and as Hank copied Angela's recent actions and knelt between her open legs, he could scent the gamey aroma to which she had referred. He loved it. Cunt. That was the word he would have used. He could smell aroused cunt. Fuck gamey. Goddamn Limey. Cunt was the word.

He reached out his fingers and opened up her fleshy pussy lips. They felt warm, and deliciously sticky. His could feel that his cock was beginning to become erect again. He leaned down and kissed her pussy. At that close range, the scent of her was really strong. His cock began

Voluptuous Venus

to throb. Almost painfully. To Hank, the smell of cunt was the finest aphrodisiac in the world, bar none. He inhaled deeply, and kissed her down there again.

She wriggled her hips. 'Oh, yes,' she whispered, just loud enough for him to hear. 'Nice. I like it. Don't stop. Please don't stop.'

He had to congratulate whoever had put together the conversational program for these robots. They were absolutely spot on. And so he didn't stop. For Angela tasted exactly like a delightful English girl would taste, and she did all the things that delightful English girls did when you sucked their pussies. She lay back, closed her eyes, and talked dirty to you. She told you when she felt that her orgasm was imminent, and then, when it came, she writhed about in the chair and made sexy, throaty little noises that told you that she was enjoying herself. And when you'd finally sucked her off, all the way, so that she could enjoy her final, multiple orgasm, then she did what all delightful English girls do, in that situation, and she said, 'Fuck me now, Hank, darling. Will you? Please? I want you inside me. I want you to fuck me. Now. Please, Hank.'

Fucking her was absolutely no problem whatsoever to Hank, at that particular moment. His cock was so stiff, it hurt. He needed a fuck as badly as Angela claimed that she did. He considered, for just a moment, fucking her up her ass (arse?) but decided that that special experience was probably best left till last, if he had any energy left. He expected that he would.

So he stood up, picked Angela up in his arms, carried her over to the bed, and laid her down. She opened her legs, in the way that all delightful English girls do in those circumstances, and he then proceeded to get what he had heard called in London 'his leg over'. More important, he thought, than getting his leg over, was getting his cock up. Which he did. Instantly. She was running wet, and he slid in, all the way, until his balls were slapping against her buttocks in the approved manner.

Angela crossed her legs behind his back, pulling him to her and thrusting her groin hard up against his. She then put up her hands, one each side of his face, and pulled his mouth down to hers. She kissed him passionately as he fucked her, exploring his mouth with her tongue. Despite his recent and excessive efforts, he soon felt his ejaculation gathering again, and he placed his hands beneath Angela's buttocks. Taking one in each hand, he pulled her up against himself. Her buttocks felt soft, but firm. Muscular, even. But eminently squeezable.

She could feel his ejaculation building. Well, put more accurately, the tiny sensor, skillfully implanted in the wall of her artificial vagina, sensed the increased tension levels transmitted to it by the thrustings of Hank's cock as he neared orgasm. It correctly interpreted this tautening of Hank's internal penile musculature, and the accompanying increase in his blood pressure, and his rise in bodily temperature, and it quite properly alerted the next item in its microprocessed programme.

Quite simply, this triggered the vocal accompaniment by Angela to their carefully timed – on her part, *meticulously* timed – mutual orgasm. 'Oh baby,' she cried. 'I'm almost there. I'm going to come. You're fucking me,

Voluptuous Venus

and you're making me come. I'm going to come now. NOW. I'm COMING NOW. Oh, God. OH JESUS. OH FUCK. OOOOHHHhhhh ... DARLING. OH YES. Oh, yes. Yes. Yeeeesss.' *Oh shit*, Hank thought, as he shot his load once more, this time into the robot's receptive vagina. *This thing is too much. I wonder if it will marry me.* He thrust as hard up into her as he could, and allowed the machine's vaginal muscles to milk his penis of the last few remaining drops of his ejaculate. *Jesus H. Christ*, he thought. He pulled out of her and she rolled over and, taking his now almost flaccid penis in her hand, she guided it into her mouth, where she gently sucked and licked it, until it was as clean and fresh as if he had just got out of the shower. But it was a lot more fun.

'OK, Hank?' she asked him. 'Was that good? Am I a great fuck? I had a lovely time. Thank you.'

'It was terrific, baby,' he told her. 'It was too much.' He turned towards her and kissed her mouth. 'And you're too much. Will you marry me, sweetheart?'

There was a pause, then an audible click, and Angela spoke to him in a quite different tone of voice to that she had been using up to now. 'I'm sorry, Hank,' she said. 'But I'm afraid that what you are suggesting is completely and totally against the contractual agreement between yourself and Aphrodite PLC, which you signed before you began the period of the agreement.'

And then her voice returned to the throaty, sexy voice to which he had, that evening, so happily become accustomed. 'But if there is any kind of sexual service or pleasure that I can perform for you, or allow you to do to me, then you only have to tell me, and I will do it. Or help you to do it to me. Please tell me what you would like.'

He didn't answer, amazed at the reply to what had been, in fact, a joke. These Brits certainly took themselves and their project seriously, he thought. And probably rightly so, upon reflection.

After a minute or two, Hank not having replied to Angela's last query about his next required sexual act, she spoke once more. 'An examination of the manual which was supplied with me when you completed your rental agreement will inform you of the complete range of sexual acts that I am programmed to perform. Over and above the basic range, it will depend upon which selection of additional microchip programs you rented with me. If you are in any doubt, or if you find that you require an act that is not listed in the information which you have, please telephone your Aphrodite rental outlet immediately, where your request will be dealt with. All Aphrodite rental outlets maintain a twenty-four-hour service facility. A courier service is available to deliver urgently required programs. Your personal agreement number, which you will need to supply, is on the first page of your rental agreement, where you will also find the telephone number of your nearest dealer. Until you make your next request, I am going into off-duty mode to prolong my battery life. All you have to do to reactivate me is to speak to me. Goodbye now.'

Angela lay back on the bed, closed her pretty blue eyes and switched herself off. At that point, Hank thought that he would call it a day. It had been a fantastic experience, and one that had convinced him that he should go ahead

Voluptuous Venus

and tie up a deal with this Aphrodite company as quickly as possible. Put at its most basic, the robot was a better fuck than most women. He went into the adjoining bathroom and showered. He dressed quickly and found his way back to the bar. Venus was waiting for him.

'So what do you think?' she asked.

'Words fail me,' Hank said. 'I need a drink. No, not another glass of champagne,' he said, as Jenny made as if to pour him one. 'I'd like a large Scotch, please. On the rocks.' Trudi went off to get him one.

Both women looked at him. 'She's unbelievable,' he said.

'You mean *it's* unbelievable,' Jenny said.

'No, you're wrong,' Hank said. 'What I mean is *she's* unbelievable. She's incredible. She's not only completely indistinguishable from the real thing, she's *better* than the real thing. She's beautiful, she's more goddamn sexy than any woman I've ever been to bed with, and she's inexhaustible.' He grinned at Venus and Jenny. 'And she's *dirty*,' he said. 'Real *dirty*. I loved every minute of it.'

'Well, I've lost my bet, that's for sure,' Jenny said. She went off to the bar and came back a few minutes later with a bottle of Dom Perignon. 'Will you drink it here, with us, or would you rather take it home with you?' she asked Venus. 'It's your choice. There's no pressure, either way. You won it fair and square.'

'I'll drink it here, with you, if I may,' Venus said. 'But hang on a sec. I've just thought of something. Has that man who wanted to know if Angela was into S&M joined her yet?'

Jenny looked over at the bar. 'No. He's still at the bar. Why do you ask?'

'Oh, nothing really. It's just a straightforward matter of hygiene. Come with me, will you, Jenny, and I'll show you how to switch Angela onto her self-cleaning mode. Just in case you ever decide to buy an Aphrodite robot.'

Jenny laughed. 'Well, from what Hank says, that's probably exactly what I should be doing. But somehow, I still don't see these things taking over from real, live, pretty young girls. In fact, I have to say, it was good of you to refuse to take my money, when I suggested a real bet, because I would have bet thousands of dollars against you. I had no idea these things were so good. But I'd love to come and see you do your thing with her.'

That'll be the day, thought Venus. *You should watch me doing my thing with anyone. Chance would be a fine thing.* But she said it to herself. Aloud she said, 'It's really not difficult, Jenny. Once you get used to it. It's all very logical, really.'

When they got to the bedroom Hank and Angela had been using, Angela was lying on the bed, on her back, and switched off, as Hank had left her. Jenny just couldn't keep her hands off her, touching and feeling her all over. Especially her breasts and nipples, and then exploring between her legs with her fingers. She even finally kissed her on the mouth.

'I just don't believe it,' she said, eventually. 'Like Hank said, she's too much. It's so real, it's not real, if you know what I mean. I guess that these things really *could* put me out of business.'

Voluptuous Venus

'Oh, no. Not really, Jenny,' Venus said. 'I mean, there will always be men who want the real thing. Yes, of course, we'll find a market with our robots. A huge market. But there will always be a market for real live women. What you're saying is tantamount to suggesting that there won't be a need for women any more, and that's just plain ridiculous, if you think about it. You're not seriously suggesting that men will stop marrying women, stop living with women, stop *fucking* women, are you?'

Jenny took a deep breath. 'Well, it has to be a possibility. After all, what's the motivation for men and women to live together? I mean, at the beginning? It's sex, isn't it? Some women kid themselves that what they feel when they are fucking is called love, but that's just a prettier name for fucking, really. If a man doesn't need a woman to fuck, or one to suck his cock – not to mention cook his meals, keep his apartment clean, do the shopping, and attend to his laundry – why get lumbered with the financial responsibility? Or even part of the financial responsibility? If he can ring up a rental company and have Angie here delivered, waiting to drop her hot knickers the moment she's through the door, why put up with a real woman, who's going to have headaches when he wants to screw her? Who'll get her period once a month, every month. And who either refuses to suck his cock, on the grounds that it's dirty – not to mention perverted – or who won't take it up her ass, for whatever reason. I mean, think about it. With these things on the loose, who'll need real women?'

Venus was about to say something, but Jenny held up a

hand. 'Hang in there a minute. I haven't finished yet.

'Now take Hank. He's the perfect example of exactly what I'm talking about. He's not married, and he doesn't shack up with anyone. Well, not for longer than a day or two. Why? Simple. Remember two things; he's so goddamn rich, he can buy any girl he wants. I don't mean literally, but with gourmet meals in smart restaurants, exotic holidays, expensive presents, flash automobiles. That sort of thing. And of course he can afford my prices, if he wants to get his rocks off without any of that kind of hassle. And the other thing is that in the business he's in, he spends all his working life amongst girls who earn their living by fucking. By performing every sexual act you can think of. If you think *my* girls are professional, Jesus, what would you call those girls who star in Hank's porno movies? *Actresses?*

'But what does Hank do, the first time he meets Angie here? He fucks his brains out with her. Not only that. He actually says she's the best fuck he's ever had. And he *knows* she's a bloody machine.' Jenny sighed a big sigh. 'Now think about it. Are these things going to do away with the need for women, or are they not? Baby, the way I see it, our days are numbered.

'If you're rich, like Hank, you don't even have to rent, although the variety that is available that way has to be a tremendous attraction. But he can buy, if he wants to. One cash payment, and she's his for life. Have her serviced regularly.' Jenny looked at Venus, and raised her eyebrows. 'How often?'

'Oh, every three months. That's about it,' Venus replied.

Voluptuous Venus

'OK, every three months. And she'll service *him* all day and all night. Every day and night. Then he can trade her in for a new model, any time he likes. No hassle. No legal costs. No maintenance. No angst. It's all so simple.'

Venus sat down on the edge of the bed and began to roll Angela over onto her stomach, in order to get at her control panel. 'Well, I hear what you're saying, Jenny,' she said. 'But what about the other things you mentioned? What about the cooking, the cleaning, the laundry, the shopping? All that sort of stuff? Angela can't do that for him, can she? Seriously.'

'No, you're right. She can't. But you can buy all those services in. And reasonably cheaply. You can buy cooks. Daily. Weekly. Monthly. Hourly, if you want to. Or you can have food delivered. The same with cleaners. No problem. Supermarkets deliver. Stores deliver. There are shopping services. People who will actually go out with your shopping list and bring the stuff back. Laundries deliver. All you need is money, which Hank isn't short of, anyway. And think of the savings any man who lives with a woman would make if he *didn't* live with a woman. All he'd have, instead, would simply be the initial purchase price, and the maintenance costs of a robot. Half the basic overheads. Food. Booze. Clothes. Restaurants. Unless of course he actually wanted to invite someone out to a meal. But that's a matter of choice. There's no real compulsion. No female doctor's bills. No gynaecologist's birth control costs. No tampons, or panty-liners. And, dear God, I've just thought of something else! Anyone actually *owning* one of these robots could probably make a profit by renting it out themselves. Jesus. Just think about that.'

Venus had the control panel open now, and she beckoned to Jenny to come over and have a look. 'Sure. I hear you. I hear you. But come and have a look at this, Jenny,' she said.

Jenny walked around the bed and leant down to look at the control panel.

'This is what makes her tick,' Venus said.

'Fuck is probably a better word,' said Jenny.

'Well, that too,' Venus agreed. 'First of all, this red knob here. You see it?'

'Yes,' said Jenny.

'You can see that it has three positions, if you look. One is off. That's where it is now. Two is on. And three is the self-cleaning mode.' Venus switched the robot's switch from one to three, without pausing in the middle. Immediately, the robot began to both hum and vibrate. Venus kept the controls open.

'It's very complicated, technologically, but the actual effect is quite simple,' Venus said. 'The robot's mouth, vagina, and anus are electronically cleaned and sterilized. It takes about seven minutes. We originated and developed the system, and we've actually sold it to the medical profession. Every hospital of any size, all around the world, now uses the same basic system. And an increasing number of private surgeries are installing it. It saves an enormous amount of time, and therefore money. And it's foolproof. No more lethal infections closing down hospitals' operating theatres. No more patients dying from the uncontrolled spread of resistant bacteria. This next unit here is where you plug in the microchip program module. This one is our top of the range, she'll-do-anything-and-everything sexual module. It's far too expensive for what it does, really. It comes from the earlier individual made-to-measure model range. Anyone renting can't actually rent this particular module. They'd have to rent it in a number of different sections. Intentionally so. It's all part of the marketing programme, and it has to do with bottom-line profitability. We put it into Angela here simply in order to save time in demonstrating the robots' abilities to Hank.'

'Mmmm,' Jenny said. 'Interesting. And what's that similar-looking unit right next to the sex program module?'

'That's the language and vocabulary module,' Venus told her. 'We obviously have to program these robots in all of the various languages for the countries in which we sell them. Added to which, the standard models come with an extensive sexual vocabulary, but with a fairly limited conversational vocabulary. If you ask Angela, when she's switched on, how she is, she'll tell you. Ask her absolutely anything you like about sex, and she's programmed to more than cope. But ask her who she thinks will win the next presidential election and she won't be able to reply. Which is fair enough. People don't buy these – and won't rent these – to have intense political conversations with them. But if you want to talk dirty, they come fully equipped!'

'Tell me,' Jenny said. 'I've been meaning to ask you, ever since you arrived earlier on. You *do* make *male* robots too, don't you?'

Eva Linczy

'We most certainly do,' Venus said. 'And they're very well equipped, too.' She laughed. 'What I mean is, they have lovely big cocks.'

Jenny laughed. 'Oh, great,' she said. 'Tell me all about them.'

'Well, they're terrific,' Venus said. 'Take it from me. One of the things that keeps my pussy muscles in good trim is the fact that I'm in charge of all product testing.'

'What exactly does that mean?' Jenny asked, curiously.

'It means a number of things,' Venus told her. 'First of all, all of our models – male and female – are based on real live human beings. Angela's tits here, for example, are an exact reproduction of those from a woman who posed, if you like, for the cast from which the plastic tits are finally made.' Venus put out a hand, and stroked Angela's nipples. 'Her breasts come from one woman, her areolae from a second, and her nipples here from a third.

'Similarly, her pussy is concocted from three different women, one of each of whom contributed her outer labia, one her inner labia, and the other her actual pussy. You see what I mean?' Jenny nodded. Venus continued. 'All the models, of both sexes, are made up in this way. Well, now, the first step in the process is for me to approve – or not – the selection of the real people who have originally been selected by a committee as possible models. With the men that means, if the man is selected for his cock, that I have to see if I believe that it is suitable for our purposes. And of course, I have to see if his cock is properly functional. And the best way to do that is to test it. Isn't it?' she asked, her eyes laughing at Jenny as she put the question.

Voluptuous Venus

'I guess so,' Jenny agreed.

'Good. So that means that – but only if I feel that it is necessary, of course – that means that I can suck it. Jack it off. Have it fuck me. Do absolutely anything I like with it, actually. It keeps me in very good shape.'

'Wow,' Jenny said. 'What a fantastic job. What else?'

'Well, the next stage for me is to test the finished product,' Venus said. 'I do a lot of that during working hours, of course. But, naturally enough, it also often involves taking the products home with me and testing them in private. After which, when I've put in my report, the models are mine to keep. There *is* in fact a second-hand market in Aphrodite models, but prior to the launch of this new rental business, that was something which we actively discouraged. Now, I guess it doesn't make much difference to us. It would be difficult to go on objecting, if you think about it.'

'Oh, sure,' Jenny said. 'But tell me the horny details. I mean, I assume that the male robots are as lifelike as Angela here? And that their cocks look and feel . . .' She paused. 'And taste and smell like *real* cocks?' she finished.

'Absolutely,' Venus told her. 'They're perfect. They never lose their erection too soon. And they always get stiff again, immediately after they've just fucked you. That's if you want them to,' she giggled. 'I always do.'

'And do they spunk when they come?' Jenny asked.

'They most certainly do,' Venus replied. 'You can buy different programs that control the exact amount of semen that they ejaculate. If you like swallowing come, like I do, there's a module made especially for you. The robots also heat it up to proper body temperature, so that you don't get a nasty cold shock in your pussy when they come. Or anywhere else, for that matter,' Venus said. She giggled again.

'Oh, come on,' Jenny said. 'You're not going to tell me that you have a robot do you up your ass.'

'I most certainly am,' Venus said. 'Why not? I love it up my arse. And I can't emphasize too much to you that these robots not only feel like the real thing, like Hank said, they're *better* than the real thing. It's your argument in reverse. With one of these' – she paused – 'actually, I've got five of them at home. Both white *and* black. But whether you've got one or five, with one of these, who needs men? These always get a hard-on, and can hold it forever. They can – and will – fuck you all night. There are tremendous foreplay programs. They'll wind you up until you're screaming for a cock in your pussy, if that's what turns you on. They'll perform the most expert cunnilingus you've ever experienced. They'll fuck you slowly. Quickly. Repeatedly. Gently. Roughly. They'll beat the shit out of you, if you want them to. Suck their cocks, and they come in your mouth. They'll tie you up and rape you. Vaginally. Orally. Anally. They'll wank you until you beg them to stop. They'll spend hours just kissing you. So who needs men?'

'But you're agreeing with me, darling,' Jenny said. 'That's exactly what I've been saying to you, this past half-hour, except that I've been saying that Angie here will replace us women, and now you're saying that these male robots will replace men.'

'Aha,' said Venus. 'Actually, no. What I'm saying is that

Voluptuous Venus

these are wonderful inventions, and every normal, hot-blooded girl should have at least one. But what I'm most particularly *not* saying is that they'll ever replace men. I'd throw away my robots and cross the Sahara desert on foot to get laid by a real man, if that was what I had to do. These things are a convenience. That's all. A sex toy. A substitute. Give me a real man, any day. A robot isn't anything more than masturbation, not really. Good-quality masturbation, but masturbation for all that. Make no mistake.'

'Oh, come on. You say that,' Jenny countered, 'but you've just been telling me what lovely big cocks these male robots have, and how they can stay hard for ever. You even said how much you like fellating them, and swallowing their semen. Now you're trying to tell me that they're just like jacking off. I guess the only way I'm ever going to know is to have one to play with. Can you arrange that for me?'

'Of course I can,' Venus said. 'My pleasure. Where do you want to play with it? Here? Or shall I have one delivered to my hotel suite for you to come there and use it? That might be the best idea, so that I can show you how it works.'

'Yes, terrific. I'll do that. Thank you,' Jenny said. 'It would be useless having it delivered here. For all that my girls spend their time getting laid, they're always complaining that they seldom get a decent fuck. They'd probably wear one of your robots out in a week, fucking themselves silly.'

Venus laughed. She looked at Angela, who had

completed her hygiene cycle some time previously. 'I guess your next customer is waiting to get his rocks off with our friend here,' she said. 'I'll stand her up, switch her on, and turn her to her getting-dressed mode, and then I'll set her up for her full sexual program. After that, we'd better get out of here.' She was turning dials and switching switches as she spoke.

Angela stood up and went over to her clothes, and began dressing. While they were waiting, Venus said, 'How does tomorrow afternoon suit you, to come over to the hotel? I can't manage the morning, because I'm going with Hank to watch his production company shooting a film. I was originally going to demonstrate Angela here for him tomorrow afternoon, but I think this evening's events have dispensed with the need for that. I think Hank's probably made his mind up already. But we can sort that out with him in a minute.'

Angela was fully dressed now. Venus went behind her, and made the necessary final adjustments. 'Have fun,' she said to Angela.

'Thank you,' Angela said. 'I'll do my best.' The two women left her standing there, looking cute.

When they got back to the bar, Jenny left Venus with Hank while she told her customer that Angela was ready and waiting for him. She then rejoined Hank and Venus. Trudi had left them, and gone off with a customer.

'Well, what did you think, honey?' Hank asked Jenny. 'She's too much, isn't she?'

'She is that,' Jenny agreed. 'We've been having a long

Voluptuous Venus

conversation about whether or not she'll put my kind of business out of business, like you suggested when you first told me about Aphrodite. In fact, I went so far as to suggest that these robot women could put us real women out of business. Permanently. But Venus doesn't agree with me on either point. Perhaps more interestingly, though, Venus is arranging for me to get laid by one of her male robots tomorrow afternoon. With your agreement, that is.'

She went on to explain that Venus felt that Hank's exploratory run just now had absolved her from the need to demonstrate the female models the following afternoon.

'Oh, sure,' Hank said. 'As far as I'm concerned, Venus baby, all we have to do now is agree terms and delivery dates. Service arrangements. Contributions to ad campaigns. That sort of thing. I'm sold.' He turned to Jenny. 'And you're more than welcome to investigate the male model tomorrow. In fact, I'd appreciate another opinion, a female one. I know what Venus thinks, and I'd love to know if you agree. I'm sure you will. So feel free. And another thing. I absolutely guarantee you, that when your client comes out of that bedroom, complete with sore ass, or whatever it was he went in for, he'll not have suspected for a moment – not for a fraction of a second – that he's been fucking with a machine. A very sophisticated machine, but it's still a machine.'

Jenny was delighted at his decision, as, of course, was Venus. 'Oh, fantastic, Hank. Thank you,' Jenny said. She turned to Venus. 'Is that agreed, then?' she asked. 'What's a good time for you?'

'Any time you like,' Venus told her.

'Three o'clock, then?' Jenny asked.

'Done,' Venus said. 'He'll be ready and waiting for you.'

'Wow,' said Jenny, laughing. 'I can't remember when I last felt excited at the thought of getting laid.'

They laughed with her. 'Have you got any special requests?' Venus asked. 'Or would you rather tell me those when Hank's not here?'

'Oh, Hank's no problem,' Jenny replied. 'He knows what I like. Simply the largest, stiffest cock you can possibly arrange. And enormous reserves of spunk.' She wriggled her hips. 'God, I'm getting turned on now,' she said. 'My panties are getting quite wet. If it goes on like this, I'll have to go turn a trick or two.'

'You'll just have to be patient,' Venus told her. 'Calm down. Take some deep breaths.'

Hank changed the subject. 'Tell me, Venus,' he said. 'Have Aphrodite done any research on the suggested rental price for this franchise operation? Right now, I haven't given much thought to what the customer is going to pay. I appreciate that it has to be tied in with overall costs and, robot maintenance aside, I've a pretty good idea of what the overheads will be, from running my video rental business. Staffing, rents, insurance, taxes, and so on. But I can't seem to put a figure on actual rental charges.'

'Not a lot,' Venus admitted. 'But deliberately so. We thought that we'd tell every franchisee what our charges to him would be, in terms of up-front money, and what percentage of his profits we would expect, and then let him decide what the market would bear in his area. In percentage terms, surely, it's got to be fairly close to your video rental mark-up? One of the things that you need to decide – and we are intentionally leaving this decision to all proposed individual franchisees – is the actual rental period. Is it twenty-four hours? Three days? A week? That obviously very much affects the rental cost.

'I appreciate that you will decide a basic rental period, and that extended rentals will be on a declining scale, so that the longer the period, the cheaper the cost per day. Or per hour. But we think that only you can decide that cost. As far as we are concerned, back in Britain, we have decided firmly that we will take a credit card reference against the full retail value of the robot. Only to be used if the robot is damaged, or lost, or anything like that. And then, of course, we'll check out credit card references thoroughly, before they are accepted in the first place. But at the time that I left to come over here, we hadn't reached a decision in the UK (where we're keeping the whole country as our own franchise) as to basic rental charges.'

She looked at Jenny. 'Talk to Jenny here. There has to be a comparison, doesn't there, between the cost of using a top quality, high class place like this, and the cost of renting an Aphrodite robot? I mean, I know they're different markets, and different products, but there has to be some kind of a relationship, in cost terms? What do you think, Jenny?'

'To be perfectly honest with you, Venus, I just don't know what the hell to think,' Jenny said. 'I'm all shook up. These sex robots have turned my little world upside down.

I think that Hank's doing exactly the right thing, in bidding to take over the entire US franchise for Aphrodite. They sure as hell won't do his video rental business any good. But mine is such a tiny business.'

Hank snorted. 'Tiny, bullshit,' he said. 'I wouldn't mind your annual turnover, against what this operation costs you to run. You don't pay the girls. The customers do. So there's no staff overhead. Well, unless you count a couple of cleaners. I suppose that your linen, and your laundry bills, are fairly high. But that's peanuts, really. Isn't it?' Jenny nodded. Hank went on. 'I don't know if you're paying off the front-of-house staff downstairs. I suspect that you are. But that's tiny, compared with what you're making. You're probably paying some tax, but I'd guarantee that you're only declaring a fraction of your real profits. You sell your booze reasonably, but you're still making a healthy profit on it. And I doubt you've got a New York State liquor licence. Have you?'

Jenny grinned at him. 'You don't expect me to answer that question, Hank, do you? But I'll answer it if you tell me how much cash *your* organization takes in a week, and what percentage of *that* you actually declare.'

Hank grinned back. 'No way, sweetheart,' he said. 'But you take my point about your "tiny" business, don't you?'

'Sure I do,' Jenny said. 'Sure I do.'

Hank looked at his watch. 'I guess I ought to be on my way. I've got an early start tomorrow.' He looked at Venus. '*We've* got an early start tomorrow, baby. If you still want to visit my movie set. I'll pick you up at the entrance to the Plaza at seven. OK? And I'll drop you back there on my

Voluptuous Venus

way now, if you like. If that's where you're going.'

'Yes, and yes, and yes,' Venus said. 'Yes to all three. Thank you. I'm looking forward to seeing the film set, and seven o'clock is fine. I'll be waiting. And yes, I'd much appreciate a lift back to the hotel. Thanks.' She turned to talk to Jenny. 'Great to meet you, Jenny. Thank you for all your kind hospitality. I love your place here. If I ever need a job, I know where to come.' Jenny laughed with her. 'But seriously, I much look forward to seeing you at the Plaza tomorrow at three. I'll have some Dom Perignon on ice. And a *very* attractive young man. Don't forget to wear your prettiest knickers.' Jenny looked at her, a bit vaguely, and Venus suddenly realized. 'Sorry, darling. Panties. Wear your prettiest panties.' She leaned over, and kissed Jenny on the cheek. 'Until tomorrow, darling,' Jenny said. 'I'll see you then. Goodbye now.'

The long-suffering limo driver was waiting outside, and he leapt out and opened the car doors as Hank and Venus came out of Jenny's apartment block. They chattered animatedly together, all the way back uptown, with Hank pointing out buildings of interest that they passed, until the driver pulled up outside the Plaza. Hank got out, and they kissed goodnight. 'I'll see you in the morning, baby,' Hank said. 'Goodnight now.'

Venus stood and watched the limo turn northwards, and then left onto Central Park South. She wondered where Hank lived. Then she turned, and slowly walked up the steps to the Plaza foyer.

CHAPTER SEVEN

In Camera

The film was being shot in what had originally been one of the old 1970s homosexual bath-houses, down on the Lower West Side of Manhattan. On the way down there, in the now customary limo, Hank was telling Venus about those early days. He had apparently made a study of them.

The bath-houses, on the surface places offering Turkish baths, showers, massage and jacuzzis, were in fact places where gay men had met for homosexual sex. Had she ever heard of Bette Midler, he asked her? Or Barry Manilow? She hadn't, and said so. 'Well, it is pushing a hundred years ago,' Hank told her. 'But you can still buy their records, you know.'

Hank went on to explain that Bette Midler was a famous star of the 1970s and 1980s who had started out as a singer in the original bath-house for which they were now headed. She had always had a gay following, and had progressed from there to become a comedienne, and then a world-famous film star. Her pianist in those early days, apparently, was a certain Barry Manilow, who had himself eventually become internationally famous as a singer and recording artist.

Like many of the old warehouses and factories in that part of New York, this particular building had been converted, in the early 1990s, into luxurious, spacious and extremely expensive apartments. Hank's film production company was renting one of these apartments from its owners at, he said, an incredibly expensive rental, for a two-week period, within which time he expected to complete the blue video that he was shooting there. The cast and technicians would have been there since six a.m., he told her, looking at his watch. It was just after seven-fifteen. By the time they got there and parked, Hank said, shooting should have begun. Had Venus ever seen one of his video productions, apart from the couple of in-flight movies she'd watched during her trip to New York, he asked?

'No,' she said. She was sorry, but she had to admit that she hadn't.

'Well, I don't know what you're expecting, but I ought to tell you that they're pretty strong stuff,' Hank said. 'Years ago, they would have been illegal. What they called hard-core pornography. You could go to prison for it. These days it's all perfectly above board, of course. But it wasn't always.' He paused for a moment or two.

And then, 'Tell me, do you like sex, Venus?' he asked. 'I mean, are you *really* into it? I know it's your job, in a way, as it is mine. But leaving that aside, do you actually genuinely like it, if you don't mind my asking?'

Voluptuous Venus

'I don't mind you asking in the least bit, Hank,' she said. 'And I love it. All of it. Fucking. Sucking. You name it, I enjoy it. OK?'

'Oh, very definitely OK, baby,' he said. 'Maybe you and I should get together, later on. Know what I mean?'

She looked at him, and grinned salaciously. 'I know exactly what you mean,' she said. 'Are you a good fuck? And have you got a big cock?'

He looked sideways at her. 'Like you said last night, honey,' he said. 'Yes. And yes. I'm a terrific fuck. And I've never had a complaint about the size of my cock. Mind you, baby,' he continued, 'I can't compete in cock size with the guys you're going to be seeing down on the film set. But they're professionals. I'm just a competent amateur. But I have brought tears to some girls' eyes, I'm pleased to be able to tell you.'

Venus laughed. 'Maybe you should join Jenny and the male robot and me, this afternoon,' she suggested. 'The four of us could have some fun together, if that's what you're looking for. And you could see the male robot for yourself, at the same time. Does that appeal? What do you say, Hank?'

'Sounds terrific,' Hank said. 'Let's do that. OK?'

'OK,' Venus agreed.

They finally arrived at the apartment block where the film was being shot. The driver let them out and drove off to the car park underneath the building. They entered the foyer, a huge glass atrium, and Hank checked in with the front desk. The block's hall porters obviously recognized him, and in moments they were on their way up to the penthouse in one of the building's elevators. The apartment, looking out over the Hudson River, was enormous, and the crew and all their equipment seemed small against the spectacular size of the room in which they were shooting. The director came over and greeted them.

Hank introduced Venus, and the director explained that they had spent some time setting up and were now just about ready to shoot. In the scene that had been prepared, the two attractive young women who could be seen relaxing, fully dressed, on a sofa at the other end of the room and who, in the film, were playing the wife of the owner of the apartment and her woman friend, would be surprised by a group of three burglars who had broken into the apartment. The burglars would then overpower the women and sexually abuse them. The director led Hank and Venus to two upright seats, just behind the two cameras, set up for this shot.

'OK, guys and dolls,' shouted the director. 'Lights. Camera. And action.' The two women were standing, talking, by the long windows that overlooked the terrace that ran all along that side of the apartment. As they conversed, a door in shot burst open, and three men ran into the room. All three were carrying hand guns. The two women screamed. The first man into the room hesitated for just a moment, and then he pointed his gun at the two women. 'Stand quite still, and stay alive,' he said. The other two men caught him up, and they too pointed their guns at the women. 'Just looka here,' said one of them, in a strong Brooklyn accent. 'Please don't hurt us,' said the wife. 'You can take anything you want, but please don't hurt us.' The two women clasped their arms about each other. 'OK,' said the first man, holding out his gun to one of his fellow thieves, 'take a holda this. I'll go first. It's your turn next.'

The second man took the gun and, holding one in each hand, he trained them both on the two women. The first man unbuckled his belt, unzipped his fly, dropped his trousers, and stepped out of them. He pulled down his jockey shorts, exposing an enormous cock which was semi-erect. He pointed at the wife. 'OK, baby,' he said. 'You. Come here.' The wife looked frightened, and didn't move. The man with the two guns prodded her in the stomach with one of them. 'Move, baby,' he said. The woman slowly moved closer to the man who had taken his trousers off.

'Kneel down,' the trouserless man said. The woman shrank away. 'Oh, please. Not that,' she said. The man stepped over to her, took hold of her by her hair, and slapped her face hard, twice. The woman began to cry. Still holding her by her hair, the man forced her down onto her knees. 'Now suck my cock,' he said. 'If you want to stay alive.' The woman took his cock in her hand, and then in her mouth, and started to suck him off. Her crying died away as she began to concentrate on what she was doing. As she fellated the first man, the third man was stripping off his trousers and underpants. He said to the man with the two guns, 'You keep them both covered. Then I'll cover whichever one you want, while you have a go.' Naked now from the waist down, his penis seemingly fully erect, he began to tear the clothes off the second woman. He quickly had her stripped down to her lingerie, which was brief, transparent, and black. The woman had good breasts, and lovely long legs. Her pubis could clearly be seen beneath her tiny knickers and was clean-shaven. The man tore her bra off, followed by her black tights and then her knickers. The woman was screaming and crying all the time that she was being stripped, and when he had her naked, the man slapped her around her face a number of times. 'Shut up, for God's sake,' he said. She stopped screaming, but made a low, snivelling noise. Then, 'Bend over,' he said. 'I'm going to fuck your ass.'

'And cut,' said the director, striding over to the actors. 'Well done. That was good.' He turned to the man who was, until the director had stopped the action, being fellated. 'Now we'll do the close-ups and the come shot, Harry,' he said to the man. He patted the girl on the head. 'All right, Carol, darling?' he enquired. 'Sure, honey,' the woman said. 'He's ready for it.'

The director turned to the others. 'OK, guys,' he said. 'Take five, will you? We'll finish off the oral shots with Harry and Carol here, and then we'll continue with you three after that. OK?' The other three agreed that it was, indeed, OK with them.

The camera crew spent a little time refocusing one of the cameras for the close-up shots of Harry and Carol, and the lighting man adjusted his lighting until he was happy. Eventually, everyone declared themselves happy, and the director called out, 'Two minutes,' at which cry a pretty young girl who had been sitting beside the script girl got up and went over to Harry and said, 'What'll it be,

Harry?' Harry thought for a moment. Then, 'Talk dirty to me while you jack me off,' he said.

The girl took hold of his almost flaccid penis and began to masturbate him. 'I'd like you to fuck me with this, Harry,' she said, looking him straight in the eye. 'I'd love your huge cock up my tiny, tight little cunt. I'd love to squeeze all the come out of your cock with my wet cunt.' She went on in this vein, and Harry's cock rapidly grew fully erect.

Hank leaned over and whispered in Venus's ear. 'She's called a starter,' he said. 'It's her job to get the men's cocks erect again, after the director has stopped a fuck scene for whatever reason.' He looked at Venus and grinned. 'That one can start me any time she likes,' he said.

Venus looked at the girl who was walking back to her seat, her job done for the moment. She had an angelic little face, sensual lips, and a terrific figure beneath her tight sweater and her short leather skirt. Her ass swung provocatively as she walked. 'And I can see why,' Venus said.

Harry and Carol signalled that they were ready to go, and the director went through his lights, camera, action routine once more. Harry quickly got to the point of ejaculation after he had taken the woman's head in his hands and begun to fuck her mouth. At the vital moment of ejaculation, he withdrew his penis from her mouth and spurted a generous amount of semen all over the woman's face. When he'd finished, the director yelled, 'Cut. Great, guys. Excellent. Got it.' Harry and Carol relaxed, and Carol stood up. 'It's just as well,' Hank said to Venus. 'If there had been any kind of a problem, we'd have had quite a wait, before Harry could do *that* shot again.'

Venus laughed. 'It's extraordinary, isn't it, that people always want to see the man actually ejaculating? I think it would be far more sexually stimulating to see the man, in medium close-up, coming in her throat. And, since this is obviously an oral rape scene, forcing her to swallow his semen. Isn't that far sexier?'

'As far as I'm concerned, I'm with you,' Hank said. 'I think that what you're suggesting is much sexier. But the research still tells us that our customers demand these so-called come shots. It's mainly men who make the actual purchase. Who buy the videos. Maybe that's got something to do with it. It's supposed to prove it's real.'

At that moment the director started getting everyone ready for the next scene. He reminded them all that Sylvia – the woman who had earlier had all her clothes ripped off – was going to be raped anally. 'You'd better get yourself well greased up, darling,' he said to her. 'It's supposed to be rape, so he won't be stopping to lubricate you before he fucks you up that pretty little ass of yours. And then, if you remember, Charlie gets fed up with waiting and he tears Carol's clothes off and fucks her while Harry's buggering Sylvia. Not to be outdone, Pete' (the man who had forced the wife to fellate him, back at the beginning) 'fucks Sylvia's mouth, while Harry's still up her ass. And then we're into the serious orgy scene, where everyone does everything to everybody. So I guess we'd better stop after Pete and Harry have finished with Sylvia, and break for lunch. How does that sound, you guys?'

'Sounds good,' they all said.

Hank leant over and whispered in Venus's ear again. 'What say we watch this next scene – I'd like to see Sylvia getting it up her ass – and then go grab ourselves some lunch, before we make our way back to your suite at the Plaza, and meet up with Jenny?' he suggested.

'That sounds good,' Venus said. 'I'd like that.'

Once more the camera and lighting crews got their acts together, but neither Hank nor Venus paid them much attention this time. They were totally preoccupied with watching the girl who was the starter – her name was Becky, it transpired – greasing the delectable Sylvia's adorable rectal passage. She was stark naked and kneeling down, the twin globes of her exquisitely curvaceous bottom spread wide and held apart by both hands as she chatted nonchalantly to Harry while Becky thrust two long crimson-painted fingers, greased with KY Jelly, up her arsehole and rotated them. After a few minutes, Becky announced that she had done her best, accepting that no grease must show around Sylvia's puckered anal entrance, so that the eventual video audience would believe that this was real rape, and that Sylvia's forthcoming screams were genuine screams of pain. Venus giggled to herself.

'What are you laughing at?' Hank asked.

'Oh, nothing, really,' Venus told him. 'Looking at Sylvia there being all greased up, I wondered if someone was a real pain in the arse, that also meant that they were a big prick.'

Hank joined her in her amusement. After which he said 'That reminds me, Venus. You Limeys kill me with your accent. Can we get the vocabularies of all the Aphrodite models that are shipped over here checked for things that our customers won't understand?'

'That's no problem,' Venus said. 'It'll be best if one of your people does the actual checking. But we'll do the corrections, of course. What sort of thing did you have in mind?'

'Well, the one that started me off on that train of thought was while I was with the lovely Angie at Jenny's yesterday,' he told her. 'She kept saying arse – like you just have – when we say ass. And then, of course, fanny means ass here in America. But I gather that it means pussy in Britain. That's a bit of a vital difference for a sex robot, if you think about it. Then there's lift, for elevator. And knickers, apparently, are your name for panties. Pavement for sidewalk. And our cars have trunks. Yours have boots. Windshields are windscreens. There's a whole slew of words that are different. Like Bernard Shaw said, we're two countries separated by a common language. But it's important.'

'Agreed,' Venus said. 'But like I said, it's not a problem.' By this time, Harry's large cock had completely disappeared up Sylvia's rectum and he was sodomizing his heart out, while Pete was enthusiastically fucking Sylvia's mouth, which at least had the advantage, Venus thought, of cutting back on Sylvia's ability to scream as she got fucked in the butt. *How's that for an Americanism*? she thought. Butt. Arse. Whatever. She had never seen another woman being sodomized before, and she found it sexually very exciting, although she felt that the earlier

Voluptuous Venus

screams were unnecessary, written in by some chauvinist who delighted in the thought of hurting women.

She found the addition of Pete, fucking Sylvia's mouth, intensely erotic, and she could feel her knickers (sorry, panties, she told herself mentally) getting wet and juicy between her legs. She wriggled around a bit on her chair, trying to get her knicker crotch out from where it had become entangled in her pussy without actually using her fingers.

Hank looked at her. 'Are you getting hot panties, baby?' he asked, provocatively.

'Hot *and* wet,' Venus told him, refusing to be embarrassed by his approach. 'But you'll be pleased, later on.'

He looked at her and laughed. 'I guess I will, at that,' he said. 'Have you had enough, here? I think you've seen enough to get a pretty good idea of what it's all about.'

'I certainly have, Hank,' she said. 'Thank you. It's been an interesting morning.' They waited for the director to call 'Cut' once more, at which point they got up and said their goodbyes. Venus never knew how Hank did it, but the limo was waiting for them downstairs when they got outside the building. 'Do you like Indian food?' Hank asked, as they got into the car. Venus said that she did. 'Strangely enough, Indian food is still quite rare in New York,' Hank told her. 'But there's an excellent little Indian restaurant on First Avenue, almost opposite the old United Nations building.'

The UN building had been converted into apartments years ago, some time in the early years of this millennium, when the fate of the United Nations Organization followed that of the even older League of Nations. But the building was still something of a tourist attraction, for all that. Their limo drew up outside a fairly ordinary-looking restaurant building, but the car door was opened by a turbaned Indian, a Sikh, his beard long and flowing, his sideburns trained back and up underneath his turban, in the approved manner. Inside, the restaurant was similar to the ones back home in England, where they seemed not to have changed in a hundred years. There was the inevitable red flock wallpaper, a generous use of gilt everywhere, and the seemingly compulsory Indian music. But the tables were laid out immaculately, and the glass and silver shone brilliantly in the sunshine coming through the windows. The menu was very similar to those back in London, apart from the fact that each dish was described in some detail beneath its listing, doubtless in deference to the fact that many New Yorkers were still completely unaccustomed to Indian food.

Venus ordered Chicken Tikka, and to her surprise Hank asked for a Prawn Vindaloo, it being the hottest of hot curries. The waiter brought them a selection of variously flavoured poppadoms and a selection of dips to nibble on while they waited for their orders.

'Jenny never did answer my question about rental costs,' Hank mused. 'But she charges three hundred bucks an hour for those girls of hers. I guess if we charged that for a twenty-four-hour rental period, that would be about right. It would show around a two hundred dollar gross profit, after basic costs, which sounds reasonable to me. What do you think?'

Voluptuous Venus

He looked at Venus, who was sitting opposite him. 'Well, it sounds reasonable,' she said. 'A lot depends on the size of your ... your ...' She paused. 'What's the collective noun for sex robots?' she asked him. 'It certainly isn't fleet. A harem? An orgy?'

'Hmmmm,' Hank said. 'I like orgy. An orgy of female sex robots. I must remember that, when I talk to the ad agency. But yes, you're right, of course. The ideal situation would be to have five hundred robots at each outlet, with all the robots permanently out on hire. I guess we'll have to start slowly, or your people will never keep up with the demand. I wonder what proportion of male to female robots we'll need? Predominantly female, I assume.'

'Why do you assume that?' Venus asked him.

'I suppose because I see these sex robots as appealing more to men than to women,' he replied. 'But I may well have to alter that viewpoint after this afternoon.'

'I think you probably will,' Venus told him. 'The male product is every bit as good as the female. And all the same advantages apply to them as to the female ones. Women simply won't need men, after you launch your business.'

Hank looked thoughtful. 'That's something that I hadn't considered,' he said, half to himself.

'What is?' Venus asked.

'Well, you'll know that New York is one of the three major gay capitals of the world,' he said. 'After San Francisco, and Sydney, Australia. London comes a very poor fourth. So I guess we could well have men renting the male robots. If only out of curiosity.'

'We always assumed that any such business would attract a degree of male gays,' Venus told him. 'And lesbians, too, for the female robots.' She thought guiltily of her own adventures in that direction. 'But we assumed that it would be quite a small percentage. In both cases. Despite that, the male robots have both oral and anal facilities for other males, and the female robots can cope both orally with other women, and with artificial penises. Dildos, if you prefer that description. We're nothing if not thorough.'

Hank grinned at her. 'I'm beginning to see just how thorough,' he said. 'Now, let me be businesslike for a moment or two. I'm totally sold on these sex robots of yours. I see the idea of rental outlets both as a threat to my existing business and as an opportunity for making a major investment. I believe that they will be the biggest and most exciting – and therefore the most profitable – thing to happen to the sex market in a hundred years. Your robots caused an international sensation when you first put them on the market, but they have always been pretty much exclusively for the very rich. Now you're making them available to anyone and everyone. It will bring about a sexual revolution. And I am determined to be part of that revolution.

'By the time that you return to London, I will have had my attorney draw up a full, complete proposition for my becoming the Aphrodite franchisee for the whole of North America. But my question, Venus, right now, is, how far have you got the patents tied up on all this equipment? The actual robots, the production processes, the materials

Voluptuous Venus

that you use, the programs? Everything? Is it all properly registered? I don't know what has been happening with your copyrights up to now, but the moment we launch these rental outlets over here in United States, everyone in the American sex business is going to be renting your robots and taking them apart. Including the Mafia, who are the biggest people of all in the sex business here. Seeing how they work. Trying to produce them more cheaply. More efficiently. With better programs. Do you know what the situation is?'

'All I can tell you is that I'm told that the copyrights and patents are tied up, totally, in every country in the world where it is possible to take out a patent,' she told him. 'And for long periods of time. Once you and my company agree, you're welcome, of course, to look at anything and everything that we have, including that information. We own everything. Nothing is licensed, or franchised, or purchased outside. We manufacture them from the bottom up.' Venus giggled. 'Oh, that sounds rude, doesn't it?'

Hank laughed. 'What a lovely girl you are, Venus,' he said. 'And I'm going to get to fuck you this afternoon. I can't wait.'

At that moment their food arrived. They both concentrated upon it. 'Mmmm, good,' Venus said. 'How's yours?'

'Good too,' Hank said. 'Good, and hot.'

'I can imagine,' Venus told him. 'Vindaloo is too hot for me. It's well past my pain threshold. I really prefer the gentler, more herby curries.'

Two hours later they were in Venus's suite at the Plaza. Both models had been delivered. The male robot was Venus's Tony, from her personal collection at home. The female was a different model to the previous Angela. This one was a black-haired girl, with, Venus informed Hank – for she was fully clothed – a shaven pussy. Tony had brown hair, was six foot six, and he too was fully clothed. Venus announced their names as Liz and Tony and told Hank they were switched off.

Then Jenny arrived and Venus dispensed drinks from her mini-bar. Everyone accepted her offer of champagne. She had made certain earlier that the fridge was well stocked with Jenny's favourite Dom Perignon. Hank had stopped the limo at a pharmacy on the way to the hotel and had purchased a toothbrush and some toothpaste in order, he said, to brush away the remains of his vindaloo curry. He disappeared into the bathroom to do exactly that. Venus took a long swallow.

'So, Jenny, my dear. How's your day been so far?' she asked.

'Oh, OK I guess,' Jenny answered. 'It's early yet, for me. I didn't get to bed until after three this morning. Your Angela robot was in unbelievable demand. She got fucked by every single customer, eventually. And they all loved it. I was so wrong with my bet of yesterday. I've lost it twenty times over. But since yesterday, I've had this terrific thought. Your robots won't put me out of business after all. Because I'll rent a couple permanently, from Hank, and then I'll be able to offer both the real thing and the new Aphrodite fuck fad as well. Don't you think that's a great

Voluptuous Venus

idea? It's always a good thing to be the first. And having a couple of the robots around the place should help Hank's sales, too. But, hey, let's have a look at this male robot, shall we?'

She went over to Tony and stood in front of him. Next, she put a hand between his legs and felt him. 'He doesn't feel like anything to write home about,' she said. 'I swear to you I've felt teenagers with bigger cocks than that.'

'Oh, hang on, Jenny,' Venus said. 'Give him a chance. He's not switched on yet, for a start. Here, let me set him up for you. What do you want him to do?'

'Fuck me,' said Jenny. 'Just that. Fuck me.'

'Where?' Venus asked.

Jenny thought for a moment. 'Everywhere,' she said. 'Just set him up to fuck me everywhere, and then I can tell him what to do as we go along. And have him set up for a bit of the old cunt-lapping, too, will you, please?'

'Oh, that comes automatically with the sexual intercourse mode,' Venus told her. She finished setting up Tony's various dials and switches, and carefully closed his concealed back-panel.

'He's all ready to go now, darling,' she said. 'He'll make with the foreplay. He'll fuck you, suck you, masturbate you, bugger you, whatever. Just tell him what you want him to do to you, or what you want to do to him.' She turned back to the robot. 'Hi, Tony, my old love,' she said. 'Meet Jenny.'

'Hello, Venus. Hello, Jenny,' he said. He had a pleasant, well-modulated voice. 'I'm pleased to be here with you.'

'So strip off, lover,' Jenny said, starting to undress herself. 'Let's not waste time.'

Tony began by taking off his blazer, quickly followed by his grey slacks. He next loosened his tie, undid it and took it off, followed by his shirt and then his boxer shorts. He then stood there, waiting for instructions. Jenny was down to a pair of pale beige La Perla panties. She kept these on and went over and knelt in front of Tony. She took hold of his penis.

'I'm glad to see you're not circumcised,' she said to him. She gave him a few semi-masturbatory strokes with her fingers. His cock became almost immediately erect. 'Well, thank God for that,' Jenny said, looking closely at the now enormous cock in her hand. 'No erection problems.' She took his cockhead between her lips and slowly sucked on him. Rather like she would a lollipop. 'Mmmmm,' she said. 'It looks good. It tastes good. And by golly, it does you good.' She turned and looked over at Venus, laughing as she said, 'It's from my history of advertising book. The trouble is, I can't remember just what it was advertising. It certainly wasn't cock. Was it Guinness?' Venus laughed too.

'I can't remember either,' she said. 'It was long before my time. But it *is* one of the famous ones, isn't it?'

'But joking aside, this is fantastic,' Jenny said. 'I mean, he's *real*. This cock tastes like real cock. It feels like real cock. And if he's up to standard, it's going to fuck rather better than real cock. Let's give it a try.'

Just then, Hank came back into the room. 'I'm just going to take Tony here off to the bedroom, Hank darling,' Jenny said. 'He's going to fuck me.' She looked up at Tony, who was a good ten inches taller than she was. His erection

Voluptuous Venus

stuck out stiffly in front of him. Impressively. 'Aren't you, honey?'

'Yes, Jenny,' said Tony.

'Looks like you're going to have fun, baby,' Hank said. 'Enjoy.'

Jenny led Tony through into the bedroom. Hank turned to Venus. 'And we're going to have fun, too, baby, aren't we?' he said.

'We certainly are, Hank,' Venus agreed. 'But would you like to have a quick look at Liz here, before we start? She's shaved her pussy for you. Especially.'

'Jesus. Shaved cunt,' Hank said. 'Let me at it.'

Venus went behind the black-haired Liz, made the necessary adjustments, and then switched her on. 'Hi, Liz,' Venus said. 'I'm Venus. And this is Hank. Hank loves shaved pussy. Would you like to show him yours?'

'Hello, Venus. Hello, Hank,' said Liz. She turned and looked directly at Hank. 'I'll show you mine, if you'll show me yours, Hank darling,' she said.

Both Venus and Hank laughed. 'It's the oldest joke in the book,' Venus said. 'But it seems to work, so we've left it there.' Liz was undressing as she too laughed with them. Beneath her smart cherry-red wool tailored suit, she was dressed like a hooker. She was wearing a black silk teddy, black silk seamed hold-up stockings, and high-heeled black patent leather shoes.

Her teddy had a velcro fastening at the crotch. Liz bent forward to find the two ends, and ripped them apart. She then lifted up the front piece, revealing a beautifully white, completely bald smooth-skinned pubis. The pink gash running down the centre of this hairless pudenda was wet at the edges, and Hank could see colourless liquid running slowly out of the bottom of it, as he looked at her. 'Oh, baby,' he said. 'Come to daddy.' Liz came and stood in front of him, and parted her legs for him. 'You like?' she asked.

'Oh, I like,' Hank said. 'I love it.' He leaned forward, put his hands behind her and, clutching her buttocks, pulled her forward onto his mouth, where he proceeded to lick and suck at her hairless, strongly scented, naked wet pussy. It was an intensely erotic sight, and Venus felt her own panties getting moist at the carnal sight before her.

After a little while, Liz put her hands down and, holding Hank's head in them, began to make fucking motions with her hips, grinding her hairless pussy hard against his lips and tongue, working for the orgasm that was apparently now well on its way. And then, moments later, Liz was succumbing to her orgasm, mouthing a host of obscenities as she appeared to enjoy a whole series of non-stop continuous orgasms. To be fair to Hank, he continued his sucking, kissing, and licking, until Liz, robot or no robot, came to the end of her orgasmic contractions. He then pulled back from her, and said huskily, 'Lie down, baby. Lie on the floor. I'm going to fuck your wet cunt now.'

Liz did as she was bidden and lay on the floor, her legs well apart. Hank's cock was rampant and he pulled Liz's teddy up and forced himself roughly into her open, wet, pink lips. Once fully home, he began to fuck her, rapidly, his erection thrusting in and out of her with increasing fervour, until – it seemed only a matter of seconds later – he was spurting his ejaculate up into her. He pulled out of

Voluptuous Venus

her almost immediately and stood up. He tucked his now flaccid cock back inside his trousers – he was still fully dressed – and Venus noticed that it was still dribbling semen as he tucked it away. *Wham, bam, thank you, ma'am*, she thought. She wondered if he would find the energy to indulge her in the long-promised fuck. The one that he had been going on about since lunch at the Indian restaurant earlier that day. 'By God, Venus. The danger is going to be – when the investment details are all worked out, and I'm in business with these robots – that I'll spend all my time fucking them, and no time at all on the business. I'm going to have to watch that.'

'Oh, don't worry about it, Hank,' Venus said. 'You must have spent some time screwing porno movie actresses when you first went into the blue video business, didn't you?'

'Well, yes. I guess I did,' he said.

'But you don't spend *all* your time doing that now, do you?' she asked.

'Well, no, actually,' he replied.

'And it will be the same with the female robots,' Venus said. 'You'll screw yourself silly for a while. And then you'll want to go back to someone who's going to play hard to get. You'll want a challenge. You'll see.'

'It's going to be a great temptation,' he said. 'But I've been wanting to fuck you since the first time we met, back at Kennedy. What was it? A couple of days ago. It seems longer than that. And you agreed yesterday that we'll make beautiful music this afternoon. So what happens when I arrive? I make a play for a collection of plastics and microchips that isn't even human. Although that's the amazing thing. Liz here does actually seem to be real. All of her.'

He looked across at Liz, who was sitting up on the floor where he'd left her. She had her arms around her knees, and was waiting, obediently, for her next instruction. Then he looked at Venus. 'I'm sorry, baby,' he said. 'Please don't be insulted.'

'I'm not insulted, Hank,' she said. 'I'm delighted. Frustrated, but delighted. Delighted because it means you really go for this rental project. Frustrated for the usual reason. I need a fuck.' She began to undress. She had intentionally put on some of her sexiest undies that morning, and as she stepped out of her skirt, Hank was mesmerized by the drop-dead sexy apparition that she presented. She wore a cream satin body by Presence that looked as if it had been tailored for her.

Its lace cups moulded her firm breasts, while the crotch fitted her like a glove. She was also wearing white hold-up stockings with lace tops. As Hank watched, she bent down and undid the fastening between her legs. She pulled the bottom of the garment up, exposing her soft blonde pubic hair.

'Don't just stand there, Hank,' she said. 'Get your clothes off.' She slowly thrust two fingers up into her pussy, and – as slowly – drew them down again. She held her fingers up in front of her.

'Look, Hank,' she said. 'Wet pussy. Wet for you.' He could see them glistening with moisture. She put her fingers up to her lips and licked and sucked at them.

'Mmmmm,' she said. 'Tastes good to me. Do you want to try my pussy juice?'

She pulled down the shoulder straps of the body and wriggled it down over her hips, and then down her legs and off. As she exposed her breasts, Hank could see that her nipples were standing out stiffly. She walked over to where Liz was still sitting on the floor and, standing in front of the robot's face, she pulled it into her crotch. 'Suck me, baby,' she demanded. 'Get me ready for Hank.'

Liz dutifully put up her hands and, clasping Venus's naked buttocks, she pulled them hard towards her, pressing Venus's pussy against her mouth as she salaciously slurped, kissed, licked, and sucked. 'Mmmmm,' said Venus again. 'That's nice, darling. Don't stop.'

Hank couldn't believe his eyes. He was so sexually excited by what was going on that his fingers were all thumbs as he tore off his clothes, an action not helped by his rampant erection. As soon as he was naked, his cock now obscenely rigid, he almost ran over to where Liz was attending to Venus's oral needs. Venus grinned at him, but made no attempt to disengage from the attentions of her robot sex slave.

'Let's be imaginative,' she suggested. 'Why don't we all three move across to that sofa over there?' She nodded her head towards a large, richly upholstered sofa set along one of the suite's walls. 'Then Liz can lie down on it, on her back. I can then lie on top of her, with my pussy over her mouth, in a *soixante-neuf* position, so that I can suck her pussy too, and you can fuck me anally, from behind.'

'Jesus,' Hank said. 'What are we waiting for?'

Eva Linczy

And so Venus took Liz by the hand and led her over to the sofa, with Hank bringing up the rear. He looked at Venus's glorious bottom as she swayed her way over to the sofa, and thought lustfully of what he would very shortly be doing to it. He waited patiently, while Liz and Venus arranged themselves comfortably, and then Venus looked over her shoulder and said, 'Use Liz's pussy juice to lubricate my anus, will you, darling? Despite the fact that it looks, feels, and tastes like real pussy juice, it is actually a very fine sexual lubricant as well. I'll be happier if you grease me up before you start. Please.'

She waited patiently as Hank scooped up fingerfuls of Liz's luxuriantly oozing pussy juice and rubbed them over, into and around her rectal passage. 'Ooooh,' she said after a bit, wriggling her bottom. 'That's nice, too.' She grinned at Hank over her shoulder. 'I reckon that's probably it. Come here, and I'll rub some on your cock.' He stood beside the sofa as Venus rubbed her fingers into Liz's pussy, and then transferred the clear, mucous liquid to his cock. 'Mmmmm,' she said. 'You told me it was a big one, and it is. You just be careful with that up my arsehole, now. Slowly, and gently, right?'

'Right,' Hank said.

'And if I say stop, you stop. OK?'

'OK,' he agreed.

'Right, then,' she said. 'I guess we're all ready now.' She put her right hand behind her. 'Just give me your cock, Hank darling, and let me ease it in. OK?'

He didn't say anything, but he took hold of her hand and placed her fingers around his swollen circumcised

Voluptuous Venus

cock. Venus applied it to her anus and pressed it carefully against the seemingly tiny aperture. It was so well lubricated that it dilated instantly, and without Hank so much as leaning forward (it was an almost irresistible temptation to him to grab her around her waist and to thrust his cock, hard, all the way up her) he was suddenly in, up to his balls.

He sucked his breath in, as if in pain. 'What's wrong, honey?' she asked.

'Wrong, baby?' he queried. 'Nothing's wrong. I think I've died, and gone to heaven.'

Venus laughed. 'Everything's OK, sweetheart,' she told him. 'So fuck me.'

He took her around the waist, just as he had wanted to moments earlier and began to fuck her. He loved watching, fascinated, as his cock disappeared deeply inside Venus's stretched anus, the distended pinkish brown membrane almost transparently thin as he thrust into her, and then seeing it reappearing once more, glistening with her juices. It wouldn't be long, he knew.

He could feel the presence of Liz's busy mouth, somewhere down below his cock and balls, as he fucked away, and he could see Venus's head, buried between Liz's thighs, busily returning the oral compliment that the robot was paying to her. Venus could feel Hank's ejaculation gathering imminently, and she pressed her pussy down harder against Liz's mouth as she at the same time slipped a finger down into the robot's pussy, found its clitoris, and began to rub it as she continued to suck and lick.

Hank was so aroused by his anal intercourse that he

knew he was going to ejaculate any moment now. In point of fact, in the end, all three came together. Venus, from long experience, adjudged Hank's orgasm absolutely correctly, and timed her own to coincide. Liz was simply programmed to orgasm when anyone else did, so that she was an imperceptible millisecond behind Venus. All three fell back, happily replete, to the unexpected accompaniment of a single-handed round of applause. Looking up, they saw that Jenny, still naked, had wandered through from the bedroom.

Satiated by her sexual exercises with Tony, she had arrived at the very moment that the three on the sofa reached the ultimate point of their sexual expression. 'Well done,' she cried, laughing, and clapping loudly. 'Very well done indeed.'

Hank and Venus got up off the sofa, rather self-consciously, and grinned at Jenny a bit vaguely. Venus reached behind Liz's back and switched her to self-clean.

'So, how was yours?' Hank asked Jenny. 'Is Tony up to the same standards as Liz and Angela are? I mean, seriously, you know? What's your recommendation to me, as far as the male robot is concerned?'

Jenny, naked as she was, went up to Hank and gave him a big hug, then she kissed his cheek. 'Hank, baby,' she said, 'I have to tell you the truth. Up until today, if anyone had actually asked me who was the best lay I had ever had in my life, I'd say in all honesty—I mean, I'm not saying this to impress you. It just happens to be the truth. I'd have said Hank. Hank Sherman is the best lay I've ever had in my entire life. And that includes a lot of lays, I tell

Voluptuous Venus

you, man. But after today, I have to say that robot next door, Tony, is the best lay I've ever had, and that I'm ever *likely* to have. And when you sign up your contract with Venus here, and her company, I wanna buy Tony there, and keep him. Just for me. For ever. Does that tell you what I think of him?'

'Wow, baby. Does it?' said Hank. 'It sure does. I thank you.'

Some hours later, showered, refreshed, dressed once more, and looking entirely respectable, the three of them were dining in the Plaza's restaurant as Venus's guests. They had finished their meal and Venus rose, albeit a tiny bit unsteadily, to her feet. A moment before she had called over the wine waiter to open yet another bottle of Dom Perignon and to fill everyone's glasses.

'Ladies and gentlemen,' she said, raising her glass. 'Dear Jenny, and dear Hank. Allow me to propose a toast. To the three of us. To our success in the United States. I give you Aphrodite. A beginning.'

Hank and Jenny raised their glasses too. 'To Aphrodite,' they repeated. 'A beginning.' They drained their glasses.

Venus sat down. 'Now let's go back upstairs,' she said. 'I'm in serious need of a fuck.'

EVA LINCZY

VAMPIRE DESIRE

INTERCOURSE WITH THE VAMPIRE!

Diabolus has lived in Hell, where he is the Master, for three thousand years. He is demon, archfiend – and vampire. He is Evil Incarnate. He forces his revolting sexual needs on the she-devils who are compelled, under duress, to pander to his every depraved erotic desire.

Bored with the sexual pleasures of the Pit, Diabolus returns to Earth. To Africa, where he conceals himself in a rare uncut red diamond – for red is the colour of blood. From this supernatural hiding place, Diabolus can assume any human form – male or female – that he wishes. His sexual excesses on earth start with Kindhu, an African tribal woman. Her torment is just the beginning . . .

In Amsterdam the diamond is cut and in London the individual stones are set in pieces of jewellery before being sent all over the world. In every one, Diabolus lurks. Which is bad news indeed for Marijka in Holland, Peggy in England, Janet in Singapore, Tania in Russia – and a myriad more . . .

Vampire Desire is a hypnotically compelling story of the outer limits of lust where the erotic and the occult meet in an explosion of terror and twisted passions.

HODDER AND STOUGHTON PAPERBACKS

DAVID JONES

THE WORLD'S BEST SEXUAL FANTASY LETTERS

WHATEVER TURNS YOU ON . . .

'Fantasies are what inject life into most of our sex lives. And one of the most frequent – and most popular – of sexual topics is, inevitably, where does real sex stop? And where do fantasies begin . . . ?'

David Jones worked in men's magazine publishing for over thirty years as journalist, editor and, ultimately, senior publisher. Top journals in the field on which he worked included *Men Only, Penthouse*, and *Forum*. During this time, the readers' letters columns were always a mainstay of the textual content. But the main difficulty with publishing such letters, especially readers' fantasy letters, was the problem of space. Almost every such letter had to be edited down from its original length, with much interesting and stimulating material ending up on, so to speak, the cutting room floor.

Now New English Library is publishing, for the first time ever, two volumes of the world's best sexual fantasy letters in their original, uncut, full-length state.

As David Jones writes: 'An historic event! Enjoy!'

HODDER AND STOUGHTON PAPERBACKS

RAY GORDON

THE DEGENERATES

WELCOME TO THE SEX WARD!

When sexy young journalist Angie Fields loses her way in the grounds of a modern hospital and stumbles across Dr Chris Martin's *very* private ward, she's in for some sensual shocks and surprises. For Dr Martin and his team are running a lucrative secret operation that has nothing to do with the NHS – and everything to do with sexual stimulation and gratification. And their equipment is the best that money can buy. It has to be to satisfy the tastes and appetites of the clientele who come from the wealthiest, most influential levels of local society.

Angie knows that she should expose these degenerates and Dr Martin's sex ward. But having experienced for herself the exquisite delights on offer, how can she bear to endanger this exciting, enticing new world of forbidden pleasures of the flesh . . . ?

In *The Degenerates*, top erotic novelist Ray Gordon once more takes the reader on an amazing journey of discovery to the wildest regions of passionate experience.

HODDER AND STOUGHTON PAPERBACKS